THE
VOROVICH
AFFAIR

S. L. STEBEL

The Vorovich Affair

A RICHARD SEAVER BOOK
THE VIKING PRESS
New York

Copyright © 1975 by S. L. Stebel
A Richard Seaver Book/The Viking Press
First published in 1975 by The Viking Press, Inc.
625 Madison Avenue, New York, N.Y. 10022
Published simultaneously in Canada by
The Macmillan Company of Canada Limited
Printed in U.S.A.

Library of Congress Cataloging in Publication Data
Stebel, S. L.
    The Vorovich affair.
    "A Richard Seaver book."
    I. Title.
PZ4.S8V0   [PS3569.T33815]   813'.5'4   75–12512
ISBN 0–670–74790–4

To
my daughter, Patricia,
my wife, Jan,
my agent and friend, Don Congdon,
for keeping the faith

*The author would like to acknowledge
the technical help given him
by agents and others in the Drug
Enforcement Administration who prefer,
for obvious reasons, to remain anonymous.*

THE
VOROVICH
AFFAIR

The men were uncomfortable with each other. It wasn't just that some were in uniform and some not, or that the border patrolmen, lean and weatherbeaten from being outdoors too much, were disdainful of these sallow men in the rum- pled loose-fitting suits, or vice versa, as that they were constantly aware of the brooding presence of the man in charge of the stakeout. He did not make small talk. And soon even their feeble attempts to needle one another about the advantages of one service over the other ceased.

All of them were used to waiting. It was part of the job. But that kind of hard, aloof attitude made it more difficult; unnecessarily so, in the men's opinion.

"What's he so bitched off about?" one of the patrolmen asked, when Vorovich, for the thirteenth time, went down the freeway embankment to the radio car, querying customs at Tijuana whether they were *sure* the people they were after had not already crossed the border.

The squat Federal agent named Dunbar hesitated, then shrugged. It wasn't exactly a secret. The entire bureau had seemed aware of it the day after it happened. "He lost out on the top job. Everyone figured he had it. Then they brought in somebody from outside."

"Tough," the patrolman agreed, squinting down the highway as a puff of chaparral went rolling across the road, then waving a green Pontiac sedan on past the barricade, a couple so old they were not even curious about the slowing.

"Yeah," Dunbar said, taking an offered stick of gum, noting the package was *hecho en Mexico,* wondering whether the wetback it had been confiscated from had dared to complain. "Especially when you figure this was probably his last chance at it. He's forty-five. The new guy's forty-two."

"Tough," the patrolman said again, and chewed his gum for a time. "If it happened to me," he said then, "I'd probably quit. I'd tell them to take my badge and shove it up sideways."

"Maybe you would," Dunbar said. "Except where would you get a job? Some hick-town police force? Head of security at some ball-bearing plant?"

"I don't know as that would be so bad," the patrolman said. "Hustling these greaseballs is beginning to pall, if you really want to know." He hesitated again. "If he's such a top honcho he was slated for the number-one job—"

"Not the number-one-A," Dunbar said. "Chief of the Enforcement Division."

"Even so," the patrolman continued. "What's he doing out here? I'd think he'd be after bigger stuff. . . ."

"Twenty minutes," Vorovich said, appearing back up over the embankment. "Six of them in a Volkswagen bus."

"What I don't understand," the patrolman persisted, when Vorovich paced some distance away, and stood hunched into his tan raincoat, too light for this December day, which, though the sun was out, chilled to the bone with every gust, "is why, if they're running dope, you didn't just bust them at the border? What if they dropped it in San Diego?"

"If they'd stopped, we'd have heard about it," Dunbar said. "If they think they're clear, they may get the stuff out of wherever it's stashed, and it won't be so difficult for us to find it."

"Oh, yeah," the patrolman said, but he was doubtful, and looked off at Vorovich, who seemed suddenly uneasy, the way he was running his hand through his short-cropped sandy hair.

"Also," Dunbar went on, breaking security somewhat, but then the pride of his Service was at stake, "we want to know which way they're headed, L.A. or up North someplace."

"Yeah?" the patrolman said, looking puzzled. "What diff . . ."

"That's them," Vorovich said, when the VW was still a silver speck down the highway, and either he was intuitive or exceptionally farsighted, since no one else could make it out without glasses.

Two of the patrolmen strode down to the barricade, hitching at their guns, and two of the others got into a car and started the engine, just in case they ignored the flags and made a run for it.

But the VW bus slowed, then docilely followed the directions of the patrolman on down the embankment to the narrow road below.

The inhabitants were not docile, however. First the young driver, who had tangled hair to his shoulders and a drooping mustache, stuck his head out the window and yelled, something inarticulate. When Vorovich got closer he could hear him protesting the stop; hadn't they been cleared at the border?

"Get them out," Vorovich said.

There were six of them, two pimply, tangle-haired youths, skinny and chicken-breasted under their long-underwear tops, and four granny-gowned girls. He didn't know why, he wasn't statistically up on the ratio of young females to males, but every snot-nose under thirty always seemed to have his choice. Not that these were any bargain. They were as unsavory as the males, with matted, greasy hair, snubby noses, and dull complexions, looking as if they had not bathed for a week—except for the last one.

She leaned in the doorway, taking her sweet time examining the scene, ignoring the agent who was offering to help her down. Though she was dressed like the others, her long light reddish hair in equal disarray, the highlights as she leaned from the van into the late afternoon sun showed that it had been recently washed. Her gray eyes and her cheeks shone with health. Her gown, though faded, was clean.

But she was pregnant. She had her swollen belly thrust out at them disdainfully. "What if I don't want to come out?" she asked. "You going to use all reasonable force to make me?"

She was sweetly contemptuous, and the agent was suddenly disconcerted, and looked around at Vorovich for instructions.

The girl followed his glance, and Vorovich became suddenly aware of his cordovan wing-tip shoes and his wrinkled coat and his frayed shirt and his tan knit tie which had a coffee stain on it.

"Drag her out," he said.

She grinned and jumped down and then yanked her arm out of the agent's grasp. "Don't you manhandle me!" she said, suddenly angry. She looked again at Vorovich, then strode over to stand with her friends.

"Clean it out," Vorovich said, and stood watching as his four men went at the little bus.

This was the hardest part, the waiting. But it wouldn't do to dig in himself. It was like the Army, you had to delegate authority to make people realize you had it. So he clenched his hands in his coat pockets and forced himself to remain still while his men brought out the dirty duffel bags and emptied the glove compartment and the ash trays and looked under the seats and the well where the spare tire was kept.

Nothing. Then he asked himself what difference it made any

more about the appearance of authority, and walked over to the bus and began undoing the bolts that held the trail bike on the back.

"Jack it up," he said to the others. "We'll take it apart if we have to."

"Hey!" the youth who had been the driver yelled as he saw them start to take off the wheels. "What the hell do you think you're doing?" A patrolman shoved him back.

Vorovich examined the bike, heeled the kick stand down, felt all around inside the luggage bags, which were empty, and, after unscrewing the gas cap, peered down into the tank. It was almost full, and so he walked a little way into the brush and found a stick and poked that down into the tank and swirled it around. Nothing.

"You must be kidding, narc," the youth yelled. "You've seen too many movies!"

Vorovich screwed the cap back on. He walked over to the little group. "Shake them down," he said to the sergeant in charge of the highway patrolmen.

It didn't take long—there weren't many hiding places when the kids wore tight-fitting pants and sandals. But these patrolmen were not skilled in this kind of search.

"Turn their pockets out," Vorovich said, and went in himself to show how it was done.

"Hey, he's groping me," the youth cried to the others, when Vorovich had his hands deep in his pockets. "He's a fag narc."

In spite of himself, Vorovich flushed. The patrolmen were looking at him strangely, and he yanked the youth's pockets inside out, and one of them ripped.

"If he's a fag he wouldn't be a narc," the pregnant girl said. "He'd be with the F.B.I. Are you with the F.B.I.?" she inquired of Vorovich.

"I'm suing you for damages," the youth said. "What's your name and badge number, narc?"

There wasn't a shred of tobacco in any of the males' pocket linings, nor in the seams of the females' handbags.

"Nothing yet," a grease-smudged agent said, when Vorovich went over to the partially demolished bus. "You find anything?"

"Nothing," Vorovich said.

"Maybe you were misinformed," the patrol sergeant said.

"They're *too* clean," Vorovich said. "There's not a shred of grass or powder from pills or anything else on them, and that just isn't natural." But he began to worry nevertheless. "We've got to search the girls," he said.

"You touch us," the pregnant girl said, "and we'll have your ass."

"A fine thing," Vorovich said. "You about to be a mother, and all. You want your kid to grow up talking dirty?" He turned to the sergeant. "Where's the nearest matron?"

"San Diego," the sergeant said.

"Get one here," Vorovich said.

The sergeant looked at the jacked-up bus and understood that it was easier to bring the matron out than to bring everyone to her—especially if they were clean, which was not impossible.

Vorovich began to wonder how good their informant was. He had ignored protocol and taken over this field operation because he did not understand how young people would have gotten their hands on the kind of dope and the quantity they were supposed to be carrying. It didn't make sense. The kids hustled grass and pills and the organic hallucinogens, but not usually the hard stuff. If it was true, it was an escalation of input that meant a whole new traffic network to be concerned about. Of course, from here on out it would be the new man's concern, but Vorovich could not resist taking one last firsthand look for himself.

"You're pretty far along," he said to the clean lovely pregnant one, after the sergeant had gone. "When are you due?"

"Any minute now," she said. "I am not supposed to be under any emotional stress. I am supposed to, like, take it easy and remain calm. . . ."

"You call a trip to Baja taking it easy?" Vorovich asked.

"I would hate to be in your shoes if I drop the kid right here and now," she said, and moaning, she put her hands to her belly.

She was probably acting, Vorovich thought. "Tell us where the stuff is," he said, "and we'll get you to a doctor."

"Stuff?" she said.

"The shit," a nearby patrolman said, and Vorovich looked at him and the other found something else to do.

"We're clean," she said, but something had made her uneasy. "Why do you think we have hard stuff?" she asked.

"Ah, that's their excuse," the youth who had been driving

said. "They have to justify all this manpower. If they were just after common ordinary dope the taxpayers would complain."

"There is no such thing as ordinary dope," Vorovich said.

"Why pick on us?" the other youth demanded. "Why ain't you worrying about organized crime?"

The lovely girl was still clutching her belly.

"If it's just grass you're running," Vorovich said, "and it's not a huge amount, and you tell us where you got it and who you're carrying it for, we can maybe let it ride this time."

"Listen at him," a snub-nosed girl with gaps in her teeth said. "He's getting worried, ain't you, narc? What's the penalty for false arrest?"

"I'm not so sure how good prison doctors are," Vorovich said to the pregnant one.

"I don't care about doctors," she said. "I'm going to do it myself."

"Well," Vorovich said, "you don't want your kid born in jail."

She shrugged, but her pale eyes had clouded.

"Nobody's going to jail," the first youth said. He and the girl looked at each other. "Why don't you give it up, narc?" the youth said then. "You're not going to find anything."

"We'll find it," Vorovich said.

"How long you going to keep us here?" the other youth demanded. "It's getting cold."

It was true. The sun had dropped behind the foothills, the day was rapidly darkening, and the gusts of wind were now penetrating the raincoat Vorovich was wearing. He looked at the girls huddling together, their bare arms pimpling and blue.

"The matron will be here shortly," Vorovich said, and started back to the jacked-up van.

"I have to go to the toilet," the pregnant girl said.

Vorovich looked at her. She was not intimidated. "Well," he said, and looked around for a place. When he looked back she was already trudging off into the brush. He caught up with her just as a "Hey!" from the first youth stopped them both.

"She's my wife," the youth said. "If you're going with her, so am I."

"Legal wife?" Vorovich said, trying to picture this scrawny snot-nose with the lovely girl.

"It's my kid anyway," the other shrugged. "I just wanna make sure you don't stand too close or . . . anything."

"She's got a long dress on," Vorovich said.

"So?" the youth said. And as Vorovich hesitated: "I need to take a leak myself."

Vorovich finally nodded. He followed the two of them out into the brush. "That's far enough," he said, when they were already beyond where he would have stopped. "Stop right there," he said, as she continued shoulder high into the chapparal.

He could have sworn she smiled, though it was hard to see in the gathering dusk.

"You have to stand that close?" she asked, no laughter in her voice, but a kind of tenseness, not exactly embarrassment, though he assumed it was partly that, too.

"I have to," he said apologetically. He looked over at the youth. "That's close enough for you, too," he said.

"I've seen her before," the youth said. He stopped, however, turned his back on Vorovich, though not on the girl, and opened the buttons on his pants, and in a moment Vorovich could hear him urinating into the almost dark.

The girl squatted in the brush like an Indian, her gown tenting around her, and she did not turn her back, but brazenly reached up under her dress, and fussed with her undergarments, and just as he was wondering why she took so long getting them down, she was waving a corset at him triumphantly.

He averted his eyes, embarrassed at having to watch a woman urinate (or worse? she was taking long enough), and by the time she stood up, keeping her skirts hitched high as she stepped over what he did not want to consider, and tossed the corset at the waiting youth, with a remark about damn the doctor, this was the first time in three months she'd been able to breathe, he was so suffused with shame over this duty he had forced on himself that he did not even think about appropriating that undergarment, as he should have.

She continued to distract him. "Try to sneak a little peek, officer?" she asked, taking his arm, and matching him step for step. She was a tall girl, almost as tall as Vorovich, and him a shade under six feet, and because he was concentrating on her expressive face, trying to see whether she was laughing at him, it took moments later than it ought for it to register that behind them in the dark that shifty youth had paused momentarily;

that is, his footsteps, by which Vorovich was peripherally keeping track of his progress, had missed a beat in that dusty shuffle through the underbrush, which, Vorovich realized a moment later, must have been the time he buckled the corset around his own waist.

The highway patrol had lights on, but pointed mainly at the half-demolished van, and while his agents were explaining that they were positive there was nothing in the van, that kid lagged back on the perimeter of the illuminated area, near the trail bike.

By the time Vorovich saw what he was wearing, and yelled at him, he was close enough to the bike to leap on. That bike must have been in marvelous condition. It started with the first kick, and while they all stood dumfounded in the circle of light, suddenly hazed with the dust the bike's rear wheel kicked up, the kid skidded in a half circle and then shot off, between two of the parked highway-patrol cars, into the night.

Vorovich's reflexes finally began working. He beat one of the two highway patrolmen to one of the Harleys, which took two kicks to get it started, and then, with the other highway patrolman right behind on another cycle, went roaring off after the kid.

Dimly, in the uproar, concentrated as he was on the chase, Vorovich heard the girl shrieking in the distance, and he assumed, wrongly, that she was ululating in triumph.

It had been a long while since Vorovich had ridden a cycle. He was not as practiced as he might
have been; the highway patrolman now pulled
ahead of him, and Vorovich had to use everything
he had not to fall more than a length behind.
When he was young, and had romantic notions about police
work, he had set out to learn a variety of skills, so he might
handle himself in every conceivable situation. He had trained
himself in judo, and the use of a variety of weapons, and the
handling of ground, sea, and airborne vehicles, large and small.

But he had not been on a cycle for ten years, and for the first
few miles it took all his energies to control that madly bucking
machine he was straddling, and so he trusted the patrolman to
keep track of their quarry, barely able to look up past the
other's rear wheel.

At first the kid had to keep his headlight on, it was that dark
on this semidesert road, but when the moon rose over the hills
the kid was heading for, even though he switched his headlight
off, the pale bluish glow over the entire brush-covered plain
made it easy enough to keep track of him. When Vorovich got
enough confidence to look up, he could make him out in the
distance, an eerie fleeting shadow.

Vorovich bounced his bike into the parallel rut and pulled
alongside the other. "Where's this road go?" he shouted.

"Nowhere," the other shouted back, and Vorovich did not
know what he meant until they reached the foothills. There the
road became a kind of path where they could only ride single
file, and then became steep, and then dipped and rose and
dipped again like some kind of carnival ride, and again it took
everything Vorovich had to keep that bucking machine under
control.

As they climbed, the noise grew almost unbearable, their
cycles' roar becoming high-pitched whines, and they had to
look down as much as up to avoid the increasing number of
rocks. Ahead, and up, the trail bike, though not as powerful, was
more agile, maneuvering more easily than they through the
thickening brush, and though they were gradually gaining, it
was becoming obvious that if they did not catch up before he
reached the wooded slopes of the mountain ahead, he might
very well dodge through a stand of trees where they would be
unable to go.

9

"Stop and open fire!" Vorovich yelled, having to repeat it before the patrolman understood. "Maybe it'll spook him, slow him down."

The patrolman did not hear this last, but he got the point, and he skidded his cycle to a stop, and was already kneeling in the dust as Vorovich continued on by, steadying his left elbow on his knee, cradling the gun while he squeezed the trigger.

The range was too great, Vorovich thought, hearing the crack of the gun behind him, and he looked for the spurt of dust and then realized the sound came after the shot, and that it was too dark to see where the bullets were falling anyway. But up ahead now the trail bike was veering from left to right, an inept attempt at zigzag. If he could just force a little more power out of the Harley, he might be able to close the gap, which he judged as not more now than a hundred and fifty yards.

Then he lost his bike. He went down into a gully and was coming back up and out when he hit a rock and the handlebars twisted half out of his hands. Before he could wrench the wheel back in line he had gone into a skid. His foot came down just a second too late, and rather than let him get caught under it his reflexes, which were perhaps too good, that is, too careful, caused him to come up off the seat and hit the ground running, letting the cycle skid out from under him and go spinning off to one side, its motor roaring as the freed wheel spun, and then backfiring. As it end-over-ended back down the hill it hit something and burst into flame, a bluish-yellow bonfire in the pale dark.

Up ahead then, as Vorovich sprawled full length, came this incredible yell, a cry of triumph, and the trail bike had apparently halted, because in the sudden silence there was only a muted *put-put-put* as the smaller motor idled. Then the kid gunned it to start back up the mountain, and Vorovich found his weapon and fired blindly in the direction of the sound.

Up ahead in the dark there was a sudden burst of flame and another yell, not of hurt but of rage and chagrin, and then Vorovich had to roll hastily to one side off the trail as, from above, out of the dark, the trail bike came cartwheeling down the mountain, spilling flames as it went. A large bush-tree stopped it, and being oily and relatively dry, went up a moment later like a gigantic torch.

Listen. Except for the crackling of the separate fires below,

Vorovich could hear nothing. Though there was still a pale glow from moon and stars over the landscape, these trees cast moving shadows on the mountainside, and he could not tell whether what he saw was anything more than wind gusts.

His eyes began to water from strain. He closed them, and that was when he heard the dribble of sand and rock somewhere high above. Without hesitation, trusting his instincts, he got up, ignoring the pain from skinned hands and knees, and moved as quickly as he was able straight up.

As he climbed he reloaded his .38 Smith and Wesson, somewhat surprised to find it empty, wondering that he had so much anger he would keep pulling the trigger without so much as a glimpse of a target. Maybe not getting that job had affected him more deeply than he knew. Had he been counting on it that much? He had tried to avoid making assumptions about his future.

And why take it out on this fugitive kid? It was true he was tired of being sneered at by the kids, of their smugness about life styles and value systems, of their willingness to cheat, lie, and steal, justifying everything on the grounds that the establishment was corrupt, but he recognized that part of his anger was because they were doing wrong things for possibly right reasons. He had never before permitted his angers to become personal, and so it must be something else.

Again, as he climbed, sweat burning his cold skin, he wondered how a girl as beautiful as that could allow this smirky kid to make it with her. This generation was something else, all right, he thought, popping the new clip home; they seemed to glory in making it all ugly.

A rock came whistling through the trees, and then another, and Vorovich ducked behind the nearest tree. He waited, straining to hear again.

Nothing. Except the wind soughing through the green branches, a clear wind that chilled Vorovich's sinuses. As he pressed his face up against the fragrant tree bark, listening, he got a sudden crazy feeling of what it would be like to be alone in these mountain woods, out here in the star-filled night with nothing to think about except survival, forgetting his life, and what he was getting, had got, would get out of it, and then he got a renewed surge of anger when he heard what might be footsteps crushing the pine needles somewhere above.

He peered carefully into the moving shadows. He edged out and dropped to one knee and felt the cold in the ground penetrate the cloth and reach the knotted ligament where he had been kicked by a female junkie more than ten years before. It was funny, he thought, as he clenched his teeth against the rheumatic ache, how they all left you with some little goodie, some memento of their hate. Out of the thousand arrests he had made, you would think that one would slip his mind. But he remembered them all. All left him something: a blow, a threat, a curse—the threats, curiously enough, never bothering him, making him feel strangely important, even valuable—it was the contempt that got to him, the way the pushers and the dealers would look him over, sneering at his rack suit and his plain shoes, reaching up to finger their own silk neckties and scarfs, making more on one drop than he would make in his lifetime. At least the kids, up until now, had not seemed only interested in the money. But if they were running smack, then that had changed, hadn't it? Somehow he felt let down, as if he had been counting on something that had never existed.

Above, through a kind of tunnel the branches created, he could make out the night sky in a cleft between giant boulders. That must be where the falling sand had come from, he reasoned, and thinking that the contemptuous fugitive must have climbed to the top and was now hustling down the other side, he rose, wincing at his stiffened knee, and hobbled as best he could up the steep path. He was very near the top when he heard the grunt, an extended moan of effort, and was transfixed as he watched one of the boulders tilt, hang precariously, and then plunge down straight at him.

For a moment he could not think what he wanted to do. He had a momentary vision of himself embracing that huge rock, pasted to it in an instant of time like a ball to a bowling pin, and then falling backward, crushed by that enormous weight, and he would always wonder why he had hesitated at all, whether he hadn't, as they say, courted death, out of curiosity or need.

But at the last instant he leaped aside; slid, rather, on those slick needles underfoot, and rolled out of the way just in time, and yelled, emptying the air from his lungs, out of fright, but also out of instinct.

He lay very still. His gun was in his right hand, outstretched, supported by his left—his momentary encounter had not shaken him so much he forgot his training—and when his vision cleared he saw that his gunsight was right on the remaining boulder, and he edged it left, holding on a star.

"Hey, narc!" came the taunting voice. "You still there?"

He did not respond. He heard another grunting, and he could see the second boulder moving, but apparently it was too heavy, because it only rocked a little, then was still.

"Narc?" came the voice again.

He moaned. It was an old trick, but what the hell, he thought. He put a lot of feeling into it, some of his rage and anguish at how close he had come to accepting death, and when he heard himself he wondered how close to the surface such feelings were, and then a shadow came between the star and his gunsight, and without hesitating a moment, without thinking about it at all, he squeezed the trigger.

The shadow screamed and then the star was there again.

Vorovich lay a moment longer, and then, sighing, but not out of sadness—the remarkable thing being that he felt absolutely nothing whatsoever—he got painfully to his feet and went up to look at the dead boy.

He knew the other was dead by the quality of that scream.

The search party came slogging up the trail, in the cold, misting dawn, two forest rangers in the lead, and one each, as a kind of delegation, from the border patrol, the Drug Enforcement Administration, and the state highway patrol.

They found Vorovich huddled over the little fire he had built in a shielding of rocks. The dead youth had been pulled to one side and turned over on his face—there had been nothing to cover him with except his coat and it was too cold, Vorovich said, to get rid of that.

"We found the sergeant back down the hill," they told him. "He's burned bad—your bike ran into him and exploded."

Dunbar, the Federal agent, turned the youth face up. He was already stiff—one of his hands was twisted palm forward, frozen in a kind of deadly protest at what was happening, and his face was contorted, but whether from fear or pain was difficult to say.

"Blew out the chest cavity," the border patrolman said. "You guys using dum-dums?"

"Don't be ridiculous," Dunbar said, but he looked curiously for a moment at Vorovich. "Perfect shooting," he said. Vorovich refused to acknowledge the compliment.

The two rangers were standing off to one side, trying hard not to look at the corpse.

Dunbar bent to the figure and went through the pockets, being careful about lifting the dirty shirt from where the blood had pasted it to the skin. Finally he looked up.

"Nothing on him," he said.

Vorovich was reluctant to leave the fire, but he finally stood up and went over to them.

"I know," he said. "I stripped him down last night. The corset wasn't on him. It must have been hampering his movements, and so he stashed it before he came back to finish me off."

"The corset?" one of the rangers asked, eyebrows to his hairline.

"He was carrying heroin," the patrolman said, pleased to be in the know. "Maybe a quarter million dollars' worth, if it was pure stuff, and they think it was."

They began to look for the corset. The two rangers went at

it with more enthusiasm than the others, who, up all night, were less eager to be climbing up and down the hill, poking into crevices, wary of snakes which might be coming out as the sun appeared, glinting pale red above the forested mountain peak.

Vorovich stood for a time staring at the corpse; then he went over to the area where the large boulder had been, proving to his own satisfaction that if the youth had been able to dislodge the rock he would have been crushed.

"Aren't you hot in that coat?" Dunbar asked: the morning was warming and the air becoming dry, and sweat had formed on Vorovich's brow.

"When's the chopper due?" Vorovich asked, looking at his watch.

"Any minute now," Dunbar said. "They promised one at daylight." He hestiated. "What about the corset? You're in trouble if we don't find it, aren't you?"

His implication was plain. "The kid was running," Vorovich said. "The girl tossed him her corset and he split. Why else would he take off like that if it wasn't loaded?"

"I agree," Dunbar said. "But the desk men like something tangible, don't they?" He hesitated. "The girl lost her baby," he said.

Vorovich heard, somewhere in his memory, that voice pealing as he had ridden out of the encampment. He swallowed hard. "The kid wouldn't have had a father anyway," he said finally, and was grateful to hear the erratic sounds of the approaching chopper.

It was a green U.S. Forest Service helicopter, and it came slanting in over the hill in that peculiar sideways motion they had, and then circled, hovered over a flat area a few hundred yards down, and floated to land, grasshopperlike.

"Damn," one of the rangers said. "We'll have to lug him down."

Dunbar gave up his coat; they wrapped the youth in that, and with a ranger at either end set off down the trail.

"Will you okay the expense on a new coat for me?" Dunbar asked, falling in beside Vorovich. He was worried, thinking about all that blood, and how hard it was to get a clothing item approved, and somewhat resentful that his superior had not offered his coat, when it was his corpse, and he high enough in the bureau they would take his voucher as submitted.

"Naturally," Vorovich said, so abruptly Dunbar fell a few steps back.

While they loaded the corpse aboard, Vorovich used the copter's radio to request a search team to comb the area for a corset whose stitching contained a large quantity of heroin. He wanted it clearly established that he knew there had been a corset, and what was in it.

"You'd better let one of our police cars bring you into headquarters," the dispatcher on the other end said. "The suspects called a lawyer, and that shyster sonofabitch called the papers. Our local guys aren't so bad, but they got an L.A. *Times* stringer down here and he's drooling all over himself over this one."

"Okay," Vorovich said, and took a deep breath and thought, yes, it was starting now, and what he had set up for himself was going to be a very long, very tough haul, and then he pulled himself up into the copter, and crowded into the side seat, and tried not to think of anything at all.

At the heliport on Federal Island the police car was waiting. The uniformed driver looked curiously at Vorovich, but Vorovich did not volunteer any information on the drive into the city. Apparently the driver had been told to avoid undue observation, for he came toward the downtown headquarters building off the side-street alley, and went at a pretty good speed even into the parking cellar itself.

"That elevator takes you up," the driver said, pointing to a steel cage. "You want five."

The fifth floor was the liaison office between the local police and other jurisdictions. This was where Vorovich should have come to set up his task force. Instead, he had asked the local agent, Dunbar, to "pick up" whatever he could and join him at the border-patrol check point.

A teletype operator looked over as Vorovich came in off the elevator, shuffled through a stack of messages, and handed the one he wanted over, winking at a stocky detective in a rumpled gray sports coat who came over to get the visitor's reaction.

NEED IMMEDIATE REPORT UNFORTUNATE INCIDENT. NEW DEPARTMENTAL POLICY REQUIRES SUBJECT OFFICER BE PLACED ON

16

INDEFINITE LEAVE UNTIL RESULTS OF INVESTIGATION IN. INSPEC-
TOR HICKERSON EN ROUTE SAN DIEGO. WAIT HIS ARRIVAL FOR
FURTHER INSTRUCTIONS. SORRY.

(signed)
H. Llewelyn Cabot,
Acting Director
Drug Enforcement Administration

What was that "sorry"? Vorovich wondered. It read like an afterthought; one of those automatic expressions of regret typical of well-bred high-mannered people like the British, or bankers from Boston.

"How is the girl?" Vorovich asked.

"Miscarried," the detective said.

"I know that," Vorovich said, irritated with their dullness, and angry with himself for it. "But how is she?"

"She's in the prison ward of General Hospital," the fellow said. "But well enough to testify."

Not so dull he hadn't picked up on Vorovich's anger.

"Probably well enough to be returned to jail right now, if you ask me," the teletype operator said. "The hospital's a soft touch."

"Let her stay, if she wants," Vorovich said.

"That's up to the doctors," the detective said.

"Bail's being posted right now," the teletyper said. "So your arguing about it is academic."

"Who's posting bail?" Vorovich asked.

"Their lawyer," the other said.

"We asked who hired him," the detective said, "and he didn't answer."

"He's deaf in that ear," the teletyper said.

"I guess I ought to go talk to her, then," Vorovich said thoughtfully.

"You can't," the detective said. He ticked the message Vorovich was holding with his middle finger. "You're on indefinite leave, remember?" He almost smiled. "You have to have an official status to get into the prison ward."

"What kind of bullshit is that?" Vorovich demanded, so loudly those behind the glass partitions turned to see what was going on. "Everytime you turn around there's a new goddam regulation. All I want to do is visit her. No interrogations."

"Then what's the point?" the detective asked.

"I'm sorry about her husband," Vorovich said, lowering his voice.

"He wasn't her husband," the detective said, loud as before.

"The father of her kid," Vorovich said.

"If there's a hearing," the detective said, "she'll testify against you." There was an unspoken "won't she?" at the end of that sentence, Vorovich thought. "Maybe," the other continued, "you ought to get a lawyer yourself."

"Right now I need sleep," Vorovich said. "I'll be in the lounge if"—he glanced at the message—"Hickerson or someone important like that wants me."

"The press wants a statement," the detective said. "You got one prepared?"

"Hickerson will handle the fucking press," Vorovich said.

"Oh, my," the teletyper said, and covered his prissy face with the outstretched fingers of his manicured hand, but this time Vorovich got to the door without being stopped.

He was momentarily tempted by the cigarette machine—Salems, that was a pretty package, and Camels, there was an abrasive taste for you—one to match what he already had in the back of his mouth—but he had not smoked for three years and he was not quite edgy enough to restart, and so he got an Oh Henry! and a Mr. Peanut and a Hershey's Almond Chocolate out of the candy machine, but he was more sleepy than he was hungry, and he fell back on the couch asleep before he had even gotten the wrapper off.

Hickerson awakened him. Vorovich opened his eyes and regarded the thin-lipped, eye-glassed fellow in the chalk-striped black suit who stood over him, a thin black attaché case in his right hand. A southpaw then, Vorovich thought, in a reflex consideration, and then remembered that internal-affairs people never carried weapons. They didn't need them. Their power came from other sources.

He'd had experience with personnel officers. Though he had worked his way up in the bureau, he had never lost the attitudes he had picked up on the streets. If anything, he had gotten worse, because it was becoming increasingly difficult to make a case, no matter how careful you were about the evidence and your testimony and all the rest of it, and so he could not resist treating the punks and pushers hard in front, knowing they might get off. They were always surprised when he got so hostile, they were used to being catered to, especially by the younger narcs, who had, after all, gone into police work because they respected or at least believed in the law, and these younger narcs found it difficult not to feel humble before the punks in their English-tailored suits and Italian shoes and Cuban cigars. And so when Vorovich became tough and even, sometimes, physical, in a way that was hard to describe legally —he *crowded* them, stood very close, breathed in their usually jowly, overbarbered faces, hemming them in against some courthouse corridor wall where they couldn't get away—more than one protest came into the bureau from a congressman on behalf of a constituent.

Hickerson had already seen his file. "You've been in trouble before," he said.

"Depends on how you define it," Vorovich said.

Hickerson ignored the jab. "They've provided us with a room," he said. "Anytime you're ready."

Vorovich got off the couch, followed the other to a small conference room, and leaned against the wall, thoughtfully munching his candy while Hickerson opened the attaché case to reveal a tiny tape recorder and a lined yellow tablet on which the questions had been scrawled.

Vorovich couldn't read the questions, though he had trained himself over the years to read documents on desk tops upside down and backward. Hickerson's handwriting was crabbed and tiny, the mark of a secretive, narrow man.

"You want to fill me in on what happened?" Hickerson asked.

"Aren't you going to switch on the tape recorder?" Vorovich asked. It wouldn't do to keep it under wraps, he thought. He had to make sure what he wanted to get out got out.

Hickerson looked at him sharply. "I thought we'd keep this informal, until I get a general idea of how much trouble you're in. The state's attorney is pissed about your borrowing the highway patrol for a dope bust. If he brings charges, he'll subpoena our records, including any tapes. . . ."

Vorovich leaned over, pressed the button marked ON.

Thin nostrils flaring, Hickerson took out an immaculate handkerchief and wiped the smeared chocolate off his machine. "January twelfth," he said, in an official tone, "investigation into the matter of the shooting of a narcotics suspect in San Diego County, California. Inspector William Hickerson, Division of Internal Affairs, questioning Timothy Vorovich, Director of Tactical Intelligence, Department of Compliance, Drug Enforcement Administration. Let the record show respondent is duly apprised of his rights, and wishes the interrogation to proceed. Question: describe the events leading up to the fatal incident."

Vorovich cleared his throat. "Information had come in," he said, "through a contact in Mexico, that a large amount of heroin would be carried across the border by six young people in a Volkswagen bus. It was decided to make our stakeout inland from the border—"

"*Who* decided?" Hickerson asked.

"I have that authority," Vorovich said.

"Go on."

"I gathered a task force composed of local, state, and Federal personnel," Vorovich said.

"Without alerting the various jurisdictions?"

"It was an informal arrangement," Vorovich said. "You can always do the paperwork later if you have to."

"You know that's in direct contradiction to normal rules of procedure?" Hickerson asked.

"What's normal?"

"Could you be more responsive to the question, please?" Hickerson said. "Weren't you aware that you were contravening established departmental procedures by setting up a stakeout without proper clearances?"

"Of course I was aware of it," Vorovich said. "I helped establish those procedures."

"Does that make you less responsible for conforming to them?" Hickerson asked.

"They're not engraved in marble," Vorovich said.

"They're printed and bound in a government handbook," Hickerson said. "And as the supervising officer, you must set an example. . . ."

"Is this an interrogation or a lecture?" Vorovich asked.

"I was merely pointing out your responsibilities as head of a department," Hickerson said, after a long moment.

"I'm aware of my responsibilities," Vorovich said.

"Then are you willing to acknowledge that you acted contrary to code in setting up a quasi-legal task force?" Hickerson asked.

"I am not," Vorovich said, holding his anger, shaping it, not wanting to use it too soon. "We needed help, and there wasn't time to go through channels to get it. . . ."

"Why wasn't there time?" Hickerson demanded.

"The information came to me late," Vorovich said heatedly. "Since the reorganization, no one knows who's supposed to do what."

"In retrospect," Hickerson said, "wouldn't you say that the size of the force you gathered was an overreaction, considering your quarry?"

"My instincts told me this was a major drop," Vorovich said.

"Your instincts?" Hickerson said.

"When you've been in the field as many years as I have," Vorovich said, "you learn to sense when something important is going to happen."

"Do you?" Hickerson said sarcastically.

"It was outside the norm to use young people as mules for heroin," Vorovich said, "and I had a feeling that—"

"Let me see if I understand you correctly," Hickerson said, interrupting. "You had received information that a group of young people of both sexes were smuggling heroin . . ."

"A large amount of heroin," Vorovich said.

"A large amount of heroin," Hickerson repeated, "and because it was outside the norm, you took personal charge of a hastily arranged stakeout on a hunch to detain a small group of young people who might have answered the description of those allegedly smuggling heroin. . . ."

"They had it all right," Vorovich said.

"But you didn't find any," Hickerson said. "Did you?" he asked, when Vorovich did not respond.

"It was in the corset," Vorovich said.

"How do you know that?" Hickerson asked.

"It wasn't any place else," Vorovich said.

"Well, unless that corset is found," Hickerson said, "you can't justify that slaying."

"It was justified," Vorovich said. "He was trying to kill me."

"How did that come about?" Hickerson asked.

"How do you suppose that came about?" Vorovich demanded. "He was on the run. . . ."

"That's precisely the area I want to explore," Hickerson said. "How did he manage that, considering the rather large force you had gathered?"

Vorovich let more of his anger show. The other was sniffing around the edges of more than incompetence, he was wondering whether Vorovich hadn't somehow set the kid up by giving him an opening—and of course he hadn't, he had merely gone with the situation as it developed. He couldn't deny to himself that this situation had turned into something a lot better than he had hoped for, but knocking some dumb kid off wasn't part of it.

"You trying to hang me?" he demanded, glaring at the other.

"I'm here to evaluate your performance," Hickerson snapped. "Any hanging will be by your own hands."

"Don't be clever with me," Vorovich said. "You got something on your mind, come out with it, don't give me any of your horseshit wit."

The tape continued to run. "I believe a playback of the tape will show that you are unfairly characterizing my remarks," Hickerson said finally, and though he seemed cool, there was a discernible tremor in his voice.

"Let's not waste the time," Vorovich said. "You were asking how the kid managed to get away."

"Yes," Hickerson said, still quivering.

"It was careless, I admit that," Vorovich said. "I had gone over by the VW van to get a report on the progress of the search, and I simply wasn't paying the attention I should have."

"Here is a pad and pencil," Hickerson said. "Would you sketch in the various positions you were in?" He handed the items to Vorovich. "In relationship to the van, the other law-enforcement personnel, and the trail bike."

"We had just come in from a toilet trip here," Vorovich said, rapidly drawing the requested positions. "The girl was here, the boy here, I was walking in this direction here . . ."

"Leaving the boy unguarded," Hickerson observed.

"It was inadvertent," Vorovich said.

"I didn't say otherwise," Hickerson said. "Was he carrying the corset then?"

"He had strapped it on under his shirt," Vorovich said.

"Didn't you think that was somewhat unusual?" Hickerson asked.

"I had other things on my mind," Vorovich said. "The girl had thrown it to him and said she wasn't going to wear it any more, it hurt her stomach too much, and I guess I assumed he threw it away in the dark."

"Then how did you know he had it strapped on?" Hickerson asked, puzzled by something in his notes.

"When he went for the bike I noticed he looked fat in the gut," Vorovich said. "That's when I remembered the corset."

"And you think the corset was loaded with dope?" Hickerson asked.

"I know it," Vorovich said. He paused a moment. "Why else did he take it when he ran?"

"Yes, of course," Hickerson said. He too paused. "And you didn't consider the corset might be the repository of the heroin until he ran away?"

Vorovich stared at him.

"Aren't you going to answer that question?" Hickerson asked.

"I have answered it," Vorovich said. And then: "You asked me that before," he said.

Again the frown from Hickerson. "Did I?" he asked.

"Yes," Vorovich said. "Can't we get this over with?"

"The girl denies there was a corset," Hickerson said.

Vorovich was taken by surprise. "She does?" he said. "Why?"

Hickerson looked at him almost pityingly. "There's no evidence of any kind that they were running dope. If she denies there was a corset, she eliminates even that possibility."

"Then why did the kid run?" Vorovich demanded.

"According to the girl," Hickerson said, "the boy had a prior conviction. He was afraid of being framed."

"Oh," Vorovich said. "Who would believe that?"

"A judge and jury, maybe," Hickerson said. Then he switched the recorder OFF. "Off the record," he said, "Mr. Cabot wants to know if there's any message you would like conveyed to him personally, outside channels."

"What kind of message?" Vorovich asked, pretending puzzlement.

"I went to college with the director," Hickerson said. "We were fraternity brothers, in fact. He said to tell you that if you wanted to take him into your confidence, you could trust me to be your go-between." Hickerson polished his glasses, careful about the handkerchief. "I might even misplace this tape, and transcribe this interview from memory."

Vorovich stared. This wouldn't do, he thought. Not just for his immediate plans, but if later, somewhere down the line, things went terribly wrong, he would have something on record to justify himself.

"What's the H. stand for?" Vorovich asked, pointing to Cabot's signature on the teletype.

"Horace," Hickerson said.

Vorovich leaned across the table and punched the recorder button to ON again. "You tell Horace for me," he said, "that any messages I would have for him are on the record, on this tape."

Hickerson flushed. "You may make a concluding statement, if you wish," he said after a moment, in a somewhat strangled voice.

"About what?" Vorovich asked. "Specifically?"

"About your handling of this field operation," Hickerson said.

"You're the one who's best at drawing conclusions," Vorovich said. "Why don't you sum it all up?"

"If you'll finish unwrapping your candy," Hickerson said. "It'll sound rather thunderous on the machine."

"Care for some?" Vorovich asked.

"Point one," Hickerson said, angrily waving the offered bar away, "you took over a function best left to people actually in the field."

"I was in the field a long time," Vorovich said. "I came up through the field."

"Point two," Hickerson continued, "you knew there were female suspects, and yet you had no female officers. Point three: a key suspect is left relatively unguarded with a questionable object in his possession, and through what can only be termed carelessness gets away . . ."

"He didn't get away," Vorovich said.

". . . and, though unarmed, is shot dead," Hickerson went on, "and a female suspect loses her baby, charging rough treatment. If you were doing the evaluating, Mr. Vorovich, how would *you* enter it into the record?"

"I'd look for extenuating circumstances," Vorovich said.

"Such as what?" Hickerson asked.

"I'd at least consider an agent's past performances before I threw him to the wolves," Vorovich said, after an appreciable pause.

"We're hardly doing that," Hickerson said. "You know that it's better to anticipate a public outcry with a departmental hearing. We are not out to *condemn* you. The department is merely evaluating your performance, and will decide, independent of any outside pressure, whether you might not—"

"Have outlived my usefulness?" Vorovich interrupted, in a cold fury.

"Have acted contrary to code," Hickerson said, eyes gleaming behind the circlets of glass.

He switched his machine to OFF, removed the cassette, began placing it all in the attaché case. "Aren't you," he said, "the department head who stressed the importance of placing agents where they may operate the most efficiently, according to character and ability? How many agents have you yourself transferred from the field to an administrative job?"

"I never pretended it was a reward," Vorovich said.

"Good luck with the state's attorney," Hickerson said, clicking his attaché case shut.

The girl lied from first breath to last. In spite of the fact that she was making him look like an absolute fool, Vorovich almost admired the way she was carrying it off, playing the sweet, innocent, bereaved spouse and miscarried mother, gazing at the fascinated spectators in that courtroom like a contrite wide-eyed child come to make her peace with her conscience and the world she loved so.

The state's attorney, determined to teach these arrogant Feds a lesson, had filed a complaint of voluntary manslaughter. The U.S. attorney representing Vorovich in this preliminary hearing, a man whose deep tan bespoke hours of tennis and golf, did not believe the other was making more than a token case, designed more for public consumption than to actually "win," but Vorovich wasn't so sure.

For one thing, the state's attorney, whose thick glasses made him seem deceptively inept, had taken pains to dress his key witness in a simple frock; she wore stockings and had her hair tied back with a bow, and with no make-up and a shiny nose she would appeal not only to these retired farmers and elderly real-estate brokers who seem to make up the majority of the population in San Diego County, but also to the judge, a thin-lipped, squint-eyed, grayish man who seemed to be hanging on her every word.

For another, she had clearly been well coached.

"Why, we would be *fools* to try and smuggle dope in," she said when the state's attorney asked her whether they had in fact contracted to bring contraband across the border. "Everyone knows how the law-enforcement people get all perturbed about transient kids and are just *looking* for an excuse to arrest them!"

"But Federal Agent Vorovich has testified that his informants gave him a specific description of you and your friends and the Volkswagen van you were traveling in, down to the license number," the state's attorney said.

"Maybe those informants," she said, "those mysterious people he won't identify, put the finger on us to *mislead* the authorities, to divert their attention from the people who were *actually* bringing dope in. Did anyone ever think of that?"

"Did you?" murmured the U.S. attorney to Vorovich.

"It was accurate information," Vorovich insisted stubbornly.

"Besides," she was going on, "I hate dope. I've seen what it can do to people . . ." she hesitated, and blinked back the tears, which, Vorovich thought, might be genuine, though very little else about her was. "I mean," she went on, looking directly at Vorovich for the first time then, "he's talking about *heroin*. I don't deny that most of us have tried marijuana or psychedelics, one time or another, but *not* the hard stuff. I mean if you follow what we're into at all, you know that we wouldn't be caught within a hundred miles of anyone fool enough to be dealing in *that!* I mean, I was carrying a baby, and I surely wasn't *about* to jeopardize a new life for something as stupid and awful as that. . . ."

Vorovich, had he not known better, had to admit that she would almost have convinced him, so intense was the look of her then, so near she seemed to breaking down.

"You deny there was any corset?" the state's attorney asked, giving her a moment to control herself.

"I don't know *what* he thinks he saw," the girl, who had said her name was Jennifer but whom the state's attorney, in another folksy touch, referred to as Ginny, said, "and I really don't understand why he was *looking*. I mean, I was pregnant, and it's bad enough for a girl to have to go to the bathroom out in the open like that without being *stared* at."

The judge was looking at Vorovich now, and in spite of himself he reddened. Everyone seemed to have forgotten that the dead youth had been there too, or if they remembered had accepted her story that he was her husband, though no record of a marriage was produced.

"Your witness," the state's attorney said.

"Let her go," Vorovich said, as the U.S. attorney started to rise.

"We shouldn't let her testimony stand unchallenged," the U.S. attorney said.

"You said there was no way they could prove the charge," Vorovich said. "What she says doesn't matter."

"It'll matter to your agency," the U.S. attorney said.

"Does the defense wish to cross-examine?" the judge asked then, in a high, testy voice.

"The defense passes," the U.S. attorney said, after a puzzled look at his client.

"Recall Timothy Vorovich, if your honor pleases," the state's attorney said.

Vorovich had to pass very near her on his way to the stand, and again he was amazed by the seeming purity of her expression. But she was unable to meet his glance.

"Were you wearing glasses during the events that took place on the day in question?" the state's attorney asked, after Vorovich had been reminded he was still under oath.

"No," Vorovich said.

"Why not?" the state's attorney demanded.

"I don't wear glasses," Vorovich said.

"You're more than forty-five years old and you don't wear glasses?" the state's attorney said.

"I've never needed them," Vorovich said patiently.

"Really," the state's attorney said, and walked to the opposite corner of the courtroom, borrowed a newspaper from a spectator in the front row, and held up a smudged black headline: FEDERAL AGENT CHARGED IN "MISTAKEN" NARCOTICS RAID SLAYING. "Can you read this?" the state's attorney called, in an unnecessarily loud voice.

Before Vorovich could respond, the U.S. attorney was protesting. "What court is the state's attorney grandstanding in, that of public opinion? Surely there are more seemly ways to determine the quality of Agent Vorovich's vision."

The judge agreed.

"Besides," the U.S. attorney said, "I think it's already been clearly demonstrated that his eyesight is excellent, considering the accuracy of his shooting. And in the dark, at that."

Though it did not square with the image of himself he was trying to project, Vorovich could not help setting the record straight. "I shot blind," he said. "By instinct."

They were all looking at him with renewed interest.

"You didn't aim?" the state's attorney asked, expressing the awe they all felt, questioning his intent, not his prerogatives.

"No," Vorovich said. "I pointed the gun in the direction I thought he might be and when I saw a shadow there. . . ."

"A shadow?" the state's attorney said. "In the middle of the night?"

"My eyes had adjusted to the dark," Vorovich said.

"But not well enough to aim, you say," the state's attorney said, pushing his glasses up on his nose.

"I just instinctively squeezed the trigger," Vorovich said.

"Instinctively?" the state's attorney said.

"It was a reflex," Vorovich insisted, as much to convince himself as this persistent other. "He was trying to tip a boulder down the hill at me."

"Was he?" the state's attorney said. "But he didn't manage to do that, did he? And your victim—pardon, suspect—was unarmed, you knew that, you had searched him yourself. And you must also have known, given your rank in the agency you serve, that firing on an unarmed suspect is contrary to your agency's Code of Conduct, isn't that true?"

"Objection," the U.S. attorney said, on his feet again. "The state's attorney is implying that Agent Vorovich was not in danger, when in fact another officer of the law was grievously wounded during the same chase. Furthermore, whether or not he conformed to his agency's regulations is irrelevant to the complaint!"

"Sustained," the judge said, though Vorovich could see he had arrived at that conclusion reluctantly.

"You are certain you saw something passed between Ginny and the dead boy," the state's attorney went on. "I'll grant you that you have remarkable night vision—but surely in a place dark enough for this girl to go to the bathroom in, what she tossed at the boy could have been something else, couldn't it? Her panties, thrown at him in a harmless bit of fun, to relieve her feelings, because, after all, two men, no matter that one was her husband, were watching her in those intimate moments we would all prefer to remain private. . . ."

"It was a corset," Vorovich said, reddening.

"How extensive a search was made for this alleged undergarment?" the state's attorney asked.

"They were out there for almost a week," Vorovich said, who had personally requested search teams comb the ground from that encampment to the foothills where the boy had been shot, so that there would not be the least doubt, among those who would know of its existence, that the corset had not been found.

"Mr. Vorovich," the state's attorney said, "won't you admit

—and may I remind you that you are under oath—that in the darkness, with your eyes averted, I am sure, because you do not strike me as the kind of a man who would stare at a pregnant girl going to the bathroom, with your modest eyes averted, and given the fact that after an exhaustive search, not only of those grounds but of the vehicle and the clothing of these young people, nothing, not a scrap or a shred of evidence against them, was found, it is possible you *imagined* this corset? Because you had gone to a great deal of trouble, brought other than Federal law-enforcement personnel into a situation that seemed hardly worth all that effort, and without full and proper authorization at that, isn't it possible that knowing how this would look on a personnel file already skewed toward the minus side, you, desperate for justification, created a corset out of whole cloth, as it were?"

Vorovich did not answer.

"I hope you don't resent my questioning your state of mind in this way," the state's attorney said. "As a representative of the public, I have a duty to question the reliability of our law-enforcement personnel."

Vorovich remained silent.

"Isn't it possible it was something other than a corset?" the state's attorney asked.

Vorovich took a deep and silent breath. It was difficult to break the habit of a lifetime. "Yes," he lied finally. "It's possible."

"Thank you," the state's attorney said, full of a triumphant kind of sadness, and sat down.

Vorovich looked at the girl, who was staring at him in puzzlement, and then it was he who couldn't hold her glance.

The U.S. attorney's move for dismissal of the indictment touched on Vorovich's long and honorable record, the quality of the information, the fact that the suspect had run, flight implying guilt, and pointing out that even then tragedy might have been averted had not the fugitive attempted bodily harm to his pursuers.

While the judge took the motion under advisement, Vorovich, fighting the urge to smoke, went to a candy-vending machine in the outside corridor, ignoring the U.S. attorney's and Hickerson's warning that he stay away from the press, now all over the place.

"When *was* the last time you had your eyes checked?" a young man, bearded and long-haired, barely into his twenties, asked.

"Who are you?" Vorovich asked.

"Underground-press syndicate," the young man barked, as if he were in a movie—*The Front Page*—and the other reporters, most graying and somewhat paunchy, laughed.

"It's all in the record," Vorovich said. "Department regulations call for an annual checkup, including the eyes."

"Is it true," an older reporter asked, "that you were up for a promotion and were passed over?"

Vorovich shrugged.

"Any special reason?" the reporter asked.

"Politics," Vorovich said, incurring the displeasure of Hickerson. The reporters laughed again, uncertainly, not sure whether Vorovich was serious or not.

"Do you resent this hearing?" the bearded young man asked.

Vorovich thought about it: thought about what he did resent, the years he had spent in the service, the deals made between lawyers, witness immunities, the use of informers, the slow upward crawl of his pay scale, bureaucratic inefficiency, the job that should have been his, and, as he had hoped, some, even a lot of that showed in his face, as he could see by the reporters' interest, and Hickerson's sudden concern.

"Wouldn't you?" he growled finally, decided now how he might use what he felt to get a message out through the press.

"That would depend," the younger man said, studying him, "on whether I thought I had goofed or not."

"The kid cut and ran, didn't he?" Vorovich said. "And along the way a cop got badly hurt—who's worried about him? That's his job, right? We're paid to bleed. And the fact is, the public, the ones who read your goddam papers, are hoping these shitheads get away with it. I mean you're always printing the net worth of our movie stars and our thousand-dollars-a-day oil millionaires and how much loot in negotiable cash our heisters make off with, and secretly the public is rooting for the criminals. They *identify* with the criminals, and when one of *us* is up before them they put it to us good, I mean God help us we should be the least bit careless, or not play by the rules. . . . How come the rules are weighted in favor of the other side? It's a no-win game. If we stay cozy within the system we won't catch many criminals, but we'll get our twenty-year pin and enough pension to eke it out in some board shack in Arizona or New Mexico. . . ."

Hickerson was beside himself. "Look here, fellows," he pleaded, as the reporters scribbled away, and those with tape recorders checked their volume control, "I don't think it is in Agent Vorovich's best interests for you to print that."

"I don't care if they print it," Vorovich said.

"Well, you should," Hickerson hissed. "Think how this will sound to the people in Washington."

"Screw the people in Washington," Vorovich said.

The underground-press-syndicate representative grinned through his beard. "Can I quote you on that?" he asked.

Vorovich permitted Hickerson to lead him away.

He was on his second candy bar when the call came that court was in session. He had a wad of chocolate in his jaw, like tobacco, when he stood to hear the verdict, and the bitter sweet trickled down his throat as the judge spoke.

"I do not find there to be sufficient evidence to convict," the judge said, "and so I am sustaining the motion to dismiss the charge against you. However, I do believe there was, within the scope of your department's own rules, contributory negligence, and certain actions believed to be contrary to your department's code, and I therefore recommend your department take appropriate action."

The U.S. attorney wanted to take exception to this last as being outside the judge's jurisdiction, but Vorovich preferred letting it stand.

"But your superiors may feel obliged to discipline you if it remains on the record," the U.S. attorney said.

"It doesn't matter," Vorovich said. "On the record or off, they're going to put it to me."

"You sound as if you wanted them to," the U.S. attorney said.

Vorovich didn't respond. But as he swallowed the melted candy, he caught the girl's curious pale-eyed gaze upon him.

Vorovich refused to return to Washington for the official reprimand, and refused also to talk with Cabot, who had left urgent messages for him in both the San Diego and Los Angeles offices. He did talk to the deputy director, an administrative man he had known since joining the bureau, who was the closest of any of them to being a friend—which wasn't very close, he thought, hanging up the department's phone. The D.D.'s reaction when he refused to "talk out" his resentments became understandably curt, and finally, with a bureaucrat's mind, he insisted Vorovich's resignation be put in writing.

The agents in the partitioned cubbyholes were all watching as he cornered the area director's secretary and dictated a one-sentence memorandum: THIS IS TO INFORM YOU THAT EFFECTIVE THIS DATE I AM RESIGNING AS AN AGENT OF THE DRUG ENFORCEMENT ADMINISTRATION. He waited for the girl to type the memo, hand-corrected a misspelling, and signed his name and the date, asking the stocky agent Dunbar to sign as a witness. Then he Xeroxed a copy for himself and walked out without a word to any of the others, either of regret or farewell.

Down three floors of that Federal building, he walked into the government vault and deposited several large manila envelopes stuffed full of personal belongings on a back out-of-the-way shelf, taking the precaution of placing them under government seal. The clerk on duty, a uniformed security guard, was so busy gossiping with another worker that he did not bother verifying the contents.

Vorovich took an apartment on De Longpre, a curving tree-lined side street just below the Sunset Strip in Los Angeles, not easy to find, which suited his emotional state perfectly.

He needed time not only to think through what he wanted to do but to sort out his feelings. At the very least, he had expected to feel some sense of loss at wiping himself out of a job he had held for almost twenty years, and to experience this lightheadedness, as if he had just gotten over a high fever, as if the hat he had worn, a kind of secret uniform, had constricted not only his forehead but his brain, was totally surprising.

Then had come uncertainty. He had trusted his instincts, and his luck, to take him through the preceding events, shaping them however he could to fit the developing situations, and everything had worked out better than he had any right to expect. So far.

But now what? If he were really smart, he told himself, he'd walk away from everything, trusting that first euphoric feeling as the true one, drift for a while, float until his severance pay ran out, then go into a new line of work, something as far removed from cloak and dagger as he could get. Maybe open a little business, buy a fried-chicken or pizza franchise. . . .

No use kidding himself, he thought then. Never before, in his twenty years' service, had he had the kind of opportunity to go to the source that might be opening up for him here. He couldn't let go of it now. Later, he reassured himself, he could always take himself out of the picture if he decided it was becoming too difficult.

His apartment, a furnished bachelor, was near the territory he wanted, the cafés and smoke shops frequented by the hip folk of the counterculture, as well as the bars and clubs of the older, better fed, mod-dressed patrons whose hair, though long, was barbered and coiffed.

He made no attempt to hide his identity. When he went to Alfie's for a hamburger and beer, and the braless mini-skirted teen-aged waitress asked him, "Aren't you the narco that, you know, like wasted the young mule in San Diego?" he sighed and nodded. And went back there again and twice again, hoping for a contact which never developed, those seemingly unaware folk always managing to leave at least one complete circle of empty tables around him.

He started having lunch at the Old World, where he ate bone-marrow soup and swinger burgers, but he was a pariah there too; no one picked up on his obvious willingness to start a conversation, instead trying to get rid of him by serving him as quickly as they could.

After the L.A. *Times* ran his picture and a series on what could be considered Excessive Force and Reasonable, and even an editorial using his quotes and deciding his resentments were invalid, a misreading of Mr. and Mrs. American, it was whispered up and down the street to watch out for him, his angers were very near the surface. When the *Free Press* gave the story its usual adolescent humorous play, and the *Rolling Stone* was surprisingly more than fair (a dramatic dialogue between Cop and Citizen, based on the fears and angers of each), he hoped

34

the threatened feeling among them would dissipate. But he could not seem to get any of them to acknowledge his existence.

He switched his beat. But they knew him at the bars, too. The first time around they pushed his money back when he ordered his whisky neats and beer chasers. After that, however, when it became apparent that he was going to keep hanging around, they charged him. And eventually started talking.

"That was pretty good shooting," a bartender at the Marquis said. "Damn freaky kids ask for it."

"Small loss," a pale curly-haired man who slid onto the stool next to him said. He looked to be about thirty-five, with effete tastes, if the frothy drink in the long-stemmed glass was any indication. Vorovich poured his whisky into his beer and watched the other wince.

"You think so?" Vorovich asked.

"They claim to be pure in heart," the other said, "and yet they're always popping pills or sniffing shit, and they won't eat anything but organically grown vegetables and yet they'll run dope. Disgusting!"

"You believe they were running dope, then," Vorovich said.

"Weren't they?" the other asked. "Not that I think some of your people are above planting evidence—do you mind if I say that? nothing personal, mind—but a man as high up in the agency as you is certainly not going to stoop to frying such small fish, are you? You must have had good information on them."

"You asking, or telling?" Vorovich asked.

"I mean," the other continued, ignoring the insulting tone, "if it was a plant, as those silly children claimed, why was no evidence of wrongdoing found?"

The bartender was looking at him expectantly. They believed he had the merchandise, Vorovich thought, and he did not know whether to be pleased or angry that such small potatoes were sounding him out. They were not what he was looking for. They were acting on their own, hoping to make a score.

He reached to pay for his drink.

"Allow me," the other said, moving quickly. "I know how quick the money goes when one is out of work."

"I have plenty," Vorovich said, shoving the money back.

"And when the severance pay is gone, what then?" the other asked. "Here," he said, sliding a card down the bar to him.

Vorovich picked up the card. It was engraved. Albert Vancouver, it said, Sales Representative, Import-Export Consultants, Ltd. "If you're ever interested in an investment opportunity," Albert said, "give me a call."

Vorovich had a sudden strong feeling that Vancouver was a Cooperating Individual, someone who covered both sides of the street. While it might be possible they were nosing around for merchandise, it was also possible that the deputy director was making a run at him—not out of suspicion, necessarily, but just as a matter of form. He took the card and carefully tore it in half, and dropped the pieces on the bar. Then he looked at the bartender, who suddenly found that he had glasses to clean.

"You're a rude man," Albert Vancouver said.

"I'm through working for other people," Vorovich said.

That was true, he thought later, when he was reconsidering his strategies. The line had come out without forethought, strong and hard, surprising himself with the vehemence of his reply, making him wonder whether his motives in all this were as straight as he had imagined them.

But he pushed all that out of his mind. Again, he told himself, time enough for that later, when—if—the connection he was looking for came.

He decided he'd better do something direct to establish his credibility. What? As dusk came, and the traffic increased, he watched as several county sheriff's cars staked out positions on the Strip and two deputies began going into and out of one shop after another. When they braced several young people, doing a quick frisk, he thought this might be his chance. And angling across the boulevard, he went into a store several doors down from where they were patrolling.

The Far-Out Smoke Shoppe, though it was thick with incense, at first glance seemed unoccupied. Entering through a glass beaded curtain, he was buffeted by Indian music, a caterwauling of reed instruments, cymbals, and untaut strings played so loudly the tendrils of smoke in the air were agitated. Then, looking down, below the level of the counters, he saw a half dozen grimy-footed, long-haired kids with faces the color of raw potato. The proprietor, however, looked healthy, his frizzy hair pony-tailed and tied with the same kind of beaded circlet that the kids in the bus had worn. Coincidence? Maybe, Vorovich thought.

"Nice," Vorovich said, picking up a long-handled opium pipe. "I imagine it takes a special blend?"

The shop owner shrugged. But some of the people sitting on the floor smirked.

"You sell the smoke stuff here too?" Vorovich asked.

"Just the equipment," the other said. "You furnish your own makings."

"Lucky for you," Vorovich said. "Because there's a couple of uniform types working their way up the street, and if they find that any of your clientele were purchasing grass they might give them a hard time."

Two of the kids got up and slipped silently out a rear door.

"Who are you?" the young shop owner demanded.

"Is your place clean?" Vorovich asked.

"Always," the shop owner said, just as the two uniformed deputy sheriffs came through the beaded curtain.

The older man came to the counter, ignoring Vorovich after one quick glance, and stared at the kids, who were concentrating on their toes.

"Okay," the older man said. "On your feet, and turn your pockets inside out, those as has pockets. The rest of you dump your handbags."

"You're exceeding your authority, aren't you, chief?" Vorovich asked.

The older man's face darkened. No wonder, Vorovich thought, he had ten years' service and no rank on his sleeve.

"What's it to you?" the other growled.

"I'm an interested citizen," Vorovich said.

The younger deputy came farther into the room. "Would you mind identifying yourself?" he asked.

"I think I do," Vorovich said.

"Why?" the older one growled.

"I don't see the point," Vorovich said.

"The point is, *sir,*" the younger one said, so that no one could say they hadn't been polite, "that you are loitering about a place in which it is known that harmful drugs have exchanged hands, and we wish to assure ourselves that this is not the case with you."

"Take my word for it," Vorovich said.

The two deputies exchanged glances.

"Okay, sir," the older man said heavily. "If you won't show

us proof of residence or solvency, we shall have to take you in."

"On what charge?" Vorovich asked.

"Soliciting," the younger one said.

"Jesus," Vorovich said. "I just bought this suit last year." He was strangely gratified to hear the younger people laugh. "You think you can justify a charge like that?"

"You a practicing lawyer, sir?" the younger one asked. "Or you been studying up on your rights, just in case?"

"Why don't you go ahead and show them identification," the shop owner said. "If they take you in you'll have to show it."

Vorovich hesitated, to make it look good, then handed over his wallet.

The older deputy didn't like what he was reading. He squinted when he looked again at Vorovich, as if he had missed something the first time around, then handed the wallet to the younger man.

"You got a shitty deal," the older man said then. "But it wasn't us give it to you."

"It is our duty," the younger one said, "to report anything out of the ordinary that we find on our tour. Now, if you will just give us a reason as to why you're here, we will not have to report that we observed you in this psychedelic head shop."

"That," Vorovich said, holding his hand out for the wallet, "is none of your fucking concern."

"I never liked the narcs myself," the older man said. "There was always something spooky about them. They get to be very like the shitheads they go after."

"Maybe," the younger man said, "there was a corset full of shit after all. Maybe that corset was found and hidden again and maybe that shit is now on the market."

"Found?" the older deputy said. "By whom?"

"By person or persons unknown," the younger man said, tossing the wallet at Vorovich. "Come on, partner, I want to go somewhere and sit down and begin thinking about what to put in our report. I want to make sure it's worded right." And after slanting a look at Vorovich he went on out, followed by the older man, who pushed through the curtain so roughly a string broke. Beads rolled about on the floor.

"Is what he said true?" the shop owner asked in a low voice, as the other young people began picking up the beads.

Vorovich smiled, and turned to leave.

"Why don't you sign our guest book?" the shop owner asked, sliding a ledger along the counter. "We'll put you on our mailing list."

"I don't like a lot of people knowing where I live," Vorovich said.

"I'll keep it just between us," the shop owner said.

"Don't worry about it," Vorovich said. "I intend to look in now and again."

"I don't think that's such a good idea," the other said. "The narcs are all over the Strip, and now that you've antagonized the pigs, they'll be all over you, like flies on sugar."

Vorovich smiled. "No problem," he said. "I've made sure my sugar is under wraps."

He stepped around the crawling figures, shouldering his way out through what was left of the beaded curtain.

He took his sweet time going down the street. He hadn't wanted to give his address to a small-time operator. If he had made an important enough contact, they would have him followed, and that would tell him he was on the right track.

He ducked through the heavy traffic, gazed into a shopwindow specializing in gay garments, saw that two people had come out of the Smoke Shoppe to look after him, though he stayed a fair distance away. He was pleased.

Then he noticed the two deputy sheriffs. Apparently he had made them angrier than he had thought, angry enough for them to want to keep him under personal surveillance for a while longer.

The problem was to lose the two deputies and still allow the other people to find out where he lived. He loitered along the crowded Strip, giving everyone plenty of time to get a fix on him. But the deputies got smart, and sicced some kid on him, someone they had busted before, no doubt. Then he was chagrined to discover the ones following him from the Smoke Shoppe were two young girls, making it less likely that the drop was as important as he had hoped it would be. They seemed so obvious, too, giggling together as they peered through angles of storefront windows at him, lighting up one cigarette after another, exchanging salutations with half the youngsters on the street . . . but then he remembered how young the kids transporting the heroin had been and he decided to follow it on through.

He went into a bar called the Hideaway, sleazy and narrow as a corridor, the stools occupied by hunch-shouldered men and pasty-faced women, where the girls couldn't go but the deputies' kid could. He ordered a beer, which the kid did too, several stools down from him. Then Vorovich asked, loud enough so the kid could hear, where the john was. Since it was in back, out of sight of the bar, he merely opened and immediately shut the bathroom door, then ducked outside, finding himself in an alley. He circled back around to the street, allowed the girls to catch sight of him, then headed down a side street, moving very fast to get himself gone before the deputies' kid would have begun to wonder what was keeping him.

On De Longpre he slowed, then stopped near a streetlight to stroke a stray cat, which permitted his followers to catch up and to see which apartment house he went into.

The elevator was available, and he delayed it, pushing the fourth-floor button when he saw them approaching. If they were intelligent at all, they could look at the lights above the elevator bank to see what floor he stopped on.

But just in case they were unsure, he turned on the lights as soon as he went in and opened the blinds facing the street. Then he mixed himself a drink; that is, he poured some Irish to sweeten the leftover coffee, and, looking at his watch, was surprised to see that it was almost nine o'clock. He fixed himself a cheese sandwich, which he ate standing up, and then, thinking there would be a certain amount of consultation before it was decided who would make the approach and how, and that it would probably not be before morning, he undressed, planning to read himself to sleep.

When the doorbell rang, his first thought was that he hadn't lost the deputies' kid after all, and second that they were all perhaps in collusion, playing some sort of elaborate charade. He didn't know how clean the L.A. county sheriff's department was, and even in the best law-enforcement circles some were corrupted, so he decided to take precautions. He strapped the little snub-nosed .32 to his lower calf, pulled his pajama leg down over it, and went to the door.

Disdaining the peephole or the chain lock, he opened it just as his visitor, impatient, was ringing the bell again.

"I'd rather not stand out here in the hall, if you don't mind," she said, and when he finally stood aside she walked past him and looked about the room as if nothing were on her mind, except, maybe, a casual visit.

She was dressed in what looked like an old fur from her grandmother's closet, a tacky brown thing that reached from a high Garbo-like collar to her ankles. He had half expected her to be barefoot, but he saw, with some kind of relief, that she was wearing ballet slippers, which was better than nothing. And she was tall enough, and her carriage regal enough, that she managed to convey something of an air of elegance, however old-fashioned.

"I didn't expect you," he said, closing the door.

"That's obvious," she said. She walked in a circle, examining the room closely. "God," she said, "the way they decorate these places is a crime, isn't it?"

"I hadn't noticed," he said finally.

"How can you stand it?" she asked, going about the room to turn each picture to the wall.

"I wasn't planning to stay here permanently," he said. He suddenly became aware of his flimsy pajamas.

"Where you going?" she asked.

"To get my robe," he said, and though he heard her saying it didn't matter, she had seen men in their natural state before, he grabbed the wrinkled cotton garment off the bathroom hook and made sure it was tied securely before he went back in.

"God, where'd you get that?" she demanded, and despite himself he felt the blood surging to his face.

"A local thrift shop," he said. "You didn't think on what we make we go Brooks, do you?" He was ashamed of his anger, but he couldn't stop it. "I don't see the folks you run around with dressing in what I would call the height of fashion."

She laughed, and he was impressed by how free it was, coming from rich areas within herself that most people left untapped.

"I guess not," she said. "But obviously, you don't entertain a lot in that outfit." She peered at the faded patch on the sagging pocket. "What country club was that?"

"A Federal hospital," he said, though he did not like admitting it.

"And you copped it?" she asked, delighted.

"A nurse packed my things," he said stiffly. "When I got home it was there."

"Sure, sure," she said, and began wandering again, finding the bottle of Irish on the divider bar. "But you didn't send it back, did you?" She held the bottle up against the light so she might gauge the contents. "You drink alone?"

"What are you, some kind of social worker?" he asked.

Again that deep, full laugh which drained his angers and drew him to her against his will.

"Not me," she said. "I don't have those kinds of skills."

He couldn't bring himself to ask the obvious question. "Want a drink?" he asked instead.

"Christ, no," she said. "That stuff desiccates your vital organs. And tastes bad, besides."

"Not Irish," he said. "It's a flavorful drink."

She removed the cap, sniffed, and wrinkled her nose. "Not by the smell. But I'll try a weensy."

"Don't do me any favors," he said. "That stuff runs a dollar an ounce."

"You spend more on whisky than you do on your clothes?" she asked.

"It was a gift," he said shortly.

"A bribe?" she asked sweetly.

"It would take more than a bottle of Irish," he said, and moved behind the bar, found two glasses, rinsed them, and poured her a short shot, himself a longer one.

"My, you're fastidious," she commented, as she lifted the

glass, and then: "Wow! It's like medicine! But it does warm you, doesn't it?"

"That's the general idea," he said.

"But so does wine," she said. "Got any wine?" And when he shook his head: "Well then, how about some grass? You've got some of that, haven't you?"

"Grass is against the law," he said.

"So was whisky once," she said. "That didn't stop people from drinking. If there was a law against it would you stop?"

"If there was a law against it when I started I might not have," he said.

"Haven't you ever broken the law?" she asked.

"Not yet," he said, and let that hang in the air.

"You keep this place awfully warm," she said, getting off the stool and going to a window. She opened it. While she was taking in deep breaths, he slipped off his ankle gun and hid it behind the bar. When he looked around she had slipped out of her coat, letting it pile up on the floor upon itself. She was wearing red leotards, nothing underneath.

"What did you come here for?" he asked, too harshly.

She looked at him so long he saw the pupils in her pale eyes expand. "I'm sorry you lost your job," she said at last.

It was not what he had expected.

"I came here to tell you that," she said.

"No other reason?" he said.

"Nothing worth mentioning," she said.

"You mean," he said, "you just happened to be in the neighborhood in your tumbling outfit, and you decided to pop in and let me know how rotten you felt about pulling that innocent crap at the hearing? Do you know how close you came to getting me burned? I suppose I should have guessed you'd have a plant somewhere like the Smoke Shoppe. But it's not you, is it? Who is it? Who's so anxious to know where the goddam corset is they sent you up here to find out?"

"You've got a lousy temper, you know that?" she said. "It's probably the whisky—alcohol's a depressant."

"How would you know?" he demanded. "You not being a drinker?" He grasped her by the wrist and shoved up the sleeve of her leotard to the elbow. "Is mainlining a better road?"

But the skin of her arm was smooth and free of needle

marks, was in fact remarkably smooth and the color of cream. She stood very still and did not try to pull away and finally, shamefaced, he dropped her arm. She pulled up her other sleeve.

"I don't believe in hard stuff," she said, "of any kind."

"Then what are you doing here?" he asked, again.

"Like I said," she went on. "To tell you how sorry I am that things worked out for you the way they have. I heard about your trying to see me in the hospital and I was touched, I mean I was really moved; this narc was concerned about me, I thought. And I thought anyone sensitive enough to worry about a girl losing her baby wouldn't deliberately kill anyone. But I can see now you're not sensitive at all, you probably pull the wings off flies in your spare time, and anyone as uptight as you are, mister, would probably get canned anyway, it was just a question of time until that lousy temper wiped you out, and now I'm not sorry about anything, except that I was sap enough to come up here!"

She swept her coat up from the floor and not even stopping to put it on went for the door. Vorovich, unable to believe she was really going, waited almost too long, but managed to stop her before she got out.

"It was a reflex," he said. "I honest to god don't think I meant to kill him."

"Billy," she said. "He had a name, you know. The least you can do is show him that much respect, not call him *him* like he was some kind of object!" There were tears in her eyes which she did not want, because tears indicated a kind of easy emotionality that got her in trouble more often than not, and trouble was something she'd had enough of.

"I never heard his name," he said. "I mean not Billy. They said William at the inquest."

"William was his given name," she said. "His loving name was Billy."

"His loving name," he said.

"He wasn't the father," she said.

"Then why are you crying?" he asked.

"Shit!" she cried. "Shit! I'm not crying!"

"You're crying," he said.

"Because you're a dumb preconditioned slob," she cried, "so

predictable. I mean, push the button and out comes the gun and bang! bang! poor dumb Billy is dead."

"Please don't cry," he said.

She started to crumple. He caught her and she leaned against him and wept. He could feel her shoulders shake. And more. He could feel something stirring inside her. And he responded to that, and she felt his response, and she in turn allowed her own feelings to rise. He held her trembling shoulders and she pressed close and put her head to his chest and he put his mouth and nose in her hair, which smelled of lemon, and he sighed, full of something he had not felt for many years. He had been so young when he held his first woman close, and felt a feeling so indescribable he had married the woman to keep the feeling and of course lost both. He knew he ought to let this girl/woman go so that he would not undergo so hellish a time again. But however much he willed it he could not.

She did not stop crying, exactly; that is, her tears kept flowing, but they were no longer bitter. As she felt his hands holding her tight against his sadness, protecting her against his own lost feelings, as she heard his soothing murmurs, a lament so soft and low it may have been, it was, that he was unaware of making any sound himself, she raised her head, leaned back to look up into his face, and he kissed her.

It was a gentle kiss, and that might have been the end of it, instead of the beginning, if she had not taken the initiative. Her hands moved up and around his back, her tongue probed his mouth, and it was suddenly as if he had been plugged into some extraordinary current. And he was no longer gentle. The kiss became hard, he groped for her breast and began squeezing it with a fierceness that made her tremble, he put his face in her long throat and bent her back so that their two bodies strained together at the waist and thighs, and he pulled her in to him, in against him, but she was not afraid. She helped him pull down her leotard until her breast was bare, and offered it to him. She continued to strip as he suckled, rolling that red cotton garment down and down, then pulled the knot on the tie of his flimsy robe, tugged at his pajama bottom, and as he shrugged out of his robe she sank back onto her coat, there on the floor, and kicked her leotard all the way off, while he did the same with his pajamas.

45

He was so incredibly excited that their lovemaking was frantic and brief, and as he felt the rush gather inside him he wondered if he could retreat, pause, get control of himself, but even as he thought that it was too late. As he exploded inside her he felt ashamed that he had taken his pleasure with no thought of hers, and he hid his face in the collar of her fur.

But she held their embrace, and would not let him go. "It was lovely," she whispered.

"For me," he said.

"For me too," she said.

He did not believe her but somehow his tense body relaxed and feeling this she released him and he rolled over on his side and was able to look at her directly.

"I guess I was pretty wound up," he said.

She smiled and stroked his face.

"I haven't been with anyone for quite a while," he said.

"Poor baby," she said. "Why not?"

"I just never seem to get around to it," he said.

"You don't have anyone you see regularly?" she asked.

"Nobody special," he said. He hesitated. "When I get—"

"Horny?" she offered.

"—I usually go to a bar, a good bar, where the hustlers, the good ones, hang out, and make it with one of them," he said. He did not know why he told her that.

"You mean you pay?" she asked.

"You think I free-load?" he asked, somewhat angered.

"I didn't mean that," she said, "I meant why go out and pay, why not find someone. . . ."

"So I don't have to get involved," he said, and did not know why he told her that either.

"Poor baby," she said again, and he looked close to see if she were laughing at him, but he could not tell for sure.

They lay for a while without talking. "Can I get you anything?" he asked.

"I would like to use your bathroom," she said. She rose, and without trying to cover herself or showing the least sign of shyness she walked where he pointed, but she was aware that he watched, because at the door she looked at him before walking through. She was beautiful, he thought, and wondered why that should make him angry, and got up to mix himself a drink.

The drink helped, but only a little. He knotted a kitchen

towel around his waist and picked up his robe and pajamas and her leotard and looked at the coat and again felt deep stirrings inside him.

Then he became aware that she was watching him from the open bathroom door. "Can I stay here tonight?" she asked.

He did not want her to, but before he could stop himself he nodded, and she disappeared into the bathroom again. He picked up her coat, and hung it in the closet, along with his robe and pajamas and her leotard, and by the time he looked around at the couch that made into a bed she was already in it, watching him gravely. Then her eyes dropped to his towel, and a dimple he had not noticed before appeared in her left cheek, and he blushed and unknotted the towel and climbed in beside her.

This time it was much better, he thought, though later she was to disagree with him about that, saying that it was wild and lovely at the first joining. But he was proud of this second encounter, because it was slow and easy and yet intense and deep, and she arched high against him and dug her hands into his back and she reached her apogee before he did himself. Later he examined himself for marks and was surprised not to find any.

They slept. He awakened at dawn, the light filtering through the palm fronds just outside the window, illuminating the venetian blinds a few strips at a time as the sun came up. The only good thing about his characterless apartment was that it had a window facing east. He liked to wake at first light, to have his eyelids become transparent, to not have to stare into the dark waiting for day so he might get moving, function, act out whatever charade life had in store for him next . . . but this morning he still awakened at the usual time, as though nothing about this day were different from any other.

But this day *was* different. She stirred with his stirring, and stretched nearer, searching for his warmth. He responded as if it were the most natural thing in the world, slipping an arm under the sweet curve of her back, pulling her close. She murmured, still asleep, and he asked, half whispering, what she had said, and she smiled, a slow delicious upturning of her wide mouth corners, and fumbled for his hand, and placed his hand on her swelling breast, and sighed and reached for him, and it wasn't till then that he realized he was ready.

47

He hadn't thought it could get any better. But it did, probably because he was not yet quite awake himself, still in a kind of dream-state, where everything moved at half-speed, in slow motion. They slipped under the covers, the heat of their bodies enclosing them in an aromatic shell, an odoriferous bower, and they exchanged positions, though never roles, first him on top and then her and then him again, and rolling side by side left and then right, both more awake now, but still under a kind of spell, communicating by touch and by gesture and by look, neither of them willing to break it by talk, and if she murmured occasionally he knew better now than to ask what she had said since it was a kind of song . . . at the end he harmonized with her and then amazed himself by laughing out loud.

"You're very passionate," she said later—much later, after they had both dozed off again, and awakened entangled in the covers and each other, and laughing about getting the bed organized.

"Well," he said, not sure she wasn't teasing, "it seemed the thing to do."

"Did it?" she smiled, snuggling close. "You mean you're not always such a stud?"

He was offended and tried not to show it. But his body gave him away.

"What is it?" she asked.

"Nothing," he said. And then: "I told you, this isn't my usual pastime."

"You like living alone?" she asked. He shrugged. "Have you ever lived with anyone?" she asked.

"Once," he said finally.

"And you didn't like it?" she asked.

"She didn't like it," he said. "I was gone a lot, and there wasn't enough money, and she was always a sucker for sweet talk, for fast talk, and I couldn't keep up."

"Where is she now?" she asked.

"I don't know," he said. He hesitated, but her eyes were so gray and direct he felt he could tell her anything. Almost. "She ran off with a hot rock salesman."

"And you didn't look for her?" Ginny asked.

"What for?" he asked, in turn, and she had no answer for that. "We were married," he said.

"I knew," she said.

"For all I know," he said, "we still are."

She looked at him for the longest time. "You should learn from the past, not live in it," she said.

"I did," he said. "Believe me."

"That's not the kind of learning I mean," she said. "You had one experience and it made you bitter and you're afraid now to open yourself up to anyone else and that's wrong. . . ."

"You're pretty young to be giving that kind of advice," he said.

"Well, you're old enough to know better," she said.

"Too old for you, probably," he said.

"I didn't say that," she said, distressed.

"Well, look at us!" he said, suddenly savage, and pulled her into a position so they caught an angle of the wall mirror. Though he was in good shape, his chest muscled and his stomach flat, his hair was streaked with gray and the lines on either side of his broad nose were deep, as were those at his eye corners, perhaps from all he had been forced to witness. She on the other hand was young, her creamy flesh firm and her lovely face without blemish or sign of death, and if anything besides her body had a woman's maturity it was in her pale eyes, which looked so calmly into his mirrored angry blue ones.

"What am I supposed to see?" she asked.

"How old are you?" he demanded.

"I lost track," she said.

"Come on," he said. "I want to know."

"Twenty-two," she said.

"I'm twice your age," he said.

"I don't doubt it," she said.

"Too old for you," he said.

"Look," she said, "if you're worrying about my trying to hang onto you, don't." She slid out from under the covers and was just as unembarrassed by her nudity in this sunny daytime as she had been by the dim artificial light. "I mean just because we slept together, Ace, you don't need to make a Federal case out of it."

"My name's Timothy," he said.

She stalked into the bathroom and did not bother to close the door. "Federal case—that's pretty funny, isn't it?" she asked.

He could hear her going to the bathroom.

"Isn't it?" she demanded.

"Funny enough," he said, and got up, and started to put on his robe, and then started not to, and then swore at himself for being intimidated by a girl half his age, and put on the robe, and went into the kitchen and began preparing breakfast.

"At least your attitude's young," she said, from behind him. "You didn't expect me to come in and scramble eggs for you."

"I might have," he said, setting the coffee pot on the flame, and cracked eggs into the mixing bowl. "But I've lived alone so long I'm used to doing for myself."

"And you prefer that?" she asked, and he turned and saw that she now wore the fur coat over her nudity. "Just asking," she said. "Nothing personal."

"How come there's nothing personal?" he demanded, suddenly and strangely irritated. "Do you go to bed with people as easy as all that?"

She was only partially amused. "You had to ask, didn't you?"

He added too much milk to the eggs but began beating them anyway.

"If it makes you feel any better," she said, "I mean if it makes you feel more like a man, why, I'm not the easiest lay in the world. Not the hardest, either, if I happen to dig someone. And I could tell you wanted me a lot, I mean I know you really needed me last night, and I dug it, I mean I felt really good about it, which is what I was trying to tell you." She watched him bang the frying pan down on the stove and put butter in. "Aren't you going to season the eggs?" she asked.

"I usually cook them with onions," he said.

"That sounds good," she said.

While he browned the onions and green peppers and then added tomatoes to the eggs, she made the toast and set the bar counter and they ate sitting side by side.

"These're great," she said. "Where'd you learn to make these?"

"I spent a lot of time in Mexico," he said.

"It gives one a thirst," she said.

He pulled two dark beers out of the refrigerator. She started to protest, then swallowed a mouthful and made an exclamation of delight. "Good," she said. And: "You always drink beer for breakfast?" she asked.

50

"Not always," he said. And: "You think dope is always better than booze?" he asked.

"Not always," she said, but she was no longer amused.

"Tell me the truth," he said. "You came up here to see if I had the corset, didn't you?"

"That was the excuse," she said. "That's what I promised ... someone ... I would do. But I wouldn't have come here just for that. I only do what *I* want to do ever, for my own private reasons."

"What are you going to tell them?" he asked.

"What I do is nobody's business," she flared.

"I mean about the corset," he said.

"Why, that you don't have it, naturally," she said.

He was both sad and delighted with what he had to tell her. And he hadn't time to sort out those conflicting emotions; he had procrastinated too long already.

"But you're wrong," he said. "I do."

She finally told him that her "people" were in San Francisco. She had not wanted to, had not, in fact, wanted him to deal at all, even remotely, long distance, with her acting as a go-between, preferring, she said, for him to destroy the merchandise rather than get involved in a situation which had already caused so much grief.

"Look," he said, "I'm tired of living lower class. I'm a slow learner, it took me all these years to figure out that everyone is on the take, one way or another; I've given the government a hundred-and-ten-per-cent effort for the best part of my life, and in return I get a half pension that will maybe permit me a three-room shack and some *frijoles* in a so-so section of Guadalajara, Mexico."

"How is selling the corset back going to bump you up in class?" she asked.

"It's a pretty good start," he said.

"It is?" she asked, surprised.

"You don't think so?" he asked in turn.

"How much is mescaline worth?" she asked.

And now he was surprised and, in a curious way, relieved. She hadn't known what they were running.

"It's worth more than you think," he said finally. "Call your people. You'll see. They'll want to meet me."

She looked at him, and went to the phone. She was a novice, he thought, and was pleased at that too.

"No," he said. "There's a pay phone in the gas station at the corner. Use that. This one may be tapped."

"By who?" she asked, skeptical.

"The narcs," he said politely, and she dropped the phone as if it were hot.

"If they agree," she said, on her way out, "when shall I tell them you'll come?"

"Right away," he said. "I can see the corner from this window," he said, pulling up the blinds and showing her. "If it's today—make it today if you can—come out and give me a thumbs up. If not, down, and I'll come out to find out why. If yes, and today, take a cab to the Burbank airport, and I'll meet you there. . . . There's a flight every hour."

After her call, she gave him a thumbs up—and more: she pantomimed a corset. He gestured an okay, though he had no intention of bringing it. Later, when he boarded the plane, and sat by her as if by chance, she asked where was the corset, was he wearing it?

"Don't be silly," he said finally.

When the stewardess came by, he ordered a beer. Ginny was remote, withdrawn, staring out the small window at the coastline as they followed it north, the winter sun, through the intermittent clouds, glinting off the steel-blue sea.

But she could not stay quiet forever. "I think in my next life," she confided, "if I'm very good and I get one, I'll be a bird."

"You expect to have a choice?" he asked.

"It's kind of a point system," she said. "If you behave particularly well, you can break your karma."

"Your what?" he asked.

"It's a Buddhist concept for the, like, kind of shell that you —that people put around themselves," she said.

"Are you a Buddhist?" he asked.

"I worked out my own system," she said. "Bits and pieces of systems I like. What happens in my system is if you behave very well you progress to a higher form of life. I think birds are the highest form. What do you think?"

"I don't have an opinion on it," he said.

"The Indians," she said, *"our* Indians, considered birds to contain the spirits of their recently departed dearly beloved, which is a charming idea, don't you think, I mean if you watch birds fly and think that's a human soul up there in the clear blue it makes the whole thing worth while."

"You think Billy's a bird now?" he asked.

She brooded about that. "Billy didn't behave very well," she said at last. "Did he?"

He shrugged.

"I mean that's why I got so upset about him," she said. "He never had a chance at breaking his karma, he died too young."

"You think he would have tried?" he asked.

"I think he would have," she said.

"No way," he said. "We're all locked into what we are."

She looked at him with those clear gray eyes. "You don't understand," she said. "We're locked into what we think we are. All the barriers are inside ourselves. Those are what we try to break down, to get in touch with our real selves. . . ."

"And what if our real selves are lousy?" he asked.

"God," she said finally. "You really do have a dark view of yourself."

He went back to his beer and she to her window and they did not speak again until the plane landed.

The car was waiting for them across the parking lot, near the international terminals, just in case he was under a domestic surveillance—which meant, Vorovich thought, that they were professional even if the girl was not.

But when he saw the car he was not so sure. It was a silver Rolls Royce with a sun roof and a right-hand drive, and not only was the car conspicuous, but so was the driver, who, though he wore the full livery of a chauffeur, had hair to his shoulders, a pair of moccasins below his polished leather puttees, and outside the corduroy jacket a hammered silver necklace dangling from his neck. He saluted Vorovich, peering curiously at him from underneath the visor pulled to the bridge of his nose, then smiled at the girl.

"Howya, Ginny?" he asked, and they embraced casually, but Vorovich felt the surge of blood. When he was introduced, he waited a moment to shake the other's flaccid, gloved hand. "Charles know you're bringin' a friend?" the chauffeur asked, as they got into the back.

"Charles knows," Ginny said.

They took the expressway into the city and then the great bridge like a poem over the bay to the valley side. The city was old and new, with Gold Rush houses and black towers like monoliths studding the hills and a modern dome-shaped cathedral holding new worshipers to an old god. From their height the water did not look dirty and if you hadn't been on it, as Vorovich had, you might think it clean enough to swim in, which it was not. But a few white-sailed boats were out, heeling beautifully, almost over in the winter wind, proving what could be done if you just put your mind to it; nearer shore, freighters and cruise liners occupied almost every dock, and as always Vorovich felt the longing, the almost unbearable urge to board and ship out, no matter what the destination. Except this time he didn't want to go alone—and when he realized that, he became suddenly afraid of and for something outside himself. That wasn't good, he thought; that made it dangerous, it made him vulnerable in an area he had not even considered.

The air in the car seemed suddenly close, and he opened the side window. It was electrically controlled, and Sam, the chauffeur, ran it back up again, locking it with the master control. "The car's air-conditioned," Sam said.

"I prefer the real stuff," Vorovich said.

"So do I," Ginny said—and Vorovich caught Sam's eyes observing them in the rearview mirror.

Nothing happened for a long moment and then just as Vorovich was about to lean across the front seat Sam ran the divider window up. They were locked in. Vorovich guessed that the glass was bulletproof, too, though he had other reasons for not making an issue of his captivity.

Ginny made an issue of it, however. "Don't be rude, Sam," she said.

"I don't know that he's clean," Sam said.

"I do," Ginny said.

Sam, disappointed, finally ran down the side windows in the back. But not the divider.

Vorovich decided not to let her know about his ankle gun. He'd had no commitments going in, it wouldn't do to acquire any now. He felt bad about it, and some of that must have showed, because cold as it got with the outside air coming in, she stayed on her own side. That was disappointing too, and he warned himself about getting involved.

Driving inland from the water to Mill Valley, they took a winding narrow road through the green rolling hills, passing great houses surrounded by enough acres to make them estates. Most were fenced in, barely visible beyond the huge pines and eucalyptus.

But the estate they went to could not be seen from the road. They drove through one gate that Sam opened with an electronic device and then over hills and through valleys for five minutes more until they came to a cluster of outbuildings, where there was another gate—this one manually controlled. Sam blipped his horn and a child stuck a shaggy head from the near building and pulled it back in, yelling something indistinguishable.

A bare-footed, disheveled girl, her patched gown sweeping the dust, came out. Vorovich couldn't be sure, but he thought she might be one of the girls they'd picked up near the border. When Sam pulled on through, and she smiled at

Ginny, revealing bad teeth, his memory was confirmed.

From what he could see these were servants' quarters, gathered about a kind of compound where repair work was done. The few people about all seemed young, even the gardener riding the power-driven mower. Along the graveled road they passed a tennis court, and then higher, surrounded by pines, a swimming pool designed like a woods pond, and finally, up on a kind of promontory, a huge gabled house, green-shuttered, with iron grillework on the windows: a kind of captain's walk went along a balcony from one shingled turret to another, giving the owner of the house private access as well as a view of the compound otherwise obscured by shrubbery.

The area immediately in front of the house was cobblestoned. When Sam stopped the car, Vorovich again found his door locked. The young chauffeur got out and grinned before walking up onto the portico and yanking a bell pull. The massive front door was opened immediately; the house had been notified of their arrival. Whoever Sam was talking to didn't come out, and in a moment Sam returned and unlocked their car doors.

"Oh, Sam," Ginny said, "stop all the horseplay. You know I've vouched for him." But she was nervous all the same.

Inside a large entryway a young black man and a young Oriental, dressed in Russian-style peasant blouses and trousers, both barefoot, were waiting.

"Wer-come to Mirr Varrey," the Oriental said, Chinese by his eyelids and snub nose. "Your coat?"

"Come off it, Chen," Ginny said, while Vorovich shrugged out of his raincoat. Chen put his hands in each of the pockets and then, grinning like a beaver in a parody of a movie Oriental, hung the coat on a hall rack.

Vorovich raised his arms while the young black (face all angles and planes), skin the color of cordovan and hair haloed "natural," started at his armpits and began patting him down. When he got to the ankle-strapped gun he hesitated, and Vorovich thought for a bewildered moment that he was not going to announce his find. He didn't have to announce it: few people were professional enough to discover it. Then the black tugged his pants leg up.

"Oh, man," the black said, "don't you reel-ee-ize you can hurt somebody with this? I'll have to confiscate it for the dooration of your visit here. But don't worry, we is a peace-loving crowd in this establishment."

"You is?" Vorovich replied, and was rewarded with a dark look from Ginny. But the black youth laughed.

"Such weaponry is strickly verboten," he said, and ushered them into an anteroom off the hallway. "Stay cool, Gin," he said, as he and Chen left. "Charles will be down toot sweet."

"I don't know why everyone's clowning around so," she said, when the door closed. "Roscoe's a college grad and Chen's in graduate school. . . ."

"Then why are they working as bodyguards?" Vorovich asked. "They get their degrees in English Lit?"

"Ha, ha," she said. "They're in sociology, doing a study on the counterculture. Charles is sponsoring them, gives them room and board and an allowance, in return for which they run the house—"

"What do you mean, run?" Vorovich asked.

"They oversee the people at the compound," Ginny said. "Charles sponsors them too, and they cook and clean and garden—"

"What do they grow, marijuana?" Vorovich asked.

"No way," Ginny said. "Charles is not about to get busted for something as sappy as that. Anyone who lives here lives by the rules."

"His rules," Vorovich said.

"It's his place," Ginny said.

"You all live off him?" Vorovich asked.

"We all contribute!" she retorted defensively. We all earn our bread, by labor or music or. . . ." She shrugged helplessly.

"Some form of entertainment," Vorovich finished for her.

"Yes," she said defiantly. "It's a self-contained community."

"But he runs it," Vorovich said.

"Someone has to," she said. "I've been in those where everyone had a voice and it's like the tower of Babel. I mean as long as we each perform our obligations and observe the amenities, we're free to live as we please. But we're all compatible. Charles saw to that. He hand-picked each of us."

"How?" Vorovich asked. "By application? Did he run ads in the *Free Press?*"

"Funny," she said. "He met all of us personally, one place or another. Like he found the whole kitchen-garden crew on an organic farm that wasn't making it, and Billy, he was playing guitar in a little club on the Peninsula. . . ."

"How'd he meet you?" Vorovich asked.

She was silent a moment. "Through my sister," she said finally.

"Where's your sister?" Vorovich asked.

"Gone," she said, and Vorovich knew she wouldn't tell him any more. He fondled a tapestry.

"How'd Charley make his money?" he asked.

"It was kind of by accident," she said. "Back in the days when acid was the thing there was so much *junk* on the market that he started making his own—I mean he was majoring in clinical psych and he was involved in consciousness-raising and mind expansion and like that and he just went into the labs. Word got out that Charles's stuff was *pure*, I mean really mind-blowing nonadulterated one-hundred-point-one percent the best. They were practically *begging* him to sell *them* some and since he couldn't *stand* it that they were being ripped off by the junk peddlers it wasn't long before he became the number-one supplier on the Coast—"

"Only acid?" Vorovich said. "Or was he into speed, too?"

"Oh, Charles wouldn't have anything to do with anything inorganic," she said.

"That was organic stuff you were running for him, was it?" Vorovich asked.

She stared at him for a moment. "It was supposed to be," she said. "It's pretty hard to adulterate mescaline."

"The only problem with you, Ginny," a voice behind them said before Vorovich could correct her, "is that you talk too much."

Vorovich had to fight his instincts not to whirl about. He wanted to do two things, both equally important: convey an appearance of calm, and listen to the other's voice. Appearances could deceive, the voice almost never. And so though his skin crawled and the short hairs on his neck rose because he had always been uneasy with people behind him, he concentrated on listening. What he heard was a spoiled tenor, a nasal drip, the hidden whine of someone used to having his way.

"I admit to everything, Charles," Ginny was saying cheerfully, looking past Vorovich's shoulder. "But must you creep up on people like that? How long have you been listening?"

"Long enough," Charles said, and Vorovich faced him in time to see the other slipping a small two-way radio into his pocket—apparently this room was wired.

Charles was dressed in a blue velvet double-breasted blazer and white hopsack pants that flared at the bottom like a sailor's. The paisley scarf at his throat was knotted at the side, gypsy-style, and his velvet slippers had a stitched rose on each toe. His hair was blond, maybe rinsed, Vorovich thought, and the cut was modified Prince Valiant.

But he had the face of a mug. His nose was thick and his skin mottled, and if it had not been not for the shrewd eyes, and the voice, Vorovich might not have recognized the intelligence, however mean.

"Long enough for what?" Vorovich inquired.

"To find out that you're awfully curious," Charles said.

"I like to know who I'm doing business with," Vorovich said.

"Really?" Charles said. "That's kind of old-fashioned, isn't it? It's the business that matters, not the people." He pulled out a silver cigar case, took one for himself, then offered one to Vorovich. "Cuban," Charles said. "A dollar a throw."

"I just quit cigarettes," Vorovich said. "If I inhale a mouthful of smoke I'm hooked again."

Charles laughed, a hostile honk that reminded Vorovich of an angry goose. "You that weak, man?" the other asked, and though it was said affably, Vorovich heard the mental note-taking. He felt the familiar chill whenever anyone probed for his soft spots.

Then Charles blew smoke in Vorovich's direction. Ginny waved it away. "You ought to quit smoking yourself, Charles," she said.

He studied her. "Maybe you have two problems," he said finally. "You are a nag, too, I'd forgotten that."

"I am what I am," she said.

"Too bad what the rest of us think then, right?" he asked.

"I can't control what anyone else thinks," she said. "Look at it this way"—and she was being kind, not patronizing, even Vorovich could see that—"because of the way I am, I'm not much of a loss to you. Right?"

"Right on," Charles drawled, but his voice was tight, and he sneaked a look at Vorovich. "Why don't you split for a while, Gin, so your friend and I can talk business?"

"I'll be at the garden house," she said.

"Your old room's still unoccupied," Charles said casually, but he was not indifferent to her answer.

"I'm with him," she said, indicating Vorovich, and without waiting for any reaction, with a kind of placid assumption that because she was honest about her feelings everyone else would be too, she left them, not seeing, as Vorovich did, the jealousy that burned in those mean eyes.

But Charles tried to hide that leap of emotion by squinting through the cigar smoke, and then he waved Vorovich over to where two chairs were set up near the flocked fleurs-de-lis wall: a nineties brothel motif, Vorovich thought, popular with bar owners and faggots.

"You buy this place furnished?" Vorovich asked.

"I had it redone," Charles said. "Why?"

"I was curious about who did the decorating," Vorovich said.

"Me," Charles said, squinting at him. He puffed at his cigar, looking too young for that senior indulgence, revealing his unsureness by asking, "You got comments?"

"It's not my taste," Vorovich said.

"When you gather enough coin," Charles said, reddening, "you can furnish your own pad."

"I was wondering when we could talk about coin," Vorovich said. "Ginny says you want your corset back."

"Where is it?" Charles asked.

"Safe," Vorovich said.

"Did Ginny see it?" Charles asked.

"You know she hasn't," Vorovich said.

"Then how do I know you really have it?" Charles asked.

Vorovich smiled. "Because I know what's in it," he said.

Charles, who had been allowing the ash on his cigar to grow, suddenly trimmed it, then looked at Vorovich directly. "I'd like to have it back," he said.

"No doubt," Vorovich said.

"I'll give you fifty thousand cash for it right now," Charles said.

Vorovich stood up and went to the door. It was locked, from the other side. He looked at the door Charles had entered.

"That's locked too," Charles said. "Until I give the word."

"Well, give the word," Vorovich said.

"What's your hurry?" Charles asked.

"We're wasting time," Vorovich said. "You either don't have the cash or you're too cheap to pay me what the shit is worth, and in either case I don't care to do business with you."

"Now take it easy," Charles said. "What figure did you have in mind?"

"Half what it's worth," Vorovich said.

Charles looked as if he couldn't decide whether to laugh or become terribly angry.

"You can't be serious," he said finally.

"Half," Vorovich said.

"Tell you what," Charles said. "I'll make it a hundred thou."

Vorovich rattled the other doorknob.

"Look," Charles said, and now there was only the one emotion. "I told you I need that corset back."

"You don't deal like a man who needs anything," Vorovich said.

"How can I offer you more than the stuff's worth?" Charles demanded.

"You forget who you're talking to!" Vorovich said. "I know what that stuff is worth—one half million dollars wholesale! Maybe a full mil by the time it's cut and hits the street! But all I want is a fair finder's fee, which is half. You're forgetting it'd be lost entirely if it weren't for me!"

"I'm not forgetting," Charles said. "Look," he said, changing his tone, "what matters now is the stuff. If it was only up to me, I'd settle for half. But I've got a partner."

"Who?" Vorovich asked.

Charles squinted at him. "A silent partner," he said.

"Well," Vorovich said, "he's your problem."

"That's not quite accurate," Charles said. "He's your problem too."

"I don't see how."

"If I settled with you for half," Charles said, "it would all come out of my share."

"Still your problem," Vorovich said. And then, as if merely curious: "Why wouldn't your partner split the tab?"

Charles licked his lips, and even with the cigar, or perhaps in spite of it, he suddenly looked very immature. "He put up all the money," he said. "It was his shit. I only provided the transportation."

Vorovich went back to his chair. He permitted himself a

smile. "And since you lost it," he said, "he's holding you responsible for the whole shot."

"You got it," Charles said, trying to return his smile. "So you can see why I can't pay what you want."

Vorovich allowed his smile to grow. "Then I'm dealing with the wrong man," he said.

Charles lost his grin, and his nostrils got very wide. "I'm willing to pay what I can afford," he said.

"Your partner can afford more," Vorovich said.

"You wouldn't want to deal with him," Charles said. "Believe me."

"If there's one thing I've learned," Vorovich said, "it's never to deal with underlings."

"He was very upset about his shit being hijacked," Charles said. "And when he heard it was being, like, held for ransom, he was infuriated. You're better off to let me buy it back. Believe me."

"Be logical, Charley," Vorovich said. "You're asking me to sell it back to you for less than it's worth and with nothing on the come. Why should I?"

"As a favor to me," Charles said.

Vorovich could not help himself: he laughed aloud. "But I don't owe you any favors," he said.

"As a favor to Ginny," Charles said.

Vorovich felt a sudden chill. Charles was young and immature, but he was mean, and capable of violence. "What's she got to do with it?" he asked.

"She lost it," Charles said, "she and the others."

"She didn't even know what was in it," Vorovich said.

"That was for her own protection," Charles said. "The less anyone knew, the better."

"Weren't they entitled to know?" Vorovich asked. "They were running the risk."

"If they knew," Charles said, "they'd have acted a lot different. This way it was just another run-of-the-mill . . ."

"If they knew," Vorovich interrupted, "you mean, they wouldn't be running it at all."

Charles smashed his cigar out, got up, and began pacing the room. Then he stopped and gave Vorovich what was supposed to be a sincere look. "I couldn't tell them," he said. "I was forced into this in the first place. These people came to me and said unless I cooperated they'd do terrible things to my people!"

"You trying to tell me this was a one-time run?" Vorovich demanded.

"One-time," Charles said. He licked his lips. Vorovich had seen that lizard flick before, the dehydrated tic of the thirsty, the frustrated. "It was a special situation, an experiment. They won't want us after this."

"Too bad," Vorovich said.

"Yeah," Charles said, studying him. "What do you say?"

"I don't see how I can help you," Vorovich said. For a moment he thought the other might come right out of his chair at him.

"Okay, you fucker," Charles said then, very quietly, but so intensely Vorovich knew the other wished him dead, "you asked for it. I'm going to have to tell my partner."

"That's what you should have done in the first place," Vorovich said.

"We'll see," Charles said, "if you still feel that way after."

"I'll take my chances," Vorovich said.

"You may never get to meet him," Charles said. "He may decide it's not worth the risk—that it's better to cut his losses, and then tell me, narc, where does that leave you?"

Suddenly Charles grinned, and that mug's face became boyish, and somehow that boyish grin was more frightening than all the deadly looks and grimaces that had passed between them before.

Vorovich did not quite understand what was going on. There seemed to be a delay in the proceedings; the series of events that he had started by appropriating the corset had come to some kind of a halt—he could feel, with the intuition developed by years of waiting on stakeout and undercover work, that something was being held in abeyance, that some decision regarding him had not yet been made.

Perhaps Charles had changed his mind. Perhaps he needed to work his courage up about approaching his secret partner with the news that the narc was being recalcitrant. Or perhaps they were going to make one more attempt to get him to change his mind.

The last seemed the strongest possibility. It was also possible that the partner was momentarily unavailable, and that Charles had to wait to get in touch with him, but Vorovich decided that he had better assume something less innocent was being contemplated.

Not that there was a lot he could do about it. He had been escorted to an upstairs room by Roscoe and Chen, and the door locked. A narrow floor-to-ceiling French window was open, but even if he wanted to risk the fifteen-foot drop, a survey of the green, rolling landscape showed him that Sam, the chauffeur, had been strategically placed to keep an eye on him. Seeing him looking out, Sam shook his head, as if he had known all along that this passenger would turn out to be unwelcome.

Vorovich stepped back from the window and sprawled on the bed, staring up at the draped ceiling. He could, he supposed, tell Charles he had decided to accept the lesser amount, and then, once away from him, ostensibly to pick up the corset, he could chuck the whole thing and be well out of it. That way he would not be getting into waters that might be over his head, the muddy waters of his own soul, where hidden dangers lurked. Maybe, he thought, the D.E.A. had known what it was doing to pass him over. Maybe their emotional evaluations, their psychological "profiles," had turned up some disfigurement that told them he would come apart in a crunch—his field record aside, maybe they had correctly determined that when confronted by choices, he could not be depended upon to make the right ones. Maybe he could never get past his feelings, make decisions for the end and never mind the means.

He had rarely questioned himself before—in the daytime. Usually his dark moods came just before dawn when the earth has shrunk in upon itself, cold and gloomy—but even then he never questioned his ability so much as his luck. His purposes were a thing apart, and did not bear thinking about. Maybe that girl whom he had made his wife too many years ago had sensed something which he'd been too young to be aware of himself, something which had made her recoil, thinking him a loser, thinking that he would never make it—whatever "it" was— thinking better to run away than spend the rest of her life harnessed to someone who would never even see the rainbow, let alone get to the end of it.

So maybe, he thought, getting up to examine the paperback book shelf, hoping to find a title to take his mind off himself, and failing, maybe he ought to chuck the whole thing, and settle down to the mediocre life he probably deserved, forget any obligations he might think he still had, even to himself, for what he figured he owed himself wasn't all that much either, and why risk so much for so little? To prove he could do it? Bullshit. Even if he pulled this off, who would care, finally? Who would be there to applaud? No one, and the sudden, ludicrous picture that came into his mind of him sitting alone in some character-less room, applauding himself, did not make him laugh.

"Something the matter?" came the soft voice from behind him.

She was standing in the door, dressed now in Cossack shirt and pants similar to those worn by his two guards, except that on her they looked sensational.

"How did you get in?" he asked.

"You're not answering my question," she said.

"You have a key?" he asked.

"I borrowed one," she said. "You had the strangest look on your face," she added then, persisting.

"It's the strain of thinking," he said.

"About what?" she asked seriously.

"My life and hard times," he said. "Now your turn. How come they're letting me out?"

"I told them I'd take the responsibility," she said. "I told them you'd give me your word not to try and split."

He had difficulty believing her. No one could be that naïve.

"And that would be enough for you?" he asked. She nodded,

waiting for his word. "Okay," he said, "I won't try to split. But that's because I want to meet your buddy Charley's secret friend. But if I thought it was to my advantage to split, I would."

"I don't believe that," she said.

"Believe it," he said. She shook her head. "Why *not?*" he demanded, for some reason angry about it. "You know about special situations. You lied in San Diego. Under oath."

"Not my oath," she said. "No one asked me what I would swear by."

"Tell me," he said. "In case I ever want you to swear to something."

She smiled, but she was absolutely serious. "By love," she said. Then: "Want a guided tour?"

The house was immaculately kept, each room a different historical period, but all-American; that is, the furnishings were from New England Colonial to rough-hewn Frontier, the antebellum South to hand-carved Hacienda, and in each room, over the stone or brick or wood mantel of the fireplaces, were the weapons appropriate to each: long rifles, dueling pistols, swords, and knives long as a forearm.

"Would you like to see Charles's room?" she asked.

"As long as he's not in it," Vorovich said.

"He's meditating," Ginny said. "The kids made a kind of chapel out of the pool house. That's where he goes when he wants to think things through. He believes in meditation. He says it's amazing what comes when you really concentrate."

"He doesn't strike me as the religious type," Vorovich said, indicating the weaponry.

"That's so he won't forget that America has a history of violence," she said. "That's why he allowed Chen to join us— to show him how other people's violence may be turned against them."

"Kung Fu?" Vorovich wondered. "Well," he said, at her nod, "a good alley fighter can beat one of those martial-arts guys five days out of six."

"I hope you never have to find out," she said, more serious than amused, and he felt childish that he had displayed this bravado.

The master bedroom was, or seemed to be, all covered with fur: there was a brown bearskin on the bed and another on the floor and the pillows were furry, and even the wall was flocked with it. All around the huge bed were controls for stereo and color TV, and within an easy stretch was a bar-sized fridge and a hot plate.

"What, no room service?" Vorovich wondered.

She smiled. "After midnight," she said, "Charles locks everyone out."

"Everyone?" he asked.

She did not answer until they were outside, under the portico; the sun had just gone down, and in that gray winter light, clear as glass, he could see her skin stippling from the cold.

"You want to know about me and Charles, don't you," she said.

"He offered you your old room," Vorovich said. "That makes you privileged, doesn't it? And you can take the responsibility for my custody—that puts you near the top of this little hierarchy, I assume."

"That was Charles's baby I lost," she said. He wanted to warm her against the chill wind. But he did not.

"And you left his house?" he said.

"I wanted the baby," she said.

"And he didn't?" Vorovich said.

"That was okay with me," she said. "I wasn't planning on spending my life with him."

"But you were carrying his baby," he said, struggling to understand, feeling a need to understand.

She was suddenly sympathetic, seeing that he was having trouble with it. "The two aren't necessarily connected," she said.

They walked down the road to the compound, and he stopped once, the oldest trick in the world, to tie his shoe, and glancing back saw Sam fading behind a tree. Where were Roscoe and Chen? That creepy feeling of being watched was too intense to be only the lackadaisical scrutiny of that hippie chauffeur; others were observing him, he felt sure, eyes for the meditating Charley, although to what purpose he didn't know. Ginny probably knew. Would she tell him if he asked? Maybe, if he picked the right moment.

In the kitchen of the "quarters," a huge place with a brick oven and black pots hanging from the ceiling, once used, Ginny told him, for hunt breakfasts and garden parties, two girls and a long-haired youth were doing things around the stove. Vorovich lifted the lid off one kettle and a puff of aromatic steam bathed his face and he sighed.

"What is it?" he asked.

"Stew," Ginny said, and seemed taken by some private amusement. "I hope you like it."

"Christ," he said, "I never smelt a stew like that."

"Wait'll you taste it," the boy said.

"You mean I'm invited for dinner?" Vorovich asked Ginny.

"Man," the boy said, before she could answer, "this dinner is in your honor."

"Lester," one of the other girls said.

"I just want to reassure him that he's gonna be fed," Lester said. "I just want him to know we wouldn't turn a dog away hungry."

"Lester," Ginny said.

"It's okay," Vorovich said, though it took him a moment. "I'm hungry as a dog."

The girls smiled at him, but Lester found something else to do. There was some joke he wasn't in on, Vorovich thought; if he weren't careful, he would be the butt of it.

"Here," one of the girls said, opening the oven. She pulled out a smoking hot loaf of bread and yelped a little as she dropped it on the wooden counter, then reached into a huge refrigerator and pulled out a ceramic crock brimful of a creamy cheese.

"Goat cheese," the girl said. "You like?"

"Well, my ancestors did," Vorovich said. "Maybe there'll be some carry-over, some . . ."

"Genetic memory," Lester said, without turning around.

"Yeah," Vorovich said, and then deliberately stumbled over the word, which made Ginny laugh. "Geneti-tic memory."

"Don't let him kid you, Lester," she said. "He's had more schooling than you."

"You don't need schooling to be a cop," Lester said.

"He's not a cop," Ginny said. "He's a Federal agent."

"He smells like a cop," Lester said, and Vorovich shuddered at that, like a deep-rooted tree in a wind, but Ginny put a restraining hand on his arm.

"Billy was his friend," she murmured. He accepted the slab of hot bread thickly spread with the cheese.

"Delicious," he said, as the pungent taste spread over his tongue. "A beer would go great with it."

"How about buttermilk?" one of the girls asked, and Vorovich wrinkled his nose.

"You got something against beer?" he asked.

"Not homemade," the other girl said. "But commercial beer's got poison in it—even the German."

"It's all organic here," Ginny said. "We grow our own vegetables and have chickens and a goat—"

"You don't eat meat?" he asked, wondering about the stew.

"Oh, sure," she said. "But we get the kind that hasn't been shot full of some synthetic goody—"

"You're so concerned about dangerous drugs," Lester said, "why don't you bust the farmers?"

"It's not the farmers," one of the girls said. "It's the big meatpackers. They own most of the farms now."

"She's from Iowa," Ginny said.

"I thought someplace like that," Vorovich said, and the girl hesitated a moment, then smiled. Lester looked at the girl hotly and motioned her back to the stove. She went, but not before she had thumbed her feeling about Lester: get him, the gesture said, asserting her independence, but a love for him too. Faintly, within himself, Vorovich felt the stirring of an understanding of what Ginny had been trying to explain. But he was still a long way from accepting it. Understanding had to do with logic, acceptance with emotion.

"You boycotting wine too?" Vorovich asked, finishing the cheesy bread in two bites.

Ginny went into a storeroom and returned with two flagons of red. The labels read BOTTLED AT THE MAISON DE CHARLES MANTEE.

"You make your own?" Vorovich asked.

"We get it in casks," Ginny said, brushing cheese curd from his mouth. "Charles owns some of a vineyard in Napa."

"I don't think Charles would dig having his business affairs told to him," Lester said.

"Let me worry about that," Ginny said.

"You better worry about it," Lester said. "He ain't been proved out yet. And what if you're wrong?"

"I'm not," Ginny said. But she seemed suddenly uncertain. "When's dinner?" she asked.

"In thirty minutes," Lester said, and somehow Vorovich knew the subject still was himself.

"Come on," Ginny said, taking Vorovich's arm and urging him out. "Let me show you the rest."

Vorovich refilled his glass with the wine, which tasted almost strong and ripe enough to have been fortified, then accompanied her through the other buildings. In one of them was the smell of leather and the stink of an acetylene torch—young people at workbenches full of belts and sandals and buckles being hammered out of silver and brass. They seemed intent on their work, but as far as he could tell, none was accomplished.

"You're not going to tell me these are the services being traded for sustenance?" Vorovich said.

For the first time she was angry. "They're all trying," she said, nostrils flared. "Charles has given them the opportunity to try and explore whatever talents they may have. This whole place is an experiment in living."

"I'll bet," he said.

"Get it off your mind," she said.

"What?" he asked, suddenly wary, afraid he had gone too far, though why he should care a damn about preserving their relationship he didn't want to think about.

"Whatever you think I traded to Charles for live-in privileges," she said.

"It's nothing to me," he said.

"At least be man enough to lay it out front," she said. "I mean, you are some kind of craven if you're going to snide and scuffle around it like some dirty-minded corporation lawyer, afraid to say what's really bubbling up through your foul mind."

"It's really none of my business, is it?" he said, trying to head her off.

"That's correct," she said. "What I am, who I am, how I live, what I do, where I do it, who I do it with—well, that's up to me, isn't it? It's my body, my mind, free and unencumbered. I mean what *is* it with you older types that two people make it and right away the lock and chains go on, we're joined at the hip, and we're supposed to three-leg it through life together. . . ."

"I was wrong," he said. "I admit it."

As quickly as that, her anger was gone. "I'm not trying to

hide anything," she said. "What I do I do of my own free will, because I want to do it, and the only thing I am careful of is that what I do is not hurtful to anyone else. Deliberately hurtful, anyway. Because if what another person is causes you to have thoughts and feelings that upset you, well, that's your problem, not mine, because how can I be responsible for anyone else's hangups?"

"You can't," he said.

She studied him. "I want you to know," she said, because she did at least feel concerned about him, "I never made it with Charles emotionally. We never got past the first layer. It was all physical, nothing more. We were like two water bugs, skittering over the surface, never taking the plunge."

She meant well, he knew that. But as he thought of this lovely vivid pale-eyed girl and that perfumed dandy with the mug's face in bed together he felt heartsick.

"What is it?" she asked.

"How can—something—just be physical?" he managed.

"Well," she said finally, sorry that he couldn't understand, "there has to be friendship."

A long, low building turned out to be a dining hall. There was a fire going, hickory by the smell. A record was playing, a kind of jazz rock, and a boy with hair tied with a piece of manila rope was playing guitar to the record, a little off tone and off beat, the effect not unpleasant. Candles in hand-crafted pottery holders guttered as they entered, then smoked and reflamed. Everyone who had been in the kitchen was there except Lester, the table already set.

Sam leaned out of the dimness into the candlelight, lighting a thinly rolled handmade cigarette. Sucking in smoke, Sam grinned at Vorovich, and through his teeth asked, "Care for a hit, narc?"

They were all watching him, the squint-eyed, pimply girls and the hirsute boys, no one amused except Sam, who was still holding his breath. Ginny was most serious of all, her usual serenity frayed at the edges, uneasy about what he would do. This was it then, he thought, the beginning of some kind of test. This was what the meditating Charles was waiting for, this divining through challenge of his prisoner's hidden character, an attempt not only to find out who he was but what he was up to.

And Vorovich hesitated. Whether he turned on or not had to do with something beyond the immediate situation. It had to do with himself as a person, and never mind that a special kind of pressure was on. This was, he knew, only the beginning, and once started it would be difficult, if not impossible, to stop. He was uneasy about more than what *they* would discover. Then he thought it was time in his life to take risks, real risks, and he reached finally for the proferred joint.

They watched as he took a hit and then another and still another, and when without strain or apparent effort he swallowed the smoke and air and handed the joint back and said "Thanks," there was a kind of sigh from the watchers, and a dimpling of Ginny's cheek that showed she was pleased.

"You've taken hits before," Sam said, doing a shame-shame with his third on index finger of the hand that held the cigarette, something effeminate, or certainly pretentious about holding it between the last two fingers like that.

"It's part of their training," one of the girls said, very serious. "When I was busted once, one of the matrons at the county jail told me they periodically volunteer under laboratory conditions so they would know what it's like."

"I guess so they can recognize someone who's stoned," another girl said.

"No," the boy with the guitar said, "it's so they can get inside our psyche. It's so they can get to where they can think like us and trap us with our own minds." He hit a dissonant chord on the guitar; to show his contempt, Vorovich guessed. "Of course they can't. I mean you can't get stoned under laboratory conditions in the same way, can you?"

Vorovich didn't know. He had taken lids of marijuana home, and in the quietness of his spartan rooms had tried to turn on, but had always quit after one or two tokes. He had been afraid to push himself to his limits. Once, as a youth, he had sat with a bottle of kerosenelike hooch and a six-pack of beer, deliberately setting out to get drunk, only to wind up insensible. He had never tried again. There was some barrier in his mind that he had always wanted to cross but could never bring himself to: he was fearful of what might transpire on that "other" side, of what might come boiling up out of his own subconscious—he was afraid, quite simply, that he might never get back.

"More?" Sam asked, holding out the joint.

Vorovich didn't hesitate; he hit it again, hard. It was risky, he knew, it was taking himself awfully close to the line. But it was necessary. And maybe he could handle this stuff; you had to go "with" pot for it to have its maximum effect.

"Man," Sam said, "do you reeleyize you could be in-car-cer-ated for dee-stroying evi-dence?" Sam's giggle was infectious, and like a glee club picking up the pitch, the notes ran around the table about which they were sitting/standing/leaning, merging into a dissonant harmonic—and Vorovich was unclear why he was laughing, since it was not all that funny. But he laughed until his eyes watered, and the dissonance was resolved by a guitar strum.

"There's hash in this," Vorovich said, outraged.

"How much?" Sam asked, laughing.

"Sixty-six per cent," Vorovich said, taking another hit, and then found the joint being taken from him—by Ginny.

Sam was astounded. "That's right *on*," he said. "How come you got taste buds like that?" He turned to Ginny, who was taking her hit. "You clued him in." She shook her head in denial. "You a *head*, man?" Sam asked him then. "I mean a big muck like you on the force a closet turn-on?"

"Hot stuff behind you!" someone yelled, and they scattered as Lester and the kitchen girls brought in two huge steaming pots and skidded them down the long table. Then Lester, with a sidelong glance at Vorovich, went to a hanging brass gong and methodically began striking it until the separate sounds merged into one. While the gong was still reverberating, Roscoe and Chen appeared, apparitionlike, out of the darkness.

"Isn't Charley eating with us?" Vorovich asked, as the two sat at the table opposite him.

"We're going to take him up some, after," Roscoe said.

"After what?" Vorovich asked.

"After you finished," Chen said, showing his teeth.

Lester spooned up a bowlful of stew and placed it before Vorovich, but Ginny took it.

"Ladies first," she said.

Lester looked at her peculiarly, then shrugged and dished up another. At least whatever it was wasn't harmful, Vorovich thought, and dug in.

With the first taste he knew he was in for it. Not that it was bad; on the contrary, he could not get over how *good* this was, how richly aromatic, maybe from the huge carrot and celery and turnip chunks and onions small as pearls and cubes of veal tender as butter—or maybe from something which had been added in the kitchen just before serving: probably, he thought, one of the so-called mind-enhancing drugs.

"More?" he asked, showing Lester his emptied bowl.

"You got quite an appetite, man," Roscoe said, as Lester spooned more in. But Roscoe took his from the other pot.

"Not just for food," Vorovich said, with a significant look at Ginny. How high he must be, he thought, surprised at himself, but not embarrassed to state publicly what he had always kept private. She returned his look, and it seemed they were staring forever, locked in a timeless situation. He gazed deep into the gray lake of her eyes, drowning there, but unafraid of a death so sweet. "What about you?" he asked.

"What you want, I want," she said.

"Restrain yourselves," Roscoe said, laughing, and when Vorovich thought he ought to be angry and reached for that emotion, he found that it was gone. He sopped up the aromatic juice with the bread, downed another glassful of wine, the rich red wine, and then looked at Roscoe and said, "What's next?"

Roscoe and Lester exchanged looks. "Don't rush it, man," Roscoe said; "let your food digest." And then, curiously, "Aren't you feelin' pretty good?"

"Not good enough," Vorovich said. Shrugging, Roscoe beckoned him to follow. In the next room, they gathered around a fireplace, and Roscoe brought out a hookah. Someone put on more music. Vorovich could feel something building in him, like a sneeze, and then the music's beat matched/slowed/rushed his heart out of sync with his mind, which began to contemplate the smoky scene as though he were on the wrong end of a telescopic lens. Slowly, so slowly each thought, like each note of music or word or movement from the others, seemed to be spinning on a record whose speed was too slow for the recorded tempo.

When they handed him the long curling tube of the water pipe he blew out instead of in and the water burbled like the laughter. For a while he thought he was the smoke and then the music, and someone (was that Sam or Lester or the uppity black?) complained that he sounded like a *bad* Lawrence Welk. He took umbrage at that. By God, just because he was of the generation of cheerful little earfuls did not mean he *dug* that music, no by God, no! and in his outrage he sucked in and in and in and in, and that smoke was cool as the morning mist and sweet as wet clover and he did not think he could get enough of it ever. Then his vision clouded and his mind too and he was hardly aware when someone took the pipe away saying, "Don't be greedy, man!" and someone else, who had to be Lester, "Pig!" and he didn't much care except enough to smile at Lester, because that was what the little dude could not stand: to be smiled at. He knew the type, had seen the type so often in the last two years—a hater. He leaned close to Lester, wanting to tell him of his sudden insight about how to love, and the little dude screamed at him to get away, get your hands off you faggot pig!

He was thoughtful about that. He had seen men whose blood drained from their faces when called that, who went into vast rages, who struck out and beat their accusers and might have continued beating to the death if not pulled off. He had never understood why such accusations should trigger such violent reactions . . . not that he hadn't questioned his own manhood, in those days when he had first been abandoned, as though unfit for cohabitation, no matter how they had in the first hot days of the marriage tumbled and groped and cried out as if in pain rather than ecstasy, and he wondered how he had failed to satisfy her, those fluttering eyelids and gasping breaths notwithstanding; and though the women he had had since reassured him, he had never realized what sex could be until the day before yesterday.

And so he continued to smile at Lester, and because he was smiling his teeth cut his lip when Lester hit him. He was too remote from himself to hit Lester back. Lester might have hit him again, while he was still, from what seemed a great height and a far distance, contemplating that enraged youth, while tasting the salt from his bloody lip, but Roscoe and Chen grabbed that frail youngster and dragged him away, screaming wordlessly the obscenities he felt apparently too profound to be spoken aloud. Then there was a thud thud and sudden silence.

When Roscoe and Chen walked back inside without Lester, it seemed Vorovich was the only one who would look at them. Ginny might have looked, but she was too busy examining his lip, dabbing at it with a handkerchief that smelled of lemon.

The others were extraordinarily shy, fussing with their clothing, rearranging the candles, poking at the fire, changing the records, everything and anything that would keep their eyes down.

"Why did he do that?" Vorovich asked Ginny, though he was watching the strutting Roscoe and Chen.

"Lester loved Billy," Ginny said.

"You told me that," Vorovich said.

"I mean he loved him," Ginny said, "passionately. And he thinks you killed him on purpose."

"Didn't you tell him I didn't?" Vorovich asked.

"Until now," Ginny said, "I didn't know for sure."

"What's different about now?" he started to ask, then stopped. Someplace deep in his head he felt a kind of click, like an oiled catch or gear sliding up a notch, and the quality of his vision changed perceptibly. He had been given a kind of truth drug. He couldn't be forced to tell the truth, but it would be impossible for him to lie.

"You gonna have a swole lip," Roscoe said, squatting next to Vorovich.

"He'll be all right," Ginny said. "But what about Lester?"

"You wolly too much," Chen said, sitting on his heels. "You get linkled fo'head wrong befo' time."

"Don't we get no thanks for heppin you?" Roscoe asked.

"No thanks," Vorovich said. The black laughed. "I don't know why you did it yet," Vorovich continued.

"We spozed to look *out* for you, man," Roscoe said. "Charles done give us the word."

"Then Charles is who you should be looking to for thanks," Vorovich said.

"Man," Roscoe said, shaking his head, "you narcs is the coolest. It must be your training, hey? But you the best I ever seen. That's why they pick you for this job, ain't it?"

"I didn't get picked," Vorovich mourned. "I got passed over."

"We know oar about you not getting plomotion," Chen said. "That eraborate proy, so you can walm you way into our affection, gain our confidence, eventuarry brow the whisser on us."

"Cut it out, Chen," Ginny said. "It's no longer funny."

"A straight-on narc is bad enough," Roscoe said, "but a fink narc is lower than scum. Tell the truth, pal. Why you here?"

Vorovich hesitated. He was so high, so literally spaced out that even if he wanted he could not twitch or blink or shrink from the question.

"Who you working for?" Chen asked, suddenly menacing without the phony dialect.

It was important not to lie, Vorovich thought. But if he told the truth, bad things could happen to him, for more reasons than one. What had old McEnery said to him once? The best agent he had ever known, knew all there was about going undercover. You had to submerge yourself in the part, Mac said, believe so much in what you were doing that the line between the acting and the reality blurred, substitute the emotions of the character you were assuming for your own, or vice versa, find the emotions in yourself like the character you were assuming, and if you were good enough, if you were absolutely first-rate, you might transcend the part, to the point where even a lie detector could not find you out. Because, in fact, you were either not who you started out to be, or you had always been something other than what you believed. Good undercover men, like good actors, were rare; the risk you ran was too great. Whether others found you out or you found yourself out, the penalty for failure was brutal. Mac had killed himself. No one had known why.

"Answer me," Chen hissed. "Who you working for?"

"You're not working for the D.E.A.?" Roscoe broke in, as Vorovich struggled to find an answer.

"Hey, man, what is that?" Chen asked, turning on Roscoe. "You're phrasing negatively—that's leading him!"

"Well, you're not getting anywhere your way," Roscoe said.

"I'm working for myself," Vorovich suddenly announced, and he was triumphant, having wanted so desperately to tell the truth.

Chen stared at him unbelievingly.

"Try her," Roscoe said, pointing at the bemused Ginny. "She scarfed from the same pot."

"What about it, Ginny?" Chen asked. "What's he doing here?"

"He's here because he loves me," Ginny said, without hesitation.

Roscoe began to laugh, and slapped his thighs, and rolled his eyes, once again parodying a vaudeville black. "Man," he managed finally, "that explains it all. He is pussy-whipped!"

"Well, that tears it," Chen said, quietly furious. "It's blown, a wasted trip."

"You don't want to tell Charles that?" Roscoe wondered.

After a moment, Chen shook his head, and the two of them walked up toward the pool area.

They were left in a bubble of silence. Faintly, outside the invisible dome which sheltered them, sounds of music and laughter and talk could be heard, as from an enormous distance, as if some distant radio were playing at its lowest volume.

"What are you thinking?" she asked.

"What if it's true, what Roscoe said?" he asked.

"What if it is?" she asked. "You going to dee-prive yourself just to prove that you ain't?"

"I suppose not," he said.

"You suppose?" she said.

"Not," he said. "They say it's fantastic when you're stoned."

"That's what they say," she said.

"I like to test these things out for myself," he said.

"Moi aussi," she said.

Her French sounded good. There was so much he didn't know about this girl. But she wasn't the subject of his investigations.

Looking up the road toward the garages, he saw Charles walking past the Rolls, where Sam stood with opened door, and getting into a Jaguar V-12, his mug's face grim, then wheeling down to the gate, honking impatiently, roaring the car on through almost before the barefooted girl got out of the way, leaving her and Sam and Roscoe and Chen clouded with dust.

"Well?" Ginny said.

"It looks like we'd have all the privacy we wanted up to the house," Vorovich said.

He had to wait until Charles got back anyway. And he couldn't think of a better way to pass the time. He didn't ask himself any hard questions about deeper motivations. That way, the truth would neither surprise nor disturb him.

They had forgotten that Roscoe and Chen also lived in the house. Even had they remembered, it was doubtful whether they would have been able to take enough precautions, since what Vorovich had taken to be a captain's walk on his first view of the house was a walk all right, designed for clandestine journeys from master to guest bedroom.

In any case, such considerations were beyond them. They were both wonderfully high, to the point of hallucination. And if, in the course of their lovemaking, they had heard sighs and muffled clicks—somewhere past consciousness, beyond the peripheries of their attention, engaged as they were in amorous acts, caught up in the exploration of all physical sensation, examining the nature of nature, uninhibited, reacting to a touch with a touch, a kiss with a kiss, entwined limb to limb, tongue to tongue, tasting all tastes, smelling all smells, all smells sweet as were all tastes, becoming one in all the ways it is possible for two to become one—if they had been aware that they were being watched, their watchers' sighs echoing their own, it wouldn't have made any difference.

Then. Now, in the very early morning, coming out of a sleep with head hammering in agonizing counterpoint to pounding heart, to see those two standing in the doorway, Chen grinning, holding up a camera, squinting through the viewfinder and taking one last picture, Roscoe indolently leaning against the jamb—for how long, sweet Jesus?—staring at them, black eyes glittering in that cordovan face, was the kind of shock that should not, could not be experienced more than once in a lifetime.

"Man," Roscoe said, "you sure do love that pussy, don't you?"

Ginny woke. She lay there rigid, and if it were not for the sound of her breathing beside him, Vorovich might have imagined her dead.

"Man," Chen parroted, "you do evlything, don't you?"

If he'd had his gun, he would have killed them. If he'd had clothes on, he'd have leaped from the bed and beat them bloody—but he hadn't his gun and he was naked under the sheet, and he could not bring himself to stand unclothed in front of those two.

Besides, it was important that he keep his cool. For Ginny's sake. He had to set a kind of example, so she might take strength from his impassivity. He was unable to look at her, not wanting to see his own humiliation mirrored on her face. He wouldn't have been able to tolerate seeing her humiliated, made less, diminishing like some creature dissolving in its own tears. One day, he thought, he might kill them. The thought gave him so much pleasure he was able to regain equanimity, enough to slide his hand over, under the sheet, to cover Ginny's. He had expected that hand to be rigid or limp and in shock, unfeeling; to have her turn her hand over and clasp his own, as if she were trying to give him some of her strength, was a surprise.

"Why are you doing this, Roscoe?" she asked.

"Charles's idea," Roscoe said. "It's sort of like insurance. A bond to keep the narc loyal and all."

"Not to wolly," Chen said grinning. "Nobody but us see photoglaphs."

"I hope not," Vorovich said quietly, but Chen lost his grin.

"Charles just called in," Roscoe said. "He says to bring your dude into town for lunch."

She nodded, and though Vorovich's mind was full of questions, she seemed to know exactly what was expected of her. She did not move. One of the young girls from the compound appeared, carrying a tray on which were covered bowls and plates of fruit and cheeses and a steaming pot of tea. Arranged there too was a bouquet of wildflowers.

"How lovely that looks, Shar," Ginny said.

Shar revealed her crooked teeth. "Where'll I put it?"

"Over there," Ginny said, pointing to the table by the French window, and, since it was apparent the two watchers were not ready to leave, she slid out of bed, and calmly, without haste, carrying herself without shame but without undue pride either, without seeming to flaunt her nudity or tease them with it, she walked to the bathroom and closed the door firmly behind her.

Vorovich wondered whether he would eventually have to do the same. He pictured himself first with the sheet, and then, not being able to bear that kind of comic appearance, without, and since the latter seemed the least of two almost unbearable alternatives, was girding himself to get up, when Roscoe said something to Chen and the two walked on out. Just like that.

Followed, moments later, by Shar, after showing him her teeth, again approvingly.

Ginny had a towel around her when she returned, and it pleased him, old-fashioned as it no doubt was. He went to the bathroom in turn, not ashamed to walk in front of her, not shy privately as he was in public. And came back to find Ginny waiting, turning her face up for a kiss.

"I could kill them for that," he said.

"I know," she said. "But nothing's worth killing about." Her vehemence surprised him, though it shouldn't have.

He needed to go on with it for his own self-respect. "An eye for an eye," he said.

She looked at him. "Then the world would be full of blind people," she said.

And the way she said it he had to laugh, and laughing, that awful tension that had been inside him dissolved.

He hadn't known oatmeal could taste that good. It was creamy and sweet and the tea was honeyed and fragrant and the cheeses pungent.

"You eat like this every morning?" he asked.

"On special ones," she said.

"You have many specials?" he asked, before he could stop himself.

She bit into an apple. "Not lately," she said.

"Excuse me for asking," he said.

"You have to ask, I know that," she said.

She drove him into San Francisco. There was a brief discussion with Sam, who wanted to chauffeur them in the Rolls, but she won out, even after Roscoe and Chen joined the argument.

"If you take the Rolls," Roscoe said, "we can all go."

"Charles tell you to come along?" Ginny asked.

"Not specifically," Roscoe said.

"I'm surprised at you, Roscoe," Ginny said.

"I meant for you to drop us off on the way," Roscoe said, "before you get wherever you're going. Like in Chinatown, say. I'll bet Chen would surely like some sweet and sour pork, hey Chen?"

"We're not going anywhere near Chinatown," Ginny said.

"I have work to do here," Chen said. "Some photographs to deverrop."

"Well I wouldn't mind some clam linguini," Roscoe said, with a disgusted look at Chen. "Smooth and buttery, a little garlic—I'm fed up to here with whole-grain curds and whey."

"You have a particular café in mind?" Vorovich asked.

"You'll just have to get there on your own, Roscoe," Ginny said, after a thoughtful glance at Vorovich.

Later as she drove them, top down on her own car, a battered white 1957 MGA, through the sparkling bright midmorning up the valley toward the city, she asked him whether he was suspicious of Roscoe. "He's always been curious," she said.

"It's more than curiosity," he said.

"You think so?" she asked doubtfully. "What more?"

"Maybe he's looking for a way to go into business on his own," he said.

"Timmy," she said then, and he was suddenly reminded by the endearment of certain moments the night before, "is this the way it's going to be, tippy-toeing around everyone, worried about what they're up to and why?"

"It's my training," he said.

They were climbing a steep road, and when they reached the top of a hill, she pulled into a view turnoff. It was a spectacular view overlooking the city, the sun glittering off the bridge spans, what remained of the morning fog drifting down the channel. In the distance a foghorn sounded, echoing the yearning inside him.

"It's not too late," she said. "The road forks here."

"Mine forked back at the border," he said.

"But why?" she demanded, a little desperately, he thought. "It can't be just the money—you must have had plenty of chances before to sell out."

"I was younger then," he said. "Ambitious. Full of principle." He looked at her. "If I had met you twenty years ago," he said, "my life might have been different."

"Why can't your life be different now?" she asked.

"There's twenty years between us," he said.

"Age is a state of mind," she said.

"Tell the body that," he said.

"You weren't worried about age last night," she said.

He couldn't help himself, he smiled, though he would never forget that pictures had been taken.

"All that counts," she said, "is what people mean to each other."

"You're wrong," he said, though he was flushed with feeling for her. "What counts is the money."

"How much do you need?" she demanded. "You—we—could raise grapes in Sonoma."

"I'm not a farmer," he said.

"It's easy," she said. "Once the seedlings are established you just maintain them. The wineries harvest the grapes for you. That pays enough to live on." She was pleading with him: deep in those gray eyes was supplication.

"What would we do if the harvest failed?" he asked. "Or the wineries lowered their price?"

"We'd find something," she said. "Someplace."

"We'd be poor," he said. "Police work is all I know. And who'd want to hire a disgraced cop?" He hastened to take that stricken look away. "I'm not blaming you," he said.

"Then why are you pushing me off?" she asked.

"I'm being realistic," he said. "What's in it for you? You're too bright for me to believe you believe it'd all be just one great big beautiful bed—and what can I offer besides that?"

"A baby," she said.

"Oh," he said.

"I want a kid," she said. "Your kid."

"I suppose I owe you one?" he said.

"That isn't what I meant," she said. "I never was all that interested before in who the father was, but now I am."

"I'm flattered," he said.

"I mean it," she said. "I never cared for anyone way deep down, like this—I never thought it was possible for two people to connect. I thought all that was a lot of sentimental middle-class horseshit. Like I had this maternal instinct and I didn't much care who planted the seed but now it's yours I want, I want the kid to have whatever it is you've got going for it, I mean he might have freckles and a weird nose but the chin would be strong and that's important—no, don't laugh, weak-chinned people have this terrible time because people *expect* them to be weak and your kid wouldn't have that problem. . . ."

"Cut it out, Ginny," he said.

"You won't even consider it?" she said.

For a moment he thought she might be going to weep, but she didn't and he wondered whether that had been his own emotion. Because she could never be self-pitying, she was too straight on to life and what it offered, too accepting to let herself go in vain regrets and fruitless melancholies.

She started the car, then let it idle in gear. "Is it that you don't trust me?" she asked.

"I don't trust anybody, including myself," he said, though even that was too great an admission for him to make.

She looked at him pityingly, and then swung the little car back onto the road and drove a little too fast on down into the city.

The moment they hit the outskirts she took little-traveled side streets, and though they turned first in one direction and then another he noticed they kept bearing toward the sea. Still, he was surprised when they arrived finally at the Embarcadero and Fisherman's Wharf, since those places were always so crowded, and mug-featured, long-haired Charles would be conspicuously out of place among these straight-looking tourists.

She let him out at the barricades, keeping the motor running. "There's an open-air fish bar about a block down," she said. "Charles will find you there."

"You're not coming?" he said.

"I found out that wasn't mescaline in that corset," she said.

He wanted to ask her how, but that would be giving too much away. She was terribly disturbed, he could see that. "Where are you going now?" he asked, finally.

"You have any suggestions?" she asked.

He closed the car door, and walked away.

It was a hard walk away, but he had always managed to do what was necessary.

Charles came out of the kitchen area of the little fish bar, and around the counter toward Vorovich, and not until he paused in front of him did Vorovich recognize who it was. He was dressed in the white coveralls of a delivery man—a fish-delivery man—and his long hair was crammed up into the low-brimmed delivery man's cap that he wore.

"I'm parked around the side," he murmured, and continued on out, and Vorovich turned to see that he had "D'Anton's Fruits de Mer" stitched in red script across his back.

It was a sea-blue-painted delivery van, parked so that Vorovich was hidden from the street the moment he walked around it. Anyone looking for him would have had only a momentary chance to see him before he climbed into the back.

"There's another pair of coveralls back there," Charles said, climbing in behind the wheel. "Put 'em on over your suit." And he started the motor and drove away in a wheeling curve which, had Vorovich not been half expecting it, might have thrown him up against the wooden cases stacked between the cleats.

The cases were cold: probably packed with dry ice, he thought, marked p-e-r-i-s-h-a-b-l-e. They were likely fish, since they smelled of salt and the sea. But he opened one all the same, to find a flensed sea bass, and another to find it literally crawling with hard-shell crab, and, because he was a methodically suspicious man, was working to open still another when Charles stopped for a traffic light.

"C'mon," Charles said, "get your ass up front. Everything's what it seems to be. It's just a cover to get us into a meeting without arousing, you know, like undue suspicion."

The drive was a short one. They began to climb the hills alongside the water toward a residential section near a park. They passed a playground and turned left and climbed again and turned left again and the homes, which had been small but expensive, became large and more expensive: row upon row of black-and-gold-painted entryways faced the street, but their back views of the bay must have been little short of sensational.

"You dig it?" Charles asked, glancing at his passenger.

"I was wondering why you don't live here instead of out in the boondocks," Vorovich said.

"Man, wouldn't I just like to," Charles said. "But I don't have the bread."

"That place you have can't be cheap," Vorovich said.

"Not like these, man," Charles said. "They don't call this the Gold Coast for nothing."

Vorovich knew about the Gold Coast, a kind of millionaire's row, where ex-ambassadors lived, and presidents of major corporations, and families whose wealth came from railroads and forests and shipping and oil. To buy one of these homes took more than money, he thought, and to be invited inside one was a rare event. What was this kinky person of no background and little worth doing turning into the alley which ran along behind the houses, convenient for service entrances? Who could *he* know that would invite him in, even through the back door?

They stopped in the second block just beyond the Row, behind the first house, and he supposed that house took on respectability from propinquity. Charles beep-beeped the horn, and moments later a plump, black-haired woman with a large mole on her cheek and an apron streaked with flour peered out. A buzzing sound and the slow rising of the garage door indicated that she had activated some sort of electronic device.

Before the door was fully open, Charles had started to pull in, showing, Vorovich thought, an anxiety about this delivery untypical of the usual service man, and though it was unlikely anyone watching would catch the little nuance it was the sort of inattention to detail that made the difference between the success or failure of sensitive operations. Charles, he decided, was unsteady.

The garage door closed behind them. For a moment they were in darkness, and then blazingly bright lights were turned on, and peering at them from either side of the van were two persons of similarly exotic, unsmiling features. One was short and slender, the other tall and burly, but both had Middle Eastern noses with eyes set too close, resembling parrots from whom all colors save black had been bleached.

"Out," the slender one said.

They were frisked, thoroughly and professionally, ankle to neck, and Vorovich wondered whether this was where Charles had learned his procedure.

"Okay," the slender one said. "Up the stairs."

"Hey," the burly one said, in a voice almost too high for a man, "what about the delivery?"

The slender man nodded, and reaching into the van, pulled out a clipboard, then read from the top sheet: "Four dozens of oysters, a dozen crab, a case of anchovy. Got that?" he said, looking at Charles and Vorovich.

Charles hesitated, then opened the side door of the van, stepped in, and began stacking the cases.

"Aren't you going to help your buddy?" the slender one asked.

"Yeah," the burly one said. "Help your buddy."

"I'm really not a delivery man," Vorovich said. "These coveralls are a disguise."

"Is that a fact?" the slender one said.

"And he's not my buddy," Vorovich said.

"C'mon," Charles said, picking a splinter out of his hand. "It's a legitimate delivery. The truck has this as part of its regular route, the last stop." He chuckled morosely. "I'm temporary help, the relief driver. That way the company records don't show anything out of the ordinary."

"Very intelligent," Vorovich said. He made no move to help as Charles jumped down, strained to put a case marked AN-CHOVY on one shoulder, and started for the stairs. When Vorovich moved to follow, he found the slender one standing in his way.

"You forgot to pick up a case," the other said.

"I didn't forget," Vorovich said pleasantly.

"Pick up a case!" the other suddenly shouted.

"You've been eating garlic," Vorovich said.

Everything stopped: Charles's footsteps on the stairs, the breathing of the two dark men, and Vorovich was bracing himself for the coming encounter when there was a sound of static, and a loudspeakered voice, from some intercom, rasped, "What's keeping you down there?"

The burly one went to the intercom. "In a minute, sir," he said. "We were unloading the order."

"Well, hurry it up," the voice said. "I'm anxious to meet our visitor."

Vorovich smiled and stepped around the slender person and walked on up the stairs past Charles. He did hold the stair door open, but Charles just glared as he went by. Vorovich held the door a moment longer, then let it swing shut just as the slender fellow, both of whose hands were holding the case stenciled OYSTERS, got to it; Vorovich watched as he struggled to keep the case from touching his blue serge suit.

"In there," the cook said to Charles, indicating a storeroom just off the kitchen, and Vorovich, spying a swinging door leading off the other way, went through it to find himself in an elegant, chandeliered dining room. He continued on through another doorway to a room filled floor to ceiling and wall to wall with books, crowded with soft leather chairs and reading lamps.

Standing in front of a burning fireplace was a small man with a large head and strong features, gray hair elegantly waved, the skin aristocratic, that is, subtly pitted, as if marked by a medieval pox. Through glasses with gold wire rims, eyes as hard and shiny-black as any Vorovich had ever seen regarded him—unfavorably.

Behind him, Charles came bursting in, followed by the two other men. That disapproving look was shifted to the latecomers.

"I find it difficult to believe," the man said, "that my instructions were unclear."

"But you said you wanted them up here," the burly man said.

"Dressed like that?" the man said, and turning his back on them bowed his head, contemplating the fire as if none of them existed.

Vorovich caught on first, and went on back through the various doors into the kitchen, where he removed the coveralls. Charles followed him, doing the same, avoiding his eyes. The cook, apparently used to such goings-on, was about to hang their coveralls in the pantry when the two others came in and, faces flushed, took them from her and began putting them on.

"Ah, much better," the man said, when Vorovich and Charles returned to the library. "You weren't told you were invited for lunch? You apparently rattled my men with your antagonistic attitude." Again he evaluated Vorovich, who shifted uncomfortably, aware that compared to the dandified Charles in his double-breasted blazer and his host in an English-cut suit, he in his worn and shapeless worsted seemed out of place in these splendid surroundings. "What would you like?"

the man asked them, indicating a bar cart filled with every conceivable kind of liquor.

"What are you having?" Vorovich asked.

"Lillet and soda," the other said. "It's not too well known, which is just as well, since the supply is limited—it's an acquired taste, I should warn you—you're welcome to try something harder, of course, but since there will be wine with lunch . . . ?"

"I'll try the Lillet," Vorovich said, pronouncing it as an Englishman would in a kind of private snobbism. Though he spoke a little French, he wasn't yet sure he wanted the other to know that.

The other nodded approvingly, then looked to Charles.

"I'll have a martini," Charles said, with an independence that was patently false: he was clearly awed by their host. "Very dry," he continued. "With an olive, over ice."

Their host made a face. "A common misconception," he said to Vorovich. "A good vermouth, like the Boissière, one part to four, enhances the gin, while the olive distorts the taste, and the ice dilutes it."

The skin on Charles's face became tight, but he said nothing, and when he got his drink he made a show of stirring the ice with the olive before popping it into his mouth.

"Perhaps it should be diluted," the other continued, amused by the little display. "To drink gin at a business lunch, and chance blurring the mental processes, seems not the most intelligent procedure. . . ."

"It's your business we'll be discussing," Charles said. "I'm just the intermediary."

"Wrong," the host said, and Charles went pale.

"This is good, Mr. D'Anton," Vorovich said, lifting his drink. "Do you import liquor as well as fish?"

"They told you my name?" D'Anton asked, frowning.

"Who else would you be," Vorovich said, "using a wholesale fish-delivery truck to slip people into your house unobserved?" He hesitated. "But what I don't understand is your giving our coveralls to your men. How were you planning to get us back out?"

"There are ways," D'Anton said obscurely, and Vorovich understood that a threat had been made.

"Well," he said, pretending to be cheerful, "your delivery system is better than Charley's, no doubt about that."

D'Anton observed him thoughtfully. "I have no system," he said. "People get trapped by systems."

A very short, slight Oriental, probably Filipino, Vorovich thought, dressed in a pale blue jacket, came into the room, waited until his employer nodded, and then announced lunch.

The dining-room table was covered with ice; that is, huge trays and bowls of ice in which were embedded oysters, cracked crab, chunks of sea bass and other kinds of whitefish, along with lemon wedges and cups of red and tartar sauces. The Filipino began tossing a huge bowl of salad greens in which red peppers and tomatoes were evident, and, on closer glance, dozens of anchovies. Then the fleshy cook came into the room bearing a steaming hot cauldron of a clear soup in which floated tiny pieces of a stuffed pasta.

"Tortellini in brodo," D'Anton said, sniffing approvingly. "Not overly cooked?" he said to the woman.

"Niente, perfetto," she responded, and waited until he had tasted one and nodded before she went back to the kitchen.

"I thought D'Anton was French," Vorovich said.

"It is," D'Anton said.

"But the food is Italian . . . ?" Vorovich said.

"Since San Francisco is, in large part, an Italian city," D'Anton said, "I find that one can entertain safely with an Italian cook."

"But why not French?" Vorovich asked, persisting.

"What is it that disturbs you?" D'Anton asked, looking up from a crab leg he was breaking.

"You don't seem French either," Vorovich said bluntly.

"I'm not," D'Anton said calmly, though there had been a hesitation so slight that had not Vorovich been looking for it, it might have been missed. "I'm Turkish. The name is legal, however. It makes it easier to deal with people socially."

"And your company?" Vorovich asked. "Is it legal too?"

"I run a legitimate business," D'Anton said, "which is quite profitable. I pay my taxes, and have never run afoul of the law, even for a minor offense."

"Then what are you doing involved with Charley here?" Vorovich asked.

"Try the oysters," D'Anton said, passing him the plate.

"They're from a special bed, twenty miles out." While Vorovich was slowly forking one from its shell, the other said, "If you insist on knowing, you should be aware that the knowledge you will then have is very special, and a danger to me. And unless you can convince me you are trustworthy, I don't see how I can permit you to leave my house with it."

Vorovich swallowed the oyster, then took a sip of the white wine, a beautifully dry gray Reisling. "Charles already had me checked out," he said. "Didn't he tell you?"

D'Anton waved a manicured hand disdainfully, and Vorovich noted the glitter of a diamond on the little finger. "A superficial test," he said. "These young people have a simple-minded faith in drugs. Truth is as complex as the human mind and personality, and can't be gotten at only by pharmaceutical methods."

Charles had restrained himself too long. "Then why did you let me bring him here?" he demanded.

"Because he wanted so much to come," D'Anton said. "And if he hadn't spoken first, I might have invited him myself." He looked hard at Vorovich. "Well?" he said.

"Don't I already know too much by having met you?" Vorovich asked.

"Hardly," D'Anton said. "What do you know now? Only that I am acquainted with a young importer of dangerous drugs. You have no way of relating me to anything illegal, unless you manage to get me to accept some contraband merchandise personally, which clearly will be impossible. You can have me watched, of course, but I think you already know such surveillances will prove fruitless." D'Anton smiled thoughtfully. "At this moment, therefore, we are both still safe. I must warn you again: the more you learn, the bigger the threat you become to me, the more dangerous for you—we will ride a rather treacherous merry-go-round together. The decision is yours."

That D'Anton had said it all in a soft, cultured voice didn't make it any the less deadly.

"I didn't come here just for lunch," Vorovich said.

D'Anton squeezed lemon on an oyster, took the shrinking crustacean off the shell with his teeth, swallowed, drained the juice. "Because of the nature of my business," he said, wiping his mouth, "I have interests and acquaintances all over the world. From time to time I am approached with investment opportunities of one sort of another, and it is my habit to study the potentials and risks of those opportunities from beginning to end. I may even venture a little capital to test the waters, so to speak, to prove its practicality."

"And that's what you were doing with Charley?" Vorovich asked.

"The key to the success of this particular investment is transportation," D'Anton said, ignoring Charles's negative headshake. "We were looking for a system off the beaten track, and one of my associates, who owns a pharmaceutical concern in Mexico, had supplied certain chemicals to Charles for one of his previous enterprises, and recommended that we try him. It was bungled, as you know—"

"It wasn't my fault," Charles said, flushing. "Whoever set up the buy goofed it. It was a plant!"

"Was it a plant?" D'Anton asked Vorovich softly—too softly, he thought.

"No," Vorovich said. "Too many people knew about the drop, probably, and someone informed on him, that's all. Since the Congress voted us a lot more money to buy information with we're getting more. Of course maybe it wasn't the money, maybe somebody just didn't like Charley."

"What difference does it make now?" Charles snarled. "I thought you were going to get him to be reasonable about the corset!"

"I am being reasonable," Vorovich said. "Half of something is worth more than all of nothing."

D'Anton laughed. "A well-thought-out position," he said. "An outrageous demand couched in reasonable terms."

Vorovich tried to hide the uneasiness that laughter made him feel. "Outrageous?" he said. "I can get more than I asked from you freelancing it."

"Someone would kill you for it first," D'Anton said. "Or turn you in for it. Certainly you of all people must know how important it is to keep as many layers as possible between you and the street."

"I can take care of myself," Vorovich said.

"Pride is the great curse," D'Anton said.

"But you have it," Vorovich said.

"Wrong," D'Anton said. "I have taste and judgment, which is something entirely different. I know how and when to take my losses, which is an art in itself, but profitable in the long run, because we learn from loss. In this case, I was quite prepared to take the loss, even after learning that the merchandise had turned up, knowing that it does not pay to deal with hijackers, even on a secondary level, until I heard how anxious you were to meet me."

"I've learned it's a waste of time to deal with anybody below the top line," Vorovich said.

"Then let's not waste any more of the time you find so valuable," D'Anton said. "Why have you really come here?"

"For the money," Vorovich said.

"I'll ask you once more," D'Anton said, "and I suggest that this time you tell me the truth. If you don't, I will know it, and I will be forced to chalk you up as a loss."

"Pride," Vorovich observed, "is the great curse."

He thought he might have gone too far. No man so sensual about food was without passion, no matter how cold and objective he thought himself; no man could achieve the position this man had without ruthlessness of the kind that had a great deal of emotion in it.

But he had gone just far enough. D'Anton smiled. "You are trying to ruffle me," he said. "Why?"

"To see if I'm in the right place," Vorovich said. "I'm here for money, as I said, but for a lot more than I could get for the corset. So you're right about me having other reasons."

D'Anton was more than interested; he was engrossed.

"I'm here to sell my services," Vorovich said.

"He never said anything about that, I swear it!" Charles cried. He had been watching them with increasing concern. "What kind of services could he provide anyway?"

"It's all right, Charles," D'Anton said soothingly. "I would like to hear what he has to say."

"The D.E.A.'s pinching off all the usual supply routes," Vorovich said. "I ought to know. I was in charge of that end of it. That's why you went to Charles—which is what I don't understand. You're smart; so you should have known in front that someone like Charley would blow it. It's one thing to run pills, another to run smack."

"You lucked in," Charles said, glaring at him.

"I took advantage of an opportunity," Vorovich said. "Which takes the kind of skill and experience you don't have. And that," he said, turning to D'Anton, "makes me pretty valuable to you, doesn't it? I know how the department thinks. I can help you end run them."

D'Anton quieted Charles with a gesture. "I'm aware of what you could do for us," he said. "I just don't understand why you want to do it." As Vorovich started to answer he said, "Think carefully. How you reply will make a difference as to whether I take you on or not."

"I've never had enough money," Vorovich said.

"To do what?" D'Anton asked.

"Anything I want," Vorovich said, hesitating only a moment, but even that moment, he thought, too long. "I'd like to travel, own a sports car, buy all the clothes I want, have a little beach place, go to expensive restaurants—"

"That all seems rather vague," D'Anton said.

"What's vague about it?" Vorovich asked. "When I see the way people like you and Charley dress, and compare it to myself, when I have to settle for a second-rate whisky instead of Black Label or Chivas Regal, when I drink the local beer instead of the imports, when I go to a hashhouse and order chicken fricassee instead of steak . . . when I see a snot-nose like Charley living on top of the world, and ask myself why, what's he done that entitles him to more right now than I used to dream about . . ."

"Keep your mouth off me," Charles began, but D'Anton stopped him.

"That's closer," D'Anton said.

"Closer?" Vorovich said, after a moment.

"To the secret truth," D'Anton said. "Money is an obvious motive. And a strong one, I grant you. But there's always an underlying reason for the acquisition of money. Some want it for power, some for the aura of success it seems to imply, very few, if any, for its own sake. All the things you describe, for example, could be yours for what you could get for the corset."

"That wouldn't be enough," Vorovich said.

"Tell me," D'Anton said, "what you were thinking when you found the corset. Besides its monetary value, I mean."

Vorovich was suddenly thirsty, but he resisted reaching for the wine. "I was thinking that was a pretty valuable load for kids to be running," he said.

"And what else?" D'Anton prompted.

"I was thinking that it was so valuable, the people behind it must be important," Vorovich continued. "And that it might be —interesting—to meet those people."

"Why didn't you tell the D.E.A. what you thought?" D'Anton asked.

Vorovich considered why he hadn't done that. "It was pretty clear to me," he said, "that the D.E.A. wasn't much interested in what I thought. About anything."

"That's when you decided to go off on your own?" D'Anton said.

Vorovich nodded slowly, surprised to find himself sweating.

"But it wasn't good enough for you to merely leave the government," D'Anton said, "the people who didn't appreciate you—you want to rub their noses in it, prove to them how wrong they were."

"Maybe," Vorovich said grudgingly.

"But what good will that do you," D'Anton asked, "if they don't know that it's you outsmarting them?"

"I'll know," Vorovich said.

D'Anton smiled, not very widely, but deeply. "More wine?" he asked.

"Where did you learn so much about people?" Vorovich asked, trying not to gulp.

"Those books on my shelves are well thumbed," D'Anton said. "Except for the fact that I had to earn my living at an early age, I might have become a psychoanalyst."

"You would have been a good one," Vorovich said. "You found out things about me I didn't know myself."

D'Anton looked at him thoughtfully, those eyes very cold behind the very expensive glasses. "Don't you ever try to con me, Vorovich. It wouldn't be wise."

"I meant it," Vorovich said, and because in a way he had, he was able to inject just the proper note of sincerity.

They went back to the library for coffee, where, over Charles's sullen objection, D'Anton filled him in on their problem.

"As you know," he began, lighting up a black cigar with an aroma so sweet it had to be Cuban, "the contraband drug market is in disarray. The decision taken at Appalachia a few years ago by the so-called 'families' to withdraw from the business left the door open for any number of would-be entrepreneurs—"

"Like Charley?" Vorovich interrupted.

95

"—and contributed to a scarcity in the market, which was driving prices up enormously," D'Anton continued, as if unaware of the interruption. "As you also know, a concerted attack is being made world-wide on the sources of supply—the Turks are now growing only under government license, the French are cooperating in closing down their clandestine laboratories, the Mexicans are blocking the normal supply routes, which leads to a further diminished supply, and even higher prices.

"An opportunity has presented itself," D'Anton continued, examining the developing ash of his cigar, "to process an extraordinary amount of raw material. As I said, I never invest without examining the potential from source to eventual buyer, and I discovered that profits increase geometrically every step of the way. So do the risks, naturally. But the profits in this case are so enormous that I have decided to take advantage of the present chaotic condition by putting together my own organization, in order to realize the maximum profit.

"We have already made contact with the owners of every secret poppy field we know of," he continued. "Harvesttime is not far off. Because I have brought some laboratory owners in as partners, we can process that crop, large as it is, without too much trouble, and package it, in a unique method I thought of myself, and get it to its shipping point. But it is there we run into a snag.

"I am trying to convince my . . . colleagues," he said, dropping a lump of sugar into his expresso, "that we should bring the entire amount in and stockpile it in this country, which is so vast, and has such a multitude of hiding places. If we stockpile it in Europe, we chance finding ourselves confronted by ever-increasing obstacles to successful imports, not to mention discovery of so large an inventory. But my partners are, understandably, reluctant to risk everything in one massive input without some pretty solid indication that the attempt will prove successful."

D'Anton motioned toward the sulking Charles. "That was why we brought Charles in. He convinced us that since the so-called dope culture was dying out and Federal agents were not as interested in young people as before, his delivery system could get through. But we should have known, 'in front' as you say, that these young people would prove unreliable.

"That," he said to Vorovich, leaning forward, "is where you *could* prove of immense value to us. A man high up enough to know not only all the procedures of our government agencies, on a local, state, and Federal level, but those in other countries as well. If I had set out to find someone, you couldn't be more perfect. Now," he said to Charles, "do you understand why I agreed to meet with him personally?"

"What I don't understand," Charles said, "is why you're telling him how valuable he is."

"Ah, Charles," D'Anton said, blowing a great cloud of smoke. "You're afraid I'll drive his price up? How little you understand people. Now that I know his underlying motives, I know that he is working as much for his revenge as for the money."

"The money is important," Vorovich said.

"I agree that it is," D'Anton said. "And we will pay you what you are worth. I believe in that. I believe in giving people incentive. You will not find a negative approach with me."

"What do you think I am worth?" Vorovich asked.

"Ah," D'Anton said, "you have that backward also. It's what you think you're worth that counts."

"One million dollars," Vorovich said.

"One million dollars?" Charles said, incredulous.

"Please, Charles," D'Anton said.

"But you don't even know whether he can do it or not," Charles said. "He doesn't even have a *plan!* "

"I'm certain he will come up with a plan," D'Anton said. "Anyone who values himself so highly has enough self-confidence to do almost anything. Your fee would, however," he said to Vorovich, "be contingent not only upon your plan, but on your being able to convince my colleagues that you are the man to do it."

"I understand," Vorovich said.

"Shall we shake on it?" D'Anton said.

"I want more than a handshake," Vorovich said.

"All right," D'Anton said, affably enough, but his complexion had darkened. "What would you suggest?"

"A down payment," Vorovich said. "Twenty-five per cent in a Swiss account."

"Ten per cent," D'Anton said, after a long puff at the cigar. "More than that might be sufficient for your needs. You might be tempted to drop out."

Vorovich hesitated; then, after a moment: "Agreed."

"Don't think I am unaware that you may wish to become part of this operation in order to break it up," D'Anton added. "Let me remind you that my colleagues will have that possibility always in the forefront of their minds. As for myself, I do not intend to engage in illegal commerce as a continuing activity, and at no time will I approve of any plan that involves me personally. Am I making myself clear?"

"Very clear," Vorovich said.

"What about the corset?" Charles said. "Make him turn over the corset."

"Excellent, Charles," D'Anton said. "I know that you speak out of personal greed, but it's a worthwhile suggestion all the same. That way, should Mr. Vorovich prove unsatisfactory, we shall lose only him, not the money. Agreed?" he said to Vorovich.

"Agreed," Vorovich said.

The arrangements they made for the exchange were simple enough. When Vorovich turned over the corset, he was to get a belt containing money, one hundred thousand dollars in hundred-dollar bills, which meant one thousand crisp new pieces of paper, arranged in such a way that worn around the waist it would cause no appreciable bulge. At the same time he was to be given five thousand dollars extra for expenses, along with an air-travel card and a tour itinerary prepared by the World-Wide Travel agency, apparently one of the "partners" D'Anton had mentioned. His first stop would be Switzerland, to open his own account.

Vorovich was not worried about being double-crossed. In the first place, it was not that easy to remove a corset from an armed man. Besides, D'Anton had more at stake than this little shipment—he was after an immense score, and it was to his advantage to go along: at least until he had decided whether Vorovich was going to work out or not.

As he had said he would, D'Anton had taken his own precautions. Alphonse and Gaston (which was how D'Anton had introduced those two parrot-beaked hoods, deadpan, so Vorovich couldn't know whether they were smart or educated enough to get the joke) had ridden with him on the plane to Los Angeles, and in the cab from the airport to the Federal building, unhappy about having to wait outside while Vorovich went in to get his "personal effects." Though they finally understood that Vorovich could not pass them through the security guards, Alphonse, the smaller man, pulled out a watch to time him.

Time therefore was important, Vorovich justified himself, when the security guard in the rear lobby told him he was wanted in Personnel, on eight, some papers to sign. Vorovich nodded, pinned the clearance badge to his lapel, got off on eight all right, but immediately took the inside fire stairs back down to seven, which held the walk-in vault.

Vorovich handed the vault clerk his receipt and walked on into the steel-reinforced interior without waiting for the other to come along. He had an anxious moment when he could not find his envelopes immediately, then picked them out from under a pile on a bottom shelf.

"Just a damn minute," the clerk said, as Vorovich started on past him again. "I have to count them. And we both have to sign this—now that we're under new management, everyone's got his asshole puckered tight about procedures."

"There's less than ten," Vorovich said finally. "What's taking you so long? Not enough fingers?"

"It doesn't say on the slip how many," the clerk said.

Vorovich didn't even blink, though his heart seemed to stop. "Well, write it in now," he said. "You were the one checked me in, and unless you enjoy demerits, no one'll be the wiser if you check me out. C'mon," he said, as the other looked at him thoughtfully, "I'm in a hurry. If anything turns up missing you'll have me to blame."

"Okay," the clerk said finally, and Vorovich thanked his luck that his clearance badge had his former rank written in. One procedure Cabot hadn't instituted was the posting of a list of those resigned or retired.

Again, Vorovich took the inner stairs two at a time, went down to six, and into the men's room, where in the privacy of a toilet stall he broke the seal on the thickest of the envelopes and pulled out the corset.

It would be an understatement to say that putting it on under his shirt made him feel strange. Not only did it have her smell, but the boy, Billy's, as well. He remembered all too vividly how he had itched with self-disgust when he had worn it before, taking it off the accusing-eyed dead boy and breaking just enough of the inner stitching to make sure that it indeed contained heroin, then, crumpling the plasticine tight to make sure none of the precious stuff would spill, he hesitated only a moment before he strapped the corset on next to his skin.

He didn't even think twice. It was as if he had known from the beginning what he would do if he got the chance. When the information had crossed his desk that a not insignificant amount of heroin was being brought across the border by kids, he had sensed that this was not an ordinary drop, and already knowing with a depressing certainty that the job he wanted, that should have been his, was going to somebody else, he had left his desk, his IN basket crammed to overflowing, his Things To Do left over from yesterday not yet transferred to the desk calendar page for tomorrow, and without even telling his secretary where he was going had flown out to the Coast.

And now the opportunity he had half sensed, half prayed for had come his way. Of course, he hadn't known things would

100

move quite so fast. It didn't give him a chance to think things through. He didn't know from one moment to the next what he would do, or even, more important perhaps, why he was doing it. But at the moment he didn't care.

A glance in the men's room mirror confirmed the excitement, the freckles over his broad nose and high Slavic cheekbones not so prominent in the flush of his skin. He ran cold water on his wrists, took several long deep breaths, discarded the empty envelope in the trash, and was ready for whatever might happen.

At the elevator bank, he waited until he saw one coming down from eight, pressed the buzzer, got on, and exited with a number of other employees.

Outside, he walked right on past the cab with the impatiently waiting Alphonse and Gaston, and hitched a ride in a government limousine leaving for the airport.

The two startled thugs pressed their cabby for speed and stared at Vorovich incredulously when they passed the limo on the way. Though he barely looked at them, he could not resist a smile.

They were waiting at the Swissair terminal. Without acknowledging their presence, Vorovich went immediately into the men's room. When the two came bursting in, Vorovich calmly indicated adjoining stalls, ignoring the middle-aged man examining his penis.

Alphonse, the smaller of the two, was the one chosen to handle the exchange. At Gaston's signal that the room was otherwise empty, the corset and the money belt changed hands under the partitions. Vorovich took longer than the other coming out, muttering aloud as if he were recounting the money.

"There's a hundred missing," he said, slamming the stall door.

Alphonse stared at him, incredulous. "That's impossible," he said.

"I'm not going to make an issue of it," Vorovich said, pumping soap onto his hands. "But I don't understand how you boys could take such an awful chance. To risk blowing a deal over a lousy hundred bucks! What if I complained to your boss? What do you think he would do? He looks like he might have a temper to me."

Alphonse began to stutter. "W-w-w-we never t-touched that

101

belt," he said, outraged. "We g-gave it to you just the way it was g-given to us."

"Don't you know enough to count the cash whenever you get some?" Vorovich asked, reaching for a paper towel.

"What's he talking about?" Gaston asked, moving in from the outside door.

"He's a-accusing us of having s-shorted him," Alphonse said.

Gaston met Vorovich's eyes in the mirror. "Can't you see he's lying, Al?" Gaston said, as Vorovich finished drying his hands and turned to go. Gaston stood in his way. "What took you so long at the Feds?" he demanded.

"They've got new security procedures I didn't know about," Vorovich said. "I had to double-talk them to get my clearance."

"Yeah?" Alphonse said. "You d-didn't have t-trouble riding in a government l-limo."

"Whyn't you ride with us?" Gaston asked.

"Don't be a sap," Vorovich said. "What if someone saw me with you? This way, no one thinks I've got anything to hide."

The door opened and several men came in. Vorovich smiled. "So long, fellas," he said, grasping each of them by the hand. "I'm late, have to run, thanks for seeing me off." And he was out the door before either of them could protest.

Vorovich hoped he had outraged them sufficiently for their report to D'Anton to be confused. His needling them about short money wouldn't bother D'Anton, since Vorovich had already established himself as truculent, with a mean sense of humor. And riding in the government limo would also make sense. D'Anton would understand the difficulty of getting contraband out of a Federal building, particularly by a discredited individual, and would even appreciate the kind of clever bravado that it took to hide under their very noses what everyone had searched for.

D'Anton wouldn't be any more suspicious than he was already. No, what worried Vorovich was that request for him to report to Personnel. He supposed it could have been routine, some paper work unfinished. God knew that was typical. And since he had not given the D.E.A. a forwarding address, they would have no other way of getting in touch. Still, he'd have to be extra careful. If someone with nothing better to do put together the fact that he'd been in the building and *not* reported together with the fact that he'd withdrawn personal belongings from the security vault, an uncounted number of unknown personal belongings, why, they just might guess what one of those personal belongings was. Until he got the money deposited, he was not in the clear.

Boarding the plane, Vorovich recognized two of the men who had come into the men's room at the airport. He considered them thoughtfully for a moment, decided they weren't Federal agents. They had neither the impassive look of policemen, to whom nothing would ever be surprising, nor the continually bewildered look of those pharmacy types who had been brought into the B.N.D.D. from Food and Drug.

"You are late," a pert little stewardess, French by her accent, said. "Your companion has already arrive, and is getting quite, you know, anxious."

Vorovich almost totaled it out right there. He had expected D'Anton to provide him with an escort once he got overseas, but to send someone along now implied either a greater distrust than he might be able to handle, or the kind of stupidity that could do him in.

But his curiosity took him down the aisle; he wanted at least to know whom they had sent.

He almost didn't recognize her. Her long red hair had been coiffed and coiled neatly under a pale green felt cloche hat that complemented the deeper lime green of her tailored velvet suit. She was no longer a somewhat disheveled, disorganized girl, but a mature woman, with the kind of poise that went deeper than her clothes.

"Surprise, surprise," she said, whispered really, for she was smart enough not to want to cause undue attention to their relationship. Stunned, he slid into the seat next to her.

"Aren't you pleased I'm along?" she asked, when he still did not speak.

When he had walked away from her along the wharf in San Francisco what seemed a lifetime ago, he had truly expected never to see her again. Now to see her so unexpectedly, to feel a rush of emotion that constricted his throat when he recognized the flamboyant girl underneath this poised mature woman, made him realize that he cared for her more than he had allowed himself to believe.

And that was bad. He could not afford any emotional commitment. Particularly to someone who had probably been sent to keep track of him.

"Well?" she asked, her teasing smile not quite hiding the apprehension she felt over his reaction.

"I guess I'm supposed to be, right?" he asked, caught between anger and desire. He wanted her badly, and they must have known that, to send her along as their spy. "Right?" he demanded, for she must have known it too, never mind that she was studying him so gravely, good little actress that she was.

They fastened seat belts, and were lost in their individual contemplations until they reached altitude on this polar flight.

"Champagne?" the stewardess asked, pouring the sparkling stuff into plastic glasses. "Good for lovers."

"That's us," Ginny said, when the stewardess had moved on. "Isn't it?"

"For as long as it lasts," he said, and drank his in a single swallow.

She looked hurt, and he could not help feeling sorry that it was he who had to destroy her gay mood, however superficial.

"I was thinking in terms of forever," she said.

"Think again," he said harshly, and motioned to the stewardess for a refill.

"You drink too much," she said.

"Only when I'm with you," he said.

"Please," she said. "Tell me why you're so angry."

"How'd they happen to pick you?" he asked.

"I volunteered," she said.

That gave him pause. "How did you even know where I was going? Or what I was going to do?" he asked.

"Charles told me," she said. "With him so worried about the corset, and your attitude about it, too, I knew it had to be more than mescaline. So when Charles came back from San Francisco, I just asked him flat out how come he had used us to run it? He told me he had to, some criminal types had threatened him, and us, and that he had to go along at least once."

"Uh huh," Vorovich said. "Why is he still involved, then?"

"Well, I asked him that too," Ginny said defensively. "And he said it was because of you. You wouldn't be reasonable about the corset, and until he gets a chance to pay them back all the money *you* cost him, he's got to stay involved."

"And you believe him?" Vorovich asked.

"What difference does it make?" she asked. "It's you I care about."

He wanted to believe her. But he simply couldn't afford to. "If that's true," he said, "wouldn't Charley know that?"

"It doesn't matter," she said patiently. "Charles doesn't believe you are what you say you are, or are going to do what you say you're going to do. And he thinks that if I find that out about you, I might tell him. If not in words, to get my friends out from under, by my attitude. He thinks I'm too straight to let someone sell him out without showing it. I'm just a kind of litmus paper for him, I know that."

He looked at her thoughtfully. She was a smart girl, no doubt about that, but her reasoning was too involved, far too clever for someone as essentially straightforward as she was. There was something that didn't quite make sense. Something she was keeping back.

"Are you telling me you *could* sell him out?" he asked.

"I was hoping that was a choice I wouldn't have to make," she said.

"Life is choice," he said.

"If it comes to that," she said then, "you'll just have to trust me to do the right thing."

He looked at her, wondering if he wouldn't be smart to hang it all up right then, and signaled the stewardess for more champagne.

Vorovich's decision to bank the money in a secret account was a major turning point for him, he knew that. It was not taken lightly, it was no un- thinking, off-the-cuff move, but something that had been brewing just below his mind's surface from the moment he realized he was actually going to get cash in advance.

Not that he had considered all the ramifications. There hadn't been time for that. He was only a few steps ahead of the D.E.A. as it was, and if he were going to get that money squir- reled away, permanently out of their reach, he had to keep moving fast.

Immediately after landing at the Zurich airport, therefore, the plane having come down seemingly at the saucered blue lake between the two incredibly high snow-capped picture- postcard mountains, he told Ginny to behave as if they were merely people who had met on the flight, going their separate ways. They would meet at the hotel later.

He had a few anxious moments going through customs. It seemed to him that they were reacting to his name in the passport, that they were going through his luggage with exag- gerated care, and that the question on the declaration form about how much money he was bringing in was scrutinized with more than ordinary concern.

But apparently not. Because they finally let him through, and he hastened to the cab stand, later than Ginny, probably, since she was nowhere in sight, and asked to be taken to down- town Zurich.

He did not spot anyone following him. But in case customs had alerted the local D.E.A. man that he had come on through, he chose a bank at random, walked in the front door and over to the information desk. He asked about opening an account but said he needed a bathroom first. He was escorted to the rear, whereupon, the moment his escort left, he exited through the back door.

Out on a narrow street not much wider than an alley, he angled across and into another building, which, as he had guessed, turned out to be another bank.

If anyone noticed that he had slipped in through the rear door, they did not react to it either by word or gesture. Secrecy was what brought the gnomes of Zurich so much of their business, and the bank had been constructed to keep business as private as possible. Vorovich had been in a lot of banks, more as an investigator than as a client, but he had never before experienced one like this. Tomblike, he thought. Attendants like mortuary or museum personnel. Business conducted not at public counters but behind partitions and closed doors. The few customers he saw looked solemn as mourners, surreptitious as thieves, slipping along the paneled mazelike corridors, heads lowered as if in shame, but actually, Vorovich thought, to conceal the avaricious glint in the eyes.

A uniformed attendant with a face of wax who spoke a German-accented English bowed reverentially and escorted him down a carpeted corridor to an inner office with a frosted glass window marked RECEPTION. Tap tap, with a deferential knuckle. The door opened. A squat little man, with glasses round and shiny as new dollars kept from slipping off his snub nose by a mole next the pinched nostril, leaned over his desk to grasp Vorovich's hand as if afraid he might back out of the closet-sized cubicle. He did not fall back into his own straight-backed chair until Vorovich was seated in the deep-cushioned one.

He tried to discourage Vorovich from opening a numbered account. "Our regular accounts are secret," he said, making a little cage with his fingers, then examining it, as if some tiny bird were hiding within. "We permit no one to examine our books or look at our records. The Swiss banking laws are quite explicit on this. . . ."

"I don't want even the bank's personnel to know I have an account here," Vorovich said, "which they would if I had one by name, *nicht?*"

He watched the other flinch, as if his pronunciation of the German were a profanity.

"You have a large amount you wish to deposit?" the fellow asked, not yet committing himself.

"What's the minimum required?" Vorovich asked. "A thousand dollars? Ten?"

The banker made a little *moue* of disdain. "I am afraid that is not sufficient," he said, and stood up, a not very subtle hint that he thought Vorovich ought to go.

"A hundred thousand?" Vorovich asked, remaining seated.

The banker remained standing. "That would be adequate,"

he said, doubting that his visitor had anything near that.

Vorovich unbuttoned his coat, pulled his shirt out of his pants, and unbuckled the money belt. He slapped that down on the banker's desk and zipped it all the way open so that the bills, which had been compressed, were revealed, some of them spilling out.

"There's a hundred thousand there," Vorovich said, pushing his shirttail back in. "I just wanted to make sure I was in the right kind of place."

"Of course," the banker said, but Vorovich watched his mole expand, and knew that the other thought him, at the least, impolite. But it was the money that mattered, in the end, wasn't it?

"Better count it," Vorovich said, and the other nodded and pressed a button hidden under the trailing edge of his desk.

In a moment a sallow, stoop-shouldered little man with scant blond hair imperfectly combed came in, and, at a gesture from the banker, came to the desk and began putting those crisp bills in stacks, lips moving slightly as he counted.

"Do you wish this sum deposited in an account drawing normal interest?" the banker asked, unlocking a desk drawer and pulling out a special form. "Or do you wish it invested in one of our stock portfolios?" He looked up at Vorovich, light reflecting off the glass. "There is a risk factor, of course. But it is insignificant." He was solemn as sin.

"What about the withdrawal factor?" Vorovich asked.

"The funds would not be quite as fluid," the other admitted. "Although within a week's notice your investment could be liquidated, with a slight penalty, of course—or you may borrow against your holdings, at a current rate of interest, if your need of cash is merely temporary. . . ."

"If I need it," Vorovich said, "I'm going to need it fast, and permanent."

"You do not need to show a legitimate cash income for tax purposes?" the other asked.

"I don't have any tax problems," Vorovich said. "Yet."

"Ah," the other said, glasses gleaming, in anticipation of vast new sums to be added to the account. Vorovich could sympathize with the feeling. He knew something about anticipation himself.

The banker handed him a golden pen and indicated a place

for the signature. Vorovich signed, including his middle name, Ogden, which not even D.E.A. records had, his father having been content merely to use an O. on the birth certificate, half ashamed, half amused that Vorovich's mother had named him that after the place of conception, a train stopped in Utah during a snowstorm.

"You wish only your signature on the account?" the banker asked.

"Only mine," Vorovich said.

"Any beneficiary?" the other asked, and Vorovich was at a loss for a moment. He had no one, he thought, no close relatives, no dear ones, no one he cared enough about, or who cared enough about him. . . . The other was looking at him expressionlessly, waiting for his reply.

Vorovich hesitated. "If I designate someone," he said, at last, "do they have to know about it?"

"Not unless something happens to you," the banker said.

"Yes," Vorovich said. "That would be the time to notify her. I can see that." But he was as unamused as the other. "The person I'm thinking of," he said, "is not related to me. What happens if some relative comes out of the woodwork and claims the money?"

"It goes to whomever you designate," the banker said.

"Secretly?" Vorovich said.

"We make no public announcements," the banker said, and suddenly smiled and said, "Who is she?"

Vorovich did not return the smile. "A lady," he said.

"Of course," the banker said, hastening to reassure him that he meant no harm. "I merely need her name and address. . . ."

"That may be a problem," Vorovich said. "She's traveling in Europe now, and I don't know that she has a permanent residence. . . ."

"Her passport number will do," the banker said. "She would have had to give your government an address to get it."

"Can I call it in to you?" Vorovich said.

"Mail it to me," the banker said, tucking the beneficiary card into an envelope and sliding it across the desk.

The scant-haired little man looked up from his counting. He said something rapidly in German.

"How much did you say was there?" he asked Vorovich.

"How much did he count?" Vorovich asked.

At a permissive nod from the banker, the little man spoke. *"Ein hundred tousand und ein hundred,"* is what it sounded like to Vorovich.

"Correct," Vorovich said.

"You said you had only one hundred thousand," the banker said.

"I was just checking your accuracy," Vorovich said, taking the hundred back.

"And our honesty?" the other asked, the mole spreading again.

"Wouldn't you?" Vorovich asked.

The banker muttered in German to the other, who handed Vorovich a very small laminated card that had nothing on it except a number.

Strapping the now empty belt back on, Vorovich pressed the card between two others of similar size in his wallet, smiled at the two men, and left. He went out through a side door and took a roundabout way back to the main street.

There he stopped the first passerby, a double-chinned little man, and asked, simply, "Cook's?"

"Ja," the fellow said, and pointed across the street and down, where Vorovich saw the familiar sign.

"I'd like to change these for some of yours," he said to the chubby blond girl in the shapeless smock at the check window inside.

She stared at the checks, then at him. "But these are perfectly good," she said. "They're as well known as ours."

"I prefer yours," Vorovich said. "Do you mind?"

She shrugged. "You must pay for the exchange," she said.

"I can afford it," Vorovich said.

Outside again, after completing the lengthy transaction, he suddenly realized how wound up he had been. A remarkable euphoria was taking place. He became so intensely aware of his surroundings it was almost hallucinatory: a sky as brilliantly pale as her eyes, the air so marvelously pure it made him giddy, the baroque stone buildings solid as forever. Why was he so light-headed? If that was the effect a large bank account gave, no wonder people went to such great lengths to acquire them.

Vorovich suddenly experienced an enormous thirst. He looked down the picture-book street. MAX'S BAR, a sign read.

The place was dim, shuttered against the light, and seemed empty. Did the Swiss not drink in the morning? A waiter in a starched white apron appeared and indicated a table. Vorovich remained standing.

"Whisky?" he said, making the classic motion of thumb to parched lips. The waiter, who had fluffy white sideburns, looked puzzled. "*Schnapps?*" Vorovich said, and was rewarded with a broad smile and a wine glass full of a liquid the color and coldness of ice. Vorovich saluted himself in the mirror and drank.

It was as if a white-hot poker had seared his gullet. But it was soothing as an anesthetic, and numbed any second thoughts that might start disturbing his pleasure.

Though he was a few miles from the hotel, he decided to walk. He strode along the incredibly clean downtown streets, past the watchmaker shopwindows glittering with timepieces whose tags went up to five thousand per, the cheese and champagne displays of restaurants, the manikins dressed in twenty-thousand-dollar furs, and began to plan how he would spend the money.

Before he had always been on per diem, which did not permit any of the little luxuries. The temptation always was to cheat the auditing, to stay in cheaper hotels and eat in hole-in-the-wall cafés and drink out of a suitcase bottle, pocketing the difference, which was slim.

This trip was not going to be like that, he promised himself. This trip was a beginning. And damn the D.E.A. There wasn't an auditor alive who could force him to account for this money.

She was waiting for him up in the hotel room. He had half thought about forcing her to book a room of her own to allow himself some breathing space, put some emotional distance between them so that he might be able to think what to do about her.

But the moment he saw her he realized he was kidding himself. Tucked into an easy chair, attempting to read a paperback—either poetry or Zen from its cover—she jumped up when he entered, and, after a quick scrutiny of his face to check his state of mind, embraced him.

"What kept you?" she murmured. "I'm supposed never to let you out of my sight, remember?"

He remembered. But she didn't give him time to worry about why she would bring it up. She had apparently just showered, for her silky skin was damp, her luxuriant hair turbaned in a towel; she was not wearing anything under that loose, pale, flimsy gown.

"You're not tired, I hope," she said.

"Not that tired," he said.

"It slips off the shoulders easier," she said.

He had that smoothly soft stuff pulled up and bunched at her magnificent thighs. "You're marvelous," he said, speaking his unbidden thought as she slipped out of her gown, some new easiness about himself—or was it her aggressiveness?—removing that censor in his brain which usually kept him on guard.

Because he had expected her to be impatient, even anxious, he missed realizing that in his absence she had reached a decisive turning point of her own. But then he was not used to close personal relationships, and as much as he cautioned himself to accept nothing at face value, he could not help being taken in by what seemed only a spontaneous demonstration of affection —to put a nice word on it.

She helped him out of his clothes. She threw his coat at a chair, and missed, and when he went to hang it and his pants up she pulled those out of his hands and tossed them aside.

"You'll have to get rid of those old fuddy-duds," she said.

"I won't have anything to wear," he protested.

"We'll take care of that later," she said.

She took him to bed. It was a good bed, wide and sturdy and deep. They were old acquaintances now, familiar lovers, their encounter passionate but steady, the territory known, the only surprise that he could please her so much. Her climactic scream was only a whisper, but it echoed from his ear into the corridors of his brain, and his own rush to the pinpoint of now was so intensely focused that when she pointed out the marks her fingers had left he could remember only dimly her folding his skin in that amorous pinch.

"It doesn't matter," he said, when she kissed those marks.

"I never want to hurt you," she said.

"That didn't hurt," he said. "On the contrary." She laughed and pinched him again. "Now it hurts," he said.

They lay together quietly for a time.

"You didn't use anything," he said then.

"How clever of you to have noticed," she said, at last. She was watching him closely to see what his reaction would be.

And he didn't know what, or how, to feel. The possibility of fathering a child had not occurred to him, not since the first years of his misbegotten marriage. To be forced to think about it now, when he had so many other things on his mind, not the least of which was personal survival, was numbing.

As the first shock wore off, possible motives for her behavior raced through his mind. Was it all a pretense? She had lied before, skillfully, when she thought it necessary. She might think this would make him believe in her loyalty. But that didn't prove anything, did it? She could want his child, as she had earlier wanted Charles's, without remaining committed to him. In fact, it would be like her to want his child even if, or even especially if, she intended to blow the whistle on him later.

"Do you mind?" she asked, as he continued to lie silent.

"I think I do," he said. "I can't take the responsibility."

"No one asked you to," she said sharply. "It's my decision, it's my body, it'll be flesh of my flesh, and mine to care for. I want to raise someone who won't have our hangups, someone unhostile, free, full of love. . . ."

"That's a lousy thing to do to a kid," he said. "The world will eat him alive."

"If you really believe that," she said, "I feel sorry for you."

"I feel sorry for the kid," he said, though it shamed him to hurt her.

She stared at him for a long moment. "God, I'm hungry," she said then, trying to hide her disappointment. "Are you?"

"I could eat," he said.

"Let's go out," she said, getting up from the bed, as always taking his breath with her body, which was spectacular, not just because her skin glowed like warm milk, or because the hair between her dancer's thighs flamed like the bush which Moses described, but because of the way she carried it, with the kind of pride called royal. "I need something to cheer me up."

They ate lunch at a little café off the boulevard which the doorman, after an appraising glance, recommended. Had he been judging affluence or appetite? But the place was charming and the food delicious. Vorovich agreed with her that he didn't need a hard drink, that the fine, yellowing German wine was perfect for after lovemaking. He tried to match her seemingly carefree but actually stagy attitude, ordering *Schnitzel mit Spaetzel* in the manner of Bogart, agreeing that the actor had been lucky, given his dental problems, not to have been born German.

They discussed their itinerary in touristic terms while they ate, carefully avoiding anything serious, not willing to destroy their mood, which was fragile as the bubbles in their *Spatlese* wine.

After lunch, though he protested that the *Strudel* had bulged his waistline two inches, she insisted they buy him some other clothes. Would she worry so about his appearance if she meant to betray him? Maybe, he thought. Maybe. He'd better believe that, if he wanted to survive.

They found the kind of shop she wanted in an arcade off the main shopping *Strasse*, run by a youth dressed like a Montana cowboy. His girl also wore a Stetson, and it was a shock to hear them speaking a thickly accented English.

He flinched at himself in the three-way mirror. It would take getting used to. But he admitted, finally, that it wasn't all that bad. The dark leather jacket and the suede pants and the buckskin boots gave him a casually tough look—and more: it somehow *changed* his appearance, bringing out some quality both disturbing and challenging, like a man given one last fling before his youth was finally gone.

The price was the equivalent of three hundred and ten dollars. That startled him; then, remembering his new attitude about money, he shelled it out without a qualm.

Outside, the air was dotted with snow, and she pulled him into another shop and bought them each a hat. "I'll pay," she insisted. "Charles laid some loot on me—just in case you were close, he said."

How could he not believe her? She wore a hat identical to his own except for the color: a low-crowned stitch-brimmed thing of gloved leather, his brown, hers a bright green.

"Look at the girls digging you," she said, as they slogged along the slushy sidewalks back to the hotel. "Maybe I'm not so smart to change your style."

"Maybe you're not," he agreed, exchanging sidelong glances with the shapely young things walking the other way.

"As long as you don't change from the inside out," she said, pushing her hands deep into the side pocket of his sheepskin-lined coat.

"What makes you think I will?" he demanded suddenly, irrationally angered.

Her sure step faltered, and then they were standing eye to eye. "It isn't that I think you will," she said, "but that I'm afraid you might."

"None of us changes," he said, and it was as if he were arguing with himself. "We just quit hiding what we really are."

They continued on through the deadening snow.

What happened next took him completely by surprise—and it shouldn't have. It was true that his fret over Ginny's motivations had taken his mind into peripheral areas, that the snow-blanketed world they walked in was so unreal, the silence so eerie, the traffic noises so faint and faraway, other pedestrians such fleeting shadows, that the place, the weather, and his thoughts all combined to damp down his finely wrought premonitory nervous system—but those were only explanations, not excuses. Dead agents couldn't make excuses.

He didn't stop at the hotel desk to ask about messages because he wasn't expecting any. If he had, the unctuously helpful desk clerk might have told him that someone *had* been inquiring after M. Vorovich, someone who had not left his name, saying he would be back later.

Even when he noticed that the hotel's MAID PLEASE CLEAN sign which Ginny had hung on their doorknob had been reversed to its DO NOT DISTURB side the significance of that did not register immediately. It was not until they were confronted by the intruder lounging in the easy chair in their bed-sitting

room that he made the connection, as if some plug half discon-
nected in his brain had been plunged into its socket.

Too late. The fellow, slight and pale with blond curly hair
and a tiny mouth pursed into a cupidlike bow, looked inoffen-
sive enough—except he was holding a gun.

"You are Vorovich?" he asked doubtfully, looking at the
newly outfitted American from head to booted foot.

"That's what it says in my passport," Vorovich said, but he
was uncomfortable for more than obvious reasons, as if he were
indeed masquerading.

The other got to his feet. Ginny was clutching her purse as
if afraid it might be taken from her.

"And who are you, Fraulein?" he asked.

"What's it to you?" Vorovich demanded, before Ginny
might answer.

The other pulled out a flopover wallet and showed them the
seal of the Swiss government. "I am with the Federal police,"
he said.

"We haven't done anything," Ginny said.

"I didn't say you had," the Swiss said. "I have been asked to
bring Mr. Vorovich in for questioning."

"At the point of a gun?" Vorovich asked.

"I was informed that you were dangerous when startled,"
the Swiss said, and ostentatiously put his gun away. "If you'll
come with me now. . . ."

"You don't have to go," Ginny said. "He has no specific
reason to bring you in. That's Swiss law."

"How do you know that?" Vorovich found time to wonder.

"I went to school in Lucerne," Ginny said, after a moment's
hesitation.

"I was given no instructions about her," the Swiss said to
Vorovich. "She can stay. But I suggest you register her at the
desk. That is a law *you* are breaking, Fraulein. Didn't your
school teach you that?"

"I'll go to the embassy," Ginny said.

The Swiss looked amused. Ginny didn't understand why.
But it began to give Vorovich an inkling of what was going on.

"Never mind," Vorovich told her. "This shouldn't take long.
But if I'm not back in an hour, call the embassy."

"Wait a minute," she said, as Vorovich started out the door.
"Don't you want your cigarettes?" And she held her opened

purse up to him. Within it, he saw his snub-nosed ankle gun.

"I'm trying to quit," he said, clicking her purse shut, and left her looking bewildered and forlorn.

A government car waited for them at the curb. It was only a short drive to the downtown Federal police building.

"Where is the merchandise?" the Swiss agent asked. "It's not in your room—I've looked. If you'll permit me . . . ?" He smiled and delicately probed Vorovich's waist.

"What merchandise?" Vorovich asked.

"Of course it makes sense that you would sell it in the States," the other said. "That is the prime market."

"I don't know what you're talking about," Vorovich said.

"I wonder if your lady friend is aware you broke the law by bringing in undeclared money?" the Swiss said.

Vorovich said nothing as the tires scrunched along the newly fallen snow.

Inside the anonymous-looking steel and concrete building, Vorovich was taken up the stairs to a corner office on the mezzanine. There two men were awaiting him. Immediately he recognized one of them. The American. Elegantly dressed, he wore a Phi Beta Kappa key dangling from a watch fob and managed to seem casual while keeping the coat spread just enough to reveal it. His silky hair was pompadoured in a cut the New Englanders still fancied, his rep-tie colors Yale, the pink rosette in his narrow lapel a decoration from some foreign government.

It was Cabot. H. Llewelyn Cabot, the bastard who had come in as acting director from the Attorney General's office, who had passed him over for the promotion, sallow face well fed but hard, so you guessed he exercised to keep fit, probably handball in a government gym.

"Well, Timothy," Cabot said, "you're looking remarkably well, considering." Before Vorovich could respond, the other man had turned to the young Swiss who had brought him in: "Good work." And to the balding, ruddy-faced Swiss behind the desk, now standing up, "I wish my agency operated as efficiently."

"Let us know if there's anything else we can do," the older Swiss said, and then Vorovich and Cabot were alone.

"You're a little out of your territory, aren't you?" Vorovich asked.

"We're expanding our operations," Cabot said. "We're reaching out to hit the enemy before he hits us. But then you know about that—you were the one who suggested we start taking the initiative, weren't you? If our allies won't do the job, then we should do it for them, is the way I believe you put it."

"I was told we couldn't do that," Vorovich said. "That it would jeopardize our foreign relations."

"That's our official stance, of course," Cabot said. "But we are pushing for greater cooperation, and as you saw here, we're getting it."

"You won't get it in Turkey," Vorovich said. "Or France."

"I believe we will," Cabot said. Vorovich shrugged. "Your stubbornness, if you don't mind my saying so," Cabot said, "might have been reason enough not to give you the promotion. We're not the C.I.A., Timothy, we simply can't operate that way."

"It's no longer my concern," Vorovich said.

"I hope there're no hard feelings," Cabot said.

"What difference would it make?" Vorovich asked.

"No one likes to make enemies unnecessarily," Cabot said.

"You didn't come here to kiss and make up," Vorovich said.

"Quite right," Cabot said, losing his affable manner. "I came here to see why it is that a top member of my agency is seen consorting with known members of the drug culture. And why it is that he ignores a direct request to report to Personnel before finally signing out."

"I'd received all the money due me," Vorovich said. "I didn't see the point of fucking with any more paper work."

Cabot's nose tip whitened at the vulgarity. "You had the corset stashed in our vault, didn't you?" he demanded then.

Vorovich couldn't help smiling.

"I don't see what amuses you," Cabot said. "You know it's a violation of D.E.A. procedure to remove evidence without authorization!"

"I'm no longer a member of the D.E.A." Vorovich reminded him.

"Even worse," Cabot snapped. "If you were acting as a civilian, that's a criminal offense!"

"Only if it can be proved I had it at all," Vorovich said softly.

Cabot hesitated; he scrutinized Vorovich, who suddenly was reminded that he wore new clothes.

"What are you up to?" Cabot asked, at last. "Baiting a trap? Come on, man," Cabot wheedled, as Vorovich stared at him. "You went out of your way to get Inspector Hickerson angry enough to tape everything you said. All those gratuitously hostile remarks—I finally understood that if you were certain the corset contained heroin, you had of course examined it firsthand. You *wanted* me to know that. Why?"

"I wanted it on the record," Vorovich said slowly, at last. "In case anything went wrong."

"So that we could pick up the pieces?" Cabot said.

"Something like that," Vorovich said.

"Or so that we would stay out of your way," Cabot said.

"Something like that, too," Vorovich said.

"It's important, then," Cabot said.

"Seems to be," Vorovich said.

"How important?" Cabot asked.

"Maybe a hundred million dollars' worth," Vorovich said reluctantly.

"Ah," Cabot said, and Vorovich knew he was thinking about newspaper headlines. "I should have realized from the start you were going undercover—you saw your opportunity, seized the moment, created the only situation dramatic enough to lend authenticity to your defection . . . frankly, I wasn't aware you had that kind of imagination."

"Your not being aware of my virtues—is that my fault or yours?" Vorovich asked.

Cabot began caressing his honors key. "It wouldn't have made any difference," he said. "You still wouldn't have gotten the job. Like it or not, Timothy, the best administrators are solid, ground-rooted men. If our man comes off as hare-brained or wispy or fey—Lawrence of Arabia was a poet, not a bureaucrat—why Congress won't trust him with money."

"You telling me I wasn't even considered?" Vorovich asked.

"Of course you were considered," Cabot said impatiently. "You must understand, Timothy, it isn't that Paul is a better man, just a different one. . . ."

"And the fact that he was a congressman himself, brief as it was," Vorovich said, "has nothing to do with it."

"It wasn't the main consideration," Cabot said, beginning to lose patience with this stubborn, obtuse man. "Just part of the total package. Be realistic, Timothy. See things for what they are, not what you want them to be."

"Not getting the job," Vorovich said, "helped me a lot in that department."

"Come on, Timothy," Cabot said. "Try to look at it from my position. It's a war we're in, a vicious, secret war, and we have to use everything we've got to win it. We're not winning, you know. They're attacking us where we're most vulnerable, at the very heart of our value system, at our will to succeed, to be the very best there is. Our troops in Southeast Asia were turned into addicts by the thousands because the hash they smoked was drenched with morphine. The government of Bulgaria has an agency, an official agency, that expedites the flow of morphine through its country to France, knowing its ultimate destination is America. Inside our own country the narcotics laws are under fire by liberals who want to legalize the stuff! Look at any country permissive about drug use: it's lazy, unproductive, no moral fiber—but I could go on for hours! The point is, we have to use our manpower where it is most effective. You happen to be a superb field man. You'd be wasted in a straight-on administrative job."

"Am I supposed to feel flattered?" Vorovich said.

"I know it's no picnic out there," Cabot said. "I know how impatient a good field man can get with rules and regulations that only seem to restrict him. That's why, the moment I got an inkling of what was going on, I decided to come into this personally. The only one you'll have to answer to is me. No one except myself—and Paul, naturally—will know what you're up to."

"That's two too many," Vorovich said.

Cabot stared at him. "You're going to try and pull this off all by yourself?" he said incredulously. Vorovich did not respond. "I know you have a reputation as a loner," Cabot said. "But with a potential haul this size, don't you think it's just plain stupid not to use whatever help's available? You have the power of an organization behind you, man—take advantage of it!"

"I will, when the time comes," Vorovich said.

"What is it, Timothy?" Cabot asked at last. "Are you so anxious to prove we were wrong about you? You want to handle this all by your lonesome to show us up publicly?"

"You can rest easy about the public part," Vorovich said. "Any press conference hailing the victory you can conduct all by yourself. Horace," he said, as an afterthought.

Cabot paled slightly, but Vorovich had to admire his self-control. "What if you get in a jam?" he asked. "I can arrange for a back-up man as protection. Someone of your own choosing."

"The fewer people who know what I'm up to the safer I'll be," Vorovich said.

"Well, what if we at least monitored your activities?" Cabot asked. "We've already got you on our "suspect keep under surveillance" list. That certainly would be an adequate cover."

"Nothing doing," Vorovich said. "The people I'm involved with are nervous enough about me as it is. Look," he said, letting just enough of his anger show, "I'm the one out there, I'm the one who'll be ducking shot and shell, so I'm going to be the one who says how it's run. No following, no monitoring, no nothing till I give the word!"

There was a silence while the two men confronted each other.

"What if something goes wrong?" Cabot asked, at last. "How will we know what to do . . . in case we need to pick up where . . . you leave off?"

"I'll make arrangements," Vorovich said after a moment's thought, seeing where this could work to his advantage too. "I'll see to it you get whatever information I've acquired."

"We can depend on that?" Cabot asked.

Vorovich nodded.

"Good luck, then," Cabot said, thrusting out his well-cared-for hand, but Vorovich was already turning away.

"One thing," Cabot said, unable to resist, since he knew the snub was deliberate. "Whatever my official position, I personally wouldn't be displeased to learn you shot that young hoodlum on purpose. It would indicate your attitude might be just hard-nosed enough to pull this off."

Vorovich couldn't believe what he was hearing. Did Cabot really expect him to admit to a cold-blooded killing, whatever the motivation? Even the possibility that he had done it subconsciously was so frightening, so full of ramifications and depths he was afraid to explore, that he had pushed it out of his mind.

"Sorry to disappoint you," Vorovich said, and left, feeling Cabot's eyes on his back. And wondering whether Cabot had bought his story.

The moment Vorovich closed the door behind him, the inside door opened, and three men entered: the two Swiss Federal police, along with a bright-eyed young American, who looked even younger than his years, dressed in a polyester wrinkle-proof khaki suit and a drip-dry button-down blue shirt.

"Did you get it all, Preble?" Cabot asked. Preble nodded. "Any comment?"

"Well," Preble said, "he's obviously determined to go it alone."

"Obviously," Cabot said dryly. "And?"

"And what, sir?" Preble asked.

"And what's your opinion of that, Preble?" Cabot snapped.

"Well," Preble said cautiously, "he is the one out there, on the line, isn't he? He's probably in the best position to judge—"

"And what if he judges wrong?" Cabot said. "What if the moment he picks to signal us is so wrong he winds up dead? What happens to the operation then? We're left high and dry. It's like a man dismantling a bomb, Preble, a brand-spanking-new-secret-weapon kind of bomb—if he doesn't detail every step to those of us behind the lines, those of us in comparative safety, and that bomb blows up, we won't have any pieces to pick up, will we? It won't do, Preble."

"I suppose not," Preble said.

"You suppose not?" Cabot demanded

"It won't do, of course," Preble said.

"Let me put it this way, Preble," Cabot said. "I hadn't wanted to bring this up—I know what an idealist you are, I've read your reasons for transferring from Food and Drug to our branch of government, and they are inspiring, I must say—and it is with the greatest reluctance that I tell you this: I have reasons to suspect our man Vorovich. His reasons for wanting to play it alone may have more to do with criminal intent than his desire to make a major arrest."

Preble, Cabot noted with satisfaction, was stunned.

"Would you mind telling Preble what you have learned?" Cabot asked the older Swiss, who was listening with considerable fascination.

"We are almost certain that he has opened a numbered account in one of our banks," the Swiss said. "Officer Klaus Handel has the details. . . ."

"I almost lost him earlier," the younger Swiss said. "He went into one bank, and out the rear door, and it took me quite a while before I saw him coming out of another bank. They refused to tell me whether he had or had not opened an account. . . ."

"Which is within their rights under our law," the older Swiss said.

"Can't you persuade them?" Cabot asked.

"We would have to have an official request from your government," the older Swiss said. "There would have to be reason to believe that the money was gained by a heinous crime. . . ."

"If he sold heroin to get the money, that would certainly fit the definition," Cabot said.

"Of course there's no proof that he actually did that," Preble said, "with criminal intent."

"Then why all the folderol about the banks?" Cabot asked.

"In case the others were following him," Preble said. "He might have wanted to make it look good."

"There is always that possibility, of course," Cabot said. "Don't imagine that I am condemning him out of hand. But until the new director has a chance to take hold of things, it's my responsibility to make sure that the D.E.A. isn't humiliated by a crooked agent."

Everyone in the room looked embarrassed.

"Do you have any suggestions as to how to avoid that, Preble?" Cabot asked. "How I can meet my responsibilities, and at the same time give Vorovich the benefit of the doubt?"

"By following him, I guess," Preble said at last, reluctantly.

"Very good, Preble," Cabot said, and the other flushed.

"But won't it be jeopardizing his position?" Preble asked. "What if someone spots whoever's following . . . ?"

"Whoever does it must operate undercover too," Cabot said. "And under no circumstances can reveal that he works for us! It's a job that calls for courage and sensitivity of the highest order—the kind you have, Preble."

"Very nice of you to say, sir," Preble said.

"Furthermore," Cabot said, "he doesn't know you, which makes it unlikely that he'll spot you. But exercise great caution, Preble. He's a contentious man, as you heard. And if he found out that we're not giving him quite the freedom to operate that he requested, he might very well throw it all in."

"I'll be careful, sir," Preble said.

"You won't be alone out there, Preble," Cabot said. "I've already put in a request for assistance to our counterparts over here. They'll monitor any border crossings he makes, so that if he should somehow lose you, you'll be able to pick him up again. That's the advantage of organization, Preble. That's what I was trying to make clear to Vorovich." He waited for Preble's nod. "Now," Cabot said, "I'll want a periodic report on his activities —where he goes, who he meets, what he does. Get them to the nearest embassy, they'll put them in the diplomatic pouch to me."

"Isn't that opening it up *quite* a bit, sir?" Preble asked.

"If worst comes to worst," Cabot said, "it'll just look like we've got him as a prime suspect. Which is close to the truth, isn't it?"

"Yes, sir," Preble said doubtfully.

"Don't worry," Cabot said. "We won't step on him unless we have to, for his own good." He turned to the younger Swiss. "Now," he said, "what about the girl?"

"She wasn't registered at the desk," the younger Swiss said. "And since there were no instructions about bringing her in . . ."

"Would you describe her?" Cabot asked.

"She is young," Klaus said. "Very attractive, tall, with reddish hair—"

"Yes," Cabot said thoughtfully, as if agreeing with something they didn't understand. "They probably came in on the same flight. We'll run down the passenger list, see if we can't get her passport number. Keep a close eye on her too, Preble."

"Yes, sir," Preble said. "You can count on me."

Vorovich walked all the way back to the hotel, the huge snowflakes like damp moths against his overheated face. That had been close, he thought. He hadn't been smart to push Cabot so hard. But then he had not expected Cabot to come down on him so soon, and his anger, his apparently inexhaustible anger, had almost done him in.

Now where was he? Caught between the proverbial rock and the hard place. All he had meant to do was cover himself, leave himself an out, give himself plenty of options when the crunch came. And instead he had cut himself off from the only people who had any reason whatsoever to help him.

He felt suddenly very alone. For a panicky moment he hesitated, there in the silent snowfall, wondering if he shouldn't go back to Cabot, tell him he had lost his nerve, let him think what he would about his motives. Maybe the stakes were too high. Maybe it was impossible to win big.

Then he remembered the money he had already put into a very private account, and the moment passed. It was amazing how reassuring the money was.

By the time he got back up to the hotel room, he was able to face the anxious Ginny with some equanimity.

"They're just hassling me on general principles," he told her, as she helped him out of his snow- and sweat-dampened clothing. "Someone in Washington asked Swiss customs to check me out, and the order was misplaced, so what you saw was a delayed reaction. Too late, by a half hour. Nothing to worry about."

"Is that what you want me to tell Charles?" she asked.

"Tell him whatever you want," Vorovich said irritably, realizing with that loss of temper how edgy he still was.

"Please," she said. "It's not Charles I care about. Don't you know that yet?"

"I don't get it," he said, exasperated. "You got pissed at Charles because you found out he was dealing in hard goods and you know that I'm doing the same and you're still going to hang in there with me?"

"I'm going to change your mind," she said.

"Don't be ridiculous," he said.

"I have to," she said. "I can be very persuasive. You'll see."

He told himself that the only reason he didn't ditch her right then was because there'd be hell to pay with Charley, who would accuse him of having something to hide. And he couldn't afford that. Not now. And if her methods of persuasion were pleasant, to say the least, it wasn't that he hadn't warned her.

Or she him, for that matter.

Vorovich did not care for the Middle East. He agreed with Ginny that the scenery was nice. The skies were the shade of blue that made poets weep and painters curse and the air could make even a hard man like himself a little drunk—but he had too much on his mind to enjoy the view.

The food did not appeal to him either. Everything tasted of honey, grape leaves, cloves, and sesame, and his palate cloyed. When he tried to wash it clean with the local wines it was worse, the resinous stuff puckering his mouth. Half under the weather most of the time, he walked around queasy and ill at ease, and it did not help him to know that his stomach roiled more from his anxieties than his oil-drenched diet.

How was he going to sell himself to the men D'Anton had arranged for him to meet? Not only did he have to come up with a plan that made sense, but he had to involve himself in such a way that he would be indispensable. Otherwise they'd blot him out early on. He had no illusions about that.

And what was he going to do about Ginny? If she was brooding over the purposes of this trip, she did not show it. She seemed determinedly gay, as if they were on the last honeymoon the world would ever know.

In Greece she stuffed her mouth full of the little sticky cakes, then kissed him so he could taste the honey on her lips. On the small steamer across the Aegean to Izmir she woke him at midnight to show him how the moon shimmered in the burgundy sea.

But her ardor gave him an excuse for changing their schedule. He wasn't aware that they were being scrutinized more than was normal at border points, considering the way he was dressed, or that he was an older man with a beautiful young girl. But just in case, they stayed an extra night in the little hotel with the blue doors overlooking the rocky beach before taking the tram into downtown Izmir. No one seemed to be following.

"You were expected yesterday," the beady-eyed clerk in the offices of World-Wide Travel said.

"Couldn't be helped," Vorovich said.

"What delayed you?" the clerk persisted. His curiosity was not inadvertent.

"Romance," Ginny said. Her leafing through travel folders

126

had not prevented her overhearing. "Surely you can understand that?"

Vorovich would not have believed it possible, but she had managed to fluster the other. "It's a problem with reservations," the clerk said, reaching for the phone. "They are not easy to come by. Your compartment was empty all the way to Ankara."

It took the clerk a number of calls. Vorovich wandered to the window, examined the crowds along the hot narrow street, looking for anyone out of place. But all the foreigners seemed part of the scene, walking as purposefully as those with business to mind, and the few loiterers were either street vendors or young bucks idling away the hours with gossip. No tourists, none that he could make out, anyway. Tourists would not be unshaven.

"You're in luck," the clerk said, finally hanging up. "A last-minute cancellation, on this afternoon's train." He handed them a ticket already made out, only the date changed. "This time I would make sure to be punctual," he said, and Vorovich recognized the warning.

The train was first class, an overnight sleeper, and didn't seem crowded enough to have warranted all that to-do over the reservations. Vorovich wondered whether a contact wasn't going to be made en route. But even after walking all the carriages forward and back, he saw no one who even blinked under his scrutiny—not even the young British climber type who wore starched shorts and knee-length hose with an aplomb Vorovich envied.

Then a few hours before dawn, while their train was switched off to a siding to allow the return express passage the opposite way, a knock on their compartment door awakened them.

Two men in bulky leather coats, skins wrinkled and dark as olives, crowded in. "Quickly!" the older of them said.

"You stay," Vorovich said, as Ginny started to get up with him. "I'll catch up with you in Ankara."

"That's not fair," she said. "I'm supposed to stick close."

"Do as I say!" he said sharply.

The older Turk had observed their exchange closely. "Let her come," he said. "She will be no trouble."

Though he was very polite, Vorovich saw that he was going to insist. But before he could argue, they heard the other train in the distance, and the two Turks helped them cram what belongings were spread about the compartment into their suitcases.

As they jumped down into the predawn darkness, the return express rushed past, throwing up a whirlwind of dust and cinders. A few moments later, as they walked to an old black Citroën parked nearby, their own train pulled out. That raised compartment blind, Vorovich thought, looking back, might only be some curious passenger unable to sleep. In any case, it was too late, they couldn't be followed now. He decided it would serve no purpose to call the Turk's attention to it.

Within minutes after leaving the siding, they were on so steep and winding a road the driver kept the car in the lower gears. It was a smuggler's car, Vorovich thought, its headlamps hooded slits that made its dim blue beams almost impossible to be seen from top or side. And the men, all of whom smoked, a sweetish blend that perfumed the air, kept the lighted ends cupped in their calloused palms, a habit of men used to danger.

"Where are we?" Ginny asked when the sun came up, showing them deep in the mountains, peaks etched like charcoal against a watercolor-pale sky.

"It doesn't matter," Vorovich said quickly.

The older Turk smiled to himself, confirming his own good judgment in bringing her.

When it seemed the car was straining itself beyond endurance to reach the highest peak, they suddenly turned off onto a rutted, precipitous path barely wide enough to allow the wheels traction. Bumping and skidding down then, they finally rounded a corner and found themselves in a flower-filled hillside meadow.

The driver stayed inside.

"I just want to see how near they are to harvest," the older Turk said.

"How beautiful!" Ginny cried. "What are they?"

"Poppies," the Turk said. *"Papaver somniferum.* The flowers of sleep."

Ginny slipped off her shoes and began doing a kind of pagan dance through the field still wet from the morning dew. The

Turk pulled out a hooked knife and made a slit in a flower pod. He squeezed it between thumb and forefinger. What looked like liquid gum oozed out.

"Not yet," the Turk said, chewing his fingers. "Another two weeks. Then all must be gathered within twenty-four hours."

"You have enough manpower?" Vorovich asked.

"The entire village turns out," the Turk said. "Everyone, from the very young to the old. It is too valuable to waste. Too valuable to risk losing in a reckless enterprise," he said, looking at Vorovich sideways.

"I've never been reckless," Vorovich said.

The Turk, with only a glance at Ginny, now gathering flowers, stroked his mustache reflectively. "It's true you were formerly one of them?" he asked. Vorovich nodded. "Formerly of high station?"

"Not high enough," Vorovich said shortly, and then Ginny arrived, all out of breath.

"Aren't they gorgeous?" she asked, showing them an enormous bouquet. "I hope you don't mind . . . do you own this field?"

"I am the representative for twenty such fields hidden all through these mountains," the Turk said. "Take all you want."

"Why is it the mind-blowing stuff always looks so marvelous?" Ginny wondered.

"The devil's creations are always so," the Turk said, admiring her openly. "God makes nettles and thorns. The devil invented paradise."

"A false one," Ginny said.

"But enjoyable," the Turk said.

"For as long as it lasts," Ginny said.

"She is a treasure," the Turk said to Vorovich. "You must be very keen on her."

"I thought we were going to discuss your crop," Vorovich said.

"But of course," the Turk said, openly amused, and led them back to the car.

The village was a ten-minute drive, literally around the mountain. Whitewashed stone huts terraced up the hillsides. The cobbled streets were barely wide enough for the car, ending in a square centered around a well. The sound of their whining gears had preceded them, ricocheting off the bluffs, and whatever villagers may have been about had long since disappeared inside.

They entered a teahouse, hissing steam from the kettle on the black iron stove the only indication that anyone was around. The Turk barked something loudly. An aproned proprietor, with a fierce nose and eyes and the shoulders of a wrestler, came in, followed a few moments later by a half dozen dark-skinned, equally fierce-looking men.

The Turks took seats at the rudely constructed wooden tables, seemingly at random, but Vorovich noted that they had been surrounded, any retreat effectively cut off.

"What's everyone staring at?" Ginny whispered.

"Your flowers," the Turk said calmly.

"Oh," Ginny said, and placed the bouquet on her lap out of sight.

At a word from the Turk, the proprietor brought them dark tea in unglazed clay mugs.

"Don't you have anything stronger?" Vorovich asked, and a moment later the proprietor brought a tall, unmarked, narrow-necked bottle containing a pale liquor the color of urine. No glass was brought. Hesitating only a moment, Vorovich drank from the bottle: it was slightly sweet and hot, like a fermented licorice. He poured some in his tea, then offered the bottle, which was passed silently among the men.

"They wish to know your proposal," the Turk said. "You can speak freely—everyone in the village shares in the fields, including the local police."

"You're not worried about informers?" Vorovich asked.

"It's a matter of economics," the Turk said. "The government does not pay as much as a share in the crop brings. Besides, the penalty for informing is severe."

"What is it?" Ginny asked.

"Death," the Turk said.

This information affected Ginny considerably. She lost her sparkle, began brooding over her tea.

"We want to purchase your entire harvest," Vorovich said. "And whatever you have in storage as well."

The Turk was silent. "You know something about us, I see," he said at last. "It would be difficult to convince them. They store a percentage of every crop against the future—in case of crop failure, or government intervention, as when they plowed the fields under last year."

"The future will be even more difficult," Vorovich said. "The Orientals are coming into the market more all the time—"

"*Feh*," the Turk said, dismissing unseen hordes with a wave of his hand. "Turkish opium is the best in the world, and ours is the best in Turkey! Here we get fifty per cent more morphine per kilo!"

"We'll pay fifty per cent over market," Vorovich said.

"They would be interested in the extra money," the Turk said after a moment's hesitation. "But dealing in such huge amounts increases the risk of discovery. It's relatively simple to sell a few kilos at a time. But this would involve bringing the opium to central gathering points, and it would take longer to convert so much into morphine. . . ."

"I thought I was dealing with men," Vorovich said.

The Turk studied him thoughtfully. "I have known these peasants for many years," he said. "And barring acts of God and the government, have always gotten them a fair return for their labors, with an equally fair return to me for mine. Yet if anything were to go wrong, if, for example, you were arranging all this in order to destroy our stockpile, I could not explain my mistake in judgment. I would not be able to remain in this province—perhaps not even in Turkey. I could lose everything I own, including my life. What will you put up of equal value?"

This man might seem only a go-between, Vorovich thought, with a comic-opera mustache, but his eyes were hard.

"I've already put everything I have on the line, just by coming here," Vorovich said.

The Turk considered this for a very long while, looking first at Vorovich and then at Ginny. Finally he spoke to the assembled men in the low, musical dialect of the province. The discussion went on for some time.

"If I say they should do it, they will," the Turk said then.

"Is there any way I can sweeten it for you?" Vorovich asked.

The Turk glanced so briefly at Ginny, Vorovich almost missed it. "A fifty per cent bonus, in advance," the Turk said.

"I'll do better than that," Vorovich said. "I'll give you a percentage point for every point over fifty toward pure."

The Turk's eyes glittered. "You want a sample," he said.

"Enough to put through the pipeline on a dry run," Vorovich said.

Again the Turk hesitated, then said something rapidly and not so musical to the men. Two of them immediately rose and went out.

"You're a cautious man. I like that," the Turk said. "Finish your tea. It will take a little while."

Later everyone, including the teahouse proprietor, walked them along a narrow hillside path that wound between the huts, arriving finally at the village outskirts, where a slanted pasture with a rusted fence held a flock of goats. Before a small shed out of which an angled pipe chimney was beginning to smoke, large sacks were being unloaded from a mule by several women, veiled before strangers.

"Why don't the men help?" Ginny suddenly wondered.

"The men save their energies for night," the Turk explained. He grinned at the expression on her face. "It's not what you think," he said then. "Their main occupation is smuggling."

Inside the shed a farmer, wearing the astrakhan cap of the province, was supervising the fire under a wooden barrel which looked large enough to store half the village's olives.

"What's that smell?" Ginny asked, wrinkling her nose.

The Turk reached into a sack and showed her a handful of camphor balls. "To mask the odor of opium. Which smells like wet grass, and might lead government inspectors to us."

"Is this a smokehouse?" Vorovich asked, peering at ropes and hooks dangling from the ceiling.

"What better place to hide what we do?" the Turk asked.

They watched the opium, a blackish-brown substance, being put into the water kept, carefully kept, just below boiling point by the man tending the fire. Sacks of lime were then added, turning the water milky white. Gradually the darker ingredients began settling until the water took on the color of bouillon.

While they waited for the next step in the process, the teahouse proprietor prepared them a dish which tasted like a peppery cheese mixed with rice, which they ate outside off clay plates, washing it down with tea.

It took four of the women to carry the barrel outside, using long poles; then the hot liquid was poured through sheets into another barrel. The process was repeated, and then the sheets spread on rocks to dry.

In that dry mountain air the afternoon sun took the moisture from the cloths very quickly; then the women took stiff whisks and meticulously brushed what looked like brown dust into lined baskets.

"Taste," the Turk said, offering the granular stuff.

Vorovich wet a finger, touched bitterness to his tongue. "Seems good," he said, spitting. "But we'll know exactly when it gets to the labs. How will you deliver it?"

"By mule to the plains," the Turk said. "Then trucks across Europe to France."

"We're talking about ten thousand pounds of opium," Vorovich said, "and if your opium is as pure as you say, that works out to almost a ton of morphine—"

The Turk shrugged. "A hundred pounds per mule, ten times twenty mules, and it is done." He rubbed thumb and forefinger together. "And the payment?" he asked.

Before Vorovich could answer, the Turk suddenly held up his hand, cried out something in Turkish. Everyone fell silent.

Then Vorovich heard it too. A sound that he at first took to be distant thunder, but continuous, and then, as it drew closer, its rumblings magnified a thousandfold in the canyons, he recognized that unsteady thrum as the whirling blades of a helicopter.

"The car!" Vorovich cried, to the driver. "Hide the car!"

The driver didn't understand, but the Turk shouted a translation, and the driver turned and ran all-out down the trail toward the village square. The others were already emptying the barrels, folding the sheets, whisking away signs of their activity.

The Turk then shouted at the men, who were beginning to scatter. They stopped, muttering among themselves. The Turk turned to Vorovich. "Have you got any money?" he demanded.

"How much do you need?" Vorovich asked, reaching for it.

"Fifty dollars," the Turk said, seeing the top denomination. Taking the bill, he flung it at the men, face turning almost black as he bellowed in rage.

Two of them, after picking up the bill, then ran toward the goats, separating one from the herd. One whipped out a long knife while the other straddled the bleating animal, lifting its chin by the beard.

Ginny's scream matched the goat's.

"If they saw the smoke," the Turk said, pointing to the gushing chimney, "we should have a reason for it." He grinned malevolently as Vorovich pocketed the rest of the money. "It's only right you should pay for all this hospitality—but at least we will have meat for supper."

Vorovich tried to comfort the sobbing Ginny while keeping a wary eye on a sky filled with echoes which alternately swelled and diminished.

"Who are they?" he asked. "Police?"

"Only the armed forces have such planes," the Turk said. "Given us by your government. They are perhaps trying to impress some visiting Americans by searching for illegal fields."

"No," Vorovich said, remembering that raised compartment blind, "they're looking for me! Listen," he said urgently. "Weren't you going to put us on the return train?"

"We can't drive the car down in daylight," the Turk protested.

"What about the mules?" Vorovich asked.

The Turk hesitated a long moment, then nodded. "We'd all better change into other clothes. You," he said to Ginny, "go with the women; they'll help you dress."

"Have them bring her clothes here," Vorovich said. "I don't want her out of my sight."

The Turk looked as if he were going to give Vorovich an argument, and then a boy cried out, pointing. There were two of them, resembling huge insects, darting in and out of the intervening hills.

"Come on then," the Turk said, and took them on a run toward the village.

While the sound of the racketing blades grew louder, they ducked into a house, where the Turk and Vorovich put on loose peasant shirts and pants, Ginny pantaloons and black caftan.

As they stepped outside again, all three wearing astrakhan hats, they could barely hear each other over the sound cannonading off the surrounding bluffs.

"Damn!" the Turk said. "Only one is landing."

One helicopter remained hovering overhead as the other came slowly down into the pasture. They could see the military markings. Several officers got out, and a civilian. His clothes, to Vorovich's anxious eye, seemed American.

"What are they going to tell them?" Vorovich asked. "Isn't

it unusual to be smoking a goat in the middle of the week?"

"I've taken care of that," the Turk said, after a quick and respectful glance at him. "It's supposed to be for a wedding."

Suddenly, as they watched the officers questioning the farmers, the hovering plane lifted and slanted away in the opposite direction.

"Now's our chance," the Turk said. "Quickly." And the Turk began moving at a fast trot down steep side streets, Vorovich and Ginny trying to keep up, slipping on the uneven stones.

The mules, three of them, were hidden below the ledges of a precipitous trail on the edge of the village, accompanied by a sinewy mule-handler and his boy.

"Grab the manes," the Turk said, showing them, and within moments they were plunged out of sight of whatever was going on above them.

Ginny, whose feet were toughened from years of going barefoot and wearing sandals, managed pretty well. But Vorovich, wearing new boots, soon felt the stinging pain of blisters. He gritted his teeth and said nothing, not willing to stop or slow them down.

That damfool Cabot had put someone on him, he thought, and somehow the Turks had gotten into the act—already defensive about American pressure, they'd be out to prove something by running him down, whether that had been what Cabot had intended or not. Now what was he going to tell this Turk when the inevitable question came?

"God," Ginny said, the first time any of them spoke in an hour, "isn't there an easier way to get there?"

The path had narrowed to the point where it was necessary to walk single file, holding onto the tails to ease around sheer corners and duck under crumbling overhangs, afraid to look at what seemed a thousand feet straight down.

"This is a smuggler's trail," the Turk said.

"Have you lost many?" Ginny gasped, as a mule kicked a stone over the edge.

"Not by accident," the Turk said.

"Maybe we ought to slow down," Ginny said, looking at Vorovich limping in the rear, the dust and the heat and the thin air making him cough for breath.

"We have to get through the difficult part by dusk," the Turk said, and slugged his mule, which had crowded him against the cliff, bringing a snort of pain from both the animal and Ginny.

By twilight, the trail had widened considerably. By dark, they had reached the foothills, and were finally able to stop for a breather.

They heard a stream nearby, and Vorovich went stumbling off to look for it. When the others came, he was not the least embarrassed that they found him sitting with his blistered bare feet soaking in the cold water.

The mules drank from the clear bubbling stream, as did Ginny, but the Turk pulled a bottle out of a mule pack, removed the cork with his teeth, offered it to Vorovich.

Vorovich drank, and at the mule-handler's gesturing, poured some on his open blisters, trying not to flinch. After that, the hurt did seem bearable.

He turned down a cigarette, and another drink, though he wanted both enormously. "How far are the tracks from here?" he asked.

"Not far," the Turk said in what was apparently meant to be a reassuring tone. But something seemed out of key, Vorovich thought. As they passed around strips of dried meat, then squatted in the growing darkness, talking, Vorovich tried to gather some meaning from the pace and inflection of their voices, though they spoke in their own tongue. When the boy could not seem to keep his large eyes off Ginny, he had the certain impression they were discussing her.

Vorovich put his arm about her, and as she snuggled in close he murmured, "Stick close. Walk in my footsteps, if you have to, but don't let any distance show between us, no matter what. Got that?"

"Why?" she whispered, tensing. "What's happening?"

"For Chrissake, Ginny," he whispered, hard put to keep his voice down, "can't you for once just do as I ask without questioning it?"

"Sor-ree," she whispered. "Sir."

"How about it?" Vorovich said then, aloud. "Shouldn't we be getting started?"

"It's not far," the Turk said, but Vorovich could hear them getting to their feet.

"Maybe now that it's flatter ground we could ride the mules," Ginny said. "Because of his feet, and all."

"Unfortunately, that is not possible," the Turk said. "Our

companions are leaving us here—they wish to return home before daylight."

"Well, if the tracks are so close," Vorovich said, "why can't they at least take us that far?"

"They live beyond the village," the Turk said. "And it is a harder trip up than down, particularly in the darkness."

While they were talking, Vorovich could hear the rustle of movement by the others; now, as the Turk murmured something in his own language, Vorovich got silently to his feet, took the hidden gun from his belt, and, reaching behind him for Ginny, pulled her along behind him as he walked as quietly as possible toward the mules.

As his eyes grew more accustomed to the dark, Vorovich could make out the shadowy forms of the mule-handler and his boy gathering up the tethers. Vorovich stopped and stood very still, keeping Ginny behind.

The mules were led away, and now Vorovich and the Turk were facing each other unobstructed; about six feet of darkness separated them.

"Is that you, my friend?" the Turk asked.

"Yes," Vorovich said, as quietly.

"Can you see me well enough to know what I'm holding in my hand?" the Turk asked.

"No," Vorovich said.

"A gun," the Turk said. "Pointed directly at your stomach. It would be impossible to miss at this distance."

"I would think a knife would be more your style," Vorovich said.

"You don't believe me?" the Turk asked. "I will strike a match."

The Turk struck his wooden match on the barrel of his gun. Both men squinted in the sudden flare, which illuminated the space between them far enough to reveal that Vorovich held a gun too.

"As you said," Vorovich said, when the match flickered out, "it would be impossible to miss, wouldn't it?"

"There are more of us," the Turk managed finally.

"What will that matter, if you're dead?" Vorovich said.

"I will put my gun away, if you do the same," the Turk said, after a moment.

"No deal," Vorovich said. He became aware of movement

in the outer darkness. "Tell them to stop," he said, "or I'll kill you where you stand."

The Turk called something. The movement stopped.

"Now hand over your gun," Vorovich said.

"But that would leave me defenseless!" the Turk protested.

"All I'm interested in is getting back on that train," Vorovich said. "What are you interested in?"

There was a silence. Then the Turk made a slight movement, and Vorovich felt something land at his feet. He stooped and picked up the other's gun.

"Do we need your friends?" Vorovich asked..

"No," the Turk said. "Shall I tell them to go home?"

"What about the morphine?" Vorovich asked.

"I have it," the Turk said.

"What was *that* all about?" Ginny asked, letting out her breath, moving up beside Vorovich as they heard the mule-handler and the boy go off into the outer darkness at the Turk's command.

"Tell her," Vorovich said.

"I thought it might be wise to have some insurance," the Turk said, now affable again. "If we kept you with us until our business was completed, it might guarantee that your companion would deal honorably with us." Even in the dark they could make out the gleam of his teeth. "No harm done. Shall we move on?"

They had been within fifty yards of the track. When they came out of the foothills, the stars were bright enough to illuminate the plain, and the moon ballooning up out of the mountains enabled them to follow the glistening rails.

"Only a few miles," the Turk said, adjusting the sack so the weight was evenly distributed along his shoulders.

Vorovich did not offer to help. The cinder roadbed made walking easier, and he wanted the Turk ahead so there would be no surprises.

The siding was near a village, shadowy huts clustered in the dark, no windows showing light. The Turk led them down into a shallow gully, which hid them as they waited.

"Does the morphine go on the train too?" Vorovich asked.

"Only this batch," the Turk said, and Vorovich guessed he was lying. "But all you need to know is that it will be delivered in France, isn't it so?"

"You mean you're going through with it, after all that's happened?" Ginny demanded.

"Of course he is," Vorovich said. "He knows that if I were running a trap on him I wouldn't have sprung it so early."

"Why are they looking for you?" the Turk asked, and Vorovich could not tell whether he was convinced or not. "Did you commit so great a crime?"

"He killed someone," Ginny said, before Vorovich could stop her.

But if she had hoped to turn the Turk against him she was to be disappointed.

"Then I'm lucky to have given in," the Turk said.

There might have been more questions, except that the ground started throbbing with the approaching train.

"If you're nervous about anything at all," Vorovich said, getting up, "you could always change the collection point."

"I will consider it," the Turk said, getting to his feet too, then holding out his hand to help Ginny.

There was an anxious moment, and then the Turk dropped her hand and picked up the sack as the train hurtled toward them along the moonlit plain.

The brakes screeched and sparks cascaded like a firefall as the train neared the siding; it rumbled and skidded past, and they had to run almost a quarter mile before they got to the proper car.

The sleeping-car steward had almost given them up. Vorovich made sure the out-of-breath Ginny was aboard before he shook hands with the Turk, then swung aboard himself, noticing, with some satisfaction, that the steward was locking the sack in his service compartment.

They had barely gotten inside their own compartment before the opposite express came roaring out of the night and past, and their own train started up.

"You tried to blow it for me, didn't you?" he asked, as she sank wearily onto the bunk.

"I told you I'd try," she said.

"No," he said. "My memory's better than that. You said you were going to persuade me."

"Well, when that didn't work . . ." she began, and then shrugged, helplessly.

"What is it with you . . . ?" he began, and then stopped also.

He was too tired himself to sustain any anger, and he didn't think he could handle whatever she might tell him next. Besides, she was doing something that worried him more: pulling out her sketchpad/journal, she was pressing a poppy between its thick pages.

As the train rattled on through the night toward the coast, the door of the adjoining compartment, which had been ever so slightly open, inched shut. Preble, dressed in his shorts and thick lederhosen and with a newly grown British-officer-type mustache, picked up a water glass and placed it against the thin veneered wall that separated the compartments. Carefully, he pressed his ear against the closed end.

At first he heard nothing except the rumble of the wheels. Then he began to hear a low murmuring that he took to be conversation, and straining to make out what they were saying, had to decide finally it was someone in the water cabinet.

At least they were not making love, he thought. Though it was his duty to monitor them, he didn't intend to embarrass himself by listening while they might be coupling.

Though by their shabby unkempt appearance they'd be too exhausted for *amour*. They looked as if they'd been through hair-raising experiences, grateful to have made the train at all.

He was grateful, too. He had been so pleased with himself on that earlier journey, congratulating himself on his choice of disguise, able to look at his quarry head on without being recognized when Vorovich made that slow tour of the train, undoubtedly looking for possible tails.

And then, later in the night, to be awakened by the unaccustomed stillness, lifting the window blind to see what was up, only to watch with a stunned incredulity as the ones he was supposed to be following were getting into a car! What could he do? Clearly, not get off himself in the middle of nowhere. And so, helpless, he had ridden the rest of the way sleepless and upset into Ankara, where at the consulate he even had difficulty proving he was of sufficient status to make an emergency call on the transatlantic phone.

How Cabot had raved! Preble flinched even now thinking about it. I don't care how you do it, Cabot had finally said—shouted. But find him. And fast!

Preble had contacted the narcotics man at the embassy, a short, swarthy type named Bucaro.

Bucaro had been full of questions. Preble, because of the admiration he could not help feeling for Vorovich, had distorted the situation, just in case Vorovich was operating on the up and up. Vorovich had been taken from the train by force, he said.

Bucaro, though urged to use the utmost discretion, immediately contacted the Turks, who reacted by ordering a sweep of those mountains by air. When Preble protested they might be endangering Vorovich, the Turks insisted the contrary—if those bandits see he's important, they said, they'll take very good care of him.

What Preble discovered was that the Turks were furious about the presence of an American agent in the Sultan mountains: it was another indication of U.S. meddling, a blatant example of distrust, of not believing Turkey serious about controlling opium production. They would prove it. They would take Americans along on the search.

Preble, however, backed out. Aghast at the events he had set in motion—why hadn't Cabot clued him in about the political implications?—he tried to convince himself that everything would turn out well, and eventually, brooding over a bitter cup of the mud the Turks called coffee, he remembered that Vorovich had not been coerced. As near as Preble could tell, he had gotten off of his own free will.

If that was the case, Preble suddenly thought, he would be coming back out of those mountains. Soon. The question was how? By car? Maybe, except a car would be easily found on those isolated mountain roads—walking was too tedious and long—he might very well, Preble realized, reverse the procedure!

Cheeks flushed with excitement over the deductive insight, Preble had hastened to the terminal and asked about the availability of compartments on the night train going back to Izmir. The one he asked for was already reserved—but he could have the one next to it.

Elated, not telling anyone where he was going, or why, or how, willing to use his own initiative, as Cabot had suggested, indeed ordered him to do, Preble got on the return express, believing with all the certainty of those touched by inspiration that his thinking was brilliantly accurate.

He questioned the steward about the locked compartment only as a matter of form, to confirm his judgment, not dispute it. But when the steward told him the compartment was occupied by a couple who had boarded early on, doubts began to assail him. He had kept his door ajar, and when he saw the steward deliver a bottle of wine and two glasses his sense of failure became overwhelming. The fact that he heard nothing through the glass proved nothing, since he wasn't at all sure the makeshift listening device would work.

Then: success! He hadn't needed his wrist-watch alarm to waken him when the train reached the midpoint siding. His anxieties monumental, he had prayed for someone to board— and was rewarded with a glimpse of the furtive pair being helped aboard by the steward.

Now he knew the glass against the wall worked, albeit poorly. He hadn't yet been able to make out a single word. As he was about to give it up when the murmuring became more distinct, argumentative in fact, and then he heard the words "flower" and "memento," though why those should produce anger was beyond him.

Then quite suddenly the murmuring stopped. A knock on their compartment door. Preble recognized the steward's voice, but not what he was saying, it was pitched so low. The response was a brief "Thanks"—and then silence.

Preble strained to hear, eyes shut. He was unaware that behind him his own compartment door was slowly opening.

Vorovich hadn't known what to expect when the steward had warned him about a foreigner with an unseemly curiosity. Ordinarily, he might have waited till morning to check him out, but the argument with Ginny had so disturbed him he almost welcomed the excuse to interrupt it.

Finding the adjoining door unlocked, his first thought was such carelessness made it unlikely the foreigner was anyone to worry about. His second was that it might be a trap. He drew his gun, used the barrel to edge it open.

When he saw the moon-faced, brush-mustached young man with his eyes shut, ear cupped against a glass next to the wall, his anger, already stirred by Ginny's behavior, spilled over. And

142

before he could stop himself he had lunged forward and shattered the glass with his gun.

Preble leaped away from the wall, hand to his now bloodied ear. There was no use going for his own weapon—it was too far away, holstered on the bunk. Besides, he had recognized Vorovich. Vorovich knew that by the flicker in Preble's apprehensive eye.

"You were on the train coming out," Vorovich said, breathing hard, studying the other's shorts and hose. "Who are you— why are you following me?"

"I'm not," Preble said, still holding his ear. "My name's Preble—I've been on a climbing holiday. . . ."

"Pretty small mountain to be back so soon," Vorovich said.

"I never got started," Preble said. "Family problems. Had to cut the trip short. Do you mind if I do something about my ear —it's cut pretty badly, I'm afraid."

"Who are you?" Vorovich said, unmoved.

"I told you," Preble said, looking at the blood on his hand, then paling and clapping it back to his ear. "You have every right to be angry about me eavesdropping, I know, but I have this insatiable curiosity about other people's bedtime conversations—I've been to a head doctor about it; hasn't helped."

"Where's your I.D.?" Vorovich asked.

"My what?" Preble asked.

"Your identification!" Vorovich snarled, unamused by the other's feeble attempts at a cover. When Preble pointed to his jacket, Vorovich, still keeping the gun on him, found a wallet in the inside pocket.

"Where's your passport?" Vorovich demanded, flinging the wallet against the wall—it held not even a driver's license.

Reluctantly Preble pointed at his knapsack. Vorovich spilled the contents out on the bunk—the usual camping gear, but unused—and found the U.S. passport wrapped in oilskin. It had a diplomatic stamp.

"Okay," Vorovich sighed. "Tell me about it."

"I'm a cultural attaché," Preble said. "The lowest of the low."

"Please," Vorovich said wearily. "Don't be more of an asshole than you have been already. Who put you on to me?"

"I don't know what you . . ." Preble began, face flushed, and then stopped at the disgusted look on Vorovich's face. "That was pretty dumb, leaving the door open, I guess," he said.

"I guess," Vorovich said. "Fix your bloody ear!" He put his gun away. "Got any alcohol?"

"Soap's an adequate disinfectant," Preble said, flinching at the sight of his ear in the washstand mirror. He gingerly began washing it.

"To drink, Preble, to drink," Vorovich said, and Preble, reddening again, shook his head no. "Maybe," he said hopefully, seeing the vast disappointment on Vorovich's face, "we could ring the steward for some?"

"Sure," Vorovich said. "That would be terrific. Let him see us getting chummy, so my ass would really be fried!"

"I guess I wasn't thinking," Preble offered.

"I guess," Vorovich said savagely. "Maybe thinking isn't part of the new administration. Maybe you guys are picked because of how you look in clothes. Why did Cabot put an asshole kid like you on me, anyway? Does he *want* me wiped?"

The red in Preble's face got so deep it matched the blood. "I'm new," he said. "They figured you wouldn't tag me."

"Christ," Vorovich said, and quite suddenly he began to shake inside, he could feel the beginning tremble from the inside out. He needed a drink. But he concentrated and the trembling stopped, if not the thirst.

"Well, you didn't, till now," Preble said. "And I figured out you'd get back on this train."

Vorovich finally nodded. "That was pretty good," he said. "Now figure out a way to get me out of this bind you put me in."

"What bind?" Preble asked.

"I've got to have some answers for the steward," Vorovich said.

"Tell them what I told you," Preble said. "And that you taught me a lesson about voyeurism." He indicated his gashed ear.

"This isn't a game, kid," Vorovich said. "If we don't play this exactly right, both of us are dead. We've got to stick very close to the truth."

"Which is what?" Preble asked, curious about more than the immediate situation.

Before Vorovich could respond, a knock sounded. "Vo, are

you all right?" came the urgent voice of Ginny.

"I'm fine," Vorovich said.

"The steward is here with me," Ginny said.

"Can you make your ear bleed?" Vorovich whispered to Preble. Preble got over his surprise and tugged at the lobe until the blood welled in the gash again. Vorovich backed to the door, unlocked it, pointed his gun at Preble again.

Ginny was there, the steward hovering behind her. She gasped. Vorovich leaned out before the steward could move. "Don't let him see you," he whispered. And aloud he said, to Ginny, "See if you can find a rope—and bring my flask too." Then he shut the door again.

"What's the rope for?" Preble asked with some anxiety.

"Would you rather I threw you off the train?" Vorovich asked. "Now what I'm going to do is take your identification, which you shouldn't be carrying anyway, and use it to prove you are what I say you are."

"But I need my passport!" Preble fretted.

"Not this kind you don't," Vorovich said. "If you're going undercover, go all the way under—you can't keep coming up for air. Hell, if . . . ah, the hell with it, I can't teach you twenty years in twenty minutes."

A knock again, and Ginny entered, the steward, as requested, staying out of sight. Vorovich showed him the bloody gun barrel, shut the door again.

"What happened to his ear?" Ginny asked, puzzled and shocked.

"He was eavesdropping," Vorovich said.

"Did you have to give him that kind of punishment?" Ginny demanded, going toward him with the flask—which Vorovich intercepted, taking a long swallow before handing it to Preble. Preble hesitated, then tried to emulate the older man, managing it with only a slight cough. Ginny took it from him with a disgusted look and poured some over the wound, which brought a subdued cry.

"Why were you eavesdropping?" Ginny asked, bandaging his ear, having talked the steward into providing a first-aid kit as well as a rope.

"He's a narc," Vorovich said before Preble could answer.

"Way over here?" Ginny said, surprised.

"We're trying to stop the flow at its source," Preble said. "Aren't you pretty young to be involved in the drug traffic?" he asked then.

"She's not as young as she looks," Vorovich said, and took an extra turn with the rope, making Preble wince. "Who knows you're on the train?" Vorovich asked.

"Why should I tell you that?" Preble asked.

"Suit yourself," Vorovich shrugged. "But if no one's expecting you, it may be a long long time till you're found—which is something I could take care of for you before you die of malnutrition."

"Nobody knows," Preble said reluctantly.

"Listen, sonny," Vorovich said, choosing his words carefully, remembering that Ginny mustn't even suspect that he had any connection with them, "I can tell you're all gung ho, and you've got this inflated idea of duty no matter what, but listen to an old hand—learn to stay out of situations that are too much for you. Keep away from me, for instance. Your cover's blown with me anyway—and I'm warning you now, if it comes down to it, if there's some situation where you're in my way, I'll run right over you."

"I'll keep it in mind," Preble said, and Vorovich, who had begun to like this very young man, felt his heart sink.

The steward saw to it that Vorovich and Ginny were among the first passengers off the train. Vorovich showed him Preble's diplomatic passport, but would not let him keep it, saying it was too valuable, he had uses for it himself. And he suggested that the steward be the one to discover the bound Preble, after waiting as long as possible to give them a running start. That would take suspicion away from him, Vorovich said, and the steward, who had been worried, relaxed and agreed.

They took a plane to Genoa. There seemed no problem with customs, though Vorovich took the precaution of putting the sample of opium he had taken into his belt buckle. He asked for, and took, the first rooming house recommended by Traveler's Aid.

A tour bus had been supposed to take them across into France, but they were now two days behind schedule, and Vorovich called the World-Wide Travel office from a street-corner booth, asking about alternate plans.

"You're in luck," the person who answered the phone said. "The bus had mechanical difficulties, and it's not leaving till tomorrow. Where are you staying?"

"Look," Vorovich said, "I'm not much for tours. So why don't I take a few days on the Riviera, and I'll check in with your office in Nice?"

"Just a moment," the voice said.

"This is Carruthers," another voice said, in an English accent so pronounced it seemed false. "Your friendly tour leader. I thought perhaps I could meet with you and give you all kinds of wonderful reasons why you shouldn't cancel out."

It was a warning, Vorovich thought. How serious, he wasn't sure. "Nothing against your tour," Vorovich said. "Maybe we could pick you up in France?"

"That would be awkward," Carruthers said. "You'd be missing some of the best parts. If you'd meet me somewhere, I could tell you about them."

"I'm not really the tour type," Vorovich said.

"What about your companion?" Carruthers asked. "Isn't she the tour type either?"

Vorovich sighed silently. "Where do you want to meet?" he asked.

Carruthers met them in a cheap bar filled with sailors and

dockworkers on the Genoa waterfront. He was a chubby little man who smiled a lot, though his teeth were very bad. He ordered Pernod: "It's like licorice, you know, has a marvelous laxative effect. Though you younger folk don't have that problem, do you?" He bared his teeth at Ginny, who had insisted on coming along. "Now, what's all this about canceling? It looks bad to the home office if I lose customers for no reason." He poured water from a chipped ceramic pitcher into the yellow liquid, which turned a chalky white. "I've never outgrown a wonderment," he said, "at how elements change through mixing—I've often thought how much *fun* to be a chemist. Laboratories are the most fascinating places. Wouldn't you say? That's why we're scheduling a laboratory on our tour—a special laboratory, which the ladies will specially enjoy."

"Why can't we meet you there?" Vorovich asked.

"I couldn't permit it," Carruthers said, losing his grin. "The other tourees might wonder why I permitted someone to join late."

"How much red tape crossing borders?" Vorovich asked.

"You have a problem about borders?" Carruthers asked.

"It's possible I may be on some kind of a list," Vorovich said.

"Well, why didn't you say so?" Carruthers wondered, all smiles again. "That's easily taken care of. No sweat, as you Yanks say." He looked over at Ginny. "Are you on a list too?"

"It's possible," Vorovich said, and Ginny flashed him a surprised glance.

"Righty-o," Carruthers said. "Everyone on the bus will be English. If you can't do a proper accent, don't talk going through, okay?" He kept smiling as Vorovich nodded and stood up to go. "I'll not ask you again where you're staying," he said. "But *please* try to be on time for the bus." He took a mouthful of his drink, puffed his cheeks with it, swallowed noisily. "There's no refunds if you miss it this time. Quite the contrary."

On the way back to their room, Ginny was full of questions about that unmistakable warning. And why should he think that *she'd* be on any list?

"The Swiss police put you on," Vorovich said. "How do you think Preble got onto us? Soon as he gets free everyone'll be looking for us. Now that I'm carrying goods I don't want to risk it."

He had thought she would give him an argument about

carrying, but she remained silent. Maybe she was carrying too, he thought—the first chance he got he must remember to look for it.

The tour bus was new, air-conditioned, and had a little bar over which Carruthers would preside—but "only after we're safely in France," he said, to a chorus of good-natured boos from the three dozen passengers, British teachers on holiday.

At the border crossing, the passengers remained seated while a customs official came aboard. Carruthers had already collected the passports. Talking all the while, he followed the officer to the roadside customs house, where they were stamped.

The luggage was not examined. After a head count, Carruthers was permitted to redistribute the passports, and the customs officer said they could go.

"Oh, I say, officer," Ginny called, in an atrocious fake of a British accent, holding the customs official in the doorway as he was about to get off. "My entry stamp is dreadfully smeared, and I did so want a clear record of where I've been . . . for my memory book, don'tcha know?"

Heads swiveled. Before the startled Carruthers could think of what to say, the customs official was climbing back in. Then Vorovich grabbed her opened passport. "It's readable," he called, after pretending to examine it. "Don't bother!"

"We are running a bit late," Carruthers said, taking the official by the elbow and ushering him off, at the same time winking at the driver to get underway.

"What the hell was that all about?" Vorovich demanded, as the door closed and the bus started across the border point.

"Well, just look at the stamp!" Ginny said, showing him, and Carruthers too as he arrived, face dark under that practiced affability.

The stamp *was* blurred, both of them could see that. Carruthers handed the passport back and, after a sidelong glance at Vorovich, went back to his place beside the driver.

"One more stunt like that," Vorovich muttered, "and I'm sending you home."

"It was a legitimate request," Ginny insisted, then sulked in her seat, not even looking at the magnificent scenery.

Carruthers opened the bar and began passing out drinks. He worked very fast, and had almost everyone laughing by the time the bus left the water's edge and turned into a stone-walled road leading up into the lush foothills.

"I've got a little surprise for all you jolly people," Carruthers said. "A serendipitous stop, which isn't printed on your agenda. But it's something I know will please the ladies, and I never tire of pleasing ladies!"

Vorovich did not join in the little chuckle. He had begun to be concerned about the battered little Volkswagen with the Swiss license plates that had been behind them ever since the customs stop, its driver hidden behind a sun visor, though they were driving west. Then the proletarian little car continued on past the turning the bus took, and as the steep road they were on turned in upon itself frequently enough to show that it did not show up on the road below, he finally relaxed and enjoyed the view.

In spite of teasing and wild guesswork, Carruthers would *not* tell them what his surprise was. But they smelled it almost twenty minutes out, the odor thick and heavy as marsh gas.

"Perfume," an ebullient lady cried, and the smiling Carruthers confirmed it. "We're going to Grasse."

The town itself was nondescript, though the streets were cobbled and the vistas extraordinary. While Carruthers kept up a stream of talk, pointing out that the sickeningly sweet smell came from pipe chimneys, venting a cloying almost invisible smoke murky as certain kinds of clear nail polish, they continued on past the town center and pulled into the parking lot of a small factory near the outskirts.

"Why so glum?" Carruthers asked, waiting by the steps as Ginny and Vorovich got off. "There'll be samples, and you can buy lots more at enormous discounts."

"I don't use perfume," Ginny said.

"Well then, you'll find the process interesting," Carruthers said, not to be put down.

What was bothering her? Vorovich wondered, as they followed the group inside. He only dimly remembered the vagaries of his fled wife's moods, having taken them to be part of a woman's cycles, but in Ginny's case he wondered whether she was still brooding over her putdown back at the border, or whether it was that no matter what she said or did, Vorovich was not going to be dissuaded.

Under a newly painted sign marked TOURISME, a young girl

in a starched blue smock announced that she was their guide.

The contact was made on the tour. The girl was explaining how only an eyedropper of essence was needed for each large vat when a well-fed, reddish-haired man, also wearing a smock, though his badge said DIRECTEUR, came through an inside door and interrupted.

"I was told one of your people was a practical chemist?" he asked of Carruthers.

"He teaches it," Carruthers said, indicating Vorovich at the rear of the group.

"Perhaps you wouldn't mind taking a look at some new equipment we're having installed?" the *directeur* asked, and the tour moved on without Vorovich—or Ginny, who again refused to be left behind. Carruthers raised an eyebrow, but moved on with the others.

The *directeur* led them down a windowless corridor and through a double-locked door marked PASSAGE INTERDIT and across a little patio and through another door unlocked only after a coded knock.

"He must be working on a helluva fragrance," Ginny said.

"Please?" the *directeur* said, holding the door open.

"Vous avez peur que quelqu'un ne découvre votre secret?" Ginny asked, before Vorovich might explain.

The *directeur* looked at her curiously, but did not respond. He ushered them into a large room whose painted windows probably led to the patio.

Large ventilator fans whirred steadily, a sound like the inside of a beehive. Huge balloon flasks were suspended in water inside what looked like laundry vats. Working intently with this equipment were four persons wearing gauze masks, like those used by hospital personnel.

Closer, they saw that each flask contained a centigrade thermometer. As they watched, the heating water moved the red column slowly upward, past eighty degrees and more, at which point one of the workers, dark-skinned above the mask, muttered something in a strange language. Two of the others immediately began adding a chemical.

"You'd think they were creating the H bomb," Ginny said.

"It's almost as delicate," the *directeur* said, "and dangerous. If the temperature falls below eighty the process ceases—if it rises above ninety the morphine is destroyed. And I don't mean to alarm you, but if it should ever reach the boiling point, this entire laboratory would explode."

"My God, the smell!" Ginny cried, and pulled a scarf from her purse to cover her nose and mouth.

"Acetyic anhydride," the *directeur* said. "A common acid."

"You don't use that in perfume," Ginny said accusingly through the cloth.

"Ah, but indeed we do," the *directeur* said. "That is why no one would ever question the shipment of certain chemicals which have a variety of uses to our little factory." He paused, slanting a look at Vorovich. "That is how your principal and I met," he said. "D'Anton supplies me with ambergris." He explained for Ginny, "That is a secretion of whales used in perfumes. Don't worry," he said, as she kept the scarf to her face. "Once the tubing is put on the flasks, the smell will disappear."

They watched as the serpentine glass tubing was placed on the flasks; almost immediately vapor began condensing inside.

"We will pull that out later with suction pumps," the *directeur* said. "Over here we wash it with water and bone black to purify and decolor it, then filter the mixture there, where we precipitate it with carbonate of soda, after which we dry and sift it. Then we wash it with water and tartaric acid, use bone black again, again filter and precipitate it after once more drying and sifting it. We finally make it water soluble by pouring it into a mixture of boiling acetone, hydrochloric acid, and ninety-degree alcohol. After it cools for twelve hours, we dry it out again in these low heat closets. *Voilà!*"

Rather dramatically, the *directeur* opened what had looked like a pantry, where on a shelf lay fine white powder.

"It was remarkably pure opium you sent us," the *directeur* said. "If the rest is as good, we can approach a ninety-eight-percent substance."

"See what this checks out as," Vorovich said, pulling the gummy ball from behind his belt buckle.

Behind the scarf, Ginny's face became grim and set. As the *directeur* tossed the opium to a worker, saying something in that foreign tongue, she walked over to sit on a bench some distance away.

"If the rest is as good, and if the dry run is successful," the *directeur* said then, "you can tell our mutual friend that I will participate gladly."

Vorovich looked at him coldly. "The dry run stops here," he said.

As he watched the *directeur*'s face change color, Vorovich knew he was taking a chance. The other, a supposedly legitimate businessman, had been tempted into joining D'Anton's scheme by the promise of an enormous profit—and the assurance that any risks would be minimal. And now Vorovich, who was supposed to bring reassurances, was about to undo what had been done, with the danger that this most essential part of the operation would be lost.

But he had suddenly seen an opportunity to get a handhold on the organization D'Anton had set up. What better way to make himself indispensable than by breaking it apart and then restructuring it? Only he would then know where all the pieces were.

"What d-do you mean?" the *directeur* stammered. "Has something gone wrong? I can't store the merchandise here, there isn't the room, I was told that as soon as it was transformed it would be taken away. . . ."

"By tour bus, you mean?" Vorovich said, sneering. "Whose idea was that?"

"Monsieur D'Anton, I thought," the *directeur* said, his face working.

"Carruthers tell you that?" Vorovich asked. The other nodded. "Well, I've been sent to examine the entire operation, and make changes wherever I think necessary," Vorovich said, lying through set teeth.

"I don't want there to be any trouble here," the *directeur* said, so worried his voice was shaky.

"There won't be," Vorovich said. "You just go ahead with your part of it as planned—you're going to package it as bath salts and powders, right?—but don't hand it over to Carruthers. Ship it as you would normally to one of your customers.

"Later I will provide a specific address. For now, send it as samples to Mr. D'Anton."

"What will I tell Carruthers?" the *directeur* asked, worrying.

"Don't tell him anything," Vorovich said. "I'll make all the explanations."

"He may already have the merchandise," the *directeur* said, looking at his watch.

"Then go on out there," Vorovich said, "tell him the packages got switched accidentally, and give him something else."

"But when he finds out, what then?" the *directeur* asked, frightened.

"I'll be there when he finds out," Vorovich said. "He'll know it was my idea."

"Very well," the *directeur* said reluctantly. "But I will have to rethink my participation in all this. Monsieur D'Anton may have to find himself another lab."

"You're in too deep to back out," Vorovich said. "If you know anything about D'Anton's other connections, you know that it'd be dangerous for you to quit."

"He would do something violent?" the *directeur* asked.

Vorovich put everything he had into his shrug. He might have gone on to be more graphic, except he didn't think it was necessary, and he had begun to wonder why Ginny was so intent on examining that fragile processing equipment.

"Be careful, mademoiselle," the *directeur* called, following the direction of Vorovich's glance. "Those fumes are very dangerous; they can mark your skin and eat out your lungs."

Ginny seemed startled to discover she was being watched. "I've been around labs before," she said. But taking her kerchief, she masked herself again before turning back to the glass tubing.

But Vorovich had seen her, thinking herself unobserved, run a section of her kerchief through the tubing where the vapors had condensed and, in a swiftly deft movement, loop the wet end into a knot before folding it into the middle of the flowered silk.

"Let's get back to our group," Vorovich called, and watched as she so very casually dropped her kerchief into her purse while walking toward them.

"It's fascinating, isn't it?" she asked, taking his arm.

"Yes," Vorovich said, "fascinating."

Carruthers was in the showroom helping the women on the tour choose fragrances. "Be careful with that one," he was saying, as the three of them entered, to a tall skinny woman who had the teeth of a horse and whinny to match. "It's aphrodisiacal, and the manufacturer won't be responsible for any sexual attacks when you wear it!"

A string shopping bag holding almost a dozen packages was

on the floor at his feet. The *directeur*, with the barest of glances at Vorovich, picked up the bag.

"But these aren't the fragrances you ordered," he said to Carruthers, looking at one and then another package. "There's been a mistake! Here," he said to the girl in the blue smock, "take these back and give Monsieur Carruthers one each from the new selections."

Carruthers was so startled he didn't have a chance to protest. He watched the girl take his bag away, looked at the nervous Frenchman, then found Vorovich in the crowd. Vorovich held his stare, then deliberately smiled in parody of Carruther's own.

As they filed into the tour bus, Carruthers took a seat across the aisle. "Any use in my opening these?" he murmured, pointing to his string bag, now filled with new packages.

"Not unless you want to smell good," Vorovich said.

"I don't understand," Carruthers said, almost plaintively, as the bus, filled with the chattering English, left the factory grounds and started down the cobbled road back the way they had come. "I work my ample rear off setting up a transportation system that took a lot of imagination, if I do say so m'self, not to mention working out complicated schedules and things, and you come along and demolish it, just like that. You have something better to take its place, I assume?"

"Not yet," Vorovich said.

Carruthers stared at him, then stood up, holding the seat rail to keep his balance. "You're either a madman or a fool," he said, and went back to his usual seat as the bus started down the looping road toward the sparkling sea.

"You're not going to tell me about it, are you?" Ginny asked finally. He shook his head. "You still don't trust me," she said.

"You had to ask, didn't you?" Vorovich said, leaning close. He opened her purse and pulled out the knotted kerchief. "Just a souvenir, like the pressed flower?" he asked.

"Charles needs to know if it's worth his while," she said, shifting uncomfortably.

"What I don't understand," he hissed, "is how you can be against me dealing in hard goods but not him."

"I'm against anybody dealing!" she suddenly flashed. "But he's deep in it and you still have time to get out!"

He nodded, as if accepting that, though he was puzzled still by some inconsistency in her. Why work at all for something she supposedly hated so? To get her friends out of a jam, she'd said, and to be with him—but even supposing all that were true, she was still leaving something out.

All would become evident in due time, he supposed. Meanwhile, he had a more urgent matter to brood over: how to redesign the shipping process so that only he would know, at any given moment, where the merchandise was hidden.

When the bus got to its lunch stop, a beachfront café in Nice, Vorovich went inside with the other passengers. But then, steering Ginny away from the crowd, they went through a side door onto the street.

Carruthers watched them go without protest. Thoughtfully, after making sure there were enough tables for everyone, he asked the café owner if there wasn't a telephone he might use in private.

At an umbrellaed curbside stand across the boulevard from the café, Preble had just sunk his teeth into one of those giant ham sandwiches made with French bread, his first food of the day, when he saw Vorovich and Ginny slip out the door. Hastily washing the giant bite down with an enormous swallow of Coca-Cola, Preble wrapped his sandwich in a napkin and, stuffing it into his pocket, took off after them.

He took care to stay well back, out of sight, though it was unlikely Vorovich would spot him. Not only was Preble now clean-shaven and very indigenously French in dress, to his beret worn at a jaunty angle, but it was unlikely that Vorovich would assume he could have picked up his trail so soon.

That showed the value of organization. Cabot was right about that. The moment he had been released from that train compartment by the slow-witted steward, Preble, not waiting for the local police, had dashed to the nearest phone, this time checking in with Interpol, who were monitoring any reported border crossings by Vorovich and the girl. Discovering that Vorovich was en route to Genoa, Preble decided to bring the Swiss in rather than the Americans—reasoning that the Swiss were already *au courant,* and he did not want to risk another debacle like the one in Turkey.

He didn't know if Cabot would understand or not. Frankly,

he no longer cared. Necessity, as Cabot himself had said, mattered more than inventions. Besides, as near as Preble could see, Cabot was condemning Vorovich out of hand. It might very well be that Vorovich was still playing for the home team.

Flying to Genoa himself, on a passport the Swiss arranged, Preble discovered that the Swiss agent, Klaus Handel, had left word that he was on the trail—and then, waiting at the offices of the airport police, Klaus called in to say he had followed them to a private home that took in overnight guests.

He and Klaus met, arranging to "leapfrog" the tailing. It was Klaus in the battered Volkswagen whom Vorovich had seen behind the tour bus—but it was Preble, in a rented Renault, following a half mile behind, who had taken the turning up into the mountainside community of Grasse.

At the perfume factory Preble debated whether to call in, but finally decided not to. Cabot had cautioned him about telling the Europeans too much, not wanting to risk them short-stopping the operation by moving in early. That consideration kept him from picking Klaus up in Nice, too. He felt bad about abandoning the Swiss in this way, after all the help he'd been, but it saved him having to avoid answering Klaus's natural questions. It went against his nature to lie.

Now, following Vorovich and the girl on foot to the local bus terminal, Preble watched them board an express bus to Marseilles. He waited until the bus pulled out to make absolutely sure Vorovich wasn't pulling a fast one, then hastened back to where he had parked the Renault.

Driving recklessly and fast, Preble managed to get to the highway on the edge of the city ahead of the bus, then relaxed enough to remember he was hungry as he drove at a more normal speed.

He gulped down the sandwich, which made him thirsty. Preble wished for that abandoned Coke. But he didn't stop. If he should get a flat, or lose a fan belt, or whatever, the bus might get by him. Not that Preble would mind all that much if Vorovich were able to give him the slip—provided that he, Preble, didn't let him do it through carelessness. Preble was very conscientious. His orders were clear. He would play his part in the game all the way out to the end. No matter what his personal feelings were.

Vorovich checked them into a shabby little hotel near the bus terminal, turned down an offer by the consumptive desk clerk to help them up the narrow five stories to their sparsely furnished suite—then had to go back downstairs when he discovered there was no phone in the room. The clerk listened openly, unperturbed by Vorovich's glare.

"I've been on one of your tours," Vorovich said to the girl who answered the phone at the local branch of World-Wide Travel, "and I got into an argument with our tour leader. It became impossible to remain under conditions like that, and so I got here on my own. Now I'd like a refund!"

"A moment, please," the girl said, and a masculine voice came on.

"Who are you, please?" the voice asked cautiously. Vorovich told him. "We are not in the practice of giving refunds," the voice said. "But perhaps there is another tour you might like in its place? If you could come into the office . . ."

"I don't know that I want to do that," Vorovich said.

"We'll send a man over," the other said. "Perhaps he can convince you, even show you some of our facilities."

"When?" Vorovich asked.

"Thirty minutes," the other said.

When Vorovich came to the first landing, where the ceiling obscured the view from the registration desk, he found Ginny.

"What don't you want to do?" she asked.

He continued on past her, and she had to hurry to keep pace as he took the stairs two at a time. "It was a ploy, that's all."

"Oh," she said, disappointed. "I thought maybe you *were* quitting."

He turned at the top landing and forced her to stop too, out of breath. "I'm in this all the way," he said. "Any ideas you might have of getting me to change my mind are not worth wasting your time on."

"You're sure?" she said, and it sounded like a warning.

"Why wouldn't I be?" he said. "What could you possibly say or do to convince me that you haven't already?"

She stared at him, eyes glistening as with a kind of fever, and for a moment he thought she was about to tell him something more private and personal than anything she had revealed to him thus far. Then the moment passed, and he thought he had just imagined it.

"Don't challenge me," she said then, with a little laugh following him into their room. "I might take you up on it."

He took out his traveling flask and poured himself a drink. "I'm supposed to meet a fellow," he said. "No need for you to come. Stay and rest up."

"I'm coming," she said.

"What if I say you can't?" he asked.

She returned his gaze steadily. "When we get back," she said, "I'll be asked whether I was with you always, day and night. You want me to say you went out for a meeting so secret I couldn't come with you?"

"You could lie," he said.

"So far you haven't given me a reason to," she said.

"You have to have reasons?" he asked, somewhat hurt.

"You won't even say trust me," she said.

"I never say anything I might regret," he said then and, opening the door, allowed her to precede him.

At first glance, the middle-aged man who approached them just outside the hotel seemed unshaven. He was dressed in a shabby tweed overcoat with a lint-covered beret pulled down so far his ears were forced out at an angle. Then they saw that he had the kind of beard which permanently shadowed his transparent skin. Squinting against the tendril of smoke that watered his eyes, he paused only long enough to ask "Vorovich?" around the saliva-drenched cigarette, and was halfway up the block before Vorovich had a chance to do more than nod.

Taking Ginny's arm, Vorovich kept a safe distance from the other, instinctively following the other as if he were tailing a suspect.

That was probably what threw him off. When he got that overly familiar tight feeling in the small of his back he reminded himself that he was the follower, not the one being followed. Though he paused at a shopwindow to look behind, he saw no one, in that sparsely pedestrianed block, who seemed out of place. Though the tight feeling persisted, he told himself his instincts were being confused by his reversal of roles.

They had walked almost twenty blocks in a zigzag pattern before the other suddenly ducked into an alley. When they arrived at the same spot he was nowhere in sight. As they hastened down the dank passageway, all the old buildings seemed "blind"; that is, the windows painted over and the doors nailed or padlocked shut.

Just as Vorovich was beginning to wonder whether they had been given the slip, the other startled them by appearing out of a recessed doorway. Quickly motioning them inside, their guide pointed to a steep stairway that led up through a murky gloom redolent of olive oil and fish, and a moment later they heard the click of a padlock being jammed shut behind them.

They climbed the creaking stairs to a kind of loft, an upper story whose windows were so grimed they could barely make out the harbor. They were apparently right on the water.

A light, so dim it wasn't much help, clicked on. A man who looked enough like the one who had led them here to be his brother stood under the swaying, bug-encrusted bulb. Without a word he turned and they followed him to a makeshift office, partitioned off by stacks of wooden cases. From the echoing sounds in the distance, they guessed they were in a warehouse.

The other had been working on ledgers spread out over a roll-top desk; now he withdrew a bottle of Lillet from a pigeon-hole, and Vorovich remembered that it was D'Anton's drink. Three glasses were found in the clutter, cleaned with a huge thumb, filled with the murky liquor.

"Health and wealth," the other said, lifting his glass, "and virility," he added, glancing at Ginny, then downed his drink at a gulp. Vorovich followed suit, and Ginny, not wanting to call any more attention to herself, did the same a moment later.

"You're behind schedule," he said then.

"Some complications," Vorovich said. "Not worth talking about."

"I disagree," the man said sharply. "I don't like it when complications arise. You might as well know I've never been too happy about being involved in this. Too risky. I'm a *pied noir*, a black foot, from Algérie, and the *flics* would like nothing better than to get something on me!"

"Then why *are* you involved?" Ginny wondered.

The Algerian looked at her more carefully. "I owe certain favors," he said at last. "But that doesn't mean I go into this with my eyes closed."

This man was not like the French perfumer, Vorovich thought, an ordinary businessman seizing an extraordinary opportunity to make a great deal of money, or the usual criminal, like the Turkish smuggler or the Englishman who transported dope—no, this *pied noir,* whose wary face and manner were that of all refugees Vorovich had known who have lived through revolution and terror, his fears could not be disposed of easily. It would not do to gloss over anything, he would smell any subterfuge in a minute.

"I don't like the setup," Vorovich said, deciding to attack it directly.

"For instance," the other said.

"The way they planned to get you the merchandise," Vorovich said. "Tour buses, for Chrissake."

"Is that what you had the falling-out with Carruthers about?" the other asked.

"Is that what he said it was about?" Vorovich countered.

The Algerian shrugged, not willing to give more than Vorovich. "It's not as stupid as it appears," he said. "Tours come to the waterfront all the time."

"To visit warehouses?" Vorovich asked.

The other stood up, walked to a painted window, forced it open. Outside they saw a low wharf, beside which a fishing boat was tied up. Crewmen in wool sweaters and waist-high, glistening rubber boots were raising a net bulging with a multitude of tiny, shimmery fish. The squirming net was lifted from boat to dock by a cable, then spilled into open vats which were wheeled away by workers in salt-grimed smocks.

Slamming the window shut again, the other led them out of the makeshift enclosure, and they walked what seemed a block to a railing at the far end of the loft, where the sounds they had heard earlier were magnified a hundredfold.

It was like looking down into a volcano or the site of some mad experiment: dozens of workers, mostly female, dressed like surgical nurses, with galoshes to keep the instep-high water out, were tending giant-sized steaming cookers. Fish streamed down watery troughs. Olive oil squirted out of greasy spouts into shiny sardine-filled tins, which were sealed by noisy machines and dropped onto a moving belt that dumped them into wooden cases, which were then nailed shut by men who stacked them in long rows.

A worker looked up and, at a sign from the Algerian, tossed a tin of sardines up. Grabbing it deftly in midair, the Algerian opened it.

161

"You own the cannery?" Ginny asked, awed.

"No such luck," the other said, offering her sardines. "I rent space from them, act as their shipping agent, that's all."

"None for you?" the Algerian asked, as Vorovich shook his head. He was too excited to eat. He had suddenly seen how it all could work—how he might use the system that had been set up but in such a way that only he, finally, would be the one who knew what or where all the elements were.

"Why don't you take that on back to the office, Ginny?" Vorovich said. He held her glare, and finally, reluctantly, she did as he asked.

The other watched with some interest. But he said nothing.

"How long were you going to keep the perfumed bath powders stored before shipping them?" Vorovich asked, when he was sure Ginny was out of hearing.

The other shrugged. "It would be brought in little by little," he said. "Weeks, even months."

"I'm changing that," Vorovich said. "I'm going to have it sent here by truck—just like a normal, everyday shipment, so that no one will have to wonder how it is that tour buses stop here.

"It'll still come in as perfumed bath powders. But it'll go out as something else."

"And how will this . . . transformation . . . be accomplished?" the Algerian asked.

"Easy," Vorovich said. He pointed to the canning operation below.

"You don't think we can get away with that?" the other said, after a long moment. But his eyes glittered.

"Why not?" Vorovich said. "Do they work twenty-four hours?"

"Only twelve," the other admitted. "Six till six."

"Well, then?" Vorovich said. "It shouldn't be too difficult to run that equipment ourselves. Three of us could probably pack all the merchandise in one night."

"Three of us?" the Algerian wondered, after a pause. "You are including the girl?"

"No," Vorovich said. "Someone else."

The other studied Vorovich appraisingly. "And this way only three of us know just where the merchandise is?"

"The fewer who know," Vorovich said, "the less chance of having the shipment knocked off."

"Then why even have three?" the Algerian asked.

"Because the people on the other end will insist on it," Vorovich said. If they didn't, Vorovich thought, he would insist on it himself. Charles was essential to the plan that was beginning to form in his mind.

"They don't trust you, then," the Algerian said.

"They don't have to," Vorovich said.

The two of them walked back to find Ginny walking that enclosure as if caged.

"You mustn't take it to heart, mademoiselle," the Algerian said. "Lovers demand too much from the other person. No offense. But never again will I risk my freedom over love, mine or anyone else's." He held up his hand, showing them a missing ring finger. "This is to remind me."

"Of what?" Ginny asked, interested now.

"I took a native woman as wife," the Algerian said, pouring them all another drink. "She bore me twin sons, never complained a day until the troubles came—then I woke one morning to find her, the boys, and my gold wedding band gone."

"But how did you lose your finger?" Ginny asked.

"I cut it off," the Algerian said. "Now," he added to Vorovich, "shall we discuss shipping dates for your bath powders?"

The telephone rang. It was a shrill sound, and so totally unexpected the two men flinched—both had gotten unexpected calls before.

"*Oui?*" the Algerian said, almost reluctantly. Then he covered the receiver so tightly Vorovich thought it might break. "Why is someone following you?" he demanded in a whisper so harsh it prickled the spine.

Vorovich made a puzzled, unknowing gesture. But he remembered that earlier feeling.

The Algerian went over to the painted window, scraped a clear place half the size of a dime, put his eye to it. After a moment, he motioned for Vorovich to come look.

There, on the corner where the alley met the waterfront street, dressed in a fisherman's black turtleneck and beret, but somehow too *neat*, clean-shaven, standing out among the scruffy waterfront types like a word misused in a foreign language, was Preble. Vorovich began inwardly cursing, steadily and long.

"You know him?" the other demanded.

"I don't think so," Vorovich said, thinking quickly, hoping Preble had taken his advice about carrying other identification, or wouldn't give it away that he even knew Vorovich, if it came to that, because if this wary Algerian discovered that Vorovich had been so stupid as to have known someone was following him and not done something about it when he had the chance—

"You," the Algerian said, motioning to Ginny. She put her eye to the window.

Vorovich prayed that *she* wouldn't give it away. Then remembering that he had no faith, he spoke before she could.

"Carruthers!" Vorovich said, as if he'd had an intuitive flash. "The sonofabitch! He's having me followed to make sure he knows where all the pieces fit. . . ."

Ginny was looking at him now, awed by his performance, stunned, and fearful because she had recognized Preble, too.

"Why would he bother?" the Algerian asked, watching him closely. "He already knew you were coming here."

"Who then?" Vorovich said, frowning as if puzzled. "Maybe D'Anton got nervous about my breaking the setup, and sent someone to keep track . . . ?" He put his eye back to the window as if hoping to find the answer there.

"I would hope Monsieur D'Anton would send someone a bit more skilled," the Algerian said.

"Well, no harm done," Vorovich said. "When we go out we'll go right back by him, and I'll make sure we lose him before we leave Marseilles—"

"Not good enough," the Algerian said.

Vorovich began to sweat at his armpits and crotch, his skin alternately hot and cold. He could sense what was coming.

"Unless, of course, you want to make other arrangements," the Algerian said. "I couldn't take part in what you propose, knowing that someone outside knew about my warehouse."

Vorovich's mind raced with alternatives. It would be difficult, if not impossible, to convince D'Anton they would be better off without this Algerian. And wasn't it likely the Algerian wasn't intending to let Preble get off in any case, but had decided to test him?

There was only one decision possible, Vorovich thought, as the Algerian waited for his answer. Why did he hesitate? He had practically begged Cabot to let him work alone. And Preble had ignored his plain warning to stay clear. No one listened. Was that his fault? Could he be blamed for the stupidity of others?

"Well?" the Algerian asked.

"We'd better do something about him," Vorovich said at last.

The other, with a satisfied grimace, picked up the phone and muttered into the receiver.

"Can someone take her back to the hotel?" Vorovich asked, unable to meet Ginny's stricken gaze.

The Algerian hesitated, but only a moment, and then he pressed a button on his desk. A thin-lipped young man appeared. "Escort mademoiselle back," the Algerian said. "Keep her company until we call," he added, and the young man took her away.

Vorovich went to the window. He watched Preble straighten in his alcove as Ginny came out, and waited, short-breathed, as the two stared at each other, but if she were trying to convey a warning, he either missed or ignored it. And then it was too late, for two men, one the man who had brought them here, came up on either side of Preble, and urged him into the warehouse.

Vorovich wasn't clear just how he knew Preble was operating under an inadequate cover. Maybe from the shamefaced way he touched his clean-shaven upper lip, nicked by a razor, or the manner in which he kind of sidled into the room, as if aware of just how unforgivably stupid it was to have been caught.

What could Vorovich do to help him now? Nothing. Either Preble would crack or make an obvious mistake, such as having something on him to give him away.

He couldn't take that chance. Before it might be too late to save Ginny, to save himself, and yes, he thought harshly, to be perfectly honest all down the line, to save all the long and arduous work that had brought him this far, he jumped in as they were searching Preble.

"He's a narcotics agent!" Vorovich said, to salvage what he could, and damn the consequences. "I didn't recognize

165

him in those clothes, and without a mustache—"

A Swiss passport was handed to the Algerian, along with a wallet, which yielded up to the Algerian's meticulous search a flimsy receipt: the fare paid on the Turkish express.

"Why are you hassling me?" Vorovich demanded, glaring at Preble, furious that he had been right, but minimally grateful too, because he couldn't be blamed for what happened now, could he? "I can't even take a two-bit tour without you bastards sticking your noses in—if I had the money, don't you think I'd be traveling first class instead of riding a lousy bus?"

"Just take it easy," the Algerian said, putting a hand on Vorovich's shoulder and pulling him away from where he had been yelling into Preble's embarrassed face.

"Why are you following him?" the Algerian asked.

"What's it to you?" Preble wondered.

The Algerian took his thumb and pressed it into Preble's Adam's apple until his eyes began to swell. "You're not a Swiss, either, are you?" the Algerian asked.

Preble took it for longer than Vorovich would have believed possible. "Even if he wanted to talk he couldn't," Vorovich pointed out.

The Algerian let go. Preble tried to clear his throat, tried again.

"He's a renegade," Preble said, coughing hoarsely. "He took dope from a runner he killed and sold it and we can't let him get away with that."

"A killer?" the Algerian said, looking curiously at Vorovich. Why was he pretending surprise? Vorovich wondered. D'Anton had given him a proper introduction, surely. Vorovich shrugged and went to pour himself another drink.

"For that you follow him all the way to Europe?" the Algerian asked, returning to Preble, who was still trying to clear his bruised throat.

"I insulted the new chief of the agency," Vorovich said. The Algerian wheeled and made a single ominous gesture to keep silent.

"I was already *in* Europe," Preble said, as if unaware of how much trouble he was in. "But we did get high priority about keeping tabs on you, so I figured it must have been something like that. The new chief's vindictive, all right, said we shouldn't stop at anything to get the goods on you."

"You couldn't have followed him all by yourself," the Algerian said. "Not with all the changes he made . . ."

"The Swiss fellows picked up the switch he made at the French border," Preble said. "That's what gave me the idea to switch myself. But I haven't had any help since then," he added almost proudly.

"Maybe you should have had some," Vorovich said sourly.

Preble's smile faded. Then Vorovich took the Algerian aside for a conference.

"He's dumb," Vorovich began. "His own people don't even know where he is. But if you want to play it absolutely safe, hold him until the whole thing's done—maybe ship him someplace on one of your freighters, Hong Kong or Taiwan, say. . . ."

"He'll know I was involved," the Algerian said.

"It'll be too late for anyone to prove anything," Vorovich said.

"My background is not immaculate," the Algerian said. "And I have many political enemies who would need nothing more than an accusation of something criminal to put me away."

"You mean you'd throw the whole thing up over a ridiculous situation like this?" Vorovich demanded. "Anyone can see he's green."

"Quite so," the Algerian said. "He hadn't even reported his location."

"How do you know?" Vorovich asked, heart sinking with the sense of what was coming.

"When my brother picked you up at the hotel," the Algerian said, "we had someone following behind, as a precaution. He did not even report the hotel you checked into."

"What are you getting at?" Vorovich asked, though he knew, as the Algerian waited expectantly.

The Algerian walked back to Preble. "If you were to drop out of sight," he said to the young man, "what procedure would your colleagues follow?"

Preble swallowed but managed a smile. "They'd start back-tracking me from my last location," he said.

"Which was where?" the Algerian asked.

Preble hesitated. For God's sake lie! Vorovich thought, trying desperately to convey the silent admonition. "The border crossing from Italy to France," Preble said, as if confessing a wrongdoing.

Vorovich stared unbelievingly at that clean-shaven, idealistic, stupidly naïve, impossibly romantic young man. How could he so casually close out the last argument for keeping himself alive? He was committing suicide, didn't he know that? Was it possible he was doing it for him, wanting to make sure Vorovich understood that *he* knew what needed to be done, and no hard feelings? It had been his goof, no one else's; it was one of the understood risks going in, and he wasn't about to penalize Vorovich, whatever he was up to, for his own stupid mistake.

For a wild moment, Vorovich considered making a fight of it. Then the moment passed. Preble, as if sensing his surge of adrenalin, had clearly signaled him no. Maybe he had something else in mind, Vorovich thought. Maybe somewhere along the way he would seize the opportunity to make a run for it. And maybe, he thought, hoping against hope, the Algerian was only testing him, wanting to see if Vorovich had the balls to go through with it, was the right man to run the operation he'd proposed.

"Okay," Vorovich said to the unspoken question. "What's the best way to handle it?"

At a sign from the Algerian, his brother and he moved in on either side of Preble and urged him to his feet. Walking close beside him then, like inseparable companions, the three of them, with Vorovich following, went down a narrow stairway into the steamy fish cannery, slogged through the wet fish-littered aisles, and came out onto the wharf, where a small boat was tied up.

The four of them were a snug fit in the small cockpit. The Algerian's brother took the wheel. Once past the breakwater into open sea, the Algerian took some plastic twine and bound Preble's feet at the ankles, his wrists behind him.

"It's not very good twine," the Algerian said. "After a few hours in the salt water, it will dissolve."

Preble's eyebrows, which Vorovich had not noticed were thin as a girl's, rose as if he appreciated the cleverness: his body would be found without mark or bruise or other sign of foul play.

Some distance out, where the water was the blue of a coldness that indicated deeps, the boat made a circular sweep, bouncing through its own wake, so they might look to make certain they were unobserved.

The Algerian motioned to Vorovich, who stood frozen.

"I thought you had killed people before," the Algerian said.

"Not in cold blood," Vorovich said, wiping salt spray from his face.

"What difference does the temperature of the blood make?" the Algerian asked.

Something was going on with Preble. What was he doing? He was leaning back, slow, oh so slowly, and Vorovich realized, with a growing horror, that Preble was trying to make it easy for him! He couldn't seem to move. And then, at the very last moment, before it would become clear to the others that Preble was throwing himself into the water, Vorovich put his hand on Preble's narrow chest, and with an almost affectionate gesture pushed him overboard.

Preble went under almost immediately. A wave lifted him briefly, long enough for Vorovich to see, or think he saw, a sweetly sad proud little smile, and then he was gone.

The Algerian's brother spun the wheel hard over and they made another slow circular sweep, and then, the hull slapping the swells, they headed straight back into the distant harbor.

"That wasn't so difficult, now, was it?" the Algerian asked, expansive again now that this questionable man of D'Anton's had, in the ultimate sense, proved himself.

"Difficult enough," Vorovich said.

But he was lying, he thought. It had seemed, in fact, all too easy.

She did not ask him any questions when he got back to the hotel. And he did not volunteer information. It was as if both were conspiring to forget everything that had happened back at the warehouse, and though he knew it was inevitable for it to come out, he almost talked himself into believing it never would, that the incident which had traumatized him was buried so deep in his subconscious he would be able to live with it, however uneasily, the only memory possibly at night, in dreams when, like poison gas in tar pits, it might, nightmarishly, bubble to the surface.

"Let's take a walk," he said, and she nodded.

Both were abnormally quiet, especially she, usually so vivacious and gay, now with dark hollows under her pale, stunned eyes, like some wild creature unable to articulate its pain. They walked the waterfront at random, hand in hand like lost children, out to the splintering ends of piers, gazing down at the murky water where oil patches produced broken rainbows. She shrank in disgust from this garbage-strewn sea. He dreamed of distant shores.

While she concentrated on the here and now, so that none of the questions which tumbled wildly through her mind would come into focus, he, his memory anesthetized by shock, lusted after the boats in the marina, particularly those ocean-worthy twin-masted schooners, picturing those sails spreading like wings to fly them to sun-drenched beaches, away from these gloomy harbors where rusting iron-hulled freighters wallowed in their own waste. She saw his despair, and could not bring herself to ask, for fear she would have to share it.

They stopped at a bistro not much bigger than a kiosk, where he ordered two glasses of the unlabeled wine, a red so deep it looked like blood. The taste was gamy too, fortified, he thought. Which probably explained why this place was thronged with blue-coveralled stevedores, each with a cigarette wetly dangling from mouth corner, squinting against the smoke which sandpapered their voices, ignoring the silent pair standing so stiffly in their midst.

"Another," Vorovich said, to the aproned *propriétaire*. But Ginny, though her glass was empty, covered it with her palm. "*Encore un,*" Vorovich said, knocking off another, whereupon his glass was filled again to the very brim.

"You know how to order a drink in every language, I bet," Ginny said then.

"Just about," he said, downing the third glass without spilling a drop.

"I've been reading up on problem drinkers," she said.

"Honey," he said, "when it gets to be a problem you'll be the first to know."

They might have quarreled then, except that neither of them was quite ready for it. They left the bistro and walked again. The waterfront was dark and gloomy, except for a few cafés whose windows threw patches of yellow out on the quay.

"Hungry?" he asked.

She had to think about it, but then, surprised and somewhat ashamed, nodded yes. He took her into the nearest café, thinking how difficult it was to control the body's appetites, no matter how stunned the mind.

Once they sat down to it, after the first tentative picks at the house paté, and a swallow of the local apéritif, the smells in that fisherman's place of sawdusted floors and bleached wooden walls brought their appetites on with a rush. The bouillabaisse, gusting steam when the lid to the red-hot ceramic pot was lifted, had a pungency that cleared their sinuses, and the stinging tastes of the saffron broth removed the last barrier to their hunger.

It seemed they ate for hours. They pried the last morsels out of the claws of the spiny fish long after their stomachs were filled, unwilling to leave this warm place of salt smells. He had a cognac with his café filtre, and then another, waiting for the muddy stuff to drip through; she had two caramel custards, but if that sweet egg pleased her she gave no sign.

Eventually, and reluctantly, they went back to the hotel. He became unaccountably nervous then, and checked for nonexistent messages, and took the stairs instead of the caged elevator up to their room, checking the hair he had pasted to the jamb (unbroken). He even examined the ledges outside the windows, salt-encrusted from the misting night, and was finally able to convince himself no one was following them, without allowing himself to think why not.

They were too emotionally exhausted to sleep. And in that dark high-ceilinged room, listening to the night harbor sounds (a lonesome buoy bell, an anguished foghorn) it was inevitable that they should touch, reach for each other in silence, make love with a gasping intensity that bordered on desperation.

In the morning they woke as far apart as they could get in that narrow bed, as if it were necessary to forget their lovemaking along with everything else. In a hurry to get to the airport, where they would pick up a connecting flight to Paris/San Francisco, they had coffee in their room.

He grabbed a morning paper on the way out and quickly thumbed through it on the short drive, but found nothing that need disturb him.

But at Orly the papers had it. She saw it first. Walking by his side through the noisy terminal she suddenly stopped, and looking where she looked he saw a front-page picture of a body that had been washed up on the Marseilles waterfront. Name of victim unknown, the story said.

The body had been wedged into the breakwater rocks by the incoming tide where two boys, out for dawn fishing, discovered it, attracted by the shrieks of the scavenger gulls. The photographers had been pleased to get pictures of such dramatic contrast: the bulging-eyed victim and those modestly grinning kids.

"Why did you bring it?" Ginny demanded, after they were airborne, and he pored over the story, the unfamiliar French making it difficult to puzzle out what the police said they knew and what they did not. He felt really lousy about the fact that he was more worried about what effect this might have on his plans than he was about the dead man. But he had to be practical. It would be even lousier to have had Preble make that incredibly noble, impossibly romantic suicidal gesture and have it all wash down the tubes because he, Vorovich, mooned too much over his own feelings.

Worrying over what was done couldn't change anything. Could it? Ignoring Ginny, Vorovich motioned the chic little French stewardess over and ordered an Irish and water.

"Look," Ginny said, "I'm sorry." She was trying hard to sheath that razor edge in her voice. "I know you did your best to save him."

"But I didn't," he said.

It was as if she didn't want to hear what he was saying. "You mustn't blame yourself," she said. "It's not your fault."

"Don't you understand?" he said, so quietly she could barely hear. "It was me who killed him!"

She sat stiffly for the longest time, trying to absorb what he had told her.

"I don't believe you," she said at last. He shrugged. "There's something you're leaving out," she said. He shook his head. "You act like you're proud of it!" she cried in a half-whisper. "Don't do that to me! If I believed you'd really done that I'd turn against you."

He waved his empty glass at the stewardess. When she brought him another Irish, Ginny rummaged in the Italian straw handbag he had bought her in Genoa and pulled out a pack of Gauloise. He should have reacted sooner. He knew she didn't smoke. And yet she pulled a cigarette out like a chainer, a flip of the pack that put a flatly thin cylinder between her lips, and she had it lit and he was smelling the sweet perfume before he realized what she was smoking.

It was such a stupid thing to do.

What if someone reported them to the captain? They might be arrested for possession and flagrant use, and that would be the end of it.

Why then did he reach across and take the burning joint out of her hand and take two enormous tokes?

The stew came by asking about dinner; he cupped the stick in his palm; yes, Ginny agreed, they would like wine with dinner, red *and* white because they were so blue—and when both of them laughed, staccato coughs, the stew looked at them closely, sniffed, rolled her eyes, and fled.

Pot made you self-sufficient, he thought, and he hit what was left of the joint, and she took a paper match and split the end and inserted the roach and took what was left in a huge inhale, the coal glowing like her eyes.

"Please," the stew said, bringing them a carafe each of red and white, "you must be, how it is you say, *discret*?" She took the roach when Ginny offered it to her away up the aisle, but Vorovich, sitting on the inside, saw that she flushed it down their little sink. A waste, he thought sadly, and wondered why he should feel so much grief over two tokes of pot.

Below them was an evening storm. After the dishes had been cleared, he turned off the overhead lights, and she pressed her face to the window, awed by those columnar thunderheads, like some kind of monuments built to reach gods, ephemeral tributes, ditto for the gods, and as the lightning flashed below them, illuminating the ominous shapes, his mind seemed to experience residual flashes, and he looked inside himself, trying to find the meaning within his own dark thoughts, and failing.

They slept the rest of the way. And though her head slipped off the pillow the stewardess had so thoughtfully provided, and he cradled her in his arms, he did not make the mistake of assuming that their physical closeness meant that their personal storm, like the one they had watched, had been passed over.

The customs inspection was too thorough. He had declared his new clothes and the bottle of Lillet, but they were making much of the fact that he had purchased so little abroad. Then the way they reacted to his passport, calling over of the supervisory officer, who went into an inner office—undoubtedly to make a phone call—made him apprehensive. Cabot again, maybe, angry and anxious for a report on how his missing agent had been killed.

Ginny, under her own letter sign, seemed to be having similar difficulty. He supposed it was how she was dressed. Before the plane had landed, an hour out, she had changed clothes, surprising him in the kind of dress that could only be characterized as hip chic: a gauzy purple micro-mini as revealing as an undergarment, full breasts loose and provocative, a golden chain necklace and a chain belt, low on her swelling hips, a chain bracelet with a scarf entwined on her bare upper arm, and no wonder the customs men wanted a closer look.

He watched her being questioned and then led toward the inner office where the supervisory officer had gone. She looked back only once, kissing her fingertips and holding them toward him like a benediction.

When the S.O. finally returned, it was to tell him he was cleared. "Sorry for the inconvenience," he said, but barely touched his cap brim.

"Mistaken identity?" Vorovich asked, slamming his suitcase back together. He said it angrily; he was beginning to sympathize with those on the run, given the hostility with which they were continually confronted.

"We had a tip," the S.O. said, "turned out to be wrong." He was clearly disappointed.

"A tip on the girl, too?" Vorovich asked.

The S.O. looked at him narrowly. "You a friend?"

"We met on the plane," Vorovich said.

"She had something she forgot to declare," the S.O. said.

"If she needs a lawyer I'll get her one," Vorovich said, his mind racing with possibilities.

"No need for that," the S.O. said. "She can either pay the duty or abandon the goods."

"What goods?" Vorovich asked, but he remembered something he should have never forgotten.

"Nothing much," the S.O. said. "And besides, it's not really any of your business, is it?"

"I'll just say good-by," Vorovich said, as casually as he could, and started toward the inner office.

"Too late for that," the S.O. said. "She used the exit on the other side. Better luck next time," he added, with a suggestive smile, as Vorovich pulled up.

"The same to you," Vorovich managed.

Outside, a World-Wide Travel limo was waiting. Gaston was the driver, complete with cap and suit. Alphonse, dressed like a businessman, was on the curb.

"Has the girl come out yet?" Vorovich demanded, not wasting time on preliminary greetings.

"What girl?" Gaston wanted to know.

"Weren't you supposed to pick up a girl?" Vorovich asked.

"Nobody said nothing about no girl," Gaston said, as he got out to take his bag.

"Shut up, Gaston," Alphonse said. "Can't you see he's stacking us up again?"

"Christ, you're quick," Vorovich said. "You're smarter than I gave you credit for."

"Listen," Alphonse snarled. "We're very good at what we do. Someday we'll prove it to you."

"I can hardly wait," Vorovich said, getting in and locking the door shut before Alphonse could get in with him.

"Right now the boss needs you," Alphonse said, sitting up front, shaking with rage, "someday he won't."

"Don't count on it, fish breath," Vorovich said.

"Why do you go out of your way to make enemies?" Gaston asked, almost plaintively, glancing at him in the rearview mirror after he forced the big car into traffic.

"I don't go out of my way," Vorovich said. "It comes easy for me."

"Wait," Alphonse said. "Just you wait."

As they came off the Bayshore Freeway into downtown San Francisco, Alphonse wheeled the car right instead of left.

"Aren't you going the wrong way?" Vorovich asked politely, though his skin went cold. He was not underestimating these two, and it was always possible that he had miscalculated the extent of his usefulness.

"No," Gaston said. "The boss wants—"

"Shut down!" Alphonse said, and the other went back to his driving.

Halfway up Nob Hill they turned into a small circular drive that led under the canopy of an apartment hotel so posh there was only a number for identification.

Inside, in a corner of the marble-tiled lobby, a discreetly lettered sign indicated the main office of World-Wide Travel, Inc. While Gaston waited with Vorovich, Alphonse went over to the desk and had a murmured word with a silver-haired clerk. He came back and led them into an elevator operated by a heavy-set, swarthy youth whose uniform seemed too small.

"Don't we need a key?" Vorovich asked.

"Take it up," Alphonse said. The operator looked amused, took them past what seemed the top floor—fourteen—to an unmarked floor above. The doors opened to reveal a wrought-iron grille. Gaston pressed a buzzer.

D'Anton appeared, elegantly dressed. He produced a key on a fob chain and unlocked the grille. Vorovich stepped out into an Empire-styled foyer, entirely mirrored with gold-mottled glass.

"Take his bag," D'Anton said to Alphonse. "Is he clean?" D'Anton asked Gaston, who for answer reached out with the toe of his shoe and lifted Vorovich's pants leg, revealing the ankle gun. "Hand it to me," D'Anton said impatiently.

"I know some city jails could use this kind of security," Vorovich said. No one seemed to have heard him except the elevator operator, whose smile broadened.

"When I ring for you," D'Anton said to the operator, "bring your cage up empty, nonstop."

"Sure thing," the operator said, and waggled his fat fingers good-by at Vorovich.

At a motion from D'Anton, Gaston settled himself uncomfortably on a red velvet courtesan's couch, bulky figure incongruous on that fragile settee, while Alphonse, too nervous to sit, took a position against the velvet-flocked wall. Then D'Anton took Vorovich inside.

It was the penthouse suite, decorated in French Empire.

"It's a sheer drop," D'Anton said.

"What happens in case of fire?" Vorovich wondered.

"The building is fireproof," D'Anton advised.

"Famous last words," Vorovich said.

"I hope they're not yours," D'Anton said.

"Why should they be?" Vorovich said, professing bewilderment.

"You tell me," D'Anton said, eyes narrowing. "I create an organization especially to handle a one-time big push, send you over to learn it, to study how to make use of it, and you leave it in a shambles!"

"It only looks that way," Vorovich said.

"Don't get smart with me," D'Anton said. "I took you on only because you convinced me you could be valuable. Now you've almost convinced me otherwise. I tell you straight—you are hanging by a thread!"

Vorovich understood that the threat was real. But he wasn't going to pull this out by becoming defensive. "I always was," he said. "You think I didn't know that? Did you think I was going to waltz back in here and hand you a plan that you could use without me?"

D'Anton didn't lose any of his anger. But he calmed down enough to listen. "Go on," he said.

"My first concern," Vorovich said, "is self-preservation. But all that aside, the system you set up had too many flaws. I had no choice but to improve it."

"How?" D'Anton said.

"In a minute," Vorovich said. He went over to a lamp, took off the shade, and examined the bulb and socket. He pushed a silk-covered couch away from the wall, lifted rugs, stood on a chair to scrutinize a chandelier, looked in back of dark paintings, and paid particular attention to telephone wires, wall plugs, and light switches.

"Who would bug this place?" D'Anton demanded.

"One of your associates, maybe," Vorovich said. "You hold meetings here, don't you?"

"Not the kind you mean," D'Anton said.

"Well, someone could have bribed a cleaning woman or a maintenance man or even laid enough legal tender on your two thugs to plant a listening device," Vorovich persisted.

"Someone?" D'Anton asked.

"Charles, maybe," Vorovich said. He scattered flower arrangements, lifted table ornaments, pulled books off shelves; then, finally, ran his fingers along the moldings and, tsk-ing gently, showed D'Anton the smudged tips.

"Nothing except dust," Vorovich said. "They deserve to lose."

"Someone is going to lose?" D'Anton asked.

"Someone always loses," Vorovich said.

"Better hope it isn't you," D'Anton said. "Whenever you're ready."

"You'll keep an open mind?" Vorovich asked.

"Do the best you can with the mind I've got," D'Anton said.

Vorovich smiled, though he shivered inside at the other's coldness, and turned to go into the bedroom.

"I don't want you leaving this room," D'Anton said.

"I brought a present back for you," Vorovich said. "I thought if I gave it to you now it would soften you up."

"Gaston," D'Anton called, and though his voice did not seem to have been raised past its conversational tone, an instant later the fat bodyguard appeared. "He'll get it," D'Anton said.

"It's a package wrapped in blue paper," Vorovich said. "You'll find it in my suitcase, unless you're color-blind. Please don't crush it, it's fragile," he called after the other.

Gaston, face flushed, glaring at Vorovich but bearing the package carefully, came back and handed it to D'Anton.

"Very thoughtful," D'Anton said, unwrapping the bottle of Lillet. He held up two fingers to Gaston, who went to the sideboard and brought back glasses, and was again dismissed to the outer anteroom.

"I formed a taste for it myself," Vorovich said, holding the glass up in a small toast.

D'Anton did not acknowledge it. "Why are you wasting time?" he asked.

"It's always worrisome to wonder whether you can convince someone else that you're right," Vorovich said. "I had that problem at the D.E.A., and I guess I'm anticipating that I may have that problem now."

"You do have that problem now," D'Anton said.

"All right," Vorovich said. "The fact is, I'm going to have to tell you things you're not going to like to hear. It's true that I've manipulated your organization in order to protect myself—but it's also true that as good as the individual elements are, the way you had it set up you were inviting disaster. The reason the government always has problems stopping the inflow of dope is that none of the elements in the chain knows anything about any of the others. The growers never meet the crop-buyers, who know nothing about who manufactures it, who don't know the shippers, who have no idea who the importers are—and so on down the line.

"But here you are," he went on, "creating your own mini-bureaucracy, every link in the chain so tied to every other that all the government has to do is find one link and they roll up the whole chain. Not very smart, would you say?"

D'Anton sipped at his drink, his only reaction a slight tightening at the corners of his mouth. "The chain would still be intact if you hadn't allowed yourself to be followed," he said.

"Allowed myself?" Vorovich wondered.

"Why didn't you kill the man the first time you caught him, in Turkey?" D'Anton asked.

The question was not polite.

"They'd have known it was me who killed him," Vorovich said at last. "And they'd have moved mountains to get me for that. Besides, I had no idea he'd ever catch up. It was a fluke."

"No fluke," D'Anton said. "They clearly have a full-scale alert out on you. If you hadn't killed him the entire operation would have had to be wiped. As it is, I'm not sure we won't have to build the whole structure all over again, from scratch. And if we do, I don't see how we have any further need for your services."

"Without me, you haven't a prayer," Vorovich said. "The D.E.A. already knows something big is going on—"

"Thanks to you," D'Anton interrupted.

"—and even though I've done you the favor of breaking your organization into separate little boxes so that those in one box don't know what's going on in any of the others," Vorovich went on, "a certain amount of information is bound to leak. More than ninety per cent of the busts made are because of informers. They're going to keep depending on what brings them results. Look at the way they're set up," Vorovich said, unfolding the little napkin that Gaston had brought with the glasses, and taking the little gold pencil D'Anton had clipped to his shirt pocket he began sketching in the D.E.A.'s organizational chart. "*Two* intelligence departments, strategic and tactical, in the Enforcement Division, as well as an over-all intelligence officer.

"Intelligence," Vorovich continued. "A bureaucratic word for compilers of information."

"I'm aware of bureaucratic terminology," D'Anton said.

"No matter how careful you are," Vorovich said, "even if you start over, the Turks are going to know that certain massive purchases have been made, the French are going to wonder how come the clandestine labs are not getting any stuff, and the folks who depend on the usual sources are going to complain about the scarcity of product—there will be plenty of rumors, none significant in themselves, but when they're correlated a kind of pattern will emerge, and the D.E.A.'s going to put the kind of pressure on that will make it almost impossible to get your shipment through."

"Almost?" D'Anton said.

"There's been a marvelous opportunity created here for us," Vorovich said.

"Has there?" D'Anton said. But he was interested. Finally.

"We'll use the D.E.A.'s own system against them," Vorovich said. "We'll see to it that not only do they get information, but that they know how to correlate it. We let them know how and where. We keep them informed every step of the way. Then we pull the plug. At the very last minute we do a disappearing act with the merchandise."

"How?" D'Anton asked, after a moment.

"By giving them some of what they're looking for," Vorovich said. "We let them turn up just enough of the merchandise to make them believe they've got hold of the real thing. While they're involved in all that, we're getting the bulk of the stuff through, free and clear."

"A diversionary tactic?" D'Anton said.

"Exactly," Vorovich said.

"And how do we manage that?" D'Anton wondered.

"We give them a fall guy," Vorovich said.

In the silence, Vorovich could hear the hum of the air conditioning—and an occasional cough and mutter from the two men in the foyer. Finally, D'Anton stirred, reached for the bottle, contemplated the label, filled his own glass, then Vorovich's. He sipped the Lillet thoughtfully, as if all he had on his mind was the quality of the drink. Vorovich knew better. D'Anton was conducting an interior dialogue, examining what Vorovich had told him, looking for the catch, not really pleased that Vorovich had turned it around, still angered by the manner in which Vorovich had fragmented his organization, having already almost decided that Vorovich would have to go. When it came to business, he had learned long ago to submerge his own feelings; revenge could wait, patience was the ultimate virtue.

"It would depend," D'Anton said at last, "on what I think the chances are for success."

"They're only as good as the trust you're willing to place in me," Vorovich said.

"I'm listening," D'Anton said.

"Whoever alerts the D.E.A. to the shipment coming in," Vorovich said, being very careful now, knowing how he explained it meant the difference between living and not, "has to be important enough to be believed. We can't leak it through some street pigeon. By the time it rises up through the hierarchy and has been hashed over by Enforcement, and studied by Tactical Intelligence, and argued about by the Strategic folks, it's bent all out of shape and doesn't look like anything the chief of intelligence would believe, let alone present to the director. It's the director has to bite the bait. Otherwise there's no way we can outflank them."

"You have someone in mind?" D'Anton asked.

"Me," Vorovich said.

D'Anton sat remarkably still. No eye blink or sound of breath disturbed the coldness of his stare. "And why should they believe you?" D'Anton wondered at long last.

Vorovich immediately knew this was the most important question he'd ever been asked. There was no room here for almosts and maybes. It had to be perfect.

"They think I've been working for them all along," Vorovich said.

D'Anton's face became incredibly dark. The veins on that flat forehead suddenly stood out, and Vorovich could guess at what kind of emotional pressure produced that rush of blood.

"But you killed one of their agents," D'Anton said hoarsely.

"That's right," Vorovich said.

"It was all a setup?" D'Anton asked. "Killing that boy, taking the contraband, selling it back to us—?"

"They think so," Vorovich said.

D'Anton took in a deep breath, and his eyeglasses actually began to fog. He was considering the possibility that he either had been or was being made a fool of, and no one living got away with that.

"They don't know anything about you," Vorovich said, as calmly as possible in the face of so murderous a rage. "I told them the only way I'd work was to go so deep undercover that no one would hear from me until the time came for the bust."

Apparently D'Anton had heard that, though the blood had unquestionably roared in his ears. He took off his glasses and began slowly wiping them dry.

"You walk a very thin line," he said.

"The stakes are worth it," Vorovich said.

"They'll know you set them up," D'Anton said.

"Not till they find out the pipeline's been filled," Vorovich said. "Too late to prove anything."

"They'll know you came into a lot of money," D'Anton said.

"I'll be spending it in foreign parts," Vorovich said.

D'Anton put his glasses back on, then scrutinized Vorovich as if testing the clarity of his vision. "You have a scenario worked out?" he asked then. Vorovich nodded. D'Anton turned slightly toward the foyer. "Alphonse," he called.

That gaunt man appeared. "I've changed my mind," D'Anton said, to the other's obvious disappointment. "I'll be eating here after all. Have them send enough for two."

Dinner was veal and peppers, salad with marinated artichoke hearts, crisped Arab bread, and two bottles of Bardolino. D'Anton did not permit Vorovich to talk until the waiter, supervised by Gaston, had served the café filtre and was dismissed.

"Now," D'Anton said, making sure his fingers were clean before twisting the lemon rind into his cup.

"Right up until the last moment," Vorovich said, "we let everyone think the stuff's going to be shipped as bath crystals."

"It's not?" D'Anton said, unprepared for this further surprise.

"Too many people know about that," Vorovich said.

"How then?" D'Anton asked.

"Sardines," Vorovich said. "We set up a dummy account, with bills of lading and all the rest of it. But when the stuff is a day, maybe two, out of San Francisco, you'll have one of your boats peel off from your fishing fleet and pick the stuff up. We'll leave just enough on the freighter to make it look good, both to the fall guy who takes delivery on the docks, and to the Feds, who will knock him off."

"And who might this fall guy be?" D'Anton asked softly.

Vorovich paused, just long enough to make his effect. "Charles, of course," he said.

D'Anton pulled out a handkerchief and blew his nose softly into the starched white linen. When he put it back, it looked to Vorovich as though the cloth were still immaculate.

"What you do is tell him it's a way to get rid of me," Vorovich said. "You send him to Europe to oversee the canning, over my strenuous objections, which will reassure him about where your loyalties are. Then you work out a separate plan where *he* is supposed to hijack the merchandise as soon as it's docked— which will leave me, he'll think, out in the cold, waiting down the line somewhere for the merchandise to be brought in—and you can tell him that as far as you're concerned, I can wait forever."

"What makes you think I don't feel that?" D'Anton asked.

"I know that you do," Vorovich said. "That's precisely the point. It'll give what you say validity."

"Yes, I can see that," D'Anton said. Now it was he who paused, searching. Then: "But what's to keep Charles from trying to implicate me?"

"The Feds would never publically admit they'd been tricked," Vorovich said. "What they'll do is inflate the amount they knock off, so Charles will think they got the whole shot. No," he said, "the only one he'll blame is me."

"Okay," D'Anton said, at last. But he had made him wait for it. "I'll bring Charles over in the morning."

When Charles got the summons to meet D'Anton prior to the breakfast meeting with Vorovich, he was surprised. Ever since he'd been forced to take a back seat to the former narc he'd had almost no contact, and from what little he'd been able to glean from Ginny it certainly seemed the narc had handled himself well in Europe.

As for her subdued air of bitter melancholy, he attributed that to Vorovich's being everything he claimed. He knew she secretly hoped the narc was still working for the forces of good. Nor had he deluded himself that her offer to keep an eye on Vorovich was for love of him, no sir, he was not so vain as all that, however much she once had seemed to be turned on by him.

But why then did D'Anton want to meet with him privately first? The dope in that torn scrap of cloth had analyzed out to an incredibly high purity rate, the overseas connections had agreed to participate . . . what more could D'Anton want?

Suspecting the worst, Charles took certain precautions. He set Chen up to make sure Vorovich did not leave the apartment and brought Roscoe to backstop Sam in case D'Anton planned to do him in.

He needn't have bothered. When Charles, accompanied by Sam, swaggered up to the front entrance of D'Anton's home at so early an hour the streets were still empty, leaving Roscoe, protesting bitterly, as protective coloration at the wheel of the Rolls, D'Anton answered the door himself and, somewhat amused at the question, told him that Alphonse and Gaston were guarding Vorovich at the downtown apartment.

Sam, still clutching the gun in his overcoat pocket, was left in the entry, while Charles was taken to the library, where D'Anton poured them coffee.

"Sorry to drag you out so early," D'Anton said. "But I think it's important we understand each other before we evaluate Vorovich's plan. Now I know you weren't pleased to have me take him on, and I must confess I salted the wound by treating you as though your objections carried no weight. That wasn't the case, as you shall see, but it was necessary in the long view."

Charles tried to cover his confusion by spooning more sugar than even he used into his cup.

"He's given us all I hoped for, and more," D'Anton said.

"After the merchandise is shipped, however, he will have out-lived his usefulness. But," D'Anton went on, not giving the now thoroughly startled Charles an opportunity to respond, "he's not unintelligent, and he's contrived the situation so only he will know where the merchandise is, as a self-protective device. It won't be easy, but I think we can force his hand—that is, if you still want to be rid of him."

Charles could hardly believe what he was hearing. He gulped his coffee, attributing the sweet bitterness to the sudden anticipation of revenge. "Supposing I do," he said cautiously, never wanting to agree to anything too hastily, "what did you have in mind?"

"I want you to take a position," D'Anton said, "become very stubborn, dig in your heels and refuse to budge—threaten to drop out entirely unless you know where the stuff is too. After all, you're the one going to take delivery. Without you, we'd have to set up a whole new storage-and-distribution pattern."

"What if he doesn't agree?" Charles asked.

"He'll agree," D'Anton said. "He'll figure we won't dare hurt him—on the basis that he could still blow the whistle on us—until you take possession, at which time he expects to get his money and be long gone." D'Anton smiled. "What he won't know is that you'll be taking delivery early, right from the docks, instead of waiting to sort it out at a downtown ware-house."

Charles almost laughed out loud. "Neat," he said, apprecia-tively. "Really neat."

D'Anton suggested they arrive at the apartment separately, Charles first, as a kind of psychological underscoring of the impartial attitude D'Anton would take in the coming argu-ment.

But Vorovich's appearance had a strange effect on Charles. Ginny had not mentioned this transformation. The man he had expected to confront in the shiny worsted of the civil servant was as nattily turned out as he was.

"You look like you've got it made, man," Charles said, look-ing at Vorovich's chamois shirt and black velvet flare cords.

"Not quite yet," Vorovich said, lounging with his brass-buck-led loafers up on the glass coffee table, ankles crossed to reveal that, like the insouciant rich, he wore no socks.

"Pretty pleased with yourself, huh?" Charles said. "Got everything worked out down to the last bath crystal."

"Who told you that?" Vorovich said, coming up off the couch.

"Why so surprised, man?" Charles asked. "Ginny's got no call to keep anything from me."

"You two still quarreling over a girl?" D'Anton wondered contemptuously, standing in the foyer.

"Not me," Vorovich said. "He can have her."

"I do," Charles said, and then D'Anton came in pushing the breakfast cart: sticky Chinese breakfast cakes, eggs foo yung, and a dark hot tea.

"I thought we might strive for the equanimity of the Oriental," D'Anton said, doing the serving himself. "So I ordered from the Chinese restaurant down the street." He sat and demonstrated a dexterity with chopsticks. "Why don't you fill Charles in?"

"He already knows too much," Vorovich said, more bitterly than he had intended.

"You can drop the act," D'Anton said. "He'll have to know they're sardines eventually."

"Why so early?" Vorovich said. "Time enough for that after the stuff arrives."

"No way," Charles said. "I'm not anybody's patsy. Either I'm wired in on the action, or I'm out right now."

"Break my heart," Vorovich said. He turned to D'Anton. "You're better off without those kids, anyway."

"I'm not using kids," Charles said, reddening but managing to keep his temper. After all, D'Anton was on his side, wasn't he? "Sam's a helluva driver—and don't be fooled by Roscoe and Chen."

"You have any reason other than personal animosity why Charles shouldn't know?" D'Anton asked. "Certainly *someone* on this end ought to know where the stuff is. . . ."

"In case anything happens to me?" Vorovich asked.

"There's always that possibility, isn't there?" D'Anton agreed.

"Okay," Vorovich finally said. "It's all on your head if he's a loose lip." He stared hard at Charles. "But no details until we're overseas."

"Fair enough," D'Anton said, and though Charles didn't

quite like that, he didn't see how, right then, he had anything to complain about.

But later, when they stopped down the street at the Chinese café to get a report from Chen, the unease that had been nagging him came to the surface.

"The nock's flee to come and go as he preases," Chen said.

"Talk straight, dammit!" Charles raged. "Wasn't he always?"

"Not according to the Arabs," Chen said. "I was at the counter when the breakfast order came in, and I talked the proprietor into letting me deliver it. They wouldn't let me take it up in the elevator, but I was doing my no talkee englee number, and while the big guy was digging up the mazooma the skinny guy was running off at the mouth something fierce about how he felt being pulled off like that, and maybe he'd follow the narc on his own, and the big guy was cooling him down, saying if D'Anton said to clear off they'd better, because D'Anton never changed his mind without he had good reason."

Charles had not become successful through chance. In spite of his flamboyant dress and arrogant manner and mug's face he was a cautious individual, a conniver who considered everyone as capable of treachery as he was, and woe to those who sold him short for brains.

Now that he thought about it, he had the feeling that Vorovich had given in too easily. He didn't doubt that D'Anton was capable of wiping someone out without a second thought, but why Vorovich rather than old Charles? In fact, from what Chen said, it sounded as if he were giving Vorovich his head—and why do that if he meant to get rid of him?

"I tell you what, Chen," Charles said. "If what you stumbled onto is the real goods, you're in for a big fat bonus. I want you to stick close to the narc, close as his shadow, and let's try to find out why the Arabs were told to get lost."

"Chen ought to have help, don't you think?" Roscoe asked. "Vorovich is an old hand, it might take two guys to tail him."

"Sure," Charles said. "Don't worry about the bonus, Chen," he said, as the other looked crestfallen. "If we're careful, and we pull this off, there's more than enough for everybody."

But as Roscoe slipped out of the chauffeur's coat and gave it back to Sam, Charles was already considering how he might approach that girl whom he had perhaps not questioned enough back at the compound.

187

Out of old cautionary habits Vorovich did not use the apartment phone to get in touch with Cabot. There were too many people with a stake in this, including Cabot, who might want to know why he felt so free with a private phone. And he wasn't sure yet just how much he was going to tell Cabot—it was all beautifully set up, they would not only knock off Charley but would also have the goods on D'Anton, who had been suckered into implicating himself through the use of his fishing boat. It had been made awfully easy for them; was it any wonder that it was going down surpassingly hard to give over control to a man he despised?

But he didn't see, then, that he had any choice. He had himself in a bind. So, after ordering a quart of Irish from the liquor-store clerk, he stepped into the booth and called Cabot collect.

When Cabot finally got on the phone, he said, with no opening amenities: "I'm ready to set up the bust."

"Well," Cabot said, barely able to contain his excitement. "Well, that's good news. We were beginning to wonder—"

"It'll take some explaining," Vorovich said. "And it'll have to be soon. The logistics are a little complicated, and I'm going back to Europe day after tomorrow."

"I'll take a plane first thing in the morning," Cabot said. "Be there by late afternoon. Meet me at the Mark—Justice keeps a suite there. . . ."

"I'm not going anywhere that smells of Feds," Vorovich said.

"Where then?" Cabot asked, but Vorovich could tell he was irked.

"There's a little hotel in Sausalito," Vorovich said, "just across the bridge, very discreet, no one minds anyone else's business. But it has to be absolutely private, just us, no watchdogs along this time, hear?"

"You don't have to worry," Cabot said. "I'm handling this one myself."

Vorovich almost had to admire the man's limitless capacity for falsehood. "Right," Vorovich said. "It's the Casa Madrano. I'll reserve the room in your name. Make yourself comfortable. I doubt I'll be able to get there before dark."

"They do have room service?" Cabot asked.

"One of the best restaurants in the city downstairs," Vorovich said, wondering what other fleshly concerns this man might have, and hung up without saying good-by.

On the way back to the apartment he passed a Chinese restaurant, perhaps the one that had sent breakfast in. Remembering that the food was good, he went inside to order some takeout. It was one thing to brood over his options without food, but it was another to drink as much as he intended.

And there, at the front counter, giggling with the girl at the cash register, was Chen. Wasn't it? Except that this young Chinese was wearing a bus boy's jacket and without even looking to see who had come into the door had faded into the dimness of the restaurant beyond.

Well, even if it wasn't Chen, better to assume that it could be, Vorovich thought. It wouldn't do to be careless. Not now, just when it was all beginning to jell.

As soon as they arrived back at the compound, Charles went looking for Ginny. He found her at the pottery wheel, hands gloved with mud, apparently naked under the lime-green granny dress, and with an apple-green bandanna over her long red hair. He wondered whether that was pride or vanity. It didn't occur to him that it might be self-respect.

"Why did you come back here, Ginny?" he asked without preliminary. "Now you're always welcome, you know that, but I'm not dumb enough to believe there's anything here for you now."

"I'm trying to talk my friends into getting out," she said without losing her concentration.

"Why?" he demanded. "You think they're getting short-sticked? You know they don't come near to balancing off what I give 'em. . . ."

"I just don't want them caught in the middle," she said.

"In the middle of what?" he wondered.

"The nasties and the narcs," she said.

"Why should the narcs be a worry?" he asked, though his heart jumped. "We've got a big one on our team just so they won't be." He watched her closely. "He *is* on our team, isn't he, Ginny?"

"Don't worry," she retorted bitterly. "He wasted one following us just so he wouldn't have to sit this out."

"So that's what's been bugging you," Charles said slowly, seeing how she had suddenly deformed the spout she was shaping. "Not that I blame you," he said. "A man who'd waste one of his own would do anything."

"You should talk," she said.

He studied her averted face angrily. "Like I told you," he said, "I've been forced into this. But even if I wasn't, I don't see where that makes me evil. I only supply what's demanded. I don't force folks to mainline. Everyone turns on one way or another, they gargle alky, like your precious narc, or pop pills or sniff glue or inhale aerosol or chew snuff and all the laws in the world ain't gonna stop people from doin' what drives 'em. At least the shit I'm providing is pure, if your sample is any . . ."

"What you're saying is you ought to get a medal," Ginny said.

"Look," he said, controlling his temper, "I'm just trying to earn a living, like everyone else. What do you want me to do, work for a corporation, the government maybe? You know I'm not pedigreed or got the proper credentials to do anything more than flush their stinking toilets! Maybe you'd rather I used my superb state-sponsored education to do social work? Well, I'm a social worker, all right, except I ain't workin' by their book, I'm not suckin' ass or hind tit—I have to make it the best way I can, and if this is the way they've left open for me, why, so much the worse for them!"

Despite himself, Charles was breathing heavily. He didn't like the sound of it, he felt close to breaking down, and he knew better than to expect her or anyone to feel sorry for him.

"But that's not your worry, I know that," Charles said, getting himself under control. "You've had your share of bad trips, and now you're concerned about your friends, and I understand and respect that, too. So I tell you what. As a favor to you, for old times' sake, I'm going to close this place down. I'm going to tell everyone to split. That'll get your friends out from under. Now what could be fairer than that?"

He had finally gotten her to look at him, and that was something. "And what do you expect in return?" Ginny asked at last.

"Boy, you're really somethin' else," Charles said. "If I didn't know you so well, my feelings would be hurt."

"You're a dealer, Charles, we all know that," Ginny said. "You don't give without getting."

"Is that so?" Charles said. "And what about the times I lose without a word of complaint? That was my kid you were carrying, that your narky friend caused you to drop, wasn't it?"

"How can you blame him for that?" she asked, stumbling over the memory. "It was you put Billy and me in the situation."

"I thought you were scamming it to get by the narcs," he said. He looked at her earnestly, but knew enough not to make too much of his sorrow. "Why didn't you tell me?" he asked. "I wouldn't have minded a son."

"That's not what you said at the time," she said, shaping the clay.

"Well, that's all passed water," he said. "I cared for you more than I let on—and still do."

"What is it you want, Charles?" she asked—but softly.

"Nothing you wouldn't want to do as a friend," he said. "All I'm asking is, if you find out the narc and Mister Big are scheming to put my nuts in a vise, you'll tell me."

She stared at him.

"I have to go with the vibes," he said. "And the vibes are not good. They may be planning to send ol' Charley-boy up. I'm like the pilot on a one-way trip. I mean I'm not supposed to know it's one way, you dig? But when I get to the old *p.o.n.r.* and the gas tanks are registering just under half and I open the sealed instructs and draw a blank, it'll be too late to turn back."

"You've been watching the late lates again," she said.

"Sleep comes hard to me, babe," he said, "when I have to sleep solo."

"I thought Sharee was helping you sleep," she said.

"I was speaking symbolically," he said. "Loneliness has to do with the heart." He glanced at her. "You're not jealous of that little gap-toothed freakout? She's not in your class."

"I'm not jealous," she said.

"Too bad," he said, genuinely disappointed. "You are something else—but to hell with that. I wouldn't insult your intelligence by saying I'd like to win you back, no matter how much I would; I'm merely asking that for old times' sake you help me find out if they're setting ol' Charley-boy up." He watched her carefully. "For your friend's sake, too."

"You're wasting your breath," she said. "I haven't talked to him since we came back from Europe. And there's no reason for us to be talking to each other now."

"It wasn't him I wanted you to talk to," Charles said.

"Who then?" Ginny asked. "I don't know anyone else involved. . . ."

"I want you to apply for a job with a man named D'Anton," Charles said, "and lightfinger through his files."

"Looking for what?" Ginny asked after a moment. "Supposing I agree."

"Looking for shipping invoices, names of boats, and arrival dates," Charles said.

"But I won't know what any of it means," Ginny said.

"I will," Charles said. Making her the peace sign, he turned to go, turned back. "I won't pretend I like your narky friend," he said. "But if you decide he's what you want, if he's true blue and like that, then I wish you both all the best, and that's from the heart, babe."

Though he had already all but decided to eliminate Vorovich, Charles thought it might be best to add that little fillip, which would not only obscure his real intentions but finagle her around so that she wouldn't be against him.

You couldn't ignore the hidden factors, like love and loyalty, Charles thought, walking away from her stricken look. He felt nothing in those areas himself, but he was aware how important they were to others. He wasn't dumb. Let no one make a mistake about that. He hadn't acquired an estate worth almost half a mil by being stupid. Let those who thought so beware.

Vorovich spent the night and half the next day hung over, in bed. There'd been more drinking than thinking since he'd found himself unable to bring what was troubling him into focus. Turning over control, sure, that was part of it, giving up a gorgeous operation before he had a chance to bring it to completion, and for what? A reinstatement, a few lines in his personnel file, maybe even a commendation? He still had the money in the Swiss bank, sure, which he'd never give up—but somehow that didn't seem like much any more, in the sense that the score ought to reflect the enormousness of the game.

He hungered for a woman, too, felt the familiar ache in his loins, and though he knew it was all over with Ginny, he just couldn't bring himself to call a hustler.

And so he drank himself into a daze, until his thoughts and his feeling of unfulfillment blurred and he was able, finally, to not so much fall asleep as pass out.

It took him until mid-afternoon to get himself back together. He forced himself to eat the cold leftover glutinous Chinese food, which reminded him of Chen, and he went out then to find him.

It wasn't hard. Chen was in the lobby, offering samples of food to the desk clerk and the elevator operator. Carefully, Vorovich eased the service stairs door shut, and went on down into the subterranean garage. With surveillance as sloppy as that, he thought, they'd never make the big time.

It wasn't that he forgot about Roscoe so much as that the only black man he saw was wearing an attendant's smock and waxing a Lincoln Mark IV. With all that was on his mind, Vorovich simply didn't think of it as anything out of the ordinary.

The Casa Madrano snugged into a hillside overlooking the bay, barely visible through the planting which had overgrown it. The sun was burning at the water's edge before Vorovich came up the winding road in a beat-up cab he had picked up in town. He'd seen one and one-half movies—a porno which had driven him out of the theater, angry with himself for having got excited in spite of his disgust, and a Marx Brothers comedy whose jokes had brought him very near tears.

"Folks don't usually go to the Madrano alone," the cabby, a youngish black man with a scarred lip, commented.

"Don't they?" Vorovich asked, relaxing as the car behind continued past the hotel turning.

"Shame to waste a romantic spot just 'cause you a stranger in town," the cabby said. "You do like girls, don't you?" he asked, pulling up past the entrance.

"Sometimes," Vorovich said, noticing the meter had not been in use.

"I provide a little introduction service to kind of supplement my income," the cabby said. "What kind you like—white-skinned or dark?"

"What do you recommend?" Vorovich asked, handing him a ten.

"The darker the better, if you want your luck changed," the cabby said, scar stretching with his grin.

"I'm thinking of changing a friend's," Vorovich said, holding out his hand for change. "Tell her Cabot's his name."

The cabby tore the bill in half. "Here," he said. "If you like what you see, give her the other half."

"Tell her to avoid the lobby," Vorovich said, getting out. "I'll pick her up in the bar. If she's good-looking enough, that is. About seven?"

"The cautious type," the cabby said, nodding, and drove off.

Vorovich, who had already made the reservation by phone, now registered in Cabot's name, explaining he wanted to save his friend the trouble. He would wait in the room. The clerk, who looked as old as the hotel, gave him the key without fuss.

What Vorovich liked about the hotel was that its warren of rooms and landings permitted guests to enter and leave without going through the lobby. Now, for instance, he was able to walk up to the rooftop observation deck without passing anyone else. There he watched the sun drop below the horizon, and was also able to see Cabot, in a rented Buick, being followed to the hotel turning by a tan Dodge that had to be government issue, which then parked on the street below.

Vorovich got back down to the room in plenty of time, so that when Cabot arrived he was lounging on the bed, a water glass half full of the whisky he had brought.

"Make yourself at home," Cabot said, unfolding and hanging his glove-leather garment bag in the closet.

"Drink?" Vorovich asked, indicating the bottle still in its paper bag.

"I had one on the plane," Cabot said.

"Better have another," Vorovich said.

"You mean I'm not going to like what you tell me?" Cabot asked.

"I'm not sure," Vorovich said truthfully, since after seeing this devious man again break his word, he felt a renewed surge of bitter dislike. The least he ought to do for himself, Vorovich suddenly thought, was to find out if the plan he'd worked out was a good one. To have taken it this far without knowing whether Cabot could be fooled would be shameful. Why not set the other up, give himself the satisfaction of pointing out how easy it would have been to sucker him?

"Pour me one, then," Cabot said, hanging up his jacket. "Perhaps, if this is going to take long, we ought to order dinner. You did say there was a good restaurant here?"

"Whatever you want, make it for two," Vorovich said, handing him a menu. "You've had more experience with fine restaurants than I have."

Cabot looked at him briefly, then picked up the phone and ordered in a precise, academic French.

"All right," he said, hanging up. "That's out of the way. Now you can proceed uninterrupted."

"What I want to know first," Vorovich said, "is whether you're going to clear the books on the contraband dope."

"You mean your secret bank account?" Cabot asked.

"I figured you knew," Vorovich said.

"The regulations are clear," Cabot said.

"It's not the government's money," Vorovich said. "I don't see where it's any skin off yours or their ass what I do with it."

"If we ignore it," Cabot said, "we're in collusion with you to break our own regulations, not to mention helping you avoid U.S. taxes."

"U.S. taxes!" Vorovich laughed. "I've got that all figured out —I'll declare that money, if the D.E.A. pays the taxes on it."

Cabot stared at him. "How can we justify that?" he asked.

"List it as a bonus," Vorovich said. "Or how about severance pay?" That had come out so fast he had surprised even himself. How long had that been stewing in his subconscious?

"You're not coming back to us?" Cabot asked, a little too casually.

"I don't know," Vorovich said. "I haven't decided yet. But

I'm giving early retirement serious thought."

"What's really bothering you?" Cabot demanded.

"You gave me your word I could operate alone," Vorovich said.

"Surely you didn't imagine an organization like ours would permit that, even if I wanted it myself?" Cabot said.

"You agreed," Vorovich said.

"Because I was forced to," Cabot said. "Haven't you been in situations where you had to give in? Besides, where's the harm —you're here, and alive."

"Preble's not," Vorovich said.

"Ah, yes," Cabot said. "Preble. Most unfortunate. Potentially a good man, too. But clearly too inexperienced for what we asked him to do. We're shorthanded, though you know that, we're forced to bring these youngsters along perhaps a bit too fast . . . I'd forgotten that you met him."

"Twice," Vorovich said.

Cabot blinked, looked at his drink, took a swallow. "His death will be justified if we break this ring, won't it?" he said.

Vorovich thought about that. That's what Preble had died for, all right. But he didn't remember making any bargains. And even if he had, how was he obligated now? Preble would still be dead when all this was over.

"I suppose it will," Vorovich said, lying, because he wasn't sure.

"You know it will," Cabot said briskly. "Now let's get back to the top of our agenda, why don't we?"

"The stuff's coming in soon," Vorovich said. "As part of a very large shipment of sardines."

"Sardines!" Cabot exclaimed.

"So large a shipment," Vorovich said, "that if anyone tried to bust it early, and their information was wrong, they wouldn't find out until they were up to their assholes in fish."

"Why are you telling me this?" Cabot asked.

"So there won't be any misunderstandings," Vorovich said. "I'm going to be part of the canning operation, but even I won't know which cans are going where until they're actually shipped —and even then I won't be sure unless I check them out myself."

"You'll let us know what boat?" Cabot asked. "The people involved and all that?"

"Only when I'm sure you understand it's to your advantage to wait for delivery before moving in," Vorovich said.

"I guess I shouldn't blame you for not trusting your own people," Cabot said after a moment.

"If you wait for delivery," Vorovich said, "you'll have them doing all the work for you. They're planning to separate out the merchandise right on the docks, and truck it away in the middle of the night—that's when you move in and bust them. You've got them actually handling the goods!"

Cabot licked his thin lips. "Sounds good," he admitted. "You're making it awfully easy for us. And awfully dangerous for you, I suspect."

Now was the time, Vorovich thought, to tell him the actual plan. If he told him now, there would be no humiliation, they might even chuckle together about Vorovich's need to get a leg up, he could say he had approached it this way, coming up on the other sideways, to show how plausible it had all seemed to the others. If he waited, however, an hour, a day or a week, after Cabot had given him the go-ahead, why, the other would never forgive him, no matter how reasonable it was to make sure that nothing got in the way of him sucking D'Anton dry.

"The only thing that worries me," Cabot said, "is that everything depends on you right up until the final moments."

"Don't think it doesn't worry me too," Vorovich said.

"It's not that I think you can't handle it," Cabot said. "But you never know when something could go wrong—and then we're left empty-handed, with nothing to go on."

"What I've been planning to do is write a comprehensive report," Vorovich said, "using names, dates, and places, which I'll leave with my banker in Switzerland. Along with instructions to mail it to you if he doesn't hear from me by a certain time."

"I suppose it's useless to argue?" Cabot asked. Vorovich shrugged. "If the operation's a success," Cabot promised at last, "I'll see what I can do about the money."

There were similarities, Vorovich thought, between this man and D'Anton.

"You'll hear from me, then," Vorovich said. "Soon." And he headed for the door.

"What about dinner?" Cabot said. "I ordered for two!"

"I'll take care of that on the way out," Vorovich said, and touching scout-salute fingers to forehead, left.

Stopping in the bar, he saw a voluptuous woman with skin the color of a ripe bananna and a tight dress two shades lighter. Her wiry hair was cropped close to her shapely skull, and when she turned at his presence, he looked into eyes dark as carbon.

"I'm spoken for," she said.

"A man named Cabot?" Vorovich asked. She nodded. "He's up in his room," Vorovich said. Making sure no one was watching, he pulled out a hundred, added the torn ten. "You're a present from me to him," he said.

"You know what turns him on, huh?" the woman said.

"Sure 'nuff," Vorovich said, and the woman laughed.

"What about you?" she asked, teeth and eyes glistening in the dark bar.

"Another time," he promised. A waiter came out of the kitchen with a cart, and he went and took care of that too—tipping the waiter, saying he would see the food was delivered.

He walked the woman upstairs, pushed the cart to Cabot's door. "In there," he said. "When he asks who you are, tell him you're his cover."

"This a surprise?" the woman asked.

"I certainly hope so," Vorovich said.

Outside, Vorovich walked away from the hotel down the winding path to the street below, where he found the tan car. Two men were inside, slumped low, probably watching for departing cabs in the rearview mirror. Vorovich tapped on the window.

A startled young man rolled the window down.

"H. Llewellyn Cabot says for me to tell you to drop the surveillance," Vorovich said. "Right now he's having dinner. Give him about thirty minutes, then go up for further instructs." And without giving them a chance to respond, Vorovich walked away, down toward the bay front, where he picked up a cab.

Roscoe was abject, he was chagrined, he was almost dog-bellied to the floor with shame over having lost Vorovich somewhere in Sausalito. It could
happen to anyone, he said: after all, it *had* been his
idea to have Chen show himself, like a magician
offering you the wrong card, while he, Roscoe, took up the trail
unobserved. Why would he lie?

"You got caught up in the porno," Charles snarled, but
Roscoe denied it, claiming that Vorovich had simply disappeared among the cluttered aisles of a two-story discount
"barn."

"What *difference* does it make?" Roscoe asked, finally. "You
know if he *is* setting you up it won't be in Europe—he'd want
to knock you off here, so he won't have to share the credit with
any foreign fuzz."

"You seem to know an awful lot about how narcs think,"
Charles said.

"How you think I keep from getting busted all these years?"
Roscoe demanded.

"By turning other folks in, maybe?" Charles said.

"Oh, man," Roscoe said, "you've got a bad sense of humor.
Even if I entertained the thought of singing, you know they's
too tight-fisted to even come close to what my share of this'll be.
'Sides, I'm no oreo cookie, I could never work for white folks."

"I'm white," Charles said.

"But you're black inside," Roscoe said.

Charles laughed, not displeased. "Tell me, soul brother," he
said, "if I was going to use a knife, where would I stick it, so's
the victim will not make any undue commotion?"

Roscoe did not much care for the question. "Right here," he
said reluctantly, pointing to his solar plexus. "But you got to be
careful you don't slide off a rib. You got a victim in mind?"

"You and Chen got it straight about the place?" Charles
asked, ignoring the question. "It has to look empty. Not even
chicks for an overnight. If anyone asks, you are caretaking for
the owner, who is sojourning abroad."

"What about Ginny, what's her story?" Roscoe asked.

"Ginny won't be here," Charles said. He called to Sam and
walked over to get into the shining Rolls.

Vorovich was at the airport early. He checked in at the Satellite terminal, where the charter flight, a French-American friendship club, originated, swore when he discovered there were no bars within walking distance, and took the shuttle bus over to the nearest lounge, where he ordered a double Irish with a beer chaser.

The more he thought about his meeting with Cabot, the more confused and upset he became. Had he all along, deep down, on the level where instincts operated, been planning to lie? Had he intended from the beginning to carry this thing all the way through? It wouldn't do to kid himself. It was possible the game had transformed him, and he was becoming what he had only been pretending to be—as Ginny had predicted.

It had happened to other men before him. One out of five agents got so caught up in the game that before they knew it they were perjuring themselves to get convictions, began trying dope, or went on the take themselves. Was that what was happening to him? Had there been some point where, without even being conscious of it himself, he had finally passed over to the other side? But it wasn't too late, he told himself. He could always pull back, call Cabot, tell him about the mid-ocean transfer—couldn't he?

He could, if he wanted nothing more than the life that had proved so tedious and unfulfilling before. All along the line he had mucked it up for himself. Was it some failing in his character that caused him to fall back at the crucial moment? Was he destined always to remain nondescript, subservient to men of lesser ability, fitting too snugly into the niche that others laid out for him?

He wanted more. But what was he willing to do to get it? All his life he had played by the rules, those unyielding rules laid down by an immigrant shoemaker father whose wife had died in childbirth, who had never mouthed a word of complaint even at his own end, when the last of his savings had been drained by illness.

His father had been proud that Vorovich worked for the police, ridding the streets of the scum that made money off man's worst instincts. Vorovich had been proud, too, until he had discovered they were cosmeticians rather than surgeons, prettying up the face of things rather than probing for cancers.

But was he being fair? he wondered. Was he blaming society

for his own lack of luck? Could he turn his back now on everything he had been brought up and trained to believe, simply because life had not been good to him?

He didn't know. He wasn't able to make up his mind. And to take care of all contingencies, he asked the bartender for two sheets of paper and an envelope, then wrote to the bank in Switzerland. On one sheet he jotted detailed instructions about what to do when certain persons did or did not get in touch with them; and on the other he asked them to notify Ginny that she was the possible beneficiary of a rather large inheritance.

He mailed both at the outside box before taking the shuttle back to the Satellite.

Coming into the terminal, he saw that there was some kind of back-up at the security check-in; pushing closer, Vorovich saw that the man causing the delay was Charles.

"It must be something you're carrying on you," the security guard was insisting as Charles stepped through without his hand baggage, and set off the alarm system again.

Charles hauled out keys, and then coins, and when that didn't clear him, finally dug deep and handed the guard a bulky metal object. The guard hefted it, then out of the bone handle pried a long thin blade.

"That's my Swiss army knife," Charles said. "It's legal, isn't it?"

"Barely," the guard said, and Charles took the knife back and snapped the blade shut himself before going on through the security archway.

Vorovich followed him a moment later. "That's not so smart, calling attention to yourself like that," he said.

"I take it with me everywhere," Charles said, "in case I get a hangnail or there's a wine cork needs pulling—how did I know that would trip it?" He thrust the knife at Vorovich. "There's more than a dozen blades," he said, "everything from a screwdriver to an awl."

"I've seen them before," Vorovich said.

The loudspeakers blared their flight, and they squeezed aboard with some three hundred others in a flurry of excess baggage, raincoats, umbrellas, and gift packages.

Vorovich found a window seat, and Charles, sticking close, took the seat next to him. "Traveling alone?" Charles asked in a too loud voice, for the benefit of other passengers. "My name's

Mariposa, but everyone calls me Charles."

"We should be traveling separate," Vorovich muttered, when he got the chance, as the motors roared during take-off.

"We'll be separate on the way back," Charles said, and calling to the stewardess as soon as they were airborne ordered a double Coca-Cola. He waited until she brought that, along with a beer for Vorovich, before he spoke again.

"Who'd you meet in Sausalito?" Charles murmured.

Vorovich was caught in mid-swallow. But he didn't choke. He'd recognized that Charles was up to something by the way he'd buddy'd up against orders.

"What's a Sausalito?" Vorovich asked.

"Don't shit me," Charles said, just low enough so that no one would overhear. "I had Roscoe tail you."

"Then you know," Vorovich said, shrugging, though his insides were cold. "Why bother to ask?"

"I want to hear it from your very own lips," Charles said.

Vorovich thought quickly. Charles had come within a hair of trapping him into some kind of damaging admission. But it was obvious that while he may have tailed him to the hotel he didn't know what had gone on inside. Either Roscoe had been unable to find out, or . . .

"Well?" Charles prodded. "Got you dead to rights, haven't I."

"I was with a chick," Vorovich said. "So what?"

Charles blinked. Immediately Vorovich was sure he didn't know anything. "A black chick," he continued, laying it on, at the same time wondering how it was that Roscoe had followed him and not reported everything.

"A spade chick?" Charles said, eyes widening. "Man, you are really indiscriminate about where you poke that thing, aren't you?"

"I felt a need," Vorovich said.

"Don't Ginny fill your needs no more?" Charles asked innocently.

"Not since I found out she's working for you," Vorovich said.

"Man," Charles said, and he couldn't seem to help grinning, "you can't win them all."

"She back at the commune?" Vorovich couldn't help asking.

Charles studied him. "I'm shutting the place down," he said, at last. "And not just because I need the place to stash the goods, neither. I know you think I'm just some kind of a wimp," he went on, "but let me tell you I have studied and brooded over and contemplated the future, and it is clear to me the party's over. There is not going to be room for no alternate life styles no more. It's been good times, and for a while there we had the straights on the run, but since it is the law of life that the upright take over in the end, we have got to recognize the inevitable. The system is a sponge, and it is sucking us up." He paused, but only for a moment. "But we do not have to be digested by the system," he went on, "and shit out again, not if we use our heads. What we do is permeate the system, *we* co-opt *it*, we shoot like sperm up into the system's vagina, we pollinate the egg, so we won't come out the system's asshole but drop from between its legs. And when we are reborn we will suck at the system's breasts and take all its vital juices. Then eventually we can put the system away in an old folks' home, and live in their houses, and run their politics, and live off the fat of the land, because you see we will *be* the system, we will have inherited it all!"

He paused, this time for effect, and the effect he was having on Vorovich was extraordinary. This man/boy had suddenly been transformed into something beyond himself, the personification of evil. Vorovich began to wonder whether he had not gotten into something that was more than he, or any one man, could handle.

"The system ain't gonna go away," Charles continued, his soft and sibilant voice like the devil's own. "But we ain't neither. We are gonna disappear for a while, is all. And when we appear again there ain't no one gonna know it's us. We're gonna look, act, and behave like them."

Vorovich suddenly understood the hold Charles had over the others. It wasn't his money, though that entitled him to a certain respect—it was his mind. It was a distorted mind, but it gave them a look at the world that was prismatic. They didn't have to understand it to believe it. Faith was stronger than reason.

Who was to say he was wrong? Not him. Not Timothy N.M.I. Vorovich, who saw that the system had created Charles as it had himself. More than ever now he was confused—who was he, and in what did he believe?

"Can you dig it, man?" Charles asked. Vorovich nodded. "Then what are *you* gonna do?"

"I'm gonna disappear too," Vorovich said.

When they arrived at Marseilles, they were picked up by the Algerian himself, who seemed displeased, apparently having expected only Vorovich and not this long-haired, shifty-eyed mug in the leather coat so expensive it drew attention to itself.

"He's the one taking delivery," Vorovich said.

Shrugging, glad his part would soon be over, the Algerian walked them to his little four-door Renault, then drove in a roundabout route to the waterfront, timing their arrival to coincide with the departure of the last shift of the cannery workers.

"I think we should wait at least an hour," the Algerian said. "Then no one will be on the docks."

"No cops either?" Charles asked.

"We police ourselves down here," the Algerian said, with a significant glance at Vorovich.

But Charles was clearly dissatisfied. He paced the confines of the makeshift office while the Algerian, to discourage conversation, worked on shipping manifests. Vorovich, having helped himself to the Algerian's liquor, sat with his back against a stack of cases, brooding over what Charles had and had not told him. Apparently Ginny had gone back to the commune after that scare at customs. But where would she go now? With her friends, to Salinas? Or was she going to hang in there with Charles, as he had implied? Vorovich couldn't imagine it—but then, it was no longer any concern of his.

Made restless by the memory of Ginny, Vorovich got up to replenish his glass—and the Algerian withheld the bottle.

"You won't be able to work," the Algerian growled, then glanced at his watch and took them down into the cannery.

While the Algerian started the machinery, Vorovich and Charles put on rubber pants and smocks, stepped into rubber boots, then joined the other, already on the line.

The heroin had been packaged in small plasticine bags. Charles manually stuffed them into empty sardine tins, then placed them on the conveyor belt. The *pied noir* operated the machinery which sealed them, leaving them seemingly indistinguishable from the other sardines. But, as Vorovich showed

Charles, he had bent the label applicator slightly out of true, which left a faint groove on the tin.

Vorovich grabbed them as they came off the conveyor, packing them in wooden cases, twelve cans among forty-eight. Five hundred cases had already been stenciled with the name of the importer: FISH IMPORTS, San Francisco, Calif. U.S.A. On the hundred cases set aside, Vorovich took a brush and stencil ink and put a dot over the I in FISH—a mark so insignificant only someone looking for it would know it was there.

Then, when Charles came over to help, Vorovich had him pack the tins while he himself trucked the cases into the warehouses. In between trips, making sure that neither the Algerian or Charles saw him, he swiftly marked dots on every other case within reach. Then, when nailing the cases containing the heroin shut, he added an extra nail to each, each in a different place, so that the only way anyone would catch it would be by knowing the number of nails used normally.

To cover his work, Vorovich asked Charles to help him stack the cases, taking a secret pleasure in the fact that once they had finished, the marked cases were so intermingled only he could now single them out.

Before daylight, an hour before the morning shift was due to arrive, they were done. Charles didn't want to wait while the Algerian removed all traces of their nighttime activity.

"Let's get out of here, man," he said to Vorovich. "While it's still dark enough out there so no one'll see us."

"A good idea," the Algerian agreed. "And don't take a cab from the docks. Go on into the city, pretend to be coming out of one of the hotels."

They removed their rubber garments, pausing only to hang them up where they had gotten them, and the Algerian let them out the door which faced on the pier.

"Careful where you walk," the Algerian said in parting. "Clean-up crews won't arrive until dawn."

They saw what he meant when the door shut behind them. That predawn darkness made the piles of rope, nets, and fish tubs an eerie gauntlet for them to pick their way through. Vorovich, as Charles hesitated, went first, striding down the pier.

"Hey, wait up," Charles whispered, swearing, already ten paces behind him. "My eyes're not as good as yours."

Vorovich hesitated, standing in the deeper shadow of a pile of fish netting. There was something strained about Charles's voice, due to more, perhaps, than fatigue from an unaccustomed night's work. Vorovich stepped deeper into the shadow, squinting through the darkness, trying to make out the other's face as Charles cautiously made his way over and around the objects scattered along the wooden pilings.

"Where are you, man?" Charles whispered, then stumbled and almost fell.

It was curious, Vorovich thought. Charles had caught himself with one hand. The other remained deep in the pocket of his leather coat. Almost instinctively, he reached behind, and felt his fingers circle a fish net.

"Over here," Vorovich said, stepping out of the shadow.

Charles acknowledged his presence by waving his free hand, then took three long steps and was on him.

Vorovich grunted aloud at the impact. He had tried to keep a pile of empty crates at his back, but Charles had taken him at an angle, and the two of them went sideways in what must have seemed a crazy dance, then crashed to the dock, Vorovich underneath. The breath whooshed out of Vorovich's lungs, and the embrace he had Charles in loosened. If he had not pushed the net between himself and his oncoming antagonist that knife might now be in his chest.

When the red-streaked blackness lifted, Vorovich could hear Charles swearing. He was struggling to free the entangled blade. Remaining limp until the very last moment, carefully taking in a deep silent breath, Vorovich waited until the blade slid free, then coming up off the dock, pulling the net with him, he flung it over Charles's head. In a moment their positions were reversed.

Vorovich had the other's knife hand in his own strong grip, and as he straddled the writhing body he began to twist and force it down until the glittering blade was inches from the other's straining neck.

"Okay, motherfucker!" Charles cried in an agonized whisper. "Do it! Do it, damn you, do it!"

Vorovich wanted to, badly. He recognized the depths of his own rage by the breath that whistled out of his mouth and nostrils, and he would have liked nothing better than to lean forward and watch that thin blade disappear into Charles's throat. But he twisted the other's wrist instead until with a cry of pain Charles opened his hand and the knife dropped out. Standing, Vorovich kicked it off the pier into the water.

A square of light suddenly illuminated the pier from a door opened in the cannery. "Is something wrong?" came the anxious call from the Algerian.

"Nothing," Vorovich called back. "He tripped in the darkness."

There was what seemed an interminable silence, and then the door eased shut.

"Whyn't you tell him?" Charles asked wonderingly. He clawed the net from his face and struggled slowly to his feet.

"If he found out we were fighting between ourselves," Vorovich said, "the stuff would never leave this dock, except to be dumped ten fathoms under."

Charles touched his throat, looked at his fingertips, which held a trace of blood. "Why didn't you waste me?" he asked, confused.

"You're supposed to take delivery," Vorovich said.

They walked the length of the pier in silence, and were almost to the main boulevard before Vorovich spoke again.

"It wouldn't have done you any good," Vorovich said. "You and D'Anton didn't think I'd be stupid enough to lose my only hole card? I fixed the cases so there's an extra hundred marked like the ones with the goods. It'd take you a week to sort it all out."

Charles brooded over that through most of the cab ride to the airport. Then, standing in front of the morning crowds at the terminal, he blurted out his question: "That means you have to be there to finger the cases," he said. "Where you gonna be till then?"

"You'll miss your plane," Vorovich said. "Hey, Chas!" he called, when the other was several angry paces away. "Better pick up some cologne. You smell kind of fishy."

Vorovich made sure Charles had boarded the San Francisco Museum charter—if anyone asked, he'd say he was an airline employee—before he himself went to board a British Airways Viscount shuttle to London, where he would take a connecting flight to the islands. He had to make sure no one would follow or anticipate his movements: with the kind of information he had, someone might decide there were other ways to get it out of him.

Ginny's friends didn't understand why she wasn't going to travel north with them. They knew she had split with the narc and that she no longer dug Charles; why then was she going to hang around San Francisco—particularly when Charles had lectured them about getting off the streets or they'd be swept away, like trash?

But after they'd packed up and shut the compound down, they offered to give her a ride into town. She accepted because she didn't want Sam or Chen or Roscoe to get even the slightest inkling of what she planned to do. She'd heard enough from Vorovich about the dangers of going underground not to risk even a friend's knowledge.

Leaving the compound was solemn and sad, but they were on the highway only a few minutes before Sharee requested that Roger get out his "gittar" and holler them a song, and soon they were all singing loudly to his hard-strummed chords as if this past year of their lives held no more significance than an overnight stop.

Then two highway-patrol cars appeared out of nowhere and bracketed their battered van, escorting them all the way into downtown San Francisco.

"I don't believe this!" Roger shouted. "Man," he screamed out the window, "why are you hassling us now?"

They drove right on down into a basement garage for an unloading, and then, manacled, protesting questions unanswered, they were ridden up in cage elevators to the interrogation rooms on the sixth floor.

It seemed Ginny was the one they were after. Her family back in Wisconsin had suggested she might have been kidnaped and was being held against her wishes, a rumpled plainclothes detective told them, and until she had been thoroughly questioned, they couldn't let anyone go.

A matron escorted Ginny into one of the rooms. But the moment they were inside, the matron went out another exit, and two men in civilian clothes came in from an outside corridor.

One she knew: Morton, the agent in charge of the San Francisco office of the Drug Enforcement Agency, a stocky, balding man in a tight brown suit.

"Hello, Ginny," Morton said. "Sorry to make this all so dramatic, but I wasn't sure when, or if, you were going to get back in touch with us. This is Mr. Cabot, from Washington."

"Ginny," the other acknowledged, and she became immediately apprehensive. "I wanted to thank you personally for everything you're doing to stop this despicable drug traffic. Leaving us that sample at customs was a big help."

"They were threatening my friends," she said, looking toward Morton. Hadn't he explained that? "I left the dope to show you how important it was that you stop them."

"I understand," Cabot said. "And we're doing everything we can to apprehend them. But quite frankly, we're operating almost completely in the dark. And unless we can gather certain information in time, I'm afraid they're going to bring a really massive amount of the stuff right past us."

"I've already told Mr. Morton everything I know." Ginny said, but she was worried, and some of that showed.

His thin brows arched skeptically. "Perhaps," he murmured. "With the best of intentions, you may have left something out —considering it unimportant, say. And that's understandable, because when it's not clear just what our knowledge means, when we don't know just where it fits into the scheme of things, it hardly seems worth while bringing the matter up."

"I don't understand what you're talking about," Ginny said, still unclear why they had dragged her here.

"Of course you don't," Cabot said. "Because it's not what, it's who. I'm speaking of Vorovich." He gave her a moment to absorb that. "What has he told you that we ought to be made aware of?" he asked.

"Why would he tell me anything?" she said.

"Because he loves you?" Cabot asked.

"What makes you think that?" she asked.

Cabot stared at her a long moment, then reached his hand out to Morton, who reluctantly handed Cabot an envelope he was carrying. Cabot, without taking his eyes from her, undid the stringed flap and took out some photographs.

Ginny didn't want to look, half guessing what she might see. The blood, which had heated her cheeks, now drained from them, leaving her cold.

"Where did you get these?" she managed finally.

"The local enforcement people got them for us," Cabot said. "They have sources inside."

Who? Ginny wondered in a sudden panic. Chen? Roscoe? Sam? Or had one of her friends gotten hold of the negs, made a copy, turned them in?

"Keep them," Cabot said, as with a shaking hand she started to hand them back. "Destroy them, if you like. I would have torn them up myself, but I wanted to give you the satisfaction."

"After you let me know you saw them," she said, shakily.

"It's a dirty business," Cabot admitted. "But I have to make you aware of just how much, and how little, we're aware of, if you're going to be able to help us fill in the missing pieces."

"I don't *have* any missing pieces," Ginny cried, a little desperately.

"Please, Ginny, credit us with some intelligence," Cabot said. "I know your motives are worthy, that you want to prevent what happened to your sister from happening to others, that you refused money to keep us informed—"

"I asked for help, not money," Ginny said. "Money always confuses things."

"I wish more people were aware of that," Cabot said. "I know too," he said, pulling a chair over and sitting down close, a little too close, to her, "that you're afraid of implicating your friends, afraid of implicating Vorovich—so I'm going to tell you something now on the assumption that you love him—"

"Me love a narc?" she said scornfully, but it came out weak.

"—because if you don't, the information you will then have can prove enormously dangerous to him." He was looking directly into her eyes now. "Unless of course he already told you," he said.

"Told me what?" Ginny asked, not sure she wanted to hear.

Cabot stared at her for a long moment. "That he was still working for us?" he asked.

Ginny flinched as if struck, then sat mute, confused and upset, not certain whether this information should give her pleasure or dismay.

"That could be a point in his favor," Morton said. "You know the first commandment of undercover work—thou must never tell anyone, neither mistress nor wife—"

"It could mean just the opposite too, couldn't it?" Cabot said impatiently.

"What are you talking about?" Ginny demanded.

"I think his mind may have given way under the strain," Cabot said at last, turning back to her. "It's never easy to go undercover, having to live the part every minute, day and night. And there's the additional factor of his personal antagonism to me—which doesn't bother me, you understand, but it's something I must take into consideration."

Cabot reached into the envelope and pulled out more photos—of Vorovich at the compound, sucking on brown cigarettes, a half dozen in sequence, after he'd eaten the stew, close-up, showing how horribly dilated his eyes were.

"I suppose one could argue he wanted to dispel any doubts the other side might have as to the depth of his commitment —but what I'm afraid of is he may have identified rather too well," Cabot said.

Ginny remained silent, uncertain what was expected of her.

"We already have enough on him to send him up for twenty years," Cabot said. "We know about his Swiss bank account, we can guess what other financial goals he has—but we would consider everything that's happened up to this point as in the line of duty, chalk it up to the stress of battle. The D.E.A. doesn't abandon its own. But if he's planning to trick me, to help them with the importation, believe me we'll get him, and then we'll throw the book at him!"

"He isn't!" Ginny cried.

"How do you know?" Cabot asked.

"He couldn't," Ginny said. "He may be trying to make a big score, but he wouldn't let the stuff come in, I know!"

Cabot stared at her, unable to conceal his surprise. It hadn't occurred to him that this arrogant, insubordinate man might be trying to play both ends against the middle! It was worse than he thought. All these months of waiting and planning, the expenditure of time, men, and money, only to wind up with nothing to show for it!

"But you don't want it to come in either, do you?" Ginny wondered anxiously, watching Cabot's face.

Again, Cabot could barely contain himself. Couldn't she, couldn't any one understand that it had to be done officially, in public view, as a symbol of government power? Not only to break the ring, but to discourage others from trying? Besides that, he had promised the people up on the Hill something spectacular, to justify a major appropriation. If he didn't deliver, he wouldn't look like a boastful fool so much as ineffectual, which was worse.

"He'll never get away with it," Cabot said, at last. "They'll tear him apart."

"Isn't there anything you can do?" Ginny cried, pressed beyond endurance, the tears coming unbidden.

"Only if you cooperate with us," Cabot said savagely. "If you tell us everything—where you went on your trip, who you met, conversations you overheard—we may be able to anticipate his moves, move in ourselves, put him in protective custody, smash the ring!"

"He'd never forgive me," she whispered at last.

"It's his only chance," Cabot said. "And eventually he'll realize what you got him out of. I tell you what: to sweeten that eventuality, I'll not only let him keep the money he has already, ah, appropriated, but I'll pay him just like any other informer, based on the amount of narcotics intercepted. That should be adequate balm for any psychic wounds he may suffer. And afterward, when the dust has settled, I'll personally see to it the two of you get a fresh start somewhere."

"Money's not his problem," Ginny said. "He'll never trust anyone in his life again!"

"Such judgmental niceties mean nothing if the man is dead," Cabot said.

Ginny thought so long about Vorovich dead that Cabot began to worry whether he had miscalculated her commitment to first principles. Then:

"Where do you want me to start?" Ginny asked.

Ginny came out into the early bright fall morning numbed and stumbling. On the sidewalk outside the county building were her friends, and Sharee embraced her fervently. But she said no to their entreaties to accompany them north—she was returning home, she said with finality, and after giving them half the money Charles had given her, bade them a tearful good-by.

Though she had given Cabot D'Anton's name, she had not

told him what Charles had asked her to do. Now she walked to clear her mind, remembering to make sure no one followed her, a little surprised to find that no one was.

Eventually, she found herself in a remote section of the waterfront, where the fishing fleets tied up. When she saw how impressively large the buildings housing Fruits de Mer were, she understood how so massive an importation was able to be financed.

Watching, she saw a limousine pause before a hole-in-the-wall café, and at the horn honk an aproned waiter hurried out with a steaming demitasse, handing it through the passenger window. The passenger was a dark, older man in a gray homburg, who drank the coffee in two swallows. Then the limo disappeared through the gates.

Thoughtfully, Ginny retreated, then walked until she came to a shopping district large enough to contain an important bank. Inside, she had a long talk with the manager about Swiss bank accounts, and though the conversation was from her point of view not entirely satisfactory, she was able, based on her connections, to obtain a loan large enough for her purposes.

She found a beauty parlor just down the street. Yes, they could cut and die her hair, though wouldn't she prefer a rinse, to deepen that already magnificent color? No. Very well, the customer's desire was their business.

Later, with scarcely a glance at her mirrored nunlike profile, Ginny went into a nearby dress shop and purchased the most tailored suit she could find, changing clothes on the spot.

At last, she was ready. She walked back, a trifle unsteady in the unaccustomedly high heels, and through the gates of Fruits de Mer, her primness discouraging whistles or comments from the men in the yard, and into the office marked EMPLOYMENT.

She had no shorthand, and her typing was rusty, but she knew how to make bookkeeping entries and was willing to take the late shift, when restaurants called in next day's orders. Yes, she could start tomorrow. References? They could start with the banker down the street.

Vorovich was supposed to board the freighter at Marina Cay, in the British Virgins. In spite of the humid, gnat-infested climate, he let no one guess he had no intention of conforming to any kind of preordained arrangements.

He took long walks along the rocky beach at dawn, again at dusk, becoming a familiar sight to local fishermen. Eventually, as he had hoped, he was invited to go out with the boats; he chose a weatherbeaten little tub owned by a gnarled fisherman so old his skin was gray as his kinky hair. Hector was grateful for the company: it was difficult to find any young blacks willing to share his already meager pickins, and Vorovich looked strong enough to hold up his end of the net.

Vorovich assumed that D'Anton was cautious enough to have him watched: he guessed it was the fat, squint-eyed black housekeeper who ran the shabby beach hotel, and her mean, thin, errand-boy son or lover, he couldn't tell which. He doubted that they would worry about his choosing such an old boat, particularly since they were so contemptuous of the old man, and when he came back and went out and came back again, seemingly inevitable as the tides, both became complacent.

The boat was seaworthy and scrupulously maintained, as was the old man himself.

Three days before the freighter was scheduled to arrive, he asked Hector to take him to St. Thomas. He didn't tell Hector what he wanted until they were at sea: but that grizzled old man put the money in his pocket without counting, and, with only a sidelong glance out of his yellowing eyes, changed course so gradually the other boats would think them merely drifting toward the horizon.

"I thought you maybe running," Hector said, when they were an hour out, and Vorovich opened them each a beer. "You do something terrible big?"

"Not so big," Vorovich said.

"You revolutionary?" Hector asked hopefully.

"I'm not political," Vorovich said. "I don't believe in anything. What I did," Vorovich continued, seeing Hector's disappointment, "was take some money from the government."

"Ah," Hector said, with satisfaction, and Vorovich knew that Hector was his ally to the death. "What you do with the money?" Hector asked.

"Spend it," Vorovich said.

"On what?" Hector asked.

"On who, you mean," Vorovich said. "A woman."

"Your woman?" Hector asked.

Hector nodded, understanding. "You have three best things in life," he said. "A woman, money, and someday maybe a child to carry on your name."

"My name's worth nothing," Vorovich said, and opened another beer.

Late that afternoon, their squat craft chugged into St. Thomas, an island whose palm-fringed harbor was crowded with ships and sailing yachts and boats, and they found the Liberian-flagged *San Pietro* just as the blazing sun reached the water's edge, limning the rusting, paint-peeled superstructure. Anyone watching from shore would be hard put to see anything against that glare of light.

The gangway ladder was down, a shoreboat with a tall, skinny, overdressed black man lounging in it bobbing underneath. Hector brought his boat alongside just long enough for Vorovich to step across; then, with scarcely a break in the rhythm of his little motor, he continued on until he was lost among all those other boats. The black man showed gold teeth; Vorovich ignored him and climbed the ladder.

The deck seemed empty. Slinging his gear over his shoulder, he walked aft toward the superstructure.

Pausing under the bridge, he looked up; no one there either. After hearing a cough, Vorovich climbed several rungs of the bridge ladder and spotted a crewman, flat-faced and dark, dressed in stained khakis, leaning over the aft rail, smoking.

"Where's the captain?" Vorovich called.

The crewman jerked around, startled, hand going to his belted knife. "Who you?" he asked. "How you get here?"

"Where's the captain?" Vorovich repeated.

The other stared at him a moment longer, then went to the bridge, where he picked up a speaking tube, blew into it twice, listened while his face grew agitated.

"I'm sorry, Cap'n," he said then. "Someone's aboard to see you." He listened a moment again, then turned. "He wants to know who you?"

"The passenger from Marina Cay," Vorovich said.

"Passenger from Marina Cay," the crewman repeated. He listened, then pointed below. "Captain in his cabin," he said. "Last one starboard side, promenade deck."

The captain was also flat-faced and dark, though quite a bit older. He appeared in the cabin doorway in a hastily thrown-on patterned-silk dressing gown, hairy legs and chest exposed.

"You aren't supposed to be aboard yet," the captain said.

"The schedule's been changed," Vorovich said. "Let's get underway—I'm in a hurry."

"I've got two passengers ashore!" the Captain protested.

"Leave them," Vorovich said.

"Impossible," the Captain said. "They were placed aboard to guard the cargo!"

"They're not doing a very good job, are they?" Vorovich said. "Now let's go!"

The captain stared at him for a long moment, then nodded, and started to close the door. Vorovich jammed his foot inside.

"I'll wait for you here," he said. He kept his right hand in his coat pocket and watched the captain's eyes go there before waving away the crewman lurking behind Vorovich.

Inside, an island girl, buxom and pretty enough except for some missing teeth, was lying half uncovered in a bunk. At a muttered word from the captain she lost her smile, got up, and angrily struggled into her dress. She held her palm out, and after a long moment the captain put some bills in it, half shoved her out of the cabin and toward the stairs. Still in his robe, he strode barefoot along the deck after her, motioned to the crewman.

"Let her pimp row her ashore," Vorovich said.

"That's our boat," the captain said.

"Small loss," Vorovich said.

Again, the captain examined the bulging right-hand pocket, turned on his barefoot heel, and climbed the ladder to the bridge. Vorovich tossed his duffel bag to the crewman and followed him up.

"No passengers on the bridge," the captain said.

"As soon as we lift anchor," Vorovich said, "get your radioman to notify the shipping agent that our estimated time of arrival has changed."

The captain's hard little eyes flickered. "To what?"

"I'll let you, and them, know that in a few days," Vorovich said.

"They won't like that," the captain said.

"Lift your fucking anchor!" Vorovich said.

The captain signaled the engine room and whistled some crewmen on deck. Underfoot could be felt the throb of the engines, and, a few minutes later, the slow groaning rasp of the rusting anchor chain.

"I'm hungry," Vorovich said, as the screws started to churn and the freighter prepared to move slowly away from the harbor. "You got a steward aboard?"

"Steward!" the captain bellowed into the ship's loudspeaker. Moments later a tall thin fellow with a mustache so perfect it appeared to have been painted on appeared. His face, like those of everyone else Vorovich had seen, was flat, as if at birth it had been pressed between bricks.

"Our passenger has arrived unexpectedly," the captain said.

"His *cabine* is prepared," the steward said.

"If you've got any interesting ideas," Vorovich said, "forget them. I'll kill any man even looks like he wants to handle me."

"It's not our cargo," the captain said. "We are only responsible for the ship."

"Sure," Vorovich said, and motioned for the steward to precede him. In the distance, against the coastline, he could barely make out the shore boat approaching the white beach. Was that his imagination, or were those two figures standing in the surf, gesticulating wildly, like puppets whose strings have gone beserk.

"Where's the cabin of the other passengers?" Vorovich asked.

"Number four," the steward said, indicating the numbers as they walked in under the bridge.

"Open it," Vorovich said.

For a moment the steward seemed about to protest; then he flipped through his key ring and did as Vorovich asked.

The place was a mess, which made the search difficult. He found what he was looking for finally in the twin shaving kits on the bathroom shelf. Two guns, snub-nosed, .32-caliber automatics, cheaply made throwaways, probably stolen, perfect for murder.

After slipping the guns into his coat pockets, Vorovich motioned the steward back out, and they continued on to the galley. A lamb stew was simmering on the stove, and the steward served him that along with a bottle of wine. Vorovich took off his coat to eat—it was hot in the cramped quarters—and placed his own gun, the familiar snub-nosed .32, on the table beside him. The pot-bellied cook and his sullen helper did not

217

seem surprised, continuing with their work impassively.

"That was good," Vorovich said, wiping his plate with a crust of bread. He pushed over what was left of the wine. "Drinks are on me."

The cooks said nothing, but they were drinking when Vorovich followed the steward out. Iron ladders took them down to the engine room, which, unlike the rest of the ship, seemed clean.

The two undershirted men in greasy caps barely glanced at him before returning to their gauges. Vorovich and the steward had to use all their strength to undo the cargo door, then entered the first hold, which held cases of olive oil destined for Mexico. The iron door leading to the inner hold, adjoining the bulkhead, was padlocked. It was a huge lock, difficult to pick or break. Vorovich had a key, given him by the *pied noir* in Marseilles. He took the padlock with him.

The interior was black and smelly as tar. Vorovich lit a match and found a wall switch; the dim illumination came from caged ceiling bulbs.

Vorovich made a hasty check of the cargo: everything was in order. But as he went along the stacked aisles he found that the coded merchandise was underneath the other cases. He swore aloud, the sound dead in the packed hold.

"I need carpenter's tools," Vorovich said to the steward. "A crowbar, a hammer, and nails."

"You want the ship's carpenter too?" the steward asked.

"I work alone," Vorovich said.

While the steward was gone, Vorovich climbed to the top of the cargo and looked for another way out. He finally found it: an inspection hatch, leading to the deck above. Though it was secured from topside, a locking screw was underneath—a few solid blows would free it.

When the steward returned, Vorovich was at the cargo door. He took the tools inside, pulled the door shut against the steward's curious look, and hooked the lock on the inside latch. He felt somewhat claustrophobic, but resisted hammering the hatch open. He knew it was there; that was enough.

Stripping to his shorts, Vorovich set to it. It was hard work. Vorovich began sweating in the fetid air of the hold, banging shoulders and elbows against the wooden cases in the cramped quarters. His first job was to uncover the marked merchandise, his second to pry open the cases and switch the contraband tins into other, unmarked crates.

He lost all track of time. Sweating, tasting salt in his dry mouth, eyes stinging, he cursed his stupidity at not bringing in something to drink with him. But he kept at it, stopping only occasionally to rest his now shivery muscles, starting again before they might tighten up.

When the ship began a slow deep roll he knew they were in the open sea, and for a while he was hard put not to become sick with the constant pitch and yaw and the odors of that airless hold.

At one point he became so weary he dozed, slumped over a partially demolished stack, until a shudder down the length of the ship caused the stack to sway, and he found himself sprawled in the aisle, a case down with him.

His left forearm was bruised, and his balance thereafter was off enough so that three times as he nailed the tops shut he hit his hand with the hammer. But finally he was done, and he surveyed the work, mentally marking off the contraband cases, having arranged them in an odd-even numerical code pattern that would be unbreakable—so long as he was.

Now he climbed back over the stacks to the "look-in" hatch, and, using a cloth to muffle the sound, he hammered the inner latch open, though he left it just far enough screwed on so that a cursory check from topside would miss it. Then he hid his weapon, pinching it between two cases, and, carrying his clothes, the two little pistols in his jacket pockets, he came out.

They were waiting for him, as he had expected. Two crewmen had rifles pointed at him, and the steward took his bundle of clothing, motioning him into the glare of the engine-room lights where they searched him.

"Where's the big gun?" the steward asked.

"I lost it," Vorovich said.

Handling him ungently, the two crewmen pushed him toward the ladder and up on deck. By the position of the sun, he judged he'd been down almost twenty-four hours. This time he was not allowed on the bridge. The captain, now in stained khakis and a Panama hat, came to the rail.

"They are very angry," the captain said. "As I knew they would be."

"Did you tell them I was in the cargo hold?" Vorovich demanded. The captain nodded uneasily. "Didn't they ask what I was doing?" Vorovich asked. "I couldn't tell them what you were doing, could I?" the captain said, now apprehensive.

"The cargo's been rearranged," Vorovich said.

"Rearranged?" the captain said.

"They'll understand," Vorovich said. "And unless they want to transfer five hundred cases instead of fifty, they might welcome my cooperation. Tell them I want my payment too!"

The captain began shouting in a language Vorovich didn't understand, and an enormously fat, double-chinned crewman appeared, by his earphones and trailing cord obviously the radioman. He listened, mouth agape, stared for a long moment at Vorovich, then disappeared back into the radio shack.

"I'd appreciate a shower and a bunk," Vorovich said. "If you think a half-naked man's dangerous, you could post a guard on my cabin until you hear back. . . ."

Again the captain muttered something Vorovich didn't understand, this time to the steward, who took one of the pistols he had found and motioned Vorovich to the stateroom area.

Inside the cabin, Vorovich saw that his duffel bag had been searched, the contents scattered over the bunk. But he ignored that and, going into the bathroom, turned on the shower, then leaned into the cabin long enough to fling his shorts at the steward.

"How long does it take to get laundry?" he asked, and shut the bathroom door in the steward's angry face. Then he stepped gratefully into the steaming hot water, not even minding that it was salt.

When D'Anton got the ship's message, relayed from the Algerian in Marseilles, he was furious. He hadn't cared much one way or the other when Charles had missed his opportunity; he had almost expected it. But when he heard that Alphonse and Gaston had been stupid enough to be left ashore by Vorovich, his expectations of picking up an extra million net cash by simply eliminating one man were gone.

He had no illusions about the controlling position Vorovich had taken—opening thousands of tins to find the right twelve hundred was out of the question. The moment they began transferring that many sardines, too many people would start wondering why. As for torturing the information out of him,

D'Anton wasn't convinced, even if the Algerian was, that Voro-vich could be made to talk—at least not quickly. And time was now of the first importance.

D'Anton buzzed for his secretary to get him a line to Mar-seilles, a roundabout move so there would be no record of his having communicated with the freighter. The woman did not answer. He came to the outer office, angered that she would leave her desk at this crucial time.

She was at the filing cabinets, showing another girl—some-one new—something about office procedures.

"Mrs. Legeri," D'Anton said sharply, and both women turned. He was struck by the exceedingly pale eyes and skin of the shapely brunette. He looked at her a moment longer, then turned his attention on Mrs. Legeri, a woman of mature years who knew better than to leave him unattended. "Would you see if you can get me the French shipping agents, please, before they go home for the night?" he asked.

Apologetic, Mrs. Legeri hurried back to her desk. The new girl, flustered by D'Anton's scrutiny, fumbled through her pa-pers, then walked awkwardly back to her own place.

It was not until D'Anton had finished informing the Algerian of this unfortunate new development that he realized some-thing bothered him about the new girl. Something about her hair; it didn't go with her skin. Her hair was badly dyed, as though it had been done in a hurry. And she seemed awkward in her high heels. Why had she come to work for him at such a time? Or was he being overly paranoid? Well, he'd better take no chances. He'd keep a careful eye on the girl for the next couple of days.

"*Ecoutez, mon ami,*" D'Anton said then, to the Algerian. "Inform them that of course we will pay—but that it will take several days to arrange for the money." He hung up and buzzed for Mrs. Legeri. "I'll be working late tonight," he said. "And I'll need someone to help me. Maybe the new girl?"

"She's a bright girl," Mrs. Legeri said, "but she hasn't many office skills—"

"I'm going to clean out my files," D'Anton interrupted, "and only need someone who can follow instructions."

"Very well, Mr. D'Anton," Mrs. Legeri said, and went out to instruct the new girl in how to conduct herself when working for the meticulous Mr. D'Anton.

Vorovich was puzzled by the second radio message. He had recognized the first as a stalling tactic, but this follow-up, a day later, made him uneasy. REPRESENTATIVE OF SHIPPING AGENT TO BOARD IN ACAPULCO. EMPOWERED TO RENEGOTIATE CONTRACT. What representative? What gave them the idea he would be willing to renegotiate? If they thought he was letting any thugs under whatever kind of euphemism aboard they had badly misjudged him . . . unless, of course, some development he knew nothing about had tipped the scales?

Acapulco. That gave him a good couple of days. To do just what Vorovich wasn't quite sure, but somehow he had the feeling that time was on his side. In a scant few hours they would be starting through the Canal, after which, he calculated, he would have some forty-eight hours before D'Anton's so-called representatives made contact. Who could they be? Vorovich had a pretty good idea, but since for the moment there was nothing he could do, he figured he might as well relax until they reached Acapulco.

On prior instructions from D'Anton, via the Algerian, they had given Vorovich back his "freedom"—though a crewman was always around to monitor his activities. He had, however, the first night after they had started up the Pacific coast, managed to undo the "look-in" hatch by slipping out of his cabin in the middle of the night, past the dozing deckhand, keeping a deck stanchion between himself and the bridge while he lifted the tarpaulin long enough to unfasten the cover.

As they approached the tropical shore, dropping anchor to windward of the island in the harbor, the tight feeling in his chest grew. As the radioman talked with the shore, Vorovich waited impatiently in the radio shack.

"Ah," the radioman said, at last, handing him the earphone. "Is for you."

"Vorovich?" came a familiar rasp. "We've got something of yours. We'll trade even for what's in your head."

Alphonse. "You've got nothing of mine," Vorovich said, "that I care about."

He didn't like the other's laugh. "I tell you what, smartass," Alphonse said. "You borrow a telescope and look at the houses back of the beach. A pink house. On the hill. Then come back and talk to me again."

Vorovich went out on deck. The steward handed him the glass. Training it on the terraced hillside leading back up off the strand, Vorovich found the house. Focusing in on the tiny figures out on a balcony, Vorovich recognized Alphonse and Gaston, the latter pushing a girl so that she faced the ship.

It was a long heartsick moment before he recognized Ginny. That black-haired short cut made the bones in her face seem exceedingly fragile.

"She's not mine," Vorovich said, back in the radio shack. "If you don't believe me, ask her."

"Vo?" came her voice then, shaky and fearful. "I ran out on you, I know. But I'll try and make it up to you—just do as they say. Please."

"No way," Vorovich said, but he was puzzled by her attitude. Her only chance was to deny any connection with him. Why was she taking the opposite stance? "I worked too long and hard to shoot it over some unfaithful broad."

"Please, Vo," Ginny pleaded. "I *want* to come aboard. They won't do anything. Mr. D'Anton promised. I'm just insurance, to see you live up to your end. Then after all this is over we can go away together."

He couldn't believe what he was hearing. She couldn't be that innocent, or stupid—no, she was deliberately putting herself into this. She was giving him no choice. He could hardly bargain with them to release her if she didn't want to be released, could he?

"Bring her aboard," he said finally, and handed the radiophone mike back to the radioman.

It was night before they boarded. They stole a small boat, to make certain no one on shore would know the freighter had taken on three new passengers.

Gaston did the rowing, and it was Gaston who climbed the ladder, sweating and blowing like a beached whale, frisking Vorovich before whispering hoarsely to Alphonse, bobbing up and down in the darkness below, that it was okay to bring her up.

Vorovich handed Ginny to the deck, feeling the unwanted but familiar longing, fighting it back, his emotions dampened when her eyes would not meet his. Alphonse was right behind, his narrow face glaring like a weasel's. Suddenly Alphonse back-handed him, the blow so unexpected Vorovich staggered and almost fell.

"That's for leaving us behind, smartass," Alphonse said.

Her outcry stopped Vorovich from swinging back. In Alphonse's other hand was the gleam of metal.

"You think I didn't cover all my bets?" Vorovich asked, when he had cleared his mouth of blood. "There's a letter with my Swiss banker he'll mail if the money isn't deposited by tomorrow night."

"Bullshit," Alphonse said, but he was uncertain.

"Maybe we better check with the boss," Gaston said.

Alphonse looked as though he would have liked to hit him again, but Gaston got between them, and Vorovich then took Ginny's arm to lead her away.

"Where you going?" Alphonse demanded.

"What are you afraid of?" Vorovich asked tauntingly. "I'm not going to try anything—at least not until the money is there. If you're really panicked, you can lock us up; I'm too big to squeeze through the porthole—and she's apparently aboard for the ride."

"You really don't mind bedding down with an old man like him?" Alphonse asked her, and was so pleased by Vorovich's reaction he let the steward escort them below.

The lock clicked shut behind them, and Ginny slumped on the bunk, looking forlorn and waiflike, the disturbing dyed hair half covering her profile. "How did they pick you up?" he asked at last.

"I was working at the fishery," she said. "And Mr. D'Anton saw through my disguise."

Vorovich didn't know whether that bellow he suppressed would be a laugh or a cry of outrage. "What were you doing at D'Anton's?" he asked, when he was able.

"I didn't know how else to find you," she said.

"You had good reason to want to, I suppose?" he said.

She stared at him. "I'm going to have your baby," she said. "Do you mind?"

Vorovich suddenly felt thirsty. He poured himself a drink. She refused to join him, watched him down it in one swallow.

"How long have you known?" he asked. She held up two fingers. "Why didn't you tell me before?"

"I didn't think you'd be interested," she said.

"What's different about now?" he demanded.

"I thought I owed you one last chance to rethink what you're doing," she said.

"Is that an ultimatum?" he wondered.

"I don't understand," she said, suddenly evasive, wringing her hands like an old woman. "How can you want your child to grow up in a world full of the shit you're going to be shoveling in? What kind of life will that be for her?"

"Her?" he asked.

"It's going to be a girl," she said. "Disappointed?"

"I've never been a father," he said, pouring himself another.

"You want to be?" she asked.

"You don't think I'm too old?" he asked, in turn.

"That's not worth answering," she said.

"Don't get pissed," he said. "You get pissed real easy, you know that?"

"If you say so," she said. "But I'm having this baby whether you want it or not."

"I want it," he said. "Her."

"But you don't care whether the world your daughter grows up in is clean?" she asked, placing his hand on her abdomen.

She put his hand under her dress to touch the warmth of this new life that was growing inside her. He tried to withdraw his hand and she pressed up against him, holding him close.

"You're pregnant," he said.

"It'll be all right," she said, "if we're careful."

He was very gentle with her. She seemed grateful for that. Their lovemaking was affectionate, possessing a kind of serenity he had never before experienced. He wished it might last forever. Then he looked more closely at her and was surprised to see the tears silently flowing.

"Am I hurting you?" he asked. She shook her head mutely, and when he tried to withdraw she held him close.

"What I don't understand about you," he said, later, "is you speak French like a whiz and you've got this classy accent and yet you spend time with a mug like Charley."

"He has his good points," she said. "After my sister died, he took me in. . . .

"You have no other family?" he asked.

"None I care about," she said. "My mother's very classy, like

225

you guessed, very particular about schools and only royalty shared her bed and cocaine is hardly dope, my dear, some of our best people lift their souls with it . . . and Millie looked like mother and wanted to be like her and when mother was going to ship her off for using her stuff Millie ran away. . . ."

He tried to comfort her and now she pushed him away. "Hey," he said. "I'm the father of your daughter."

She did not smile. "Will you give it up, Vo?" she asked.

"Give what up?" he said, knowing full well what she meant.

"You haven't thought it through," she said. "The money has turned your head. You've been hurt. Something. But you don't really plan to sell that stuff, do you? It's turning your back on what you've believed your whole life."

"Maybe I have turned my back on my whole life, Ginny. Maybe I've just begun to get smart."

"I don't believe that," she said, and she made no effort to hide her bitterness. "Promise me, Vo, that you won't go through with it."

"I don't see how I can," he replied, logically enough, but she turned her face to the wall and refused to discuss it any further.

When Charles came back from Europe he showed up at D'Anton's warehouse office to make his report personally. Though he became uneasy when he didn't see Ginny anywhere around, he didn't dare ask any questions. Then Roscoe told him yes, there had been a new chick gone to work for D'Anton, and according to some men he knew on the docks she had been driven off late one evening in D'Anton's limo, never to be seen again.

Charles immediately became agitated, all his anxieties rushing to the surface. He put Roscoe and Chen and Sam to watching the offices around the clock.

It was Roscoe, too, who found out about the standby crew. He had followed D'Anton one early morning, he said, to a boardinghouse near the docks, where a grizzled man in a knit cap and sailor's dungarees came out and got into D'Anton's car, which drove them to the pier where D'Anton's boats unloaded their catches. They boarded a boat which had not gone out, needing, so it was said, repairs. Apparently it was now ready, for both men seemed pleased when they returned from the inspection.

Charles sent Sam up to get a room in the boardinghouse, but Sam was told the place was full. In two days, however, he could have his choice, since five of the roomers were a "standby fishing crew" who had just given notice they were shipping out.

The next morning Chen managed to board D'Anton's boat. There wasn't much trouble, except for an anxious moment when a security patrol car stopped him as he carried his duffel bag along the pier.

"Cook arways one day early, make shuah garrey in tip-top shape," he said. They let him continue. The duffel bag contained a short-barreled Czech-made submachine gun.

He stowed away forward, in a compartment just under the wheelhouse reserved for safety gear, managing to cram himself in among the lifejackets. When the five men came aboard just before a foggy dawn the next day, they remained on deck only long enough to cast off; then four of them went down into the galley for coffee.

Chen squirmed out of the compartment and silently mounted the ladder to the wheelhouse. The wheelman did not hear him, all his faculties concentrated on working his way down the channel through the heavy fog. Chen shifted the submachine gun to his left hand, pulled a belaying pin out of his belt with his right, and slugged the wheelman at the point where the knit cap ended and his blue shirt collar began. The wheelman slumped. Chen pushed him aside and took the wheel.

Sam had trained him well, pointing out there were only two controls: all he had to do when he neared the buoy at the channel entrance was to ease the throttle into idle, and hold the wheel steady. A small rubber boat with Roscoe and Sam and Charles loomed out of the fog, and with the aid of grappling hooks Sam had picked up in a naval supplies store they scrambled aboard, pulling the lightweight craft up after them.

Sam took the wheel then, and the others, carrying pistols, stationed themselves at the ladder leading to the galley. They were in no hurry. On the compass table was a chart, neatly affixed, showing the rendezvous point. Roscoe had started to tie up the wheelman, but a glance sufficed to show he was dead.

They passed under the bridge. The ocean currents began dealing a series of hard swipes at the boat. In those nausea-producing shifts and dips the four below came piling up for air.

Roscoe did the frisking, finding handguns and knives. A yellow-toothed man with a mouth like a fish had a gun with a silencer. Charles took it from Roscoe, very pleased.

"Now why didn't we think of that?" he said. Making sure the silencer was properly screwed on, Charles walked along where Roscoe had the men facing the rail and shot each in the back of the head. The whole operation took less than a minute.

"You know," he said wonderingly to the grim-faced Roscoe and Chen, "I've never shot a man before."

They weighted the men down with sinkers cut from the nets, but did not throw them overboard until they were almost a hundred miles out. Then the noon sun burned through the mist, and Roscoe said the bodies would start to smell.

"We're restoring the balance of nature, man," Charles said to Roscoe as he and Chen swung each of them over. "Don't look so glum. When the scavenger fish get through, just imagine how delish-ioso all the crab, lobster, and shrimp will be, sliding down rich folks' gullets."

Charles laughed as Roscoe turned away. "Why don't you take your medicine, man?" he asked.

On the way to the docks, Roscoe had asked Charles to stop at a drugstore, claiming a deathly fear of seasickness. Inside, he told the pharmacist he needed something more potent than the packaged stuff, and was told for that he needed a prescription.

"Hey, man, what're you doing?" Charles had called from the front of the store, where he was buying gum and candy. "We can't be late!"

"Forget it," Roscoe said, grabbing the packaged medication from the startled pharmacist after he had given him a number. "Just tell the doc I've gone fishing, and if this stuff's not potent enough, he can send the Coast Guard to the rescue."

Now, as he contemplated that vast and empty horizon, Roscoe thumbed open the plastic tube and swallowed a bitter pill under Charles's watchful eye.

"That's it," Charles said. "I don't want you sick when the action starts. I'm going to need every hand."

When the message confirming the one-million-
dollar deposit came in, Vorovich experienced a
feeling like none he had ever known in his life. He
was euphoric. His head and his heart sang. Clutching the paper, he left the radio shack and half ran
down the deck to his cabin, where he pulled Ginny up off the
bed and waltzed her around the cramped quarters.

"Isn't that fan-fucking-tastic?" he asked, letting her go only
in order to shove the document at her, then leaning over her
shoulder to read it again, though the words shone in his mind.

VERIFYING ONE REPEAT ONE MILLION DOLLARS U.S. REPEAT ONE
MILLION DOLLARS U.S. DEPOSITED TO YOUR ACCOUNT. AWAITING
INSTRUCTIONS RE DISPOSITION LETTERS, MONEY ETC.
F. MAYER, MGR. ZURICHSBANKE

"We've got a chance now!" Vorovich cried. "The money's
out of his reach, and he'll let me handle the transfer so he can
get what he paid for!"

"And then what?" Ginny asked.

He hesitated, not wanting to scare her. "We'll go off on the
smaller boat," he said finally.

"You're not going to try and take that over?" she demanded,
and he motioned to her to keep her voice down.

"What choice do I have?" he asked, when certain no one was
eavesdropping. "I can't stay on the freighter—Cabot's waiting
for it in San Francisco."

"You could radio Cabot," she whispered after a long moment, "and get him to help you. . . ."

"Even if I wanted his help, which I don't," Vorovich said,
"we'd be wiped out before he could get here. And supposing we
weren't?" he continued over her protest. "You think D'Anton's
going to hold still for me ripping him off for a million bucks?"

"You could give him his money back," she said.

"You're being ridiculous," he said. "He expects to make a
hundred times that off the stuff."

Then, as she started to ask about Cabot again, the cabin door
was pushed open, and a disgruntled Alphonse thrust a new
message at him.

CONFIRM RENDEZVOUS SIX HOURS EARLY. V TO REMAIN COM-
PLETE CHARGE. OBSERVE RADIO SILENCE HEREAFTER.
D.

229

"Vo . . ." she began, as the elated Vorovich started to follow Alphonse out. But when he turned, she had apparently changed her mind.

For some reason, the moment held a particular poignancy. When she continued to say nothing, however, he brushed her cheek with a kiss, then continued up on deck.

On the bridge, the captain stopped his pacing long enough to point out the fog bank they were moving toward.

"I can give you two crewmen, and that's all," he said. "In this kind of weather, I need every available hand on deck."

"You two will have to pitch in," Vorovich said to Gaston and Alphonse.

"What about you?" Alphonse demanded.

"I'm a millionaire now," Vorovich said. "Millionaires don't work." And he escorted the four men below.

It was steamy hot in the engine room. The squat chief engineer and his greasy wiper watched the silent little parade without comment as Vorovich opened the first hold, then led the way through the aisles of bagged sugar and barreled olives to the inside hold, which was locked with that massive padlock.

The men watched sullenly as Vorovich unlocked it and pulled the door open—taking care to lock the padlock shut around the handle so no one could remove it.

"These," Vorovich said, showing them the cases he had worked so hard to arrange. "Carry them over by the bulkhead doors, then tie them down so they won't shift—in case we run into heavy seas. And keep them stacked in order."

While the men started to work, Vorovich went down the dark aisles on the pretext of making sure all the cases were out —and found his snub-nosed .32, which he shoved into his boot beneath his pant leg.

"Make sure he does his share," Vorovich said, of Alphonse to Gaston, his voice strangely without timbre in the dead air of the hold. "Otherwise I'll report him to his chief."

On deck again, Vorovich saw they were close to the fog bank, which hung like a huge steel-wool curtain between the lowering sky and the water's edge. As Vorovich hastened along the promenade deck, the ship's horn began sounding, a deep agonized blare like some beast sensing danger.

"What is it?" Ginny asked, in something of a panic as she met him at the cabin door.

"Fog," he said, and making sure the door was locked, offered her the gun.

She recoiled from it as from something obscene.

"I can't handle it alone," he said.

"I could never shoot anyone," she said.

"I'm not asking you to shoot anyone," he said patiently. "Just the threat of it will stop most people. And if worst comes to worst you can shoot in the air. That usually stops even the desperate ones."

"And if it doesn't?" she asked.

He shrugged. "You may have at least given me time to get the situation under control," he said.

She shivered, and when it seemed she couldn't stop, he took her to the bunk and laid her down, crawling in beside her. Gradually, her cold skin warmed to his touch, and that awful trembling stopped. Finally, she dozed off.

When Ginny awoke, Vorovich was gone. She looked at her watch, thought for a moment it had stopped, then realized she had slept for almost twelve hours! She was undressed, and under the covers, and understood then that he had made her comfortable—when? How long had he been gone?

Quickly dressing in shirt and pants, she hurried out on the open deck, not forgetting the gun, though its metal was clammy.

It was so dark she found it difficult to believe that somewhere on the other side of that dismal gray blanket was daylight. The sea, except for the sound of it hissing alongside the hull, had disappeared. They were shrouded in mist, a thick cloud billowing all about them, dank and mind-numbing. She found Vorovich at the forward rail, up on the observation platform, lifting binoculars whenever he thought there might be a gap in the fog.

"What is it?" she asked, feeling his tenseness.

"They're late," he said. "Hours late."

"Because of the fog, probably," she said.

"That shouldn't bother them," he said. "They have radar equipment and enough maneuverability to get out of a bigger ship's way, even at a normal rate of speed."

"Maybe the earlier rendezvous threw them off," she said.

"They're experienced seamen," he said. "That shouldn't give them any problems whatsoever."

"You don't suppose the Coast Guard intercepted them?" she asked hopefully.

"Not in this stuff," he said, though her tone had given him pause. "And even if the Guard lucked in, they'd look like a legitimate fishing boat. No," he said, slamming the rail, "something's gone wrong. I can feel it."

"You're just nervous," she said, without conviction.

He put his arm around her for a moment, felt the gun in her pea coat pocket, and hugged her. Then he sent her back below and continued scanning the ocean.

If the freighter had not cut its speed, maintaining just enough power to make way against the southerly current, it might have crushed the smaller boat, so suddenly did that fishing craft appear out of the fog. As it was, only a last-minute hard turn by the wheelman of the sixty-foot *Neptune's Pride* prevented a collision. The *Pride* came about almost directly under the freighter's bow and, its wake boiling yellow in the sudden throttling up, slipped into the fog bank again as if racing to put distance between itself and that near miss.

When it approached again the *Pride* came out cautiously, at half-speed, wallowing like a sea hippo as it bucked through the waves, sidling toward the starboard side, afraid now to close too fast for the risk of a sudden swell.

Where was the crew? Only the wheelman could be seen, and he only obscurely through the salt-encrusted windows. Vorovich focused the binoculars, wondering what was familiar about the way the other handled the smaller craft, and then, when the other had to lean out to judge the diminishing gap, Vorovich saw, even through the unshaven beard, the knit cap pulled down to the eyebrows, and the pea-coat collar up to his ears that it was Sam!

No wonder the others had gone below. They were waiting until the last possible moment before having to come out to make fast, not knowing if anyone was on the freighter who might know them.

Carefully then, without showing undue concern or haste, Vorovich stepped back from the rail. But as soon as he was out of sight of the boat below, he went on a dead run to their cabin.

"Get dressed!" he said to Ginny. "I'll need your help!"

He pulled on another pair of pants and a bulky sweater over the ones he was already wearing. He had no time for explanations. Barely giving her a chance to get her shoes tied, he cautioned her to silence and led her out on deck.

They heard two shots, and two cartridge-propelled grappling hooks came sailing up and over the rail. Below, two crewmen dressed in oilskins, wet and slick as fish, were making fast. A youngish man in a master's cap, visor jammed low on his forehead, looking remarkably pale for someone who made his living from the sea, was shouting instructions.

The captain put a LoudHailer to his mouth. "What took you so long?" he rasped.

"We were ducking a Coast Guard weather plane," came the reply, through a battery-powered megaphone handed the young master by his wheelman. Even through the hoarseness of the amplification Vorovich recognized that nasal drone—and so did Ginny!

"Come on!" Vorovich whispered urgently.

As they ducked down the first ladder they heard the captain asking anxiously, "You lost them?"

"We better get a hustle on," the other replied. "If this shit lifts we could be in *mucho* trouble!"

As they approached the engine room Vorovich motioned her back. The engineer and his wiper were having a smoke.

"Got a cigarette?" Vorovich asked. They did not understand English. Vorovich pantomimed smoking. Smiling, the engineer handed him a grease-stained pack, and the wiper a packet of matches. Taking both, nodding his thanks, Vorovich lit up, blew an enormous puff of smoke, tossed the cigarettes at one, the matches at the other, and while both were distracted, pulled out his gun.

They did not resist. Using their own belts, Vorovich bound their hands behind them, then marched them into the toilet and, after finding his carpenter's tools, nailed the door shut.

Ginny followed him then into the first hold, watching wide-eyed as Vorovich dragged the barrels of oily rags he had found along.

"Here's what I want you to do," Vorovich said, pushing the barrels under the ventilating shafts. "After I've been in there fifteen minutes, set fire to the rags. When the fire gets going," he continued, ripping open a sugar sack and throwing a handful into the barrel, "throw more sugar on it—that'll make it really smoke. These shafts come out on deck through funnels, and when the smoke starts pouring out it will look like a disaster." He showed her how to close the padlock. "After I've gone through," he said, "make sure it's locked. I'll be all right," he said, noting her worried look. "You know where the hatch I showed you is, up on the foredeck? That's where I'll be coming out. If you make sure it's unlocked, that is. But don't go up on deck until you're sure the fire's started. Take your time, no one should bother you—if someone should come and ask about the engine-room crew, just play dumb. If they get nasty, show them the gun."

And without giving her a chance to protest, Vorovich stepped through into the inner hold and clanged the door shut behind him. He waited long enough to hear Ginny banging at the huge lock to get it closed, then moved swiftly on.

The two crewmen were using sledgehammers on the bulkhead.

"About time you got down here," Alphonse muttered, without looking up from the splinters he was picking out of his hands.

Once the latches were hammered free, Vorovich stepped in—it took two men on each wheel and one with a plank shoving against the seam to even move the huge doors—and then slowly, with each turn, the doors began groaning outward.

"You'd think the sonsabitches coulda had 'em greased," Alphonse said, panting with the strain.

As the doors began moving more easily, Vorovich dropped the plank and went to make sure the portable gangway was ready to drop into place. Put aboard by the Algerian, it was a flimsy affair, a series of aluminum slats for steps, held together by rope, with canvas underneath and on either side, held also by rope and posts to enclose it. As Vorovich pulled it forward Gaston looked at it skeptically.

"It'll hold ten times your weight," Vorovich said.

The two crewmen shoved the gangway through the opening. Its segments laddered into place as it dropped toward the boat below, and they secured the top end with rope around the latches.

"Jesus," came the complaint from the fishing-boat bridge. "Took you long enough!"

Gaston stepped to the opening and peered down. "Ain't that the guy come with you to the boss's house?" he asked Vorovich, frowning.

"Sure as hell looks like him," Vorovich admitted, after taking a quick glance, then stepping back so he wouldn't be seen.

"What's he doing here?" Alphonse demanded. "The boss didn't say nothing about him!"

"He didn't?" Vorovich said, trying to sound even more worried than he was. "Maybe something's gone wrong! Listen: go ahead with the unloading—we can't leave the stuff here—while I figure out a way to take them by surprise. Play it cool, but stay alert, and wait for my signal."

Before they had a chance to ask what he had in mind, Vorovich was heading down the cramped aisles toward the connecting—and now padlocked—door to the outer hold. But as soon as he disappeared from view, he crouched low and ducked back into the hold toward the forward hatch.

Meanwhile, from below, after having fastened the gangway to the fishing-boat deck, Roscoe and Chen came tentatively up the swaying aluminum-slatted canvas, clinging to the rope on either side, which alternately popped and sagged with the movement of the two ships in the uneasy sea. They reached the hold and paused, trying to see past Alphonse and Gaston into the dimness, feeling very nervous with the light behind them.

"There it is," Alphonse said, indicating the stacked cases.

Sam came up the gangway then, making a game of it by using the crowbar he held over his head for balance. "I'm supposed to check out the goods," he explained. He pried the top off one of the cases, removed a sardine tin, peeled the lid back. Pulling out a sardine, he showed it to the figure waiting anxiously on the fishing-boat bridge below, then popped the oily little fish into his mouth.

"Not from the first row, dummy!" came a scream from below. "I told you—two over from the side and two down!"

Sam tried again. The next tin held plasticine bags of white powder. He displayed it triumphantly.

"Bring them aboard!" Charles yelled. "And make it snappy!"

As Sam and the two flat-faced crewmen began carrying the cases down the gangway, Charles motioned for Roscoe and

Chen to move on inside the hold. If the goods were there, then so was Vorovich, somewhere. Their job was to find him. But as Roscoe and Chen moved on inside, Alphonse and Gaston went with them.

Considering the situation above, Charles thoughtfully sorted through the arsenal of weapons in the locker and chose a short-barreled repeater shotgun. It just fit under the folds of his bulky seaman's coat. Then he stationed himself at the foot of the gangway, waiting for Vorovich to show himself.

By this time Vorovich had crawled across the top of the lashed-down cargo to the hatch. Kneeling, he undid the inner cross screw, then pushed against the cover with both hands.

It refused to budge. Lying on his back then, Vorovich brought his feet up, and pushed against it with all his strength.

If it moved at all, Vorovich still could not feel it. He lay for a moment, breathing heavily, staring into blackness. What could have happened to Ginny? Surely no one would have any reason to stop her now, what with all the activity of the mid-ocean transfer. And what about those oily rags? Hadn't they been lit? By this time there should be sufficient smoke to raise an alarm.

Bracing himself again, no longer trying to muffle the sound, Vorovich began kicking at the hatch cover. He had to get out, no matter how. Otherwise the situation would become impossible. Again he kicked, and again, to no avail. Suddenly, just as he was about to give up, the hatch cover came loose. Probably just stuck, Vorovich thought, breathing a sigh. Or maybe he had jammed it down too tight when he had secured it, and the wood had swelled. He pulled himself through the hatch and stood up —to find himself facing the steward.

"Where's the girl?" Vorovich demanded, the question answered as she was pushed from behind a stanchion, arm half-twisted behind her by the radioman.

"She try send an S.O.S.," the steward said, showing the gun.

"I knew you couldn't do it alone," Ginny said, half weeping, as he stared at her, dumbstruck.

"I didn't think I *was* alone," he managed, finally. "Who do you think's out there," he went on then, "could get to us be-fore—"

"Cabot," she whispered, cutting him short.

"Cabot?" he repeated, incredulous, trying to make sense of what he was hearing. Once again, he thought, against all the smarts he had labored to accumulate over the years, knowing that life double-dealt every time you gave it a chance, he had been stupid enough to let down his guard.

"She soft in heart," the steward said, grinning. "When I tell Sparks to not send message she not able to pull trigger."

"Next time experiment with your own life," Sparks said bitterly, and gave Ginny's arm an extra twist for the fear she had brought out in him.

"Why you come out this place?" the steward wondered then, pointing to the loosened deck hatch. "Why you not arrive on deck normal way?"

Vorovich, looking away from the anguished Ginny, bent down and grasped the cover, as if to secure the hatch. "Those aren't the right people," he said. "They're not the ones we were expecting."

The steward stared at him, for a moment disbelieving. "But we must tell the captain!" he said then, turning to go, and Vorovich, rising with the hatch cover thrust before him like a shield, came up and across the deck at him.

The steward was raising the gun when Vorovich slammed into him, bouncing him off a stanchion. As the steward slumped with the double impact, Vorovich grabbed the gun and pointed it at the radioman—who had not moved.

Vorovich motioned the radioman back to the radio shack. He grabbed Ginny, half shoving her along too. They crowded inside, where Vorovich yanked out the transmitting unit, bringing a cry from both the others.

"I don't want Cabot's fucking help!" Vorovich told her, shoving the radioman into a chair and binding him with an electrical cord.

"He promised not to bring charges if you'd call him in," Ginny cried.

"His promises aren't worth shit!" Vorovich almost yelled. "Don't you know that? How long have you been working for him?"

"I haven't," she said, shrinking from him.

"You telling me this is a coincidence?" he demanded, and his anger reverberated in the little room.

"Not exactly," she said, denying what she saw in his face.

"Mr. Cabot had us busted so he could interrogate me—"

"And how did he know about you?" Vorovich asked.

"Back when Charles said the syndicate was threatening him," she said, after a moment, "I went to the D.E.A. They didn't seem very interested, telling me to keep my eyes and ears open and if I got anything specific, to let them know—so I left them a sample of the stuff from Turkey."

The radioman cried out. In his shock and anger Vorovich had been binding him too tight. Remembering the scene at customs, he had half known a contact was being made, but he should have totaled it all out right then. The scarf: she had probably given them the scarf. Too caught up in the flow of events, he had denied what his own instincts told him.

"He doesn't have any hard feelings," Ginny said.

"Doesn't he?" Vorovich said, as sarcastically as possible.

"He thinks you've freaked out," Ginny said.

"Why would he think that?" Vorovich asked, jamming a gag in the radioman's mouth.

"From the pictures," she said.

"He told you he'd seen them?" Vorovich asked, reddening.

"He gave them to me," she said, "to tear up."

"You're not telling me he bought you for those lousy photos?" Vorovich cried. "You never gave a damn who saw you bare-assed!"

"I tore them up for you," she said.

"What difference does it make now?" he asked, edging the door of the radio-shack opening, looking to see if the deck was clear. "They can publish it in *Rolling Stone*, for all I give a shit—"

"He kept the others," she said. "The ones of you stoned at the commune," she explained, at his puzzled look. "He promised that if I told him everything I knew, and if I could signal him in time, he'd help you, even give you a bonus—"

"And you sold me out for that?" he demanded, and there was an edge of undeniable hate to his anger.

She heard it, and unable to hold it back any longer, she wept. "What are you going to do now?" she cried, as Vorovich, seemingly unmoved by her tears, stepped out the door.

"Salvage what I can," Vorovich said, cold and bitter.

"Let me help," she begged, running after him down the promenade deck toward the port rail aft.

"Help?" he demanded, stopping to face her, his throat constricting with the rage that came boiling up out of him. "You couldn't even light the goddam fire for me!" And he came as close as he had ever in his life come to striking a woman when out of the deck funnels he saw the beginning wisp of smoke.

"Maybe," she said, following his glance, "I threw too much sugar on. I was in an awful hurry. . . ."

"Here," Vorovich said, handing her the gun. "Protect yourself. If you can." And pushing aside a deck tarp, he took up the coiled rope, fastened one end to the anchor chain, slung part of it under his butt, and started over the side.

"Can't I come too?" Ginny wailed.

Vorovich stared at her, a great hollowed-out place in his chest where his heart had been. "The water's too cold," he managed finally. "You might cramp up and lose the baby."

Then as smoke, thick, greasy, and black, came pouring out of the funnels, he left her, left that grieving wild-eyed girl, and went up and over the rail. Bells on the ship started clanging and someone reactivated the foghorn as crewmen ran everywhere.

It was not as easy as he hoped it would be. The hull was slick from the fog, and it took all his strength to walk himself down. Though his back was to the water, he forced himself to move deliberately, planting each foot against the slippery metal before lifting the next. Then the rope began to burn his thighs and his hands.

He slipped, and his legs dropped vertically and he came slamming up against the side, dangling from the rope. He heard her cry out above, but, not looking up, he used his knee to get leverage and finally managed to plant his opposite foot.

Almost straight out then, he continued his slippery backward walk down, every muscle in his arms and chest burning. He felt, rather than saw himself, close to the water line.

The edge of the bow rose and fell like a guillotine blade. Though the ship's engines were at the lowest possible speed, the freighter was still moving forward. Somehow he would have to swing around the bow. But his arms and shoulders were already stretched beyond endurance, and he didn't know if he had any more reserves of strength.

Then he remembered that Cabot was somewhere close, and bending his knees he allowed his weight to swing inward, then pushed out with all the anger he had. He swung out and around the knife-edge prow, made sure he was clear, let go of the rope, and dropped the few feet into the churning water. It was colder than he would have believed possible. His genitals immediately constricted, the pain traveling all the way up to his teeth. He would have to get to the smaller boat very fast, before the water numbed him to the point he would be unable to swim.

His double layer of clothes made him awkward. But without them the cold would have knocked him out immediately. Swimming as fast and hard as he could, he reached the fishing boat's bow and, clinging to a vertical plane, heard, above the ringing din of the alarm bells, Charles screaming at those loading to finish up.

He had to get up on that boat quickly. But he could not quite manage it at the prow, and he dropped back into the water, that bone-cold water. He swam toward the stern and was finally able, with a desperate kick and lunge, to grasp a side sandbag bumper. Hanging for a moment, he prayed for strength, and somehow pulled himself up and over the rail.

He sprawled on the deck, exhausted. He could not seem to get enough air into his aching lungs. Faintly, from the freighter far above, he heard the cries of the men loading as they discovered they were locked in. In the cacophony of strident voices, he recognized those of Gaston and Chen.

"Never mind that!" Vorovich heard Charles yell. "Get those goddam cases transferred!"

There couldn't be many cases left, Vorovich thought. Cautiously he raised his head. The two dark-faced crewmen were nowhere to be seen, presumably trying to claw their way out of the locked hold. Roscoe and Chen were at one side of the bulkhead opening; Alphonse and Gaston at the other. Sam was in between, struggling with a sardine case on each shoulder.

"Come on, dammit!" Charles screamed, to make himself heard above the din. "Everybody grab a case!" Charles was standing halfway up the gangway.

None of the four men moved. Alphonse and Gaston, already nervous about the transfer, now even more agitated at the idea that people who weren't supposed to receive the goods were about to get away with it, edged around to get Sam between them, clearly undecided about what to do. Roscoe and Chen, recognizing what a dangerous situation they were in, were afraid to turn their backs on them.

Vorovich stood up, quickly unwrapped the oilcloth he had used to sheath the gun, and stepped out from behind the wheelhouse.

"Alphonse!" he shouted. "Gaston! Let's take them now!"

For what seemed like the eternity captured by a photograph, everyone froze. Then everyone moved at once.

Charles whirled on the gangway and fired without quite getting the shotgun out from under his coat and up to his shoulder. The impact knocked him sprawling. Vorovich, anticipating the shot, ducked back behind the wheelhouse, the shotgun blast taking out a window. Then, scuttling crablike along the deck, he came around the other way, peering over the rail.

Sam, he saw, was caught in a crossfire. Both pairs had drawn their guns and were firing. At first the only effect Vorovich could see was that bullets were splintering the cases that Sam held, and he was turned first one way and then another, like a wide-eyed shooting-gallery figure. Then between one of the turns Alphonse shot Sam in the chest, and the impact was enough to send Sam staggering backward, dropping first one case and then another; vainly clutching at one case as it went over the side, he leaned too far himself, and went spinning end over end down into the sea.

Gaston got Chen, whose reflexes, good as they were, were not as good as the professional's. Chen, shot in the throat, had his scream suddenly muted by the gout of blood.

Roscoe, who was also a professional, hit Gaston a split second after in the ear; Gaston dropped to his knees as if in prayer. His prayers unanswered, the big man toppled sideways and rolled down the gangway toward Charles.

Charles, who had snapped the repeater into readiness for another shot and was peering down at the fishing boat for Vorovich, did not see Gaston's tumbling body.

Above and behind Charles, Alphonse and Roscoe were firing at each other. Vorovich came up and snapped off a shot at Alphonse. The bullet smashed up against the iron plate and skidded in a snarling whine, causing Alphonse to flinch. His shot at Roscoe was off just enough to catch him across the cheekbone instead of the nose. Roscoe, in a reflex before he went down, fired again, hitting Alphonse in the stomach.

Now Charles had a clear shot at Vorovich. But just as he squeezed the trigger, Gaston's body hit him back of the knees, and Charles went sprawling, this time forward, on his face. The shotgun blast tore a gaping hole in the gangway.

Quickly Vorovich grabbed a fire ax from its holder on the wheelhouse and began hacking at the gangway ropes wound around the deck cleats. In his haste he was not very efficient, and he still had one rope to go when Charles, nose bleeding, from its misshapen look probably broken, struggled to his knees and pumped the receiver action again.

Vorovich heard the shot only after he had been hit. The impact took him all the way across the deck and up against the wheelhouse. He looked in surprise at his right arm, which hung by his side, useless. The shoulder of his jacket was gouted and frayed—but there was no blood. The fact that he had worn two sweaters beneath the jacket had saved him from an open wound, but not from a broken arm.

He had dropped the ax. Now he reached for the gun in his belt. Charles was already on his feet, braced against the gangway rail, sagging and askew from its severed rope, and the clatch-clack of the repeater action was distinct.

"Okay, you cock-sucking narco sonofabitch," Charles screamed.

And then, up in the bulkhead opening, a slim figure, dressed in dungarees, pea coat, and knit cap, stepped forward. "Charles!" the figure screamed. It was Ginny.

How had she gotten there? The hatch. Vorovich remembered the hatch.

Charles was as incredulous as Vorovich. Half turning, but still keeping the barrel of his shotgun on Vorovich, he looked up at Ginny, who was pointing a gun at him.

"Jesus H. fucking Christ," Charles said. "Are you out of your freaking mind?"

"Put your gun down, Charles," Ginny cried, but her voice was quavering.

"Or what?" Charles demanded. "Or what? Or you'll shoot me? You've never hurt anyone in your life. You've told us all often enough that you can't kill a chicken or even clean a fish, and now you're threatening to *shoot* me? *Me?*"

"Put your gun down, Charles," Ginny repeated, and now she could barely be heard. *"Please."*

"We were close once, Gin, remember?" Charles asked. "You carried my kid!"

Then the totally unexpected happened. Sam came up out of the water, streaming blood like a wounded Neptune, grabbed at the gangway, but clearly hadn't the strength to pull up.

"Don't move, narco!" Charles shouted, as Vorovich went for him.

"Help him, Charles!" Ginny screamed, as Sam flopped back in the water, now holding on with only one hand. "He's your *friend!*"

"If I do that," Charles said, as if trying to be perfectly reasonable, "the narco will kill me. He kills very easily, you know that. He killed Billy, didn't he?"

Sam let go and slid under the water and the two boats kissed hulls. When they separated again Sam did not appear. Ginny gave an inarticulate cry.

Charles started to lift his shotgun.

"Don't, Charles!" Ginny whispered.

"The sonofafucking bitch worked a number on me," Charles screamed, completely turning his back on her, snugging the shotgun up into his shoulder, making sure this time he wouldn't flatten his now oh-so-tender nose. "Him and that freaking spic tried to whipsaw me, and you let them get away with it."

"Charles!" Ginny screamed, needing all the strength she possessed in both hands to lift the gun. He ignored her. Closing her eyes, she squeezed.

Charles coughed, a discreet little cough. Slowly, he lowered the shotgun. He looked back once at Ginny, then at Vorovich, as if wanting an explanation for this surprising thing that was happening. Then his puzzled frown was replaced by the glow of revelation.

Taking a step forward, as if meaning to explain it to Vorovich, Charles sagged and crumpled over the rail, like a doll out of which all the stuffing has leaked. The rail, already ripped, parted. Charles fell into the sea.

When Ginny opened her eyes, Charles was not there. She stared as if awakening from a nightmare. But the gun in her hand was hot, and there, on the boat below, Vorovich was picking up the ax with his good hand.

"Wait!" Ginny screamed, and came sprinting down the sagging gangway as, awkwardly, Vorovich hacked at the remaining rope. She averted her eyes as she passed the spot where Charles had stood, then leaped to the deck just as Vorovich slashed the last rope, and the gangway fell back against the freighter's side.

Vorovich had hesitated, he wouldn't admit to himself why, just long enough for her to make it. He hadn't time now to think through his reasons. The boat was out of control. Vorovich ran inside the wheelhouse, then yelled at her to help.

While she took the wheel, he tried to start the engines. The motor coughed, and quit, and the starter ground, and he forced himself to take his finger off the button and wait. Though she did her best with the wheel, on the next swell, without the engines, the boat came jarringly up against the freighter again. Guns fired, and another window shattered as both of them ducked.

He pressed the starter again. The engines caught. Working as best he could with one hand, Vorovich tried to throw the gear into forward. It wouldn't go. She helped him jam the lever into reverse, and he gave it all the throttle it would take.

The boat wallowed for an instant, then another, and then finally responded, sliding back alongside the freighter in that heavy sea as Vorovich helped her yank the wheel hard over starboard.

Slowly, the *Pride* began to arc away from the freighter. Up on the freighter's deck, the steward appeared. He slid a rifle over the rail. He had a clear bead on Vorovich through the shattered window. Vorovich was too busy running his boat to even sense, let alone see him, and when Ginny looked up, it was almost too late.

Then behind the steward a form appeared. Roscoe. He had a handkerchief pressed against his shattered cheek. He was also holding his gun, and he hit the steward in the back of the head.

At Ginny's gasp, Vorovich looked up and saw Roscoe just as the steward's rifle fired and missed. But Roscoe didn't acknowledge them. He slipped back away from the rail, out of sight.

"Now why did he help us?" Ginny wondered.

"He must be the one gave the pictures to Cabot," Vorovich

said. "He's an informer, maybe—or maybe working as an undercover narc for a local jurisdiction. Either way, we'd better get away from here fast, before he brings Cabot booming down on us."

Already the freighter was lost in the fog, only the steady booming of the foghorn reminding them it still existed. It took their combined efforts to work the gear into neutral, then, finally, into forward. After helping her bring the boat about in a large heeled-over circle, he plotted a southerly course toward Mexico.

"Where are we going?" she asked, as he worked over the charts.

"We'll stay in the fog bank as long as we can," he said, "and work our way down the coast. There's a little out-of-the-way fishing village I know on the inside of the Baja penninsula. We can hole up there till the heat's off."

"And then what?" she asked.

"I'll try and figure a way to get at the money," he said. "It'll be difficult, because they'll be watching—"

"I tried to give it away," she said.

He was surprised, and he shouldn't have been. By this time he should have realized how clear and strong was the flow of her resolve never to profit from dope, no matter from which side the money came.

"I asked the banker to set up a foundation to rehab drug addicts," she said. "It can't be done without your permission."

"Jesus Christ, Jennifer," he said, after a long incredulous moment. "You're not expecting me to do that? After all I've been through to get it?"

"I guess not," she shrugged hopelessly, blinking furiously to keep the tears back as she tried to match course to compass.

"Look," he said, trying to find the least painful position in which to bind his arm, feeling the angers working in him again, "I may have to let that money sit there five, even ten years as it is. If Cabot can manage it, he'll put a freeze on it by declaring it was obtained feloniously . . . I have no way of proving it wasn't, have I?"

"He won't care," she said. "I Xeroxed shipping papers in Mr. D'Anton's files and sent them to Cabot. When he finds the freighter, he'll be able to put a case together against D'Anton."

"He'll still care," Vorovich said. "It won't be as spectacular a bust without those." And he pointed to the cases of heroin-stuffed sardines scattered about the deck.

"Then why not give them to Cabot?" Ginny asked. "That way you'll be straight with him, and—"

"I'd sell them first!" he said.

"You can't be serious," she said, staring at him.

"Can't I?" he demanded. "Don't you have any idea what those cases are worth? One hundred thousand dollars—*each!*"

"About a dollar a life," she said bitterly.

"You can't hold me responsible for what people want to do to themselves," he said, shrugging angrily.

"That's what Charles claimed!" she cried. "You're not beginning to think like him, are you?"

"I'm thinking there's ten million dollars right here that you're asking me to give away," he said. "Why? Because the money wouldn't be nobly earned? How do you think the great fortunes got started? People robbed and polluted and cheated and connived and sold each other out, but who remembers any of that three or four generations later? It's the money that counts, in the end. I'll set you up a dozen foundations. I can see my name now, honored in our history books, right alongside Morgan and Rockefeller!"

"Now I know you're not serious," she said.

"I've never been more serious in my life," he said.

"You *have* changed," she whispered, her face so drained he thought she might faint.

"Everyone changes," he said, and he might have reminded her she'd killed to get on this boat. "That's what life is: change. And when there's no more change you're dead." But he remembered too that she had saved his life. "Don't worry," he said, his anger suddenly spent. "I'll dump the stuff."

She looked at him doubtfully. But, moving gingerly, he stepped down to the deck. He stooped down to one of the cases and was able with some effort to pick it up with his good arm.

Recovering, Ginny lashed the wheel in place and jumped down to help. "Someone's got to start being straight somewhere," she said, as Vorovich balanced the case on the rail, the case worth a hundred thousand dollars.

"Like Preble?" Vorovich wondered.

"Yes," she said defiantly. "Like Preble."

"Here's to Preble," he said then, and pushed the case into the sea.

Ginny struggled up to the rail with another. "For Billy," she said, and shoved that case over.

"For my old man," Vorovich said to himself with the next case, wondering if that uncomplaining, hard-working old man would consider him a hero—or a fool.

Working together then, it was not long before they had all but one over the side. The fog had lifted enough so they could see the crates forming a lazy, moving chain in their wake. When they got to the last case, Vorovich pried open the lid with an ax. He removed a few tins of sardines, and a few that contained heroin.

"We'll stash some on the boat," Vorovich explained. "When we're ready to leave it, we can tip off the Federales, and they'll have another piece of evidence against D'Anton."

Then they shoved the last case over, and her lips silently formed a name he had heard her mention only once: Milly.

Weary and sweating with their efforts, they both stood watching the cases bob and twist, some taking longer than others to sink. As the last one settled beneath the waves, Vorovich turned his eyes away, climbed back up in the wheelhouse, and took over the wheel.

"Now what?" Ginny asked, following him.

"We'll hole up for a while," Vorovich said. "Then, when my arm heals and we figure it's safe, we'll make a run at the border. I know more about crossing borders than any man alive. Then we can head north to that wine country you're always raving about," he went on. "I doubt anyone will look for us there. But we'll change our names just in case. I'll grow a beard, make a down payment on some acreage, settle in and plant some vines until the kid is born—what you've always wanted.

"It'll be a good life," she said when it had all finally sunk in. "A full life, too—it'll keep you so busy you won't even have time to think about the million dollars sitting in that bank!"

"Don't you believe it," he said.

"If you don't give the money away, Vo, I'll leave you," she said evenly. It wasn't a threat. It was a simple statement of fact.

"How about making some coffee?" he said finally.

"Sure," she said at last, knowing better than to push him

now. She headed for the galley, but at the ladder she stopped. "Want some Irish in it?" she asked.

"If you can find some," he said, "that would be great.

She managed a smile and disappeared below.

He went back to his navigation. Why was life always full of impossible choices? He wanted the money. But he wanted her too. Did he have to lose one to gain the other?

Maybe, he thought, it wouldn't be such a bad life. Maybe even someone like himself could get to like it, working those grape-heavy vines under the hot dry sun. At least he would have a loving wife and a beautiful daughter. And who knew, maybe, if he worked long enough and hard enough and the sun was hot enough, he might even sweat the memory of all that money clean out of his mind.

Maybe.